ISAAC ASIMOV Presents

THE GREAT SCIENCE FICTION STORIES

Edited by
Isaac Asimov and
Martin H. Greenberg

DAW BOOKS, INC.
DONALD A. WOLLHEIM, PUBLISHER

1301 Avenue of the Americas
New York, N.Y.　　　10019

Copyright ©, 1979, by Isaac Asimov and
Martin H. Greenberg.

All Rights Reserved.

Cover design by Jack Gaughan.

Complete list of copyright acknowledgments for the contents will be found on the following pages.

First Printing, March 1979

1 2 3 4 5 6 7 8 9

DAW BOOKS

PRINTED IN U.S.A.

ACKNOWLEDGMENTS

BLACK DESTROYER by A.E. van Vogt. Copyright 1939 by Street & Smith, Inc., 1967 © by Condé Nast Publications, Inc. By permission of the author's agent, Forrest J. Ackerman.

HEAVY PLANET by Milton A. Rothman. First published under the by-line of Lee Gregor. Copyright 1939 by Street & Smith Publications, Inc. By permission of the author.

THE STRANGE FLIGHT OF RICHARD CLAYTON by Robert Bloch. Copyright 1939 by Robert Bloch. By permission of the author and the author's agent, Scott Meredith Literary Agency, Inc.

TROUBLE WITH WATER by H.L. Gold. Copyright 1939 by Street & Smith, Inc., 1967 © by Condé Nast Publications, Inc. By permission of the author's agent, Forrest J. Ackerman.

THE FOUR-SIDED TRIANGLE by William F. Temple. Copyright 1939 by Ziff-Davis Publications, 1967 by Ultimate Publishing Co., Inc. By permission of the author's agent, Forrest J. Ackerman.

THE CLOAK OF AESIR by Don A. Stuart (John W. Campbell, Jr.). Copyright 1939 by Street & Smith, Inc., © 1967 by Condé Nast Publications, Inc. By permission of the Scott Meredith Literary Agency, Inc.

PILGRIMAGE by Nelson Bond. Copyright 1939, 1945, 1949 by Nelson Bond. By permission of the author.

GREATER THAN GODS by C.L. Moore. Copyright 1939 by Street & Smith, Inc., © 1975 by C.L. Moore. By permission of Harold Matson Company, Inc., agents for the author.

THE GNARLY MAN by L. Sprague de Camp. Copyright 1939 by Street & Smith, Inc., © 1966 by L. Sprague de Camp. By permission of the author.

THE BLUE GIRAFFE by L. Sprague de Camp. Copyright 1939 by Street & Smith, Inc., © 1967 by L. Sprague de Camp. By permission of the author.

I, ROBOT by Eando Binder. Copyright 1938 by the Ziff-Davis Publishing Company. By permission of the author's agent.

RUST by Joseph E. Kelleam. Copyright 1939 by Street & Smith, Inc., © 1967 by Condé Nast Publications, Inc.

THE ULTIMATE CATALYST by John Taine (Eric Temple Bell). Copyright 1939 and 1949 by Better Publications, Inc. Reprinted by permission of the Estate of John Taine.

LIFE-LINE by Robert A. Heinlein; MISFIT by Robert A. Heinlein. Copyright 1939 by Street & Smith, Inc.; renewed © 1967 by Robert A. Heinlein. Reprinted by permission of Lurton Blassingame, author's agent.

ETHER BREATHER by Theodore Sturgeon. Copyright 1939 by Street & Smith, Inc., © 1967 by Theodore Sturgeon. Reprinted by permission of the author's agent, Kirby McCauley.

THE MISGUIDED HALO by Henry Kuttner. Copyright 1939 by Street & Smith, Inc., renewed © 1975 by Catherine Moore Kuttner, Executrix for the Estate of Henry Kuttner. Reprinted by permission of the Harold Matson Company, Inc.

TRENDS by Isaac Asimov. Copyright 1939 by Street & Smith, Inc., © 1966 by Isaac Asimov. By permission of the author.

STAR BRIGHT by Jack Williamson. Copyright 1939 by Popular Publications, Inc. Reprinted by permission of the author's agents, Scott Meredith Literary Agency, Inc.

THE DAY IS DONE by Lester Del Rey. Copyright by Street & Smith, Inc., © 1967 by Condé Nast Publications, Inc. Reprinted by permission of the Scott Meredith Literary Agency, Inc.

TABLE OF CONTENTS

Introduction		8
I, ROBOT	Eando Binder	11
THE STRANGE FLIGHT OF RICHARD CLAYTON	Robert Bloch	25
TROUBLE WITH WATER	H. L. Gold	35
CLOAK OF AESIR	Don A. Stuart	56
THE DAY IS DONE	Lester Del Rey	103
THE ULTIMATE CATALYST	John Taine	118
THE GNARLY MAN	L. Sprague De Camp	141
BLACK DESTROYER	A. E. Van Vogt	163
GREATER THAN GODS	C. L. Moore	194
TRENDS	Isaac Asimov	229
THE BLUE GIRAFFE	L. Sprague De Camp	248
THE MISGUIDED HALO	Henry Kuttner	272
HEAVY PLANET	Milton A. Rothman	289
LIFE-LINE	Robert A. Heinlein	299
ETHER BREATHER	Theodore Sturgeon	318
PILGRIMAGE	Nelson Bond	332
RUST	Joseph E. Kelleam	353
THE FOUR-SIDED TRIANGLE	William F. Temple	363
STAR BRIGHT	Jack Williamson	385
MISFIT	Robert A. Heinlein	412

Introduction

In the world outside reality, it was a very bad year indeed. On March 28 Madrid fell to the forces of Francisco Franco, ending the Spanish Civil War. On April 15, President Roosevelt sought assurances from Hitler and Mussolini that they would not attack a long list of nation states (they said they would consider the request). On May 4 Vyacheslav Molotov (not yet named for the cocktail) replaced Maxim Litvinov as Soviet Foreign Minister, paving the way for the Hitler-Stalin Pact a few months later. On May 22 Hitler and Mussolini signed the "Pact of Steel."

On September 1 Germany grew tired of conquering without war and invaded Poland. On the 3rd Britain and France reluctantly declared war on the Third Reich. On September 17 the U.S.S.R. invaded Poland from the East—by September 30 Germany and the Soviet Union had agreed on the partition of Poland between them, and Hitler's master plan had passed another hurdle triumphantly.

On October 10 the deportation of Polish Jews to "reserves" began, and the Soviet Union invaded Finland on November 30, while Great Britain and France maintained a firm inactivity and the United States pretended it was on another planet.

During 1939 D.D.T. was invented. Pan American began "Clipper" flights between the United States and Europe. John Dewey's CULTURE AND FREEDOM was published. Texas A. & M. was the National Collegiate Football Champion. Picasso painted "Night Fishing at Antibes." The record for the mile run was still the 4:06.4 set in 1937 by Sydney Wooderson of Great Britain. "Grandma" Moses became famous. Bobby Riggs became the USTA Champion by defeating S. Welby Van Horn (Billy Jean King was not yet born). Jacob Epstein created "Adam" out of marble. Alice Marble was the National Women's Singles Champion. William Walton wrote his *Violin Concerto*. Byron Nelson won the U. S. Open. Robert Graves published THE LONG WEEK-END. Ralph Guldahl won the Masters Tournament. John Steinbeck published THE GRAPES OF WRATH. Johnstown won the Kentucky Derby. THE MAN WHO CAME TO DINNER by George S. Kaufman and Moss Hart made it big on Broadway, as did William Saroyan's THE TIME OF YOUR LIFE. Oregon won the NCAA Basketball Championship. GONE WITH THE WIND and GOODBYE MR. CHIPS were the movies of the year. Joe DiMaggio led the majors with a .381 average before he turned to selling coffee-makers. "Roll Out the Barrel," the prophetic "The Last Time I Saw Paris," and "Hang Out the Washing on the Siegfried Line" were hit songs. New York defeated Cincinnati four games to none to take the World Series. Joe Louis beat a bunch of turkeys to retain his heavyweight boxing championship.

And the distant knell of doom went unheard as in Germany Hahn and Strasseman discovered uranium fission, Lise Meitner in Sweden let the cat out of the bag, and Niels Bohr carried the news to the United States.

Death took Zane Grey, William Butler Yeats, Ford Maddox Ford, and the recently exiled Sigmund Freud.

Mel Brooks was still Melvin Kaminsky.

But in the real world it was a very good and important year.

In the real world the very first World Science Fiction Convention was held in New York as Sam Moskowitz and Don Wollheim fought for control of The Movement. In the real world UNKNOWN was published as a fantasy companion to ASTOUNDING: STARTLING STORIES; SCIENCE FICTION; FANTASTIC ADVENTURES; FUTURE FICTION; FAMOUS FANTASIC MYSTERIES; and PLANET STORIES all saw the light of day for the first time.

In the real world, John Campbell spent his first full year as editor of ASTOUNDING and the "Golden Age" was born with a flurry of writers Campbell was either to conceive or develop. Important people made their maiden flights into reality: in March—Isaac Asimov with MAROONED OFF VESTA; in April—Alfred Bester with THE BROKEN AXIOM; in July—A. E. van Vogt with BLACK DESTROYER; in August—Robert A. Heinlein with LIFE LINE and Fritz Leiber with TWO SOUGHT ADVENTURE; and in September—Theodore Sturgeon with ETHER BREATHER.

More wondrous things occurred in the real world: SINISTER BARRIER by Eric Frank Russell and LEST DARKNESS FALL by L. Sprague de Camp were published in UNKNOWN. ONE AGAINST THE LEGION by Jack Williamson and GREY LENSMAN by Doc Smith were serialized in ASTOUNDING (the last installment of the latter appearing in 1940). WAR WITH THE NEWTS by Karel Capek and THE OUTSIDER AND OTHERS by H. P. Lovecraft appeared in hard covers, as did the late Stanley Weinbaum's THE NEW ADAM.

The New York World's Fair influenced a generation of New York (and a few others) sf fans, editors, and writers-to-be. HARPER'S published an attack on science fiction—"Doom Beyond Jupiter" by one Bernard De Voto—no one cared.

And distant wings were beating as Barry N. Malzberg, Michael Moorcock, and Peter Nicholls were born (the last to a critical reception).

Let us travel back to that honored year of 1939 and enjoy the best stories that the real world bequeathed to us.

I, ROBOT *Amazing Stories*, January
by Eando Binder (1911–1975)

"Eando Binder" was the name used by the brothers Otto and Earl Binder on a number of science fiction stories, although after 1940 Otto worked alone. The Binder brothers are best known for three series published from the late thirties to the early forties—"Anton York," an immortal man, stories collected as ANTON YORK, IMMORTAL (1965); the "Via" stories under the name "Gordon A. Giles," all appearing in Thrilling Wonder Stories; *and the "Adam Link" stories about a robot, collected as ADAM LINK—ROBOT (1965).*

I, ROBOT was the first of the tales, most interesting because it was one of the very few science fiction stories told from the point of view of a nonhuman. Adam Link captured the imagination of the readers of Amazing Stories *with adventures like this one.*

(It certainly caught my attention. Two months after I read it, I began "Robbie", about a sympathetic robot, and that was the start of my positronic robot series. Eleven years later, when nine of my robot stories were collected into a book, the publisher named the collection I, ROBOT over my objections. My book is now the more famous, but Otto's story was there first. IA)

My Creation
Much of what has occurred puzzles me. But I think I am be-

ginning to understand now. You call me a monster, but you are wrong. Utterly wrong!

I will try to prove it to you, in writing. I hope I have time to finish. . . .

I will begin at the beginning. I was born, or created, six months ago, on November 3 of last year. I am a true robot. So many of you seem to have doubts. I am made of wires and wheels, not flesh and blood.

My first recollection of consciousness was a feeling of being chained, and I was. For three days before that, I had been seeing and hearing, but all in a jumble. Now, I had the urge to arise and peer more closely at the strange, moving form that I had seen so many times before me, making sounds.

The moving form was Dr. Link, my creator. He was the only thing that moved, of all the objects within my sight. He and one other object—his dog Terry. Therefore these two objects held my interest more. I hadn't yet learned to associate movement with life.

But on this fourth day, I wanted to approach the two moving shapes and make noises at them—particularly at the smaller one. His noises were challenging, stirring. They made me want to rise and quiet them. But I was chained. I was held down by them so that, in my blank state of mind, I wouldn't wander off and bring myself to an untimely end, or harm someone unknowingly.

These things, of course, Dr. Link explained to me later, when I could dissociate my thoughts and understand. I was just like a baby for those three days—a human baby. I am not as other so-called robots were—mere automatized machines designed to obey certain commands or arranged stimuli.

No, I was equipped with a pseudo-brain that could receive *all* stimuli that human brains could. And with possibilities of eventually learning to rationalize for itself.

But for three days Dr. Link was very anxious about my brain. I was like a human baby and yet I was also like a sensitive, but unorganized, machine, subject to the whim of mechanical chance. My eyes turned when a bit of paper fluttered to the floor. But photoelectric cells had been made before capable of doing the same. My mechanical ears turned to receive sounds best from a certain direction, but any scientist could duplicate that trick with sonic relays.

The question was—did my brain, to which the eyes and

I, ROBOT

ears were connected, hold on to these various impressions for future use? Did I have, in short—*memory?*

Three days I was like a newborn baby. And Dr. Link was like a worried father, wondering if his child had been born a hopeless idiot. But on the fourth day, he feared I was a wild animal. I began to make rasping sounds with my vocal apparatus, in answer to the sharp little noises Terry the dog made. I shook my swivel head at the same time and strained against my bonds.

For a while, as Dr. Link told me, he was frightened of me. I seemed like nothing so much as an enraged jungle creature, ready to go berserk. He had more than half a mind to destroy me on the spot.

But one thing changed his mind and saved me.

The little animal, Terry, barking angrily, rushed forward suddenly. It probably wanted to bite me. Dr. Link tried to call it back, but too late. Finding my smooth metal legs adamant, the dog leaped with foolish bravery in my lap, to come at my throat. One of my hands grasped it by the middle, held it up. My metal fingers squeezed too hard, and the dog gave out a pained squeal.

Instantaneously, my hand opened to let the creature escape! Instantaneously. My brain had interpreted the sound for what it was. A long chain of memory-association had worked. Three days before, when I had first been brought to life, Dr. Link had stepped on Terry's foot accidentally. The dog had squealed its pain. I had seen Dr. Link, at risk of losing his balance, instantly jerk up his foot. Terry had stopped squealing.

Terry squealed when my hand tightened. He would stop when I untightened. Memory-association. The thing psychologists call reflexive reaction. A sign of a living brain.

Dr. Link tells me he let out a cry of pure triumph. He knew at a stroke I had memory. He knew I was not a wanton monster. He knew I had a thinking organ, and a first-class one. Why? Because I had reacted *instantaneously*. You will realize what that means later.

I learned to walk in three hours. Dr. Link was still taking somewhat of a chance, unbinding my chains. He had no assurance that I would not just blunder away like a witless machine. But he knew he had to teach me to walk before I could learn to talk. The same as he knew he must bring my brain alive fully connected to the appendages and pseudo-organs it was later to use.

If he had simply disconnected my legs and arms for those first three days, my awakening brain would never have been able to use them when connected later. Do you think, if you were suddenly endowed with a third arm, that you could ever use it? Why does it take a cured paralytic so long to regain the use of his natural limbs? Mental blind spots in the brain. Dr. Link had all those strange psychological twists figured out.

Walk first. Talk next. That is the tried-and-true rule used among humans since the dawn of their species. Human babies learn best and fastest that way. And I was a human baby in mind, if not body.

Dr. Link held his breath when I first essayed to rise. I did, slowly, swaying on my metal legs. Up in my head, I had a three-directional spirit-level electrically contacting my brain. It told me automatically what was horizontal, vertical, and oblique. My first tentative step, however, wasn't a success. My knee joints flexed in reverse order. I clattered to my knees, which fortunately were knobbed with thick protective plates so that the more delicate swiveling mechanisms behind weren't harmed.

Dr. Link says I looked up at him like a startled child might. Then I promptly began walking along on my knees, finding this easy. Children would do this more only that it hurts them. I know no hurt.

After I had roved up and down the aisles of his workshop for an hour, nicking up his furniture terribly, walking on my knees seemed completely natural. Dr. Link was in a quandary how to get me up to my full height. He tried grasping my arm and pulling me up, but my 300 pounds of weight were too much for him.

My own rapidly increasing curiosity solved the problem. Like a child discovering the thrill of added height with stilts, my next attempt to rise to my full height pleased me. I tried staying up. I finally mastered the technique of alternate use of limbs and shift of weight forward.

In a couple of hours Dr. Link was leading me up and down the gravel walk around his laboratory. On my legs, it was quite easy for him to pull me along and thus guide me. Little Terry gamboled along at our heels, barking joyfully. The dog had accepted me as a friend.

I was by this time quite docile to Dr. Link's guidance. My

impressionable mind had quietly accepted him as a necessary rein and check. I did, he told me later, make tentative movements in odd directions off the path, motivated by vague stimuli, but his firm arm pulling me back served instantly to keep me in line. He paraded up and down with me as one might with an irresponsible oaf.

I would have kept on walking tirelessly for hours, but Dr. Link's burden of years quickly fatigued him and he led me inside. When he had safely gotten me seated in my metal chair, he clicked the switch on my chest that broke the electric current giving me life. And for the fourth time I knew that dreamless non-being which corresponded to my creator's periods of sleep.

My Education

In three days I learned to talk reasonably well.

I give Dr. Link as much credit as myself. In those three days he pointed out the names of all objects in the laboratory and around. This fund of two hundred or so nouns he supplemented with as many verbs of action as he could demonstrate. Once heard and learned, a word never again was forgotten or obscured to me. Instantaneous comprehension. Photographic memory. Those things I had.

It is difficult to explain. Machinery is precise, unvarying. I am a machine. Electrons perform their tasks instantaneously. Electrons motivate my metallic brain.

Thus, with the intelligence of a child of five at the end of those three days, I was taught to read by Dr. Link. My photoelectric eyes instantly grasped the connection between speech and letter, as my mentor pointed them out. Thought-association filled in the gaps of understanding. I perceived without delay that the word "lion," for instance, pronounced in its peculiar way, represented a live animal crudely pictured in the book. I have never seen a lion. But I would know one the instant I did.

From primers and first-readers I graduated in less than a week to adult books. Dr. Link laid out an extensive reading course for me in his large library. It included fiction as well as factual matter. Into my receptive, retentive brain began to be poured a fund of information and knowledge never before equaled in that short period of time.

There are other things to consider besides my "birth" and "education." First of all the housekeeper. She came in once a week to clean up the house for Dr. Link. He was a recluse, lived by himself, cooked for himself—retired on an annuity from an invention years before.

The housekeeper had seen me in the process of construction in the past years, but only as an inanimate caricature of a human body. Dr. Link should have known better. When the first Saturday of my life came around, he forgot it was the day she came. He was absorbedly pointing out to me that "to run" meant to go faster than "to walk."

"Demonstrate," Dr. Link asked as I claimed understanding.

Obediently, I took a few slow steps before him. "Walking," I said. Then I retreated a ways and lumbered forward again, running for a few steps. The stone floor clattered under my metallic feet.

"Was—that—right?" I asked in my rather stentorian voice.

At that moment a terrified shriek sounded from the doorway. The housekeeper came up just in time to see me perform.

She screamed, making more noise than even I. "It's the Devil himself! Run, Dr. Link—run! Police—help—"

She fainted dead away. He revived her and talked soothingly to her, trying to explain what I was, but he had to get a new housekeeper. After this he contrived to remember when Saturday came, and on that day he kept me hidden in a storeroom reading books.

A trivial incident in itself, perhaps, but very significant, as you who will read this will agree.

Two months after my awakening to life, Dr. Link one day spoke to me in a fashion other than as teacher to pupil; spoke to me as man to—man.

"You are the result of twenty years of effort," he said, "and my success amazes even me. You are little short of being a human in mind. You are a monster, a creation, but you are basically human. You have no heredity. Your environment is molding you. You are the proof that mind is an electrical phenomenon, molded by environment. In human beings, their bodies—called heredity—are environment. But out of you I will make a mental wonder!"

His eyes seemed to burn with a strange fire, but this softened as he went on.

"I knew I had something unprecedented and vital twenty years ago when I perfected an iridium sponge sensitive to the impact of a single electron. It was the sensitivity of thought! Mental currents in the human brain are of this micro-magnitude. I had the means now of duplicating mind currents in an artificial medium. From that day to this I worked on the problem.

"It was not long ago that I completed your 'brain'—an intricate complex of iridium-sponge cells. Before I brought it to life, I had your body built by skilled artisans. I wanted you to begin life equipped to live and move in it as nearly in the human way as possible. How eagerly I awaited your debut into the world!"

His eyes shone.

"You surpassed my expectations. You are not merely a thinking robot. A metal man. You are—life! A new kind of life. You can be trained to think, to reason, to perform. In the future, your kind can be of inestimable aid to man, and his civilization. You are the first of your kind."

The days and weeks slipped by. My mind matured and gathered knowledge steadily from Dr. Link's library. I was able, in time, to scan and absorb a page at a time of reading matter, as readily as human eyes scan lines. You know of the television principle—a pencil of light moving hundreds of times a second over the object to be transmitted. My eyes, triggered with speedy electrons, could do the same. What I read was absorbed—memorized—instantly. From then on it was part of my knowledge.

Scientific subjects particularly claimed my attention. There was always something indefinable about human things, something I could not quite grasp, but science digested easily in my science-compounded brain. It was not long before I knew all about myself and why I "ticked," much more fully than most humans know why they live, think, and move.

Mechanical principles became starkly simple to me. I made suggestions for improvements in my own make-up that Dr. Link readily agreed upon correcting. We added little universals in my fingers, for example, that made them almost as supple as their human models.

Almost, I say. The human body is a marvelously perfected organic machine. No robot will ever equal it in sheer efficiency and adaptability. I realized my limitations.

Perhaps you will realize what I mean when I say that my eyes cannot see colors. Or rather, I see just one color, in the blue range. It would take an impossibly complex series of units, bigger than my whole body, to enable me to see all colors. Nature has packed all that in two globes the size of marbles, for *her* robots. She had a billion years to do it. Dr. Link only had twenty years.

But my brain—that was another matter. Equipped with only the two senses of one-color sight and limited sound, it was yet capable of garnishing a full experience. Smell and taste are gastronomic senses. I do not need them. Feeling is a device of Nature's to protect a fragile body. My body is not fragile.

Sight and sound are the only two cerebral senses. Einstein, color-blind, half-dead, and with deadened senses of taste, smell, and feeling, would still have been Einstein—mentally.

Sleep is only a word to me. When Dr. Link knew he could trust me to take care of myself, he dispensed with the nightly habit of "turning me off." While he slept, I spent the hours reading.

He taught me how to remove the depleted storage battery in the pelvic part of my metal frame when necessary and replace it with a fresh one. This had to be done every forty-eight hours. Electricity is my life and strength. It is my food. Without it I am so much metal junk.

But I have explained enough of myself. I suspect that ten thousand more pages of description would make no difference in your attitude, you who are even now—

An amusing thing happened one day, not long ago. Yes, I can be amused too. I cannot laugh, but my brain can appreciate the ridiculous. Dr. Link's perennial gardener came to the place, unannounced. Searching for the doctor to ask how he wanted the hedges cut, the man came upon us in the back, walking side by side for Dr. Link's daily light exercise.

The gardener's mouth began speaking and then ludicrously gaped open and stayed that way as he caught a full glimpse of me. But he did not faint in fright as the housekeeper had. He stood there, paralyzed.

"What's the matter, Charley?" queried Dr. Link sharply. He was so used to me that for the moment he had no idea why the gardener should be astonished.

"That—that thing!" gasped the man finally.

"Oh. Well, it's a robot," said Dr. Link. "Haven't you ever heard of them? An intelligent robot. Speak to him, he'll answer."

After some urging, the gardener sheepishly turned to me. "H-how do you do, Mr. Robot," he stammered.

"How do you do, Mr. Charley," I returned promptly,

seeing the amusement in Dr. Link's face. "Nice weather, isn't it?"

For a moment the man looked ready to shriek and run. But he squared his shoulders and curled his lip. "Trickery!" he scoffed. "That thing can't be intelligent. You've got a phonograph inside of it. How about the hedges?"

"I'm afraid," murmured Dr. Link with a chuckle, "that the robot is more intelligent than you, Charley!" But he said it so the man didn't hear and then directed how to trim the hedges. Charley didn't do a good job. He seemed to be nervous all day.

My Fate

One day Dr. Link stared at me proudly.

"You have now," he said, "the intellectual capacity of a man of many years. Soon I'll announce you to the world. You shall take your place in our world, as an independent entity—as a citizen!"

"Yes, Dr. Link," I returned. "Whatever you say. You are my creator—my master."

"Don't think of it that way," he admonished. "In the same sense, you are my son. But a father is not a son's master after his maturity. You have gained that status." He frowned thoughtfully. "You must have a name! Adam! Adam Link!"

He faced me and put a hand on my shiny chromium shoulder. "Adam Link, what is your choice of future life?"

"I want to serve you, Dr. Link."

"But you will outlive me! And you may outlive several other masters!"

"I will serve any master who will have me," I said slowly. I had been thinking about this before. "I have been created by man. I will serve man."

Perhaps he was testing me. I don't know. But my answers obviously pleased him. "Now," he said, "I will have no fears in announcing you!"

The next day he was dead.

That was three days ago. I was in the storeroom reading—it was housekeeper's day. I heard the noise. I ran up the steps, into the laboratory. Dr. Link lay with skull crushed. A loose angle-iron of a transformer hung on an insulated platform on the wall had slipped and crashed down on his head while he sat there before his workbench. I raised his head, slumped over the bench, to better see the wound. Death had been instantaneous.

These are the facts. I turned the angle-iron back myself. The blood on my fingers resulted when I raised his head, not knowing for the moment that he was stark dead. In a sense, I was responsible for the accident, for in my early days of walking I had once blundered against the transformer shelf and nearly torn it loose. We should have repaired it.

But that I am his *murderer*, as you all believe, is not true. The housekeeper had also heard the noise and came from the house to investigate. She took one look. She saw me bending over the doctor, his head torn and bloody—she fled, too frightened to make a sound.

It would be hard to describe my thoughts. The little dog Terry sniffed at the body, sensed the calamity, and went down on his belly, whimpering. He felt the loss of a master. So did I. I am not sure what your emotion of sorrow is. Perhaps I cannot feel that deeply. But I do know that the sunlight seemed suddenly faded to me.

My thoughts are rapid. I stood there only a minute, but in that time I made up my mind to leave. This again has been misinterpreted. You considered that an admission of guilt, the criminal escaping from the scene of his crime. In my case it was a full-fledged desire to go out into the world, find a place in it.

Dr. Link and my life with him were a closed book. No use now to stay and watch ceremonials. He had launched my life. He was gone. My place now must be somewhere out in the world I had never seen. No thought entered my mind of what you humans would decide about me. I thought all men were like Dr. Link.

First of all I took a fresh battery, replacing my half-depleted one. I would need another in forty-eight hours, but I was sure this would be taken care of by anyone to whom I made the request.

I left. Terry followed me. He has been with me all the time. I have heard a dog is man's best friend. Even a metal man's.

My conceptions of geography soon proved hazy at best. I had pictured earth as teeming with humans and cities, with not much space between. I had estimated that the city Dr. Link spoke of must be just over the hill from his secluded country home. Yet the wood I traversed seemed endless.

It was not till hours later that I met the little girl. She had been dangling her bare legs into a brook, sitting on a flat

I, ROBOT

rock. I approached to ask where the city was. She turned when I was still thirty feet away My internal mechanisms do not run silently. They make a steady noise that Dr. Link always described as a handful of coins jingling together.

The little girl's face contorted as soon as she saw me. I must be a fearsome sight indeed in your eyes. Screaming her fear, she blindly jumped up, lost her balance, and fell into the stream.

I knew what drowning was. I knew I must save her. I knelt at the rock's edge and reached down for her. I managed to grasp one of her arms and pull her up. I could feel the bones of her thin little wrist crack. I had forgotten my strength.

I had to grasp her little leg with my other hand, to pull her up. The livid marks showed on her white flesh when I laid her on the grass. I can guess now what interpretation was put on all this. A terrible, raving monster, I had tried to drown her and break her little body in wanton savageness!

You others of her picnic party appeared then, in answer to her cries. You women screamed and fainted. You men snarled and threw rocks at me. But what strange bravery imbued the woman, probably the child's mother, who ran up under my very feet to snatch up her loved one? I admired her. The rest of you I despised for not listening to my attempts to explain. You drowned out my voice with your screams and shouts.

"Dr. Link's robot!—it's escaped and gone crazy!— shouldn't have made that monster!—get the police!—nearly killed poor Frances!—"

With these garbled shouts to one another, you withdrew. You didn't notice that Terry was barking angrily—at you. Can you fool a dog? We went on.

Now my thoughts really became puzzled. Here at last was something I could not rationalize. This was so different from the world I had learned about in books. What subtle things lay behind the printed words that I had read? What had happened to the sane and orderly world my mind had conjured for itself?

Night came. I had to stop and stay still in the dark. I leaned against a tree motionlessly. For a while I heard little Terry snooping around in the brush for something to eat. I heard him gnawing something. Then later he curled up at my feet and slept. The hours passed slowly. My thoughts would not come to a conclusion about the recent occurrence. Monster! Why had they believed that?

Once, in the still distance, I heard a murmur as of a crowd of people. I saw some lights. They had significance the next day. At dawn I nudged Terry with my toe and we walked on. The same murmur arose, approached. Then I saw you, a crowd of you, men with clubs, scythes, and guns. You spied me and a shout went up. You hung together as you advanced.

Then something struck my frontal plate with a sharp clang. One of you had shot.

"Stop! Wait!" I shouted, knowing I must talk to you, find out why I was being hunted like a wild beast. I had taken a step forward, hand upraised. But you would not listen. More shots rang out, denting my metal body. I turned and ran. A bullet in a vital spot would ruin me, as much as a human.

You came after me like a pack of hounds, but I outdistanced you, powered by steel muscles. Terry fell behind, lost. Then, as afternoon came, I realized I must get a newly charged battery. Already my limbs were moving sluggishly. In a few more hours, without a new source of current within me, I would fall on the spot and—die.

And I did not want to die.

I knew I must find a road to the city. I finally came upon a winding dirt road and followed it in hope. When I saw a car parked at the side of the road ahead of me, I knew I was saved, for Dr. Link's car had had the same sort of battery I used. There was no one around the car. Much as a starving man would take the first meal available, I raised the floorboards and in a short while had substituted batteries.

New strength coursed through my body. I straightened up just as two people came arm in arm from among the trees, a young man and woman. They caught sight of me. Incredulous shock came into their faces. The girl shrank into the boy's arms.

"Do not be alarmed," I said. "I will not harm you. I—"

There was no use going on, I saw that. The boy fainted dead away in the girl's arms and she began dragging him away, wailing hysterically.

I left. My thoughts from then on can best be described as brooding. I did not want to go to the city now. I began to realize I was an outcast in human eyes, from the first sight on.

Just as night fell and I stopped, I heard a most welcome sound. Terry's barking! He came up joyfully, wagging his stump of tail. I reached down to scratch his ears. All these hours he had faithfully searched for me. He had probably tracked me by a scent of oil. What can cause such blind devotion—and to a metal man!

Is it because, as Dr. Link once stated, that the body, human or otherwise, is only part of the environment of the mind? And that Terry recognized in me as much of mind as in humans, despite my alien body? If that is so, it is you who are passing judgment on me as a monster who are in the wrong. And I am convinced it is so!

I hear you now—shouting outside—*beware that you do not drive me to be the monster you call me!*

The next dawn precipitated you upon me again. Bullets flew. I ran. All that day it was the same. Your party, swelled by added recruits, split into groups, trying to ring me in. You tracked me by my heavy footprints. My speed saved me each time. Yet some of those bullets have done damage. One struck the joint of my right knee, so that my leg twisted as I ran. One smashed into the right side of my head and shattered the tympanum there, making me deaf on that side.

But the bullet that hurt me most was the one that killed Terry!

The shooter of that bullet was twenty yards away. I could have run to him, broken his every bone with my hard, powerful hands. Have you stopped to wonder why I didn't take revenge? *Perhaps I should!* ...

I was hopelessly lost all that day. I went in circles through the endless woods and as often blundered into you as you into me. I was trying to get away from the vicinity, from your vengeance. Toward dusk I saw something familiar—Dr. Link's laboratory!

Hiding in a clump of bushes and waiting till it was utterly dark, I approached and broke the lock on the door. It was deserted. Dr. Link's body was gone, of course.

My birthplace! My six months of life here whirled through my mind with kaleidoscopic rapidity. I wonder if my emotion was akin to what yours would be, returning to a well-remembered place? Perhaps my emotion is far deeper than yours can be! Life may be all in the mind. Something gripped me there, throbbingly. The shadows made by a dim gas jet I lit seemed to dance around me like little Terry had danced. Then I found the book, *Frankenstein*, lying on the desk whose drawers had been emptied. Dr. Link's private desk. He had kept the book from me. Why? I read it now, in a half-hour, by my page-at-a-time scanning. And then I understood!

But it is the most stupid premise ever made: that a created man must turn against his creator, against humanity, lacking a soul. The book is all wrong.

Or is it? . . . .

As I finish writing this, here among blasted memories, with the spirit of Terry in the shadows, I wonder if I shouldn't. . .

It is close to dawn now. I know there is not hope for me. You have me surrounded, cut off. I can see the flares of your torches between the trees. In the light you will find me, rout me out. Your hatred lust is aroused. It will be sated only by my—death.

I have not been so badly damaged that I cannot still summon strength and power enough to ram through your lines and escape this fate. But it would only be at the cost of several of your lives. And that is the reason I have my hand on the switch that can blink out my life with one twist.

Ironic, isn't it, that I have the very feelings you are so sure I lack?

(signed) ADAM LINK

THE STRANGE FLIGHT OF RICHARD CLAYTON

Amazing Stories, March

by Robert Bloch (1917–   )

Robert Bloch has been around the science fiction world for a long time, being one of the members of the "Lovecraft Circle" in his youth. Although he is primarily a writer of the supernatural and macabre story, he also produced some excellent science fiction, most of which is available in his collections ATOMS AND EVIL (1962) and THE BEST OF ROBERT BLOCH (1978). His skill as an after-dinner speaker masks a real talent for the shocking and the unexpected, as his non-sf novel PSYCHO illustrates. He also had the unusual distinction of winning a Hugo Award for a work of fantasy, "That Hell-Bound Train" (1958, Award in 1959).

Space travel is science fiction for too many people, although the exploration of the great unknown of space has provided us with many wonderful stories—as has the voyages that take place between our ears.

(This story appeared in the magazine issue that contained my own first published story, "Marooned Off Vesta." Bob's story was the only one in that issue which, in my eyes, was better than mine. I was not unduly troubled with excessive modesty even then, you see. IA)

Richard Clayton braced himself so that he stood like a diver waiting to plunge from a high board into the blue. In truth he was a diver. A silver spaceship was his board, and he meant to plunge not down, but up into the blue sky. Nor was it a matter of twenty or thirty feet he meant to go—instead, he was plunging millions of miles.

With a deep breath, the pudgy, goateed scientist raised his hands to the cold steel lever, closed his eyes, jerked. The switch moved downward.

For a moment nothing happened.

Then a sudden jerk threw Clayton to the floor. The *Future* was moving!

The pinions of a bird beating as it soars into the sky—the wings of a moth thrumming in flight—the quivering behind leaping muscles; of these things the shock was made.

The spaceship *Future* vibrated madly. It rocked from side to side, and a humming shook the steel walls. Richard Clayton lay dazed as a high-pitched droning arose within the vessel. He rose to his feet, rubbing a bruised forehead, and lurched to his tiny bunk. The ship was moving, yet the terrible vibration did not abate. He glanced at the controls and then swore softly.

"Good God! The panel is shattered!"

It was true. The instrument board had been broken by the shock. The cracked glass had fallen to the floor, and the dials swung aimlessly on the bare face of the panel.

Clayton sat there in despair. This was a major tragedy. His thoughts flashed back thirty years to the time when he, a boy of ten, had been inspired by Lindberg's flight. He recalled his studies; how he had utilized the money of his millionaire father to perfect a flying machine which would cross Space itself.

For years Richard Clayton had worked and dreamed and planned. He studied the Russians and their rockets, organized the Clayton Foundation and hired mechanics, mathematicians, astronomers, engineers to labor with him.

Then there had been the discovery of atomic propulsion, and the building of the *Future*. The *Future* was a shell of steel and duraluminum, windowless and insulated by a guarded process. In the tiny cabin were oxygen tanks, stores of food tablets, energizing chemicals, air-conditioning arrangements—and space for a man to walk six paces.

It was a small steel cell; but in it Richard Clayton meant to realize his ambitions. Aided in his soaring by rockets to get him past the gravitational pull of Earth, then flying by means of the atomic-discharge propulsion, Clayton meant to reach Mars and return.

It would take ten years to reach Mars; ten years to return, for the grounding of the vessel would set off additional rocket-discharges. A thousand miles an hour—not an imaginative "speed of light" journey, but a slow, grim voyage, scientifically accurate. The panels were set, and Clayton had no need to guide his vessel. It was automatic.

"But now what?" Clayton said, staring at the shattered glass. He had lost touch with the outer world. He would be unable to read his progress on the board, unable to judge time and distance and direction. He would sit here for ten, twenty years—all alone in a tiny cabin. There had been no room for books or paper or games to amuse him. He was a prisoner in the black void of Space.

The Earth had already faded far below him; soon it would be a ball of burning green fire smaller than the ball of red fire ahead—the fire of Mars.

Crowds had swarmed the field to watch him take off; his assistant Jerry Chase had controlled them. Clayton pictured them watching his shining steel cylinder emerging from the gaseous smoke of the rockets and rushing like a bullet into the sky. Then his cylinder would have faded away into the blue and the crowds would leave for home and forget.

But he remained, here in the ship—for ten, for twenty years.

Yes, he remained, but when would the vibration stop? The shuddering of the walls and floor about him was awful to endure; he and the experts had not counted on this problem. Tremors wrenched through his aching head. What if they didn't cease, if they endured through the entire voyage? How long could he keep from going mad?

He could think. Clayton lay on his bunk and remembered—reviewed every tiny detail of his life from birth to the present. And soon he had exhausted all memory in a pitifully short time. Then he felt the horrible throbbing all about him.

"I can exercise," he said aloud, and paced the floor; six steps forward, six back. And he tired of that. Sighing. Clayton went to the food-stores in the cabinet and downed his capsules. "I can't even spend any time eating," he wryly observed. "A swallow and it's over."

The throbbing erased the grin from his face. It was maddening. He lay down once more in the lurching bunk; switched on oxygen in the close air. He would sleep, then; sleep if this damned thrumming would permit. He endured the horrid clanking that groaned all through the silence; switching off the light. His thoughts turned to his strange position; a prisoner in Space. Outside the burning planets wheeled, and stars whizzed in the inky blackness of spatial Nothingness. Here he lay safe and snug in a vibrating chamber; safe from the freezing cold. If only the awful jarring would stop!

Still, it had its compensations. There would be no newspapers on the voyage to torment him with accounts of man's inhumanity to man; no silly radio or television programs to annoy him. Only this cursed, omnipresent vibration. . . .

Clayton slept, hurtling through Space.

It was not daylight when he awoke. There was no daylight and no night. There was simply himself and the ship in Space. And the vibration was steady, nerve-wracking in its insistent beating against the brain. Clatyon's legs trembled as he reached the cabinet and ate his pills.

Then, he sat down and began to endure. A terrific feeling of loneliness was beginning to assail him. He was so utterly detached here—cut off from everything. There was nothing to do. It was worse than being a prisoner in solitary confinement; at least they have larger cells, the sight of the sun, a breath of fresh air, and the glimpse of an occasional face.

Clayton had thought himself a misanthrope, a recluse. Now he longed for the sight of another's face. As the hours passed he got queer ideas. He wanted to see Life, in some form—he would have given a fortune for the company of even an insect in his soaring dungeon. The sound of a human voice would be heaven. He was so *alone*.

Nothing to do but endure the jerking, pace the floor, eat his pills, try to sleep. Nothing to think about. Clayton began to long for the time when his nails needed cutting; he could stretch out the task for hours.

He examined his clothes intently, stared for hours in the little mirror at his bearded face. He memorized his body, scrutinized every article in the cabin of the *Future*.

And still he was not tired enough to sleep again.

THE STRANGE FLIGHT OF RICHARD CLAYTON 29

He had a throbbing headache constantly. At length he managed to close his eyes and drift off into another slumber, broken by shocks which startled him into waking.

When finally he arose and switched on the light, together with more oxygen, he made a horrible discovery.

He had lost his time-sense.

"Time is relative," they had always told him. Now he realized the truth. He had nothing to measure time by—no watch, no glimpse of the sun or moon or stars, and no regular activities. How long had he been on this voyage? Try as he might, he could not remember.

Had he eaten every six hours? Or every ten? Or every twenty? Had he slept once each day? Once every three or four days? How often had he walked the floor?

With no instruments to place himself he was at a total loss. He ate his pills in a bemused fashion, trying to think above the shuddering which filled his senses.

This was awful. If he lost track of Time he might soon lose consciousness of identity itself. He would go mad here in the spaceship as it plunged through the void to planets beyond. Alone, tormented in a tiny cell, he had to cling to something. What was Time?

He no longer wanted to think about it. He no longer wanted to think about anything. He had to forget the world he left, or memory would drive him frantic.

"I'm afraid," he whispered. "Afraid of being alone in the darkness. I may have passed the moon. I may be a million miles away from Earth by now—or ten million."

Then Clayton realized that he was talking to himself. That way was madness. But he couldn't stop, any more than he could stop the horrible jarring vibration all around him.

"I'm afraid," he whispered in a voice that sounded hollow in the tiny humming room. "I'm afraid. *What time is it?*"

He fell asleep, still whispering, and Time rushed on.

Clayton awoke with fresh courage. He had lost his grip, he reasoned. Outside pressure, however equalized, had affected his nerves. The oxygen might have made him giddy, and the pill diet was bad. But now the weakness had passed. He smiled, walked the floor.

Then the thoughts came again. What day was it? How many weeks since he had started? Maybe it was months already; a year, two years. Everything of Earth seemed far away; almost part of a dream. He now felt closer to Mars than to Earth; he began to anticipate now instead of looking back.

For a while everything had been mechanical. He switched light on and off when needed, ate pills by habit, paced the floor without thinking, unconsciously tended the air system, slept without knowing when or why.

Richard Clayton gradually forgot about his body and the surroundings. The lurching buzz in his brain became a part of him; an aching part which told that he was whizzing through Space in a silver bullet. But it meant nothing more, for Clayton no longer talked to himself. He forgot himself and dreamed only of Mars ahead. Every throb of the vessel hummed, "Mars—Mars—Mars."

A wonderful thing happened. He landed. The ship nosed down, trembling. It eased gently onto the gassy sward of the red planet. For a long time Clayton had felt the pull of alien gravity, knew that automatic adjustments of his vessel were diminishing the atomic discharges and using the natural gravitational pull of Mars itself.

Now the ship landed, and Clayton had opened the door. He broke the seals and stepped out. He bounded lightly to the purple grass. His body felt free, buoyant. There was fresh air, and the sunlight seemed stronger, more intense, although clouds veiled the glowing globe.

Far away stood the forests, the green forests with the purple growth on the lushly-rearing trees. Clayton left the ship and approached the cool grove. The first tree had boughs that bent to the ground in two limbs.

Limbs—limbs they were! Two green arms reached out. Clawing branches grasped him and lifted him upward. Cold coils, slimy as a serpent's, held him tightly as he was pressed against the dark tree-trunk. And now he was staring into the purple growth set in the leaves.

The purple growths were—*heads*.

Evil, purple faces stared at him with rotting eyes like dead toadstools. Each face was wrinkled like a purple cauliflower, but beneath the pulpy mass was a great mouth. Every purple face had a purple mouth and each purple mouth opened to drip blood. Now the tree-arms pressed him closer to the cold, writhing trunk, and one of the purple faces—a woman's face—was moving up to kiss him.

The kiss of a vampire! Blood shone scarlet on the moving sensuous lips that bore down on his own. He struggled, but the limbs held him fast and the kiss came, cold as death. The

THE STRANGE FLIGHT OF RICHARD CLAYTON

icy flame of it seared through his being and his senses drowned.

Then Clayton awoke, and knew it was a dream. His body was bathed with moisture. It made him aware of his body. He tottered to the mirror.

A single glance sent him reeling back in horror. Was this too a part of his dream?

Gazing into the mirror, Clayton saw reflected the face of an aging man. The features were heavily bearded, and they were lined and wrinkled, the once puffy cheeks were sunken. The eyes were the worst—Clayton did not recognize his own eyes any more. Red and deep-set in bony sockets, they burned out in a wild stare of horror. He touched his face, saw the blue-veined hand rise in the mirror and run through graying hair.

Partial time-sense returned. He had been here for years. Years! He was growing old!

Of course the unnatural life would age him more rapidly, but still a great interval must have passed. Clayton knew that he must soon reach the end of his journey. He wanted to reach it before he had any more dreams. From now on, sanity and physical reserve must battle against the unseen enemy of Time. He staggered back to his bunk, as trembling like a metallic flying monster, the *Future* rushed on in the blackness of interstellar Space.

They were hammering outside the vessel now; their iron arms were breaking in the door. The black metal monsters lumbered in with iron tread. Their stern, steel-cut faces were expressionless as they grasped Clayton on either side and pulled him out. Across the iron platform they dragged him, walking stiffly with clicking feet that clanged against the metal. The great still shafts rose in silvery spires all about, and into the iron tower they took him. Up the stairs—clang, clang, clang, pounded the great metal feet.

And the iron stairs wound round endlessly; yet still they toiled. Their faces were set, and iron does not sweat. They never tired, though Clayton was a panting wreck ere they reached the dome and threw him before the Presence in the tower room. The metallic voice buzzed, mechanically, like a broken phonograph record.

"*We—found—him—in—a—bird—oh—Master.*"

"*He—is—made—of—soft—ness.*"

"*He—is—alive—in—some—strange—way.*"

"*An—an—im—al.*"

And then the booming voice from the center of the tower floor.

"*I hunger.*"

Rising on an iron throne from the floor, the Master. Just a great iron trap, with steel jaws like those on a steam-shovel. The jaws clicked open, and the horrid teeth gleamed. A voice came from the depths.

"*Feed me.*"

They threw Clayton forward in iron arms, and he fell into the trap-jaws of the monster. The jaws closed, champing with relish on human flesh. . . .

Clayton woke screaming. The mirror gleamed as his trembling hands found the light-switch. He stared into the face of an aging man with almost white hair. Clayton was growing old. And he wondered if his brain would hold out.

Eat pills, walk cabin, listen to the throbbing, put on air, lie on bunk. That was all, now. And the rest—waiting. Waiting in a humming torture-chamber, for hours, days, years, centuries, untold eons.

In every eon, a dream. He landed on Mars and the ghosts came coiling out of a gray fog. They were shapes in the fog, like slimy ectoplasm, and he saw through them. But they coiled and came, and their voices were faint whispers in his soul.

"Here is Life," they whispered. "We, whose souls have crossed the Void in death, have waited for Life to feast on. Let us take our feasting now."

And they smothered him under gray blankets, and sucked with gray, prickling mouths at his blood. . . .

Again he landed on the planet and there was nothing. Absolutely nothing. The ground was bare and it stretched off into horizons of nothingness. There was no sky nor sun, merely the ground; endless in all directions.

He set foot on it, cautiously. He sank down into nothingness. The nothingness was throbbing now, like the ship throbbed, and it was engulfing him. He was falling into a deep pit without sides, and the oblivion closed all about him. . . .

Clayton dreamed this one standing up. He opened his eyes before the mirror. His legs were weak and he steadied himself with hands that shook with age. He looked at the face in the glass—the face of a man of seventy.

"God!" he muttered. It was his own voice—the first sound he had heard in how long? How many years? For how long had he heard nothing above the hellish vibrations of this ship? How far had the *Future* gone? He was old already.

A horrid thought bit into his brain. Perhaps something had gone wrong. Maybe the calculations were at fault and he was moving into Space too slowly. He might never reach Mars. Then again—and it was a dreadful possibility—he had passed Mars, missed the carefully charted orbit of the planet. Now he was plunging on into empty voids beyond.

He swallowed his pills and lay down in the bunk. He felt a little calmer now; he had to be. For the first time in ages he remembered Earth.

Suppose it had been destroyed? Invaded by war or pestilence or disease while he was gone? Or meteors had struck it, some dying star had flamed death upon it from maddened heavens. Ghastly notions assailed him—what if Invaders crossed Space to conquer Earth, just as he now crossed to Mars?

But no sense in worrying about *that*. The problem was reaching his own goal. Helpless, he had to wait; maintain life and sanity long enough to achieve his aims. In the vibrating horror of his cell, Clayton took a mighty resolve with all his waning strength. He *would* live and when he landed he would see Mars. Whether or not he died on the long voyage home, he would exist until his goal was reached. He would fight against dreams from this moment on. No means of telling Time—only a long daze, and the humming of this infernal spaceship. But he'd live.

There were voices coming now, from outside the ship. Ghosts howled, in the dark depths of Space. Visions of monsters and dreams of torment came, and Clayton repulsed them all. Every hour or day or year—he no longer knew which—Clayton managed to stagger to the mirror. And always it showed that he was aging rapidly. His snow-white hair and wrinkled countenance hinted at incredible senility. But Clayton lived. He was too old to think any longer, and too weary. He merely lived in the droning of the ship.

At first he didn't realize. He was lying on his bunk and his rheumy eyes were closed in stupor. Suddenly he became aware that the lurching had stopped. Clayton knew he must be dreaming again. He drew himself up painfully, rubbed his eyes. No—the *Future* was still. It had *landed!*

He was trembling uncontrollably. Years of vibration had done this; years of isolation with only his crazed thoughts for company. He could scarcely stand.

But this was the moment. This was what he had waited for ten long years. No, it must have been many more years. But he could see Mars. He had made it—done the impossible.

It was an inspiring thought. But somehow, Richard Clayton would have given it all up if he could only have learned what time it was, and heard it from a human voice.

He staggered to the door—the long-sealed door. There was a lever here.

His aged heart pumped with excitement as he pulled the lever upward. The door opened—sunlight crept through—air rushed in—the light made him blink and the air wheezed in his lungs—his feet were moving out—

Clayton fell forward into the arms of Jerry Chase.

Clayton didn't know it was Jerry Chase. He didn't know anything any longer. It had been too much.

Chase was staring down at the feeble body in his arms.

"Where's Mr. Clayton?" he murmured. "Who are you?" He stared at the aged, wrinkled face.

"Why—it's Clayton! he breathed. "Mr. Clayton, what's wrong, sir? The atomic discharges failed when you started the ship, and all that happened was that they kept blasting. The ship never left the Earth, but the violence of the discharges kept us from reaching you until now. We couldn't get to the *Future* until they stopped. Just a little while ago the ship finished shuddering, but we've been watching night and day. What happened to you, sir?"

The faded blue eyes of Richard Clayton opened. His mouth twitched as he faintly whispered.

"I—lost track of Time. How—how long was I in the *Future?*"

Jerry Chase's face was grave as he stared again at the old man and answered, softly.

"Just one week."

And as Richard Clayton's eyes glazed in death, the long voyage ended.

TROUBLE WITH WATER

Unknown, March

by H. L. Gold (1914–   )

One of the most significant figures in the history of science fiction, Horace Leonard Gold was the founding editor of GALAXY SF, and under his direction it quickly became the leading magazine in the field during the Fifties.

Unfortunately, his fame as an editor has obscured his talent as a writer. Gold was an original, clever author, and a more than competent stylist. His best work was collected in 1955 as THE OLD DIE RICH AND OTHER SCIENCE FICTION, a book that strongly deserves reprinting.

"Trouble With Water" is arguably his best story—and not because the protagonist's name is Greenberg. Think about this one the next time you feel thirsty.

(This was the funniest fantasy I had ever read, in my opinion, at the time it appeared. It appeared in the maiden issue of UNKNOWN FANTASY FICTION, and though the lead novel was Eric Frank Russell's classic SINISTER BARRIER, Horace's story was my favorite in the issue. IA)

Greenberg did not deserve his surroundings. He was the first fisherman of the season, which guaranteed him a fine catch; he sat in a dry boat—one without a single leak—far out on a lake that was ruffled only enough to agitate his artificial fly.

The sun was warm, the air was cool; he sat comfortably on a cushion; he had brought a hearty lunch; and two bottles of beer hung over the stern in the cold water.

Any other man would have been soaked with joy to be fishing on such a splendid day. Normally, Greenberg himself would have been ecstatic, but instead of relaxing and waiting for a nibble, he was plagued by worries.

This short, slightly gross, definitely bald, eminently respectable businessman lived a gypsy life. During the summer he lived in a hotel with kitchen privileges in Rockaway; winters he lived in a hotel with kitchen privileges in Florida; and in both places he operated concessions. For years now, rain had fallen on schedule every week end, and there had been storms and floods on Decoration Day, July 4th and Labor Day. He did not love his life, but it was a way of making a living.

He closed his eyes and groaned. If he had only had a son instead of his Rosie! Then things would have been mighty different—

For one thing, a son could run the hot dog and hamburger griddle, Esther could draw beer, and he would make soft drinks. There would be small difference in the profits, Greenberg admitted to himself; but at least those profits could be put aside for old age, instead of toward a dowry for his miserably ugly, dumpy, pitifully eager Rosie.

"All right—so what do I care if she don't get married?" he had cried to his wife a thousand times. "I'll support her. Other men can set up boys in candy stores with soda fountains that have only two spigots. Why should I have to give a boy a regular International Casino?"

"May your tongue rot in your head, you no-good piker!" she would scream. "It ain't right for a girl to be an old maid. If we have to die in the poor-house, I'll get my poor Rosie a husband. Every penny we don't need for living goes to her dowry!"

Greenberg did not hate his daughter, nor did he blame her for his misfortunes; yet, because of her, he was fishing with a broken rod that he had to tape together.

That morning his wife opened her eyes and saw him packing his equipment. She instantly came awake. "Go ahead!" she shrilled—speaking in a conversational tone was not one of her accomplishments—"Go fishing, you loafer! Leave me here alone. I can connect the beer pipes and the gas for soda water. I can buy ice cream, frankfurters, rolls, sirup,

TROUBLE WITH WATER

and watch the gas and electric men at the same time. Go ahead—go fishing!"

"I ordered everything," he mumbled soothingly. "The gas and electric won't be turned on today. I only wanted to go fishing—it's my last chance. Tomorrow we open the concession. Tell the truth, Esther, can I go fishing after we open?"

"I don't care about that. Am I your wife or ain't I, that you should go ordering everything without asking me—"

He defended his actions. It was a tactical mistake. While she was still in bed, he should have picked up his equipment and left. By the time the argument got around to Rosie's dowry, she stood facing him.

"For myself I don't care," she yelled. "What kind of a monster are you that you can go fishing while your daughter eats her heart out? And on a day like this yet! You should only have to make supper and dress Rosie up. A lot you care that a nice boy is coming to supper tonight and maybe take Rosie out, you no-good father, you!"

From that point it was only one hot protest and a shrill curse to find himself clutching half a broken rod, with the other half being flung at his head.

Now he sat in his beautifully dry boat on an excellent game lake far out on Long Island, desperately aware that any average fish might collapse his taped rod.

What else could he expect? He had missed his train; he had had to wait for the boathouse proprietor; his favorite dry fly was missing; and, since morning, not a fish struck at the bait. Not a single fish!

And it was getting late. He had no more patience. He ripped the cap off a bottle of beer and drank it, in order to gain courage to change his fly for a less sporting bloodworm. It hurt him, but he wanted a fish.

The hook and the squirming worm sank. Before it came to rest, he felt a nibble. He sucked in his breath exultantly and snapped the hook deep into the fish's mouth. Sometimes, he thought philosophically, they just won't take artificial bait. He reeled in slowly.

"Oh, Lord," he prayed, "a dollar for charity—just don't let the rod bend in half where I taped it!"

It was sagging dangerously. He looked at it unhappily and raised his ante to five dollars; even at that price it looked impossible. He dipped his rod into the water, parallel with the line, to remove the strain. He was glad no one could see him do it. The line reeled in without a fight.

"Have I—God forbid!—got an eel or something not kosher?" he mumbled. "A plague on you—why don't you fight?"

He did not really care what it was—even an eel—anything at all.

He pulled in a long, pointed, brimless green hat.

For a moment he glared at it. His mouth hardened. Then, viciously, he yanked the hat off the hook, threw it on the floor and trampled on it. He rubbed his hands together in anguish.

"All day I fish," he wailed, "two dollars for train fare, a dollar for a boat, a quarter for bait, a new rod I got to buy—and a five-dollar-mortgage charity has got on me. For what? For you, you hat, you!"

Out in the water an extremely civil voice asked politely: "May I have my hat, please?"

Greenberg glowered up. He saw a little man come swimming vigorously through the water toward him: small arms crossed with enormous dignity, vast ears on a pointed face propelling him quite rapidly and efficiently. With serious determination he drove through the water, and, at the starboard rail, his amazing ears kept him stationary while he looked gravely at Greenberg.

"You are stamping on my hat," he pointed out without anger.

To Greenberg this was highly unimportant. "With the ears you're swimming," he grinned in a superior way. "Do you look funny!"

"How else could I swim?" the little man asked politely.

"With the arms and legs, like a regular human being, of course."

"But I am not a human being. I am a water gnome, a relative of the more common mining gnome. I cannot swim with my arms, because they must be crossed to give an appearance of dignity suitable to a water gnome; and my feet are used for writing and holding things. On the other hand, my ears are perfectly adapted for propulsion in water. Consequently, I employ them for that purpose. But please, my hat—there are several matters requiring my immediate attention, and I must not waste time."

Greenberg's unpleasant attitude toward the remarkably civil gnome is easily understandable. He had found someone he could feel superior to, and, by insulting him, his depressed

TROUBLE WITH WATER

ego could expand. The water gnome certainly looked inoffensive enough, being only two feet tall.

"What you got that's so important to do, Big Ears?" he asked nastily.

Greenberg hoped the gnome would be offended. He was not, since his ears, to him, were perfectly normal, just as you would not be insulted if a member of a race of atrophied beings were to call you "Big Muscles." You might even feel flattered.

"I really must hurry," the gnome said, almost anxiously. "But if I have to answer your questions in order to get back my hat—we are engaged in restocking the Eastern waters with fish. Last year there was quite a drain. The bureau of fisheries is coöperating with us to some extend, but, of course, we cannot depend too much on them. Until the population rises to normal, every fish has instructions not to nibble."

Greenberg allowed himself a smile, an annoyingly skeptical smile.

"My main work," the gnome went on resignedly, "is control of the rainfall over the Eastern seaboard. Our fact-finding committee, which is scientifically situated in the meteorological center of the continent, coördinates the rainfall needs of the entire continent; and when they determine the amount of rain needed in particular spots of the East, I make it rain to that extent. Now may I have my hat, please?"

Greenberg laughed coarsely. "The first lie was big enough—about telling the fish not to bite. You make it rain like I'm President of the United States!" He bent toward the gnome slyly. "How's about proof?"

"Certainly, if you insist." The gnome raised his patient, triangular face toward a particularly clear blue spot in the sky, a trifle to one side of Greenberg. "Watch that bit of the sky."

Greenberg looked up humorously. Even when a small dark cloud rapidly formed in the previously clear spot, his grin remained broad. It could have been coincidental. But then large drops of undeniable rain fell over a twenty-foot circle; and Greenberg's mocking grin shrank and grew sour.

He glared hatred at the gnome, finally convinced. "So you're the dirty crook who makes it rain on week ends!"

"Usually on week ends during the summer," the gnome admitted. "Ninety-two percent of water consumption is on weekdays. Obviously we must replace that water. The week ends, of course, are the logical time."

"But, you thief!" Greenberg cried hysterically, "you murderer! What do you care what you do to my concession with your rain? It ain't bad enough business would be rotten even without rain, you got to make floods!"

"I'm sorry," the gnome replied, untouched by Greenberg's rhetoric. "We do not create rainfall for the benefit of men. We are here to protect the fish.

"Now please give me my hat. I have wasted enough time, when I should be preparing the extremely heavy rain needed for this coming week end."

Greenberg jumped to his feet in the unsteady boat. "Rain this week end—when I can maybe make a profit for a change! A lot you care if you ruin business. May you and your fish die a horrible, lingering death."

And he furiously ripped the green hat to pieces and hurled them at the gnome.

"I'm really sorry you did that," the little fellow said calmly, his huge ears treading water without the slightest increase of pace to indicate his anger. "We Little Folk have no tempers to lose. Nevertheless, occasionally we find it necessary to discipline certain of your people, in order to retain our dignity. I am not malignant; but, since you hate water and those who live in it, water and those who live in it will keep away from you."

With his arms still folded in great dignity, the tiny water gnome flipped his vast ears and disappeared in a neat surface dive.

Greenberg glowered at the spreading circles of waves. He did not grasp the gnome's final restraining order; he did not even attempt to interpret it. Instead he glared angrily out of the corner of his eye at the phenomenal circle of rain that fell from a perfectly clear sky. The gnome must have remembered it at length, for a moment later the rain stopped. Like shutting off a faucet, Greenberg unwillingly thought.

"Good-by, week-end business," he growled. "If Esther finds out I got into an argument with the guy who makes it rain—"

He made an underhand cast, hoping for just one fish. The line flew out over the water; then the hook arched upward and came to rest several inches above the surface, hanging quite steadily and without support in the air.

"Well, go down in the water, damn you!" Greenberg said

viciously, and he swished his rod back and forth to pull the hook down from its ridiculous levitation. It refused.

Muttering something incoherent about being hanged before he'd give in, Greenberg hurled his useless rod at the water. By this time he was not surprised when it hovered in the air above the lake. He merely glanced red-eyed at it, tossed out the remains of the gnome's hat, and snatched up the oars.

When he pulled back on them to row to land, they did not touch the water—naturally. Instead they flashed unimpeded through the air, and Greenberg tumbled into the bow.

"A-ha!" he grated. "Here's where the trouble begins." He bent over the side. As he had suspected, the keel floated a remarkable distance above the lake.

By rowing against the air, he moved with maddening slowness toward shore, like a medieval conception of a flying machine. His main concern was that no one should see him in his humiliating position.

At the hotel he tried to sneak past the kitchen to the bathroom. He knew that Esther waited to curse him for fishing the day before opening, but more especially on the very day that a nice boy was coming to see her Rosie. If he could dress in a hurry, she might have less to say—

"Oh, there you are, you good-for-nothing!"

He froze to a halt.

"Look at you!" she screamed shrilly. "Filthy—you stink from fish!"

"I didn't catch anything, darling," he protested timidly.

"You stink anyhow. Go take a bath, may you drown in it! Get dressed in two minutes or less, and entertain the boy when he gets here. Hurry!"

He locked himself in, happy to escape her voice, started the water in the tub, and stripped from the waist up. A hot bath, he hoped, would rid him of his depressed feeling.

First, no fish; now, rain on week ends! What would Esther say—if she knew, of course. And, of course, he would not tell her.

"Let myself in for a lifetime of curses!" he sneered. "Ha!"

He clamped a new blade into his razor, opened the tube of shaving cream, and stared objectively at the mirror. The dominant feature of the soft, chubby face that stared back was its ugly black stubble; but he set his stubborn chin and glowered. He really looked quite fierce and indomitable. Unfortunately, Esther never saw his face in that uncharacteristic pose, otherwise she would speak more softly.

"Herman Greenberg never gives in!" he whispered between savagely hardened lips. "Rain on week ends, no fish—anything he wants; a lot I care! Believe me, he'll come crawling to me before I go to him."

He gradually became aware that his shaving brush was not getting wet. When he looked down and saw the water dividing into streams that flowed around it, his determined face slipped and grew desperately anxious. He tried to trap the water—by catching it in his cupped hands, by creeping up on it from behind, as if it were some shy animal, and shoving his brush at it—but it broke and ran away from his touch. Then he jammed his palm against the faucet. Defeated, he heard it gurgle back down the pipe, probably as far as the main.

"What do I do now?" he groaned. "Will Esther give it to me if I don't take a shave! But how? . . . I can't shave without water."

Glumly, he shut off the bath, undressed and stepped into the tub. He lay down to soak. It took a moment of horrified stupor to realize that he was completely dry and that he lay in a waterless bathtub. The water, in one surge of revulsion, had swept out onto the floor.

"Herman, stop splashing!" his wife yelled. "I just washed that floor. If I find one little puddle I'll murder you!"

Greenberg surveyed the instep-deep pool over the bathroom floor. "Yes, my love," he croaked unhappily.

With an inadequate washrag he chased the elusive water, hoping to mop it all up before it could seep through to the apartment below. His washrag remained dry, however, and he knew that the ceiling underneath was dripping. The water was still on the floor.

In despair, he sat on the edge of the bathtub. For some time he sat in silence. Then his wife banged on the door, urging him to come out. He started and dressed moodily.

When he sneaked out and shut the bathroom door tightly on the flood inside, he was extremely dirty and his face *was* raw where he had experimentally attempted to shave with a dry razor.

"Rosie!" he called in a hoarse whisper. "Sh! Where's mamma?"

His daughter sat on the studio couch and applied nail-polish to her stubby fingers. "You look terrible," she said in a conversational tone. "Aren't you going to shave?"

He recoiled at the sound of her voice, which, to him, roared out like a siren. "Quiet, Rosie! Sh!" And for further emphasis, he shoved his lips out against a warning finger. He heard his wife striding heavily around the kitchen. "Rosie," he cooed, "I'll give you a dollar if you'll mop up the water I spilled in the bathroom."

"I can't papa," she stated firmly. "I'm all dressed."

"Two dollars, Rosie—all right, two and a half, you blackmailer."

He flinched when he heard her gasp in the bathroom; but, when she came out with soaked shoes, he fled downstairs. He wandered aimlessly toward the village.

Now he was in for it, he thought; screams from Esther, tears from Rosie—plus a new pair of shoes for Rosie and two and a half dollars. It would be worse, though, if he could not get rid of his whiskers—

Rubbing the tender spots where his dry razor had raked his face, he mused blankly at a drugstore window. He saw nothing to help him, but he went inside anyhow and stood hopefully at the drug counter. A face peered at him through a space scratched in the wall case mirror, and the druggist came out. A nice-looking, intelligent fellow, Greenberg saw at a glance.

"What you got for shaving that I can use without water?" he asked.

"Skin irritation, eh?" the pharmacist replied. "I got something very good for that."

"No. It's just— Well, I don't like to shave with water."

The druggist seemed disappointed. "Well, I got brushless shaving cream." Then he brightened. "But I got an electric razor—much better."

"How much?" Greenberg asked cautiously.

"Only fifteen dollars, and it lasts a lifetime."

"Give me the shaving cream," Greenberg said coldly.

With the tactical science of a military expert, he walked around until some time after dark. Only then did he go back to the hotel, to wait outside. It was after seven, he was getting hungry, and the people who entered the hotel he knew as permanent summer guests. At last a stranger passed him and ran up the stairs.

Greenberg hesitated for a moment. The stranger was scarcely a boy, as Esther had definitely termed him, but Greenberg reasoned that her term was merely wish-fulfillment, and he jauntily ran up behind him.

He allowed a few minutes to pass, for the man to introduce himself and let Esther and Rosie don their company manners. Then, secure in the knowledge that there would be no scene until the guest left, he entered.

He waded through a hostile atmosphere, urbanely shook hands with Sammie Katz, who was a doctor—probably, Greenberg thought shrewdly, in search of an office—and excused himself.

In the bathroom he carefully read the direction for using brushless shaving cream. He felt less confident when he realized that he had to wash his face thoroughly with soap and water, but without benefit of either, he spread the cream on, patted it, and waited for his beard to soften. It did not, as he discovered while shaving. He wiped his face dry. The towel was sticky and black, with whiskers suspended in paste, and, for that, he knew, there would be more hell to pay. He shrugged resignedly. He would have to spend fifteen dollars for an electric razor after all; this foolishness was costing him a fortune!

That they were waiting for him before beginning supper, was, he knew, only a gesture for the sake of company. Without changing her hard, brilliant smile, Esther whispered: "Wait! I'll get you later—"

He smiled back, his tortured, slashed face creasing painfully. All that could be changed by his being enormously pleasant to Rosie's young man. If he could slip Sammie a few dollars—more expense, he groaned—to take Rosie out, Esther would forgive everything.

He was too engaged in beaming and putting Sammie at ease to think of what would happen after he ate caviar canapes. Under other circumstances Greenberg would have been repulsed by Sammie's ultra-professional waxed mustache—an offensively small, pointed thing—and his commercial attitude toward poor Rosie; but Greenberg regarded him as a potential savior.

"You open an office yet, Doctor Katz?"

"Not yet. You know how things are. Anyhow, call me Sammie."

Greenberg recognized the gambit with satisfaction, since it seemed to please Esther so much. At one stroke Sammie had ingratiated himself and begun bargaining negotiations.

Without another word, Greenberg lifted his spoon to attack the soup. It would be easy to snare this eager doctor. A *doctor!* No wonder Esther and Rosie were so puffed with joy.

In the proper company way, he pushed his spoon away from him. The soup spilled onto the tablecloth.

TROUBLE WITH WATER 45

"Not so hard, you dope," Esther hissed.

He drew the spoon toward him. The soup leaped off it like a live thing and splashed over him—turning, just before contact, to fall on the floor. He gulped and pushed the bowl away. This time the soup poured over the side of the plate and lay in a huge puddle on the table.

"I didn't want any soup anyhow," he said in a horrible attempt at levity. Lucky for him, he thought wildly, that Sammie was there to pacify Esther with his smooth college talk—not a bad fellow, Sammie, in spite of his mustache; he'd come in handy at times.

Greenberg lapsed into a paralysis of fear. He was thirsty after having eaten the caviar, which beats herring any time as a thirst raiser. But the knowledge that he could not touch water without having it recoil and perhaps spill, made his thirst a monumental craving. He attacked the problem cunningly.

The others were talking rapidly and rather hysterically. He waited until his courage was equal to his thirst; then he leaned over the table with a glass in his hand. "Sammie, do you mind—a little water, huh?"

Sammie poured from a pitcher while Esther watched for more of his tricks. It was to be expected, but still he was shocked when the water exploded out of the glass directly at Sammie's only suit.

"If you'll excuse me," Sammie said angrily, "I don't like to eat with lunatics."

And he left, though Esther cried and begged him to stay. Rosie was too stunned to move. But when the door closed, Greenberg raised his agonized eyes to watch his wife stalk murderously toward him.

Greenberg stood on the boardwalk outside his concession and glared blearily at the peaceful, blue, highly unpleasant ocean. He wondered what would happen if he started at the edge of the water and strode out. He could probably walk right to Europe on dry land.

It was early—much too early for business—and he was tired. Neither he nor Esther had slept; and it was practically certain that the neighbors hadn't either. But above all he was incredibly thirsty.

In a spirit of experimentation, he mixed a soda. Of course its high water content made it slop onto the floor. For breakfast he had surreptitiously tried fruit juice and coffee, without success.

With his tongue dry to the point of furriness, he sat weakly on a boardwalk bench in front of his concession. It was Friday morning, which meant that the day was clear with a promise of intense heat. Had it been Saturday, it naturally would have been raining.

"This year," he moaned, "I'll be wiped out. If I can't mix sodas, why should beer stay in a glass for me? I thought I could hire a boy for ten dollars a week to run the hot-dog griddle; I could make sodas, and Esther could draw beer; but twenty or maybe twenty-five a week I got to pay a sodaman. I won't even come out square—a fortune I'll lose!"

The situation really was desperate. Concessions depend on too many factors to be anything but capriciously profitable.

His throat was fiery and his soft brown eyes held a fierce glaze when the gas and electric were turned on, the beer pipes connected, the tank of carbon dioxide hitched to the pump, and the refrigerator started.

Gradually, the beach was filling with bathers. Greenberg writhed on his bench and envied them. They could swim and drink without having liquids draw away from them as if in horror. They were not thirsty—

And then he saw his first customers approach. His business experience was that morning customers buy only soft drinks. In a mad haste he put up the shutters and fled to the hotel.

"Esther!" he cried. "I got to tell you! I can't stand it—"

Threateningly, his wife held her broom like a baseball bat. "Go back to the concession, you crazy fool. Ain't you done enough already?"

He could not be hurt more than he had been. For once he did not cringe. "You got to help me, Esther."

"Why didn't you shave, you no-good bum? Is that any way—"

"That's what I got to tell you. Yesterday I got into an argument with a water gnome—"

"A what?" Esther looked at him suspiciously.

"A water gnome," he babbled in a rush of words. "A little man so high, with big ears that he swims with, and he makes it rain—"

"Herman!" she screamed. "Stop that nonsense. You're crazy!"

Greenberg pounded his forehead with his fist. "I *ain't* crazy. Look, Esther. Come with me into the kitchen."

She followed him readily enough, but her attitude made him feel more helpless and alone than ever. With her fists on her plump hips and her feet set wide, she cautiously watched him try to fill a glass of water.

"Don't you see?" he wailed. "It won't go in the glass. It spills over. It runs away from me."

She was puzzled. "What happened to you?"

Brokenly, Greenberg told of his encounter with the water ghome, leaving out no single degrading detail. "And now I can't touch water," he ended. "I can't drink it. I can't make sodas. On top of it all, I got such a thirst, it's killing me."

Esther's reaction was instantaneous. She threw her arms around him, drew his head down to her shoulder, and patted him comfortingly as if he were a child. "Herman, my poor Herman!" she breathed tenderly. "What did we ever do to deserve such a curse?"

"What shall I do, Esther?" he cried helplessly.

She held him at arm's length. "You got to go to a doctor," she said firmly. "How long can you go without drinking? Without water you'll die. Maybe sometimes I am a little hard on you, but you know I love you—"

"I know, mamma," he sighed. "But how can a doctor help me?"

"Am I a doctor that I should know? Go anyhow. What can you lose?"

He hesitated. "I need fifteen dollars for an electric razor," he said in a low, weak voice.

"So?" she replied. "If you got to, you got to. Go, darling. I'll take care of the concession."

Greenberg no longer felt deserted and alone. He walked almost confidently to a doctor's office. Manfully, he explained his symptoms. The doctor listened with professional sympathy, until Greenberg reached his description of the water gnome.

Then his eyes glittered and narrowed. "I know just the thing for you, Mr. Greenberg," he interrupted. "Sit there until I come back."

Greenberg sat quietly. He even permitted himself a surge of hope. But it seemed only a moment later that he was vaguely conscious of a siren screaming toward him; and then he was overwhelmed by the doctor and two internes who pounced on him and tried to squeeze him into a bag.

He resisted, of course. He was terrified enough to punch wildly. "What are you doing to me?" he shrieked. "Don't put that thing on me!"

"Easy now," the doctor soothed. "Everything will be all right."

It was on that humiliating scene that the policeman, required by law to accompany public ambulances, appeared. "What's up?" he asked.

"Don't stand there, you fathead," an interne shouted. "This man's crazy. Help us get him into this strait jacket."

But the policeman approached indecisively. "Take it easy, Mr. Greenberg. They ain't gonna hurt you while I'm here. What's it all about?"

"Mike!" Greenberg cried, and clung to his protector's sleeve. "They think I'm crazy—"

"Of course he's crazy," the doctor stated. "He came in here with a fantastic yarn about a water gnome putting a curse on him."

"What kind of a curse, Mr. Greenberg?" Mike asked cautiously.

"I got into an argument with the water ghome who makes it rain and takes care of the fish," Greenberg blurted. "I tore up his hat. Now he won't let water touch me. I can't drink, or anything—"

The doctor nodded. "There you are. Absolutely insane."

"Shut up." For a long moment Mike stared curiously at Greenberg. Then: "Did any of you scientists think of testing him? Here, Mr. Greenberg." He poured water into a paper cup and held it out.

Greenberg moved to take it. The water backed up against the cup's far lip; when he took it in his hand, the water shot out into the air.

"Crazy, is he?" Mike asked with heavy irony. "I guess you don't know there's things like gnomes and elves. Come with me, Mr. Greenberg."

They went out together and walked toward the boardwalk. Greenberg told Mike the entire story and explained how, besides being so uncomfortable to him personally, it would ruin him financially.

"Well, doctors can't help you," Mike said at length. "What do they know about the Little Folk? And I can't say I blame you for sassing the gnome. You ain't Irish or you'd have spoke with more respect to him. Anyhow, you're thirsty. Can't you drink *anything?*"

"Not a thing," Greenberg said mournfully.

They entered the concession. A single glance told Greenberg that business was very quiet, but even that could not lower his feelings more than they already were. Esther clutched him as soon as she saw them.

"Well?" she asked anxiously.

Greenberg shrugged in despair. "Nothing. He thought I was crazy."

Mike stared at the bar. Memory seemed to struggle behind his reflective eyes. "Sure," he said after a long pause. "Did you try beer, Mr. Greenberg? When I was a boy my old mother told me all about elves and gnomes and the rest of the Little Folk. She knew them, all right. They don't touch alcohol, you know. Try drawing a glass of beer—"

Greenberg trudged obediently behind the bar and held a glass under the spigot. Suddenly his despondent face brightened. Beer creamed into the glass—and stayed there! Mike and Esther grinned at each other as Greenberg threw back his head and furiously drank.

"Mike!" he crowed. "I'm saved. You got to drink with me!"

"Well—" Mike protested feebly.

By late afternoon, Esther had to close the concession and take her husband and Mike to the hotel.

The following day, being Saturday, brought a flood of rain. Greenberg nursed an imposing hang-over that was constantly aggravated by his having to drink beer in order to satisfy his recurring thirst. He thought of forbidden icebags and alkaline drinks in an agony of longing.

"I can't stand it!" he groaned. "Beer for breakfast—phooey!"

"It's better than nothing," Esther said fatalistically.

"So help me, I don't know if it is. But, darling, you ain't mad at me on account of Sammie, are you?"

She smiled gently, "Poo! Talk dowry and he'll come back quick."

"That's what I thought. But what am I going to do about my curse?"

Cheerfully, Mike furled an umbrella and strode in with a little old woman, whom he introduced as his mother. Greenberg enviously saw evidence of the effectiveness of icebags and alkaline drinks, for Mike had been just as high as he the day before.

"Mike told me about you and the gnome," the old lady said. "Now I know the Little Folk well, and I don't hold you to blame for insulting him, seeing you never met a gnome before. But I suppose you want to get rid of your curse. Are you repentant?"

Greenberg shuddered. "Beer for breakfast! Can you ask?"

"Well, just you go to this lake and give the gnome proof."

"What kind of proof?" Greenberg asked eagerly.

"Bring him sugar. The Little Folk love the stuff—"

Greenberg beamed. "Did you hear that, Esther? I'll get a barrel—"

"They love sugar, but they can't eat it," the old lady broke in. "It melts in water. You got to figure out a way so it won't. Then the little gentleman'll know you're repentant for real."

There was a sympathetic silence while his agitated mind attacked the problem from all angles. Then the old lady said in awe: "The minute I saw your place I knew Mike had told the truth. I never seen a sight like it in my life—rain coming down, like the flood, everywhere else; but all around this place, in a big circle, it's dry as a bone!"

While Greenberg scarcely heard her, Mike nodded and Esther seemed peculiarly interested in the phenomenon. When he admitted defeat and came out of his reflected stupor, he was alone in the concession, with only a vague memory of Esther's saying she would not be back for several hours.

"What am I going to do?" he muttered. "Sugar that won't melt—" He drew a glass of beer and drank it thoughtfully. "Particular they got to be yet. Ain't it good enough if I bring simple sirup—that's sweet."

He pottered about the place, looking for something to do. He could not polish the fountain on the bar, and the few frankfurters boiling on the griddle probably would go to waste. The floor had already been swept. So he sat uneasily and worried his problem.

"Monday, no matter what," he resolved, "I'll go to the lake. It don't pay to go tomorrow. I'll only catch a cold because it'll rain."

At last Esther returned, smiling in a strange way. She was extremely gentle, tender and thoughtful; and for that he was appreciative. But that night and all day Sunday he understood the reason for her happiness.

She had spread word that, while it rained in every other place all over town, their concession was miraculously dry. So, besides a headache that made his body throb in rhythm to its vast pulse, Greenberg had to work like six men satisfying the crowd who mobbed the place to see the miracle and enjoy the dry warmth.

How much they took in will never be known. Greenberg made it a practice not to discuss such personal matters. But it is quite definite that not even in 1929 had he done so well over a single week end.

Very early Monday morning he was dressing quietly, not to disturb his wife. Esther, however, raised herself on her elbow and looked at him doubtfully.

"Herman," she called softly, "do you really have to go?"

He turned, puzzled. "What do you mean—do I have to go?"

"Well—" She hesitated. Then: "Couldn't you wait until the end of the season, Herman, darling?"

He staggered back a step, his face working in horror. "What kind of an idea is that for my own wife to have?" he croaked. "Beer I have to drink instead of water. How can I stand it? Do you think I *like* beer? I can't wash myself. Already people don't like to stand near me; and how will they act at the end of the season? I go around looking like a bum because my beard is too tough for an electric razor, and I'm all the time drunk—the first Greenberg to be a drunkard. I want to be respected—"

"I know, Herman, darling," she sighed. "But I thought for the sake of our Rosie— Such a business we've never done like we did this week end. If it rains every Saturday and Sunday, but not on our concession, we'll make a *fortune!*"

"Esther!" Herman cried, shocked. "Doesn't my health mean anything?"

"Of course, darling. Only I thought maybe you could stand it for—"

He snatched his hat, tie, and jacket, and slammed the door. Outside, though, he stood indeterminedly. He could hear his wife crying, and he realized that, if he succeeded in getting the gnome to remove the curse, he would forfeit an opportunity to make a great deal of money.

He finished dressing more slowly. Esther was right, to a certain extent. If he could tolerate his waterless condition—

"No!" he gritted decisively. "Already my friends avoid me. It isn't right that a respectable man like me should always be drunk and not take a bath. So we'll make less money. Money isn't everything—"

And with great determination he went to the lake.

But that evening, before going home, Mike walked out of his way to stop in at the concession. He found Greenberg sitting on a chair, his head in his hands, and his body rocking slowly in anguish.

"What is it, Mr. Greenberg?" he asked gently.

Greenberg looked up. His eyes were dazed. "Oh, you, Mike," he said blankly. Then his gaze cleared, grew more intelligent, and he stood up and led Mike to the bar. Silently, they drank beer. "I went to the lake today," he said hollowly. "I walked all around it hollering like mad. The gnome didn't stick his head out of the water once."

"I know," Mike nodded sadly. "They're busy all the time."

Greenberg spread his hands imploringly. "So what can I do? I can't write him a letter or send him a telegram; he ain't got a door to knock on or a bell for me to ring. How do I get him to come up and talk?"

His shoulders sagged. "Here, Mike. Have a cigar. You been a real good friend, but I guess we're licked."

They stood in an awkward silence. Finally Mike blurted: "Real hot, today. A regular scorcher."

"Yeah. Esther says business was pretty good, if it keeps up."

Mike fumbled at the Cellophane wrapper. Greenberg said: "Anyhow, suppose I did talk to the gnome. What about the sugar?"

The silence dragged itself out, became tense and uncomfortable. Mike was distinctly embarrassed. His brusque nature was not adapted for comforting discouraged friends. With immense concentration he rolled the cigar between his fingers and listened for a rustle.

"Day like this's hell on cigars," he mumbled, for the sake of conversation. "Dries them like nobody's business. This one ain't, though."

"Yeah," Greenberg said abstractedly. "Cellophane keeps them—"

They looked suddenly at each other, their faces clean of expression.

"Holy smoke!" Mike yelled.

"Cellophane on sugar!" Greenberg choked out.

"Yeah," Mike whispered in awe. "I'll switch my day off with Joe, and I'll go to the lake with you tomorrow. I'll call for you early."

Greenberg pressed his hand, too strangled by emotion for speech. When Esther came to relieve him, he left her at the concession with only the inexperienced griddle boy to assist her, while he searched the village for cubes of sugar wrapped in Cellophane.

The sun had scarcely risen when Mike reached the hotel, but Greenberg had long been dressed and stood on the porch waiting impatiently. Mike was genuinely anxious for his friend. Greenberg staggered along toward the station, his eyes almost crossed with the pain of a terrific hang-over.

They stopped at a cafeteria for breakfast. Mike ordered orange juice, bacon and eggs, and coffee half-and-half. When he heard the order, Greenberg had to gag down a lump in his throat.

"What'll you have?" the counterman asked.

Greenberg flushed. "Beer," he said hoarsely.

"You kidding me?" Greenberg shook his head, unable to speak. "Want anything with it? Cereal, pie, toast—"

"Just beer." And he forced himself to swallow it. "So help me," he hissed at Mike, "another beer for breakfast will kill me!"

"I know how it is," Mike said around a mouthful of food.

On the train they attempted to make plans. But they were faced by a phenomenon that neither had encountered before, and so they got nowhere. They walked glumly to the lake, fully aware that they would have to employ the empirical method of discarding tactics that did not work.

"How about a boat?" Mike suggested.

"It won't stay in the water with me in it. And you can't row it."

"Well, what'll we do then?"

Greenberg bit his lip and stared at the beautiful blue lake. There the gnome lived, so near to them. "Go through the woods along the shore, and holler like hell. I'll go the opposite way. We'll pass each other and meet at the boathouse. If the gnome comes up, yell for me."

"O. K.," Mike said, not very confidently.

The lake was quite large and they walked slowly around it, pausing often to get the proper stance for particularly emphatic shouts. But two hours later, when they stood opposite each other with the full diameter of the lake between them, Greenberg heard Mike's hoarse voice: "Hey, gnome!"

"Hey, gnome!" Greenberg yelled. "Come on up!"

An hour later they crossed paths. They were tired, discouraged, and their throats burned; and only fishermen disturbed the lake's surface.

"The hell with this," Mike said. "It ain't doing any good. Let's go back to the boathouse."

"What'll we do?" Greenberg rasped. "I can't give up!"

They trudged back around the lake, shouting half-heartedly. At the boathouse, Greenberg had to admit that he was beaten. The boathouse owner marched threateningly toward him.

"Why don't you maniacs get away from here?" he barked. "What's the idea of hollering and scaring away the fish? The guys are sore—"

"We're not going to holler any more," Greenberg said. "It's no use."

When they bought beer and Mike, on an impulse, hired a boat, the owner cooled off with amazing rapidity, and went off to unpack bait.

"What did you get a boat for?" Greenberg asked. "I can't ride in it."

"You're not going to. You're gonna walk."

"Around the lake again?" Greenberg cried.

"Nope. Look, Mr. Greenberg. Maybe the gnome can't hear us through all that water. Gnomes ain't hardhearted. If he heard us and thought you were sorry, he'd take his curse off you in a jiffy."

"Maybe." Greenberg was not convinced. "So where do I come in?"

"The way I figure it, some way or other you push water away, but the water pushes you away just as hard. Anyhow, I hope so. If it does, you can walk on the lake." As he spoke, Mike had been lifting large stones and dumping them on the bottom of the boat. "Give me a hand with these."

Any activity, however useless, was better than none, Greenberg felt. He helped Mike fill the boat until just the gunwales were above water. Then Mike got in and shoved off.

"Come on," Mike said. "Try to walk on the water."

Greenberg hesitated. "Suppose I can't?"

"Nothing'll happen to you. You can't get wet; so you won't drown."

The logic of Mike's statement reassured Greenberg. He stepped out boldly. He experienced a peculiar sense of accomplishment when the water hastily retreated under his feet into pressure bowls, and an unseen, powerful force buoyed him upright across the lake's surface. Though his footing was not too secure, with care he was able to walk quite swiftly.

"Now what?" he asked, almost happily.

Mike had kept pace with him in the boat. He shipped his oars and passed Greenberg a rock. "We'll drop them all over the lake—make it damned noisy down there and upset the place. That'll get him up."

They were more hopeful now, and their comments, "Here's one that'll wake him," and "I'll hit him right on the noodle with this one," served to cheer them still further. And less than half the rocks had been dropped when Greenberg halted, a boulder in his hands. Something inside him wrapped itself tightly around his heart and his jaw dropped.

Mike followed his awed, joyful gaze. To himself, Mike had to admit that the gnome, propelling himself through the water with his ears, arms folded in tremendous dignity, was a funny sight.

"Must you drop rocks and disturb us at our work?" the gnome asked.

Greenberg gulped. "I'm sorry, Mr. Gnome," he said nervously. "I couldn't get you to come up by yelling."

The gnome looked at him. "Oh. You are the mortal who was disciplined. Why did you return?"

"To tell you that I'm sorry, and I won't insult you again."

"Have you proof of your sincerity?" the gnome asked quietly.

Greenberg fished furiously in his pocket and brought out a handful of sugar wrapped in Cellophane, which he tremblingly handed to the gnome.

"Ah, very clever, indeed," the little man said, unwrapping a cube and popping it eagerly into his mouth. "Long time since I've had some."

A moment later Greenberg spluttered and floundered under the surface. Even if Mike had not caught his jacket and helped him up, he could almost have enjoyed the sensation of being able to drown.

CLOAK OF AESIR

Astounding Science Fiction, March

by Don A. Stuart
(John W. Campbell, Jr., 1910–1971)

"Don A. Stuart" was the name employed by the late John Campbell for a group of stories that helped change the texture of science fiction. Although Campbell was a legendary editor, his innovations as a writer have not received enough analysis (we badly need a first-rate critical biography of this complex and fascinating man)—indeed, future historians of the field may some day view the literary trends he established as equal in importance to his editorial skills. Primarily known as a writer of superior space opera like the Penton and Blake stories and THE MIGHTIEST MACHINE 1934 in the Stuart persona he changed to an emphasis on reflection and the responses of human beings to technology and the human condition. In this sense, he started the "Golden Age" all by himself.

"Cloak of Aesir" is an independent sequel to "Out of Night" 1937 and was the last story Campbell wrote under the Stuart byline. It is a memorable and moving contribution to the literature of science fiction.

(To science fiction fans who remember the 1930s, there has always been something sad about having had to choose between John Campbell, Writer and John Campbell, Editor. There was no way in which we could have given up the Editor and yet now and then we mourn the Writer and what we might have had. IA.)

The Sarn Mother's tiny, almost-human face was lined with the fatigue of forty hours of continued strain. Now, she feared greatly, a new and greater tension was ahead. For the eight City Mothers, taking their places about the Conference Hall of the Sarn, were not going to be sympathetic to the Mother's story.

To them, the ancient Sarn Mother well knew, the humans of Earth were slaves. Slaves bred for work, of little mentality and no importance. Earth was the planet of the Sarn, the planet the Sarn had taken, some four thousand years before, from the race of small-bodied, small-minded weaklings called Man that had originally inhabited it.

And that idea was going to be extremely hard to change. Particularly, it would be hard for the Sarn Mother to change that idea, for she was somewhat—not of them. The Sarn Mother was the Immortal. She was, therefore, disliked.

These eight, these Mothers of Cities, were the matriarchic governors of Earth under the Sarn. Each had risen to overlordship of a continent, or near-continental area, by competitive brilliance among all their people. They had won their places, merited them, they felt.

But the Sarn Mother? The ultimate ruler of all Earth, all Sarn and humans alike? She had not *inherited* her position exactly—she had simply been there forever. Her winning of it was forgotten in the mists of antiquity. The Sarn were a long-lived people—some lived a thousand years—but the Sarn Mother was immortal; she had lived in the mythical days of the Forgotten Planet, before the home world of the Sarn had disrupted in cosmic catastrophe, forcing the race to seek new worlds.

The Sarn Mother had won this world for them, but that—and all others who had fought mankind in that four-thousand-years-gone time—was forgotten. The Sarn Mother was simply a hang-over from an era that should have died. So felt the Mothers of Cities, ambitious Sarn who saw a place above them that—because of the Mother's cursed immortality—they could never hope to reach.

The Old Sarn Mother knew that, and knew, too, that only her own possession of secret science those millenniums of her life had given her, made her place safe. The City Mothers feared two things: that well-held secret science, and the jealousy of their sisters.

The old Sarn was tired with mental struggle, and she knew, as soundly as she knew the City Mothers hated her, that she was facing another struggle. The humans of Earth were rising in a slow, half-understood revolt. She and these eight City Mothers knew that.

But the City Mothers did not, and would not, admit that those humans were capable of revolt. For all their lives humans have been slaves, pets, a sort of domesticated animal. That they or the similarly domesticated cows might attempt to set up a civilization—

For the Sarn Mother alone had been alive the four thousand years that had passed since mankind's defense of Earth all but succeeded in defeating the invading Sarn. The City Mothers could not understand. Subconsciously they had no intention of understanding anything so unpleasant.

The Sarn Mother's pointed, elfin face smiled weary greeting. Her fluting, many-toned speech betrayed her fatigue as she spoke to them. "I call you together, daughters, because something of grave importance has arisen. You have heard, perhaps, of the judging of Grayth and Bartel?"

"Rumors," said the Mother of Targlan, the city perched high in the crystal clarity of the mighty Himalaya Mountains. "You reversed your judgment, I heard." Her voice was silky smooth—and bitter.

The Sarn Mother's small, pointed face did not change. The trouble, definitely, was beginning. "I told you at the last Council that the human stock was rebuilding, that the submerged intelligence and will that built, before our invasion of this planet, a high civilization, were mounting again. It is, I believe, equal in power to that before the Conquest. And, under our rule, it has been purified in some respects. There is less violence, and more determination.

"It is somewhat hard for you to appreciate that, for you do not remember human beings as other than slaves.

"I recognize a certain growing restlessness at restraint. The majority of those humans do not yet know—understand—the reason for a vague restlessness that they feel. Their leaders do. They are restless of government and restraint, and I hoped to use that vagueness of feeling to destroy the tendency toward rebellion. I thought the rebellion might be turned

CLOAK OF AESIR

against their own, proxy government. Therefore, I caused the humans to revolt against their government under us, instead of against the Sarn.

"Even I had underestimated them. Grayth and Bartel, the leaders of mankind, appeared before me accompanied by Drunnel, the rival leader. I will not detail their quarrel, save to say that Drunnel was my tool. I sentenced Grayth and Bartel.

"Then—Aesir, he called himself—appeared. He was a blackness—a three-dimensional shadow. He stood some four feet taller than I, nearly twelve feet tall, twice the height of humans. But he was shaped like a human in bulk, though the vague blackness made any feature impossible. He claimed that he was not made of any form of matter, but was the crystallization of the wills of all humans who have died in any age, while seeking freedom.

"Aesir spoke by telepathy. Mind to mind. We know the humans had been near that before the Conquest, and that our own minds are not so adapted to that as are the humans'. Aesir used that method.

"He stood before me, and made these statements that were clear to the minds of all humans and Sarn in the Hall of Judgment. His hand of blackness reached out and touched Drunnel, and the man fell to the floor and broke apart like a fragile vase. The corpse was frozen glass-hard in an instant of time.

"Therefore, I released Grayth and Bartel. But I turned on Aesir's blackness the forces of certain protective devices I have built. There is an atomic blast of one-sixteenth aperture. It is, at maximum, capable of disintegrating half a cubic mile of matter per minute. There was also a focused atomic flame of two-inch aperture, sufficient to fuse about twenty-two tons of steel per second.

"These were my first tests. At maximum aperture the blackness absorbed both without sound or static discharge, or any lightening of that three-dimensional shadow."

The Sarn Mother's mouth moved in a faint, ironic smile. "There are," she went on softly, "certain other weapons there. The Death of the Mother, which I employed once on a rebellious City Mother, some thirteen hundred years gone. Tathan Shoal, she was, of Bishop Waln." The Sarn Mother's slitted eyes lit amusedly on the present Mother of Bish-Waln, capital city of the continent of Africa.

"Tathan Shoal had the mistaken idea that she might gain

by attacking me. She came with many devices, including a screen capable of turning all the weapons she knew. It cost me the South Wall of the Hall of Judgment and an effective and efficient administrator to convince her. For she had been effective and efficient.

"Daughter of Targlan, it is best for the Race that we share knowledge. Tell your sister of Bish-Waln the remarkable progress your physicist has made with the field she knows as R-439-K."

The Mother of Targlan's face remained unchanged, save for a faint golden flush that spread over it, and the sudden angry fire of her eyes. Field R-439-K—her most treasured secret——

"It is a field," she said in a pleasant, friendly tone, "which causes the collapse of atoms within it, bringing about a spreading disruption that continues so long as the generator is activated. It is necessarily spherical in shape, destroying the generator very quickly, however. It would be excellent as a sort of bomb." She added that last as a sort of afterthought, a hazy, bitter dream in her voice.

The Sarn Mother smiled and nodded toward the Mother of Bish-Waln. That City Ruler's eyes were angry as had been her predecessor's as she responded to the unspoken command. But her voice betrayed no emotion.

"No, sister, it can be projected to some extent. The generator need not be destroyed, though the projector is, if you employ a field of ellipsoidal form."

The Mother of Uhrnol smiled, but her smile was only half amusement. "The projector can be saved, too. It is too bad I could not have known of your efforts. I could have saved you considerable work."

The three smiled at each other in seeming friendliness. Each felt slightly relieved; she stood alone neither in her chastisement nor in the loss of treasured secrets.

"The point of interest," the Sarn Mother pointed out softly, "is that none of you can stop that field. There is no protection. Some twenty-two centuries ago I discovered that interesting modification of the atomic-blast field, and within a century I had projected it. Ten centuries ago I had it tamed to the extent of a cylindrical tube of force of controllable dimensions. If Tathan Shoal had waited another five centuries before attacking me, she would not have cost me the South Wall. It still does not match perfectly the other three. But I cannot screen that force."

CLOAK OF AESIR

"Nor I," admitted the three City Mothers, in turn. There was a hint of bitter defeat in their tones, for each had hoped that field that could not be screened might make them safe in disposing of the old harridan, the Immortal Sarn Mother, who ruled them from a forgotten generation. She was a bitter, anachronistic hang-over from a forgotten time, from even the Forgotten Planet, and should have been forgotten with it.

"Aesir," said the Sarn Mother softly, "took the Death of the Mother into his blackness, and seemingly drew strength from it. At any rate, both the apparatus and the atomic generator which fed it were blown out from sudden overload.

"It might be wise to coöperate more closely than in the past. Once, remember, our race had a very bitter struggle with this race. What do you Mothers of Cities believe this Aesir to me?"

The Mother of Targlan stirred angrily. "There are clowns among the humans of my district who amuse their fellows by trickery. Humans have stiff legs, bending only in certain, few joints. That lack of flexibility gives them amusing powers. They can, for instance, advance the stiffness by the use of poles of light metal, representing longer, artificial bones. I have seen such clowns walk on legs that made them not twelve, but seventeen feet high."

"Yes," said the Sarn Mother sweetly, "the clowns of my North America are of a very inferior brand. They can appear but twelve feet tall. But—"

"Many," said the Mother of Bish-Waln, "of my humans have shown they can talk mind to mind among themselves. If it is new among your people here, it is—"

"Yes," said the Sarn Mother sweetly, "the humans of my North America are of an inferior brand, evidently. But—I am curious of these clowns and mind-talkers. Do they, perhaps, absorb atomic-blast beams for nourishment, and warm themselves at a focused flame? Do they so overload your atomic-collapse field generators as to burn them in molten rubbish?

"Or do they, perhaps, unlike yourselves, remember that the Sarn Mother has watched humans, and the minds and tricks of humans, for some eight times your not-inconsequential five hundred years?

"There were, in the Hall, humans, Sarn, and myself. By telepathy, Aesir spoke to us all, telling a myth of his origin among immaterial wills. He was, in his way, quite noisy, and quite conspicuous. Also, he was an excellent psychologist.

Had I been warned—had I known beforehand and had time to think—I would not have turned the blast, the focused flame, nor, certainly, the Death of the Mother against him.

"Now do any of you, who see so clearly through the trickery of my poor little, twelve-foot clown, and the trickery of my slow-developing telepathist—do any of you see through to the message Aesir meant for my intellect, and not my mind? A message he did not speak, but acted?" The Sarn Mother's elfin face looked down the Council table, and there was nothing of laughter in it.

The City Mothers moved uneasily under the lash of biting scorn. The Sarn Mother's voice dropped, softer still, till the tinklings of the atom flame above muffled her words.

"Mummery for fools, my daughters. I am interested that you are so attracted by the mummery as to forget the purpose, and so pleased with your cleverness that saw the human behind it.

"But I am—irritated that you underestimate, not merely of the mind of a human of deadly, blazingly brilliant intellect, but, even more, my own mind.

"Humans are a smaller people, better adapted to this somewhat heavier planet than we are. But we are no longer on the Forgotten World. The humans have learned to respect height; the ruling Race is tall.

"Is Aesir a fool, then, to make himself yet taller, and to fill out his slenderness with vague blackness?

"We have no hair on our skulls, as have humans, but the more useful *sterthan* which seems, to humans, practical telepathy, since we can talk among ourselves by what they know only through microwave radio sets.

"Is Aesir a fool, then, to use telepathy himself, talking truly mind to mind? Men know the limitations of microwave radio, that it ends at the horizon. But they do not know what vague limits telepathy may or may not have, and it is very wonderful, therefore.

"That mummery, my daughters, was intended only for humans, that mass of restless humans who do not know what they want. That was not meant for me—save that he wanted me to know what others heard.

"I am proud of my humans, daughters. But I am afraid, for you. You have not shown the intelligence that that man expected. That mind telepathy he used was not the message he meant for me. To me he said: 'Mother, a new balance must be reached. You are the ruler of Earth—but for me I

CLOAK OF AESIR

challenge you to try your weapons—which I know, as does everyone on Earth, you have in your throne—and see if you can destroy me.' And when I, not thinking, but reacting spontaneously to the evident menace of his blackness, did just this, he said more. He touched Drunnel, and Drunnel fell dead. 'I have an impregnable shield' his actions spoke, 'and it is more; a weapon. You cannot destroy me, Mother of the Sarn—but I can destroy you.

" 'Therefore, we seek a new balance. You could destroy all my people—but not destroy me. And I could destroy you, or any of your people.

" 'Release these two, Grayth and Bartel, and we will think again. This is not the time for hasty action.'

"Aesir, daughters, is no fool. He is no trickster—save for his own sound purposes—but a mind of astounding brilliance. He has discovered a principle, a weapon, unknown to us and of immense power.

"And, my daughters, I respect him. I released Grayth and Bartel, since they are, evidently, pawns in this game. Or, at least, they are two of the few humans on Earth I know are not—Aesir.

"And I have more liking"—the Sarn Mother's voice was bitter and ironic—"for one who expects my mind to see beyond mummery to a deep and important sincerity, than for those who explain trickery and point out the inferiority of my humans."

"You are reading words that are not written," said the Mother of Targlan flatly.

For an instant the eyes of the Sarn Mother burned with a white anger, a blazing intolerance of such sheer stupidity. Then it faded to a look of deep concern.

The Sarn Mother was unhuman, unhuman in the same way her elfin face was. It was very wrong, taken as a human face, with its pointed chin and tiny mouth, the slit-pupiled, golden eyes, and peaked hairline that was not hair. But there was the fundamental parallelism of two eyes, a mouth, a high, rounded forehead. Her body was grotesquely unhuman, but again there was a parallelism of articulated arms carried high on a strong torso and legs, though her arms were like four powerful snakes.

And—she was un-Sarn. The Mother was immortal, an unchanging intellect in a world that waxed and waned and changed about her. She had living memories of a world crushed in cosmic dust. She had memories of great Sarn who had dared and won a world, of a human civilization of magnitude near equal to this present Sarn world.

And the process that had made her immortal, had made her unable to have descendants. There was no direct link from her to this newer generation. Her only link was through a planet wiped from the face of time.

Four thousand years she had ruled this planet. Two thousand more she'd lived on the Forgotten World before the desperate colonization attempt had been conceived. These creatures—these Sarn—were ephemeral things about her, for all their five hundred years.

Sixty centuries are long, for any intellect. All things exhaust themselves in that long time, save one: the curiosity of the mind, the play and counterplay of intellect. The Mother was the perfect seeker after knowledge, for no other thoughts could ponderably intrude. Those others she had met long ago.

She was un-Sarn by her immortality, by her separation of six thousand years from all direct contact with her equals.

She was unhuman only by a different in body. And the body is wearied and forgotten in that time. Only the intellect, the mind, remains of interest, expanding and changing forever.

The intellect behind Aesir's cloak of blackness was the keenest, the finest, this planet had ever seen. And—that human appreciated that she, the Sarn Mother, was a keen intelligence.

The City Mothers did not.

The Sarn Mother turned her eyes slowly from the Mother of Targlan. "The words that spell the secret of that blackness are not written," she said mildly. *(These were the daughters of her race. These were the descendants of Sarn she had known and worked with and liked during six thousand years. These were—)*

"I must see more of that cloak, and investigate it more adequately." She sighed. "And you, my daughters, must not underestimate an enemy. And the humans are, I fear—or will be soon.

"They have been slaves for many generations—very short generations—and they have evolved. They evolve more swiftly than we, because of that short life span. And, remember this: at least one of them is sufficiently brilliant, of sufficient mental caliber, to develop a screen weapon superior to anything we know of. That alone makes him, potentially, extremely dangerous."

The City Mothers sat silent for long seconds. The thought was, as the Mother had known, extremely upsetting. Their matriarchic minds rebelled at the thought that there was a human—and a *male* human, at that—who was capable of developing something scientifically superior to anything in their possession.

"If," said the Mother of Targlan, "he has this remarkable weapon—proof against all ours, and deadly to us—I am extremely thankful that he has shown such kindliness toward our race." Her fluting voice was sugary. "He has not equipped any of his compatriots nor attacked us in any way."

The seven other City Mothers twitched slightly straighter in their chairs and looked with pleased smiles at the Sarn Mother's fine, small face.

The Mother smiled bitterly. "Undoubtedly that would be your own reaction were you possessed of such a weapon," she admitted. The Mother of Targlan stolidly continued to look into the Mother's half-angry, half-annoyed eyes.

"But you," the Mother explained, "have never done more than to say 'a thousand pounds of tungsten' when you had need of it. Or order fifty No. 27-R-29 oscillator tubes, when you hoped to make a satisfactory lie detector. Incidentally, daughter, I have an effective invisibility generator. And your lie detector will not operate. You'd do far better to use common sense and simplicity instead of outrageously expensive mummery that doesn't work. That spy you sent to—one of the other cities—last week had a very slipshod invisibility. I watched her a whole afternoon from here. She set off seven different alarms, and finally was caught in a delightful booby trap. Your sister believes in simplicity instead of gadgets."

The Mother of Targlan sat silent and stony. Her slitted eyes contracted slowly in flaming hatred. The old harridan was becoming cattish.

The old harridan was tired. She was wearied to death of the bickerings and annoyances of these City Mothers with too little to do to occupy their time. Furthermore, she hadn't slept in forty hours, and knew it. And the Mother of Targlan was being unbearably stupid.

The Mother of Bish-Waln was interested. So—that was the source of that spy. And the old Mother, for all her foolishness about these humans, had some sense. The secret of success is simplicity. Though that Targlan spy *had* had a fearful and wonderful array of apparatus strapped about her, it also had made her—even when dead—remarkably hard to see. She'd sounded like a collapse in a glass factory when she fell, though.

"To get back to my remarks," said the Sarn Mother abruptly, "you have never had to want something without getting it. Except," she added with a flash of tiny, pointed, green-white teeth, "understanding. If you want materials, they are brought.

"If a human wants materials, he steals them. And I will say this for you: you have all been remarkable organizers. The anti-theft measures you have developed are outstanding. But I should think that the fact that humans still succeed in thieving would convince you they are clever."

"So," snapped the Mother of Targlan, "are rats. But they aren't intelligent."

"Quite true," admitted the Mother. The Mother of Targlan was becoming annoyed, which vaguely pleased the old Sarn Mother, who was very annoyed. "But humans are both. It took me twelve years to find exactly how it was approximately thirty ounces of platinum disappeared each month, despite my electrostatic balance detectors. Now I make all workers clip their fingernails and hair. It was truly startling how much dust they could carry that way.

"To acquire materials, humans must steal them. And they must find it extremely difficult to gather such things as metallic caesium, gaseous fluorine, and rare gases like helium and neon. Unfortunately, I believe a considerable quantity of material is obtained from ingeniously acquired atom-flame lamps." The Mother nodded toward the softly rustling lamps overhead.

"So your workers secrete complete atom-flame lamps under their nails?" said the Mother of Targlan. "Your theft measures are indeed remarkable. The atom destructor of one atom lamp would power a dangerous weapon. They will stand a load of nearly ten thousand horsepower."

The Sarn Mother smiled. "How many atom-flame lamps have you lost through theft, daughter?"

"None. Not one!" snapped the Mother of Targlan.

"And what," asked the Mother kindly, "of lamps destroyed in burning human homes?"

"Perhaps ten a year."

"I'd say five a year, then, are acquired by humans. I've

proven two homes were burned to the ground to secure the atom-lamps the occupants wanted."

"We," said the City Mother loftily, "require that the wreckage be produced."

"Excellent," sighed the Mother. "An excellent provision. Do you have a chemist analyze the molten waste? The humans generally find it very difficult to obtain scandium, and the analyses usually skimp badly on that. But the other elements you'll find. They smelt up a careful mixture of all the proper elements, with the exception of gallium. But they can always claim that boiled away."

The Mother of Targlan looked startled. The Sarn Mother's eyes twinkled slightly in satisfaction. She had discovered *that* trick only four days before, herself.

"As I said, the humans find it hard to get materials and appartus. But they are really ingenious, and I rather respect them for it. If you wish to assure yourselves of your cities," she added, looking about the table, "I'd advise you to acknowledge the power of your opponents.

"That is the reason this human, Aesir, has not done more. He has a weapon and a protection—for one. So long as he cannot obtain material, he cannot do more.

"But he will obtain materials." The Mother's annoyed air was dropped now. This, she knew, meant the safety of the Sarn race. "If he obtains sufficient materials before we learn the secret of that cloak, *the Sarn will not rule this planet.*"

The Mother of Bish-Waln looked at the Immortal steadily. Suddenly she spoke. "I have always considered the humans stupid. That they had the cleverness of other lower animals, in greater degree, I realized. But we, Mother, have no memories of their civilization before we came. How far advanced was it, actually?"

The Sarn Mother looked at the City Mother keenly for a moment. It was anomalous; this City Mother, less than one twentieth the Immortal's age, looked far older. Her face, pointed in the manner typical of her race, was graven with fine lines. There was a power and strength of purpose in its deeply tanned, leathery molding. Ruler of a tropical continent, her city centered in the warmth and cloudless air of the Sahara, she was one of the most active of the City Mothers.

The old Sarn Mother smiled slightly and nodded. "I can tell you very little now. But call in your archeologist. She is a brilliant and learned Sarn. Briefly, when we landed, the humans had had civilization for some fifteen thousand years. It was, by their calendar, 1977. They had recently developed atomic power of the first order, involving vapor turbines heated by atomic combustion, driving electromagnetic generators. They mined the world, their transportation systems were heavily interlinked and efficient.

"And—of our fifty-two ships, we lost thirty-nine during the Conquest. They were intelligent, efficient and deadly fighters. We captured and enslaved only the scum of the race; the best of humankind died fighting with a grim tenacity that appalled us. They were a fighting breed, slightly given to attack, but utterly and insanely given to defense.

"It is worth nothing in this case. If they once attack us, then we will, of course, attack, in reply. Whereupon their inherited defensiveness will come into play. If it does, I seriously assure you that, whether they have weapons or not, even if they fight with their bare hands, you will find the human race a perfectly deadly thing to tangle with. They have no conception of when to stop. It is good military tactics to stop, if any reasonably equitable settlement can be reached, after losing ten percent of your forces. The human race does not know that, and never will. They stop when, and only when, they are convinced they have won their point. They simply do not show good sense.

"But they are extremely deadly.

"That is true of the mass of humanity. They have leaders now, and Aesir is the principal leader. We can, and must, control them through him. He knows, instinctively, the attitude of his people, and will try, therefore, to prevent suicidal war.

"Wherefore, if we obtain the secret of his cloak of blackness, we can proceed."

"I will ask my archeologist, Mother," said the Mother of Bish-Waln.

"Whatever you may say of the dreadful, deadly, human race," said the Mother of Targlan ironically, "it would be interesting to know the mechanism of that shield. But—maybe he will not explain. And it would be extremely difficult to force him to, if what you say of it is true."

"We shall have to analyze it, of course," said the Mother wearily. There were many more hours of work and sleeplessness ahead. "Some hours ago I instructed my physicists to set up all the instruments they thought might be useful in the House of the Rocks."

The Mother of Targlan stared blankly; then, acidly, commented: "Of all places in the Sarn City here, I should say that that would show the absolute minimum of probability for an appearance of Aesir."

"And," continued the Mother, wearied of interruptions, "they will be ready for him in about an hour and a half. It is evident that Aesir will come to the aid of Grayth, if we capture him. To make assurance doubly sure—since Grayth is not, actually, absolutely necessary to them—we will take also Deya, Spokeswoman of Human Women. Grayth plans to marry her, and I am sure that Aesir will aid in releasing her."

The Mother of Bish-Waln frowned slightly. "Is it not bad policy, Mother, to arrest, and then release this man again? And—again at the insistence of Aesir."

"Therefore, the House of the Rocks. No human can approach. No human will know of the actual escape—save those humans already closely associated with Grayth, and, therefore, Aesir. Those humans already know what powers Aesir has, even better than we, and they will recognize this maneuver not as an arrest that failed, but as a test that did not fail. Our policy will be good, not bad, to those who know. The mass of humans simply will not know."

"They will not, I suppose," said the Mother of Drulon, at the far, stormy tip of South America, "notice that Grayth, their spokesman, is being taken in Sarn custody—and returns?"

"They will not," smiled the Mother. With an uncoiled finger, she pressed a tiny button.

At the far end of the long Council room, a silver door opened in the jet black of the wall. The heavy metal portal swung aside, and a guard snapped to attention in its opening, a giant Sarn standing over eight feet tall. Her powerful, supple arms were corded with the smooth-flowing muscles of a boa constrictor. Vaguely, her trappings indicated the rank of a Decalon—a commander of a Ten. Her cloak, though, with a deep, rich maroon, and in the center the gold, silver, and bright-purple metal threads wove a pattern that was the Mother's personal symbol.

And her face—to one who knew Sarn physiognomy—was not that of a mere Decalon. The slitted eyes were deepset and widely separated. Her mouth was firm, and the face, small and pointed to human experience, was square and powerful in a Sarn. The golden skin had been tanned to a leathery, weather-beaten brown, crossed by a myriad of fine lines of character. This was no mere commander over ten guards.

"Decalon," said the Mother softly, "bring the Cloaks of the Mother, and your command. There is an errand."

The Decalon turned sharply, noiselessly, closing the metal door.

"Once," explained the Mother, "Darath Toplar was Commander-in-chief of the Guard of the Sarn City. She is now a Decalon. That is because there are but ten in my personal guard.

"Now this is a time of emergency. I have revealed to each of you something of the things each thought a secret, and some of the things that I held secret. I am showing you the Cloaks of the Mother. That they existed, rumors have stated. They do. They have the properties the rumors suggest. Because it is necessary, they will be used."

The Decalon was back, behind her ten guards dressed in the same type of maroon uniform. Ten powerful, eight-foot Sarn warriors. On the face of each was stamped a keen, loyal intelligence. In the arms of the Decalon was a case of dark hardwood, inlaid with heavy, silvery metal straps. She put it down at the end of the great Council table, and the Mother's hand flicked out as her supple arm uncoiled to shoot a scrap of carefully cut metal the length of the polished table. The Decalon fitted it into a concealed lock with a motion of familiar dexterity.

The case, opened, revealed a space two by three by one-half foot. In it, racked neatly along one side, were twenty little battery cases, with coiled, flexible cables attached, and twenty headsets, bearing curiously complex goggles. The case was practically empty.

The Decalon reached in, and with practiced movements passed to her command the goggles and battery cases. Then she reached more carefully into the body of the case. The reaching hand vanished. Presently, queerly section by section, the Decalon was wiped out, till only a pair of feet remained, dwindling off into space. These vanished as some unseen boots were pulled over them.

In a moment, only the City Mothers and the Mother of the Sarn remained in the room—seemingly. The City Mothers stirred uneasily. The eyes of the Mother of Targlan were golden fires of anger and chagrin. These—these picked eleven of the Mother's personal guard and spy force—knew every secret of her laboratories.

And the old immortal harridan knew them, too. Her crack-

CLOAK OF AESIR

ling laughter must have been spurred a thousand times by the futile attempts and doomed plans the Mother of Targlan had made and thought over. The Mother of Targlan felt a rising pressure of helpless anger well up, an anger that was suppressed by its very helplessness. Even the satisfaction that the Mother was old, a cackling hag, was denied. For—salt on her wounded pride—the Mother had done, seemingly centuries ago, what the Mother of Targlan struggled with vainly! The Mother was a far better scientist.

It was a very different Council room, this chamber where the Spokesmen of Man had met—an inner office of the elected representative of mankind, the Spokesman of Mankind. It was a warm room, mellowed by a thousand years of time; ancient woods, waxed and cared for for ten centuries and more, had taken on a fine, soft patina. Long-slanting fingers of afternoon sunlight did not glare on cold jet stone here; it was softened by the richness of the panels. Each was of a different wood; one from each of the continents, and one for each continental spokesman.

The great table in the center was worn in soft hummocks and swales by the arms of forty generations of Spokesmen, the thick rubberlike floor carven by their feet.

But as in the great Council room of the Hall of the Sarn in nearby Sarn City, here, too, atom-flame lamps rustled softly with dying atoms, whitening the light of the setting sun. Four men only were at this Council table, four who sat motioning, gesturing with a curious alertness, their faces intent. Yet—utterly silent.

Grayth, tall, lean, keen-faced Spokesman of Mankind, an elected representative who had won his honor by a keen understanding of the practical psychology of the men he represented before the Sarn Mother, political leader of mankind. Bartel, shorter, more solidly built Spokesman of North America, close friend of Grayth, who had stood beside him before the Sarn Mother, when—Aesir—had come.

And Carron, the gigantic commander of the legion of peace, the only semblance of an army allowed humans. A police force armed with tiny gas throwers capable of a single, stupefying shot, and rubber truncheons.

Also, one more. Darak, Grayth's subspokesman. He sat silent now, making occasional pothooks on the pad of paper, his round, uninteresting face bored and boring. Darak's office was appointive, given him at Grayth's order for the blankly unimpressive face and uninteresting character of the man made him few friends—as he had found by many years of careful study of the subject. Few friends, and few who paid him any attention whatever.

Darak had no need of the Cloak of the Mother; his own, based not on laws of physics but of psychology, was nearly as effective. People did not see Darak. He wasn't worth seeing.

Four humans at the ancient Council table, four men as free as possible in this day of the Sarn, each wearing on his cloak the symbol of his rank in human society. Each wearing on a band round his forehead the medallion given every human at the age of eighteen. The band of Manhood or Womanhood, the Sarn informed them. The mark of Mankind's submission to the Sarn.

Or was, till Ware made certain slight alterations, alterations that hollowed out the solid three-inch disk of silver to contain a minute thing of spider-web coils and microscopic crystal oscillators. The first of the telepaths that rendered this soundless Council meaningful.

And rendered quite useless the listening devices that had followed every Council of Mankind for a thousand years. Grayth smiled upward to the swell of the atom-flame lamp. In the mechanism of that device, in a dozen other places in the room, the Sarn had long ago hidden radio transmitters. For a millennium, every Council of Mankind had been directly open to the strange radio-sense of the Mother and her advisers. For the hairlike growth on the Sarn's skulls were the sense organ of a type Man did not have, directly sensitive to radio.

"Four men in here," Grayth thought to his companions, "four men rustling papers. But the Sarn must be very curious as to the silence."

Carron's broad, tanned face broke into a wide grin. "After a thousand years, a bit of silence from this room is due. The Mother knows well enough we aren't minding her business. But I don't think she'll be anxious to investigate after—Aesir."

"The Sarn Mother," the thought whispered in their minds from a more distant telepath, "is busy holding a conference of her own. I've been trying for weeks to get the pattern of Sarn thoughts. I get annoying flashes, but no more. The Mother is tired, and the City Mothers are being stubborn, I gather. But the thought patterns are just enough different from human thought to make the telepaths ineffective at more than about one hundred feet. And the most assiduous electrotechnician can't spend *all* his time tracing conduits in the Sarn Palace."

"I'd suggest you do absolutely nothing that an ordinary electrotechnician wouldn't do, Ware," Grayth hurriedly advised. "And for Aesir's sake, stay home when you're supposed to have off hours."

"Have you reached any conclusions? I've been sleeping, and woke only a few minutes ago." Ware's mental voice seemed to yawn. "I've been trying to think of some way to get more metal. Ye gods, if I could just get into one of the Sarn electrical plants for a day, I'd have a dozen things I need fixed up. The math was none too simple, but I've gotten it, I think." He chuckled. "Thanks, in fact, to a very wise old Sarn.

"Just below conscious level, a thought came to him, a bothersome equation. While a certain electrotechnician fussed with conduits fifty feet away, he fussed with the equation. The Sarn have some mathematical methods our ancestors never developed, and that I haven't had a chance to learn. Carron, if you ever feel urged to crack the skull of old Rath Largun, spare him for that."

"Can you use him again?" asked Carron amusedly.

"Oh, I have. He's old, and his mind wanders. Nearly a thousand years old, I think, which is exceptionally old for even a Sarn male. Since he is a male, he gets less credit among his people than he deserves, but he's the most brilliant mathematician the Sarn have. Because his mind wanders—he believes he thinks up the equations."

"Might they give him a clue later?" asked Grayth sharply.

"T . . . P . . ." said Ware easily. "What word am I spelling? When you have correctly answered that, the Sarn may get that clue."

"Good." Grayth nodded silently. "Ware, Carron has seven technicians in his legion of peace who will procure some of those things you need. They have volunteered."

"I have not said what I wanted, nor will I," Ware answered instantly. "Every technician caught stealing metal now will be destroyed by the Sarn instantly. No man is going to lose his life on something I wouldn't attempt myself. Further, we need two classes of men now more vitally than ever before: technicians and fighters. Humans haven't fought and are not fighters. Carron's legionnaires are the only trained, experienced fighters—with the will and emotion needed for fighting—that we have. And when they are also technicians, we can't spare them.

"Have you told Darak what's to be done, and given him the disks?" Ware changed the subject abruptly, with an air of "that's that." It was because Carron didn't know what metals Ware wanted; had he, he would have gotten them somehow, anyway.

Darak replied softly: "I have been told, and I have the disks. Twenty-five telepaths, each equipped with destroying apparatus reacting to one key thought. I know how the destroying mechanism is to be disconnected if successful delivery is made. Grayth has supplied me with sufficient official dispatches for both Durban City and Targlan. I am starting in twenty-two minutes."

"Then—good luck, Darak."

"Thank you. The wish is, perhaps, the luck of the gods?"

"Yes. The luck of Aesir—very appropriate." Ware chuckled. "You will lose contact with me, except when I use the large telepath here in the laboratory. You know the schedule hours for that?"

"Yes, thanks."

"We will be going, too, I think." Carron rose ponderously. His huge form dwarfed even the great Council table. And, since he spoke for the first time, his heavy voice seemed to explode in the room. "I'll see you to the Sarn City gates, Darak."

He glanced down at the subspokesman's busy fingers. They were chubby, soft-looking fingers, rather thick and clumsy. An ink bottle flickered and wavered in and out of existence under the flicking, incredibly deft fingers. Then it flickered, without seeming to move under his caressing, chubby hand, from a round, red ink bottle to a square black one. "Thank you, Carron. The dispatches, Grayth?" Darak's voice was rather high for a man, quite undistinguished. Darak was, next to Ware, the cleverest human on Earth in that era. But his mentality was as utterly different as was Grayth's. Grayth was a practical psychologist, the only living man capable of unifying and moving the masses of mankind. Ware was the scientist, the epitomization of centuries of the Sarn efforts to develop capable human technicians. And Darak?

Darak had the curiosity of the scientist in Ware, the psychological sense of Grayth, and the love of action that made giant Carron what he was.

CLOAK OF AESIR

Grayth tossed a mass of papers toward the subspokesman, a mass that bulged and crinkled. Darak leafed them swiftly into a brief case that he carried. "One thing I will have to remedy," he telepathed silently. "The metal gleams." Twenty-five silvery disks flickered momentarily among the rapidly leafed papers, and vanished as his thick fingers passed them. "All here," he said aloud. "Good-by. I should be back in about four days."

His feet made no noticeable noise on the floor—an accomplishment far more difficult than a soundless tread. An unnoticeable step involves exactly sufficient sound to satisfy the ear, without enough to attract it. A soundless tread is very startling, particularly in a rather stout, heavily built man.

He walked through the outer office, past a battery of secretaries and clerks working over statistics from all the human world, correlating and arranging them for Grayth and the human government. Two looked up as he passed, but neither saw him. They missed him as completely as they missed the passing of eleven eight-foot Sarn guards walking past in the opposite direction on the soundless toe pads nature had given them. For neither party wished to be seen, and each had its own unseen cloak wrapping it.

The door stood open a moment as giant Carron and Grayth spoke a few last words. Bartel stepped out, and then Carron, holding the door wide for his own exit, lingered a moment longer. Soundless feet carried the three Sarn, larger even than Carron's six feet six, through the door.

The door closed behind the commander of the legion of peace, and Grayth stood alone, silent. "Aesir—Aesir—Aesir—" his telepath was sending out.

"Yes?" snapped Ware.

"Three Sarn are standing in the room, invisible to me. Eight more are in the outer office. Both Carron and Bartel are trying to call you—they stood in the door delaying the entrance of the invisible three. All are invisible. Their thoughts I can detect, but not decipher."

"I know. I've learned to 'hear' their thoughts. It takes a little adjusting, due to the different patterns. I'm trying to get them now. Too distant. I don't like it."

"Grayth, Spokesman of Mankind." The Decalon spoke from the air in the curious accents of the Sarn, speaking the tongue common to humans and Sarn.

Grayth started, looked about him, shook his head violently, and reached for a call button with a look of unhappy doubt.

"Stop," snapped the Sarn. Grayth's hand halted in midair. "The Sarn Mother sent us for you. Stand up."

"Wh-where are you? Are you—"

Grayth stopped abruptly. A Sarn's powerful, muscle-corded arms gripped him suddenly, and simultaneously an intense blackness fell over him. A blackness more utterly complete than could have been produced by any substance thin enough and flexible enough to give the clothlike sensations that accompanied it. A very faint, rubbery rustling sound came to his ears, and simultaneously the jerking and pulling of the Sarn guard adjusting the cloak.

"We wear the Cloak of the Mother," the guard fluted sharply. "You will be quiet. You will make no sound, say no word. It is understood?"

"Yes," sighed Grayth. Then silently: "You've caught my impressions, Ware?"

"Yes." It whispered in his mind, the reassuring solidity of another human in close contact. The blackness, the utter blackness, baffled and brought a welling of panic. The huge corded arms of the Sarn, the secrecy of this invisible arrest, all brought a feeling of irrepressible panic.

Then Ware's calm mind obtruded powerfully, silently. "The blackness is not related to mine. It is caused, I suspect, by the complete refraction of light about your body. To be invisible, you must be rendered blind to visible light, since any organ capable of seeing must, by its nature, intercept light. Struggle slightly. Strike the face of one of the Guard."

Grayth shuddered. A guard was working swiftly at his feet. A tremor passed through him, and for a moment he fought off the powerful arms, surprising their grip by a sudden thrust and a gasp of panic. His arm flailed out gropingly. Then with a second gasp, half-sob, he quieted at the soft, tensely sharp command of the Decalon.

"Goggles," said Ware softly. "Transformers, probably, operating on ultravisible light, thus making vision possible with invisibility."

Tensely, in Grayth's mind came the impression of half a hundred other human minds attending this exchange, half a hundred humans throughout this central city, the Sarn City, capital alike of human and Sarn affairs.

"You must stop them," Grayth felt a mind whisper urgently. "Ware—you must release him. Secret capture—they hope to loose him where Aesir cannot find him to release him." Deya's mind, turbulent and fearful, now. Leader of hu-

CLOAK OF AESIR   77

man women, determined and ready to defy the age-long, mind-burdening hold of the Sarn, this sudden, half-magic descent of the invisible guards terrified her for the sake of the man she loved.

"Stay where you are, Ware," Grayth rapped out mentally. "They're moving me now—leading—no, carrying me out through my office. In thirty seconds, I'll be lost utterly; the darkness is totally blinding and bewildering." Grayth felt solid ground under his feet suddenly, then he was standing, and spinning in the four cable arms of the giant Sarn. The darkness spun madly about him for a moment, then he stood waveringly on his feet, without the faintest idea of position as powerful arms urged him forward. "Stay where you are. I don't know where I am, anyway, and I'm convinced this is intended as a trap to bring you where the Mother's prepared weapons can destroy you and all hope of the revolution. She wants me only as bait for you. Stay!"

Softly in Grayth's mind came Ware's easy chuckle. "If I knew where you were, my friend, I would come. I will know soon enough. In good time, the Mother will see that you—and hence I—know. She realizes you have telepathic communication with me. Never, to my knowledge, has she revealed these invisible cloaks—"

"There have been other unexplained disappearances; this is the first time a telepath has been available to carry word," Deya snapped out.

"No matter. In good time, for no force, no power, no weapon or ray, no bomb or any other thing can serve to disrupt the—Cloak of Aesir. No energy, however great, can break down that shield. That is not the Mother's hope, for this morning in the Hall of Judgment she tested that cloak to all her powers—and one or two, Grayth, no other Sarn of all Earth knows, save the Mother alone. It did not fail then, nor can it. She makes no further trial of it, but wants an analysis of its forces." Ware's easy jubilance rode through to Grayth, lessening the tension.

"She will not learn one iota of that, Grayth. No, she wants a demonstration, a demonstration on her own terms, at her own time, in her chosen place. By Aesir and all the gods of Earth, Grayth, we'll give her the demonstration she seeks. By every god from Mithra to Thor, we'll give her one, I'll chill her prized palace there on the Sarn Hill till her old bones ache. No Sarn yet ever had rheumatism, but, by Earth and man, we'll find out this night whether a Sarn's thousand bones can't breed a mighty case!"

"You'll stay where you are, you braggart fool," Grayth howled through his telepath. "You are the revolution, not I. Bartel's an abler man, if he does lack a bit in fine words and simple phrases. The Sarn Mother's lived five centuries to your year; she has studied space and time and all of energy with tools and instruments you never guessed, or will guess. You are a child, a prattling fool of a child, to her, Ware. Stay where you are! You may not know of any way to analyze or defeat that shield of yours, but what do you know of the Sarn's ten-thousand-year-old science?"

Ware's bubbling laughter echoed queerly in telepathy. "All Sarn science, Grayth, that has been published. The telepath, my friend, is not without its powers as an educator, tuned inward to catch, amplify and reflect each thought to a solid impression. And all human science, Grayth. Under my house—when I was trying to make a lab the Sarn wouldn't find—I found an ancient subway and a buried lab some striving humans had contrived in the last days before explosives and gas killed them. Books and periodicals, tons of them, heaped clumsily. A forgotten legacy."

Grayth groaned. The skin of his back seemed suddenly oppressed in the queer manner a telepath contrives when absolute rapport is established between two powerful minds. A heavy pack strapped on Ware's back. The screaming hiss of an atom-flame-lamp unit readjusted, rebuilt to carry a million times the load it had been designed for, a scream that vanished in inaudible shrillness. Sketchily, waveringly, the rock-walled, hidden laboratory of Ware's contriving stood out before Grayth's eyes, lighted against the utter blackness that shrouded him. Then that, too, became a blackness, a stranger, straining blackness and chill as Ware pressed a contact at his belt.

"Ware," pleaded Grayth, "I don't know where I am. If you don't promise now to stop this expedition at least until I give further intelligent information, I'll grind the Mother's medallion under my heel, and by the gods, you'll never know."

"I'll wait," sighed Ware.

"But—you'll go later, Ware—you'll go?" demanded Deya.

"I'll promise that, too, Deya." Ware's mind smiled to her.

"Grayth, I shall continue." Darak's thoughts, faint with distance, came in.

"Right," replied Grayth. "Bartel!"

CLOAK OF AESIR 79

"Yes."

"And Carron and Oburn, Tharnot, Barlmew, Todd—all of you, continue your duties, without any change or shift. Do not hint you know of my disappearance till the appropriate time. Todd, you take charge of that outer office; you did a good job, apparently, when you knew I was being carried by, invisible, ten feet from you. You are in charge there. Keep the girls out of my inner office, for any reason, until I can give some idea of what is to take place. Got it?"

"Right."

"Deya," said Ware, "has stopped sending. Further, she does not answer; she's blanked her mind."

"We've been walking—stopped now!" Grayth's mind raced. "Deya . . . Deya, answer me!"

There was a tense silence of mind; only the low, multitudinous mutter of a thousand human minds in normal thought about him.

"Oburn, where are you?" snapped Ware.

"At home."

"Stroll out in front; you live within three doors of Deya. Grayth, stumble in the dust—do you feel dust under your feet?"

"Yes." Grayth stumbled awkwardly against a giant Sarn guard, dragging his foot sharply across a dusty walk, unseen.

"Dust rose," said Oburn softly. "Deya, will you answer me?"

"Yes." Her telepath thoughts were half angry, half miserable. We're moving again, though, so—they spun me. I don't know which way."

"You will stop dragging your foot." A Sarn voice low and tense in Grayth's ear warned him.

"Ware, I . . . I don't like this." Grayth's thought was tense and very worried.

Deya's was bitter. "It was well enough when you were the one; now you are not so anxious that Ware stay back, I take it. Ware, you stay right where you are, because if that was wise for Grayth, the only one of us who can really move the men of his following, it is a hundred times wiser so far as I am concerned."

"I think," said Ware, annoyed, "that I had better start designing a telepath locating device. It should be relatively simple, and if this continues, we'll need one. I'll join you as soon as I know where you are. In the meantime, I have a little work to do preparing. Please stop ordering and counterordering. We need you both; the Mother wants to study this apparatus, and she won't stop taking people until she gets the chance. It won't do her any good whatever, so she'll get that chance."

"I fear you're right," Grayth agreed. "It should be getting dark now."

"It is. The moon rises at 1:45, so we have plenty of time. I think . . . I think it is going to be heavily overcast," predicted Ware suddenly. A chaos of thoughts raced suddenly through his mind, thoughts too lightly touched for others to follow.

Utter jet, and the sound of people moving, voices and low laughter. Hasty side steps to avoid unseen passers that brushed by, feet sounding softly on the dusty walks or grassy lanes. Then rough cobbles under their feet, rounded by the tread of more than a hundred generations of mankind, and behind them, the low murmur of the square fading away.

The rough cobbles gave way, suddenly, to the smooth, glassy pavement of the roads of the Sarn City. They had passed the low, ancient wall that marked the boundaries where men might walk unchallenged. Only low, sleepy cheeps of birds in nearby parklike gardens now, and the shrill notes of crickets and night insects tuning up.

The pace of the Sarn guards accelerated, their long legs, and the curious manner in which they retracted them with each step, making a pace swift for the humans to match. Grayth heard Deya's soft breathing accelerate as they moved at a near trot up the low rise that led to the Sarn Palace.

Then steps under his feet, strong Sarn arms guiding him upward, steadying stumbling feet. The echo of corridors answered to his tread, and for an instant he knew where he was; this was no unfamiliar walk to him now, and he was mentally readjusted. To the right, and a half-dozen turns, and he was beyond any area of the vast, sprawling Sarn Palace that he knew.

An arm detained him; he stood motionless in utter darkness, while, beyond, something hummed for an instant, then a soft shuffling of a sliding door, two steps forward, and the soft clang of the door's return. The sensation of a sudden drop in a swift elevator was nerve tearing in this darkness, this total unknowingness of place, time or intent of captors. Grayth stiffened, heard Deya's soft gasps as the floor seemed cut from beneath her. Then the steadiness of the floor returned, and only the soft humming of the gravity controls told of their movement downward. Time became confused, there was no clue to their speed, yet Grayth was certain that they dropped many thousands of feet. The air pressure mounted till swallowing had relieved it so many times he lost track of that crude barometric method. More than five thousand feet, though—

More than a mile! No human had ever guessed at the depths of the Sarn Palace. Only once had humans ever been permitted to see those depths, and then it was the upper caverns only, when Drunnel and his men had been given a few feeble weapons by the Mother's orders. Weapons to overcome Grayth and Ware.

"More than a mile—we're slowing, Ware. The air is thick; it must be nearly two miles down. The air itself seems denser and richer in my lungs. Unless we are brought upward again—"

"I'll come down to you," Ware's calm mind replied. "Can you receive there clearly?"

"Perfectly," Grayth acknowledged.

"Two facts I wanted; antigravity units of the cars do not disturb the reception. Two miles of solid rock do not disturb it. Thought waves are a level below all known radiations, a force unto themselves. The Cloak of Aesir stops all other things."

"We are walking down a corridor, wide, rock floored and walled, low ceilinged. There are columns," said Deya. "Ahead, I hear Sarn."

They halted, and the echoes of their feet died away slowly, the curious *zing-zing-zing* of sound reflected from rows of columns disappeared in unknown, unseeing distances.

"Mother of Sarn! Decalon Toplar reports with her Ten, and the two humans for whom she was sent," the Decalon's fluting voice called out.

"Remove the Cloak of the Mother, Decalon. Place all of the cloaks in this case, and with them the visors."

A giant Sarn tugged at Grayth, the curious rustle of the cloak rose about him, then abruptly he was blinded by a flood of intolerably brilliant light. Gradually his eyes adjusted themselves; it was no more than normal illumination from a score of giant atom-flame lamps set high above in the arched and groined stone of the ceiling. Black, glittering, granitic rock, studded with two huge plaques on opposite sides. A twenty-foot disk of gold mapping Earth, a twenty-foot golden disk mapping the Forgotten Planet. From a concealed atom-flame lamp in the lofty dome, two projectors shot stabbing rays against the golden disks. On Earth's, a ray of brilliant yellow-white; on the other, a ray of dim, chill blue.

The Mother sat on a chair of state, about her the eight Mothers of the Cities and a score of giant Sarn guards. From air, eleven more were emerging, as Deya emerged piecemeal, while goggled Sarn packed into the silver and hardwood case on the long table something unseen and tenderly treated. The Decalon stood by the case, tucking unseen folds carefully into its corners, taking goggles and batteries from the guards to place on tiny pins.

"It is the Given Law that no being, human or Sarn, shall twice be accused of a single thing," said Grayth. "Yesterday in the Hall of Judgment I was tried and acquitted. It is the Given Law that no being, human or Sarn, shall be brought for judging without an opportunity of defense, save he waive that right.

"Neither I nor this woman, Deya, has committed any offense against any being, human or Sarn. As is our right, we ask our accuser to appear and explain before us and the Mother the reason for this arrest."

The Mother's slitted eyes closed slowly and opened sleepily. Her powerful body remained as motionless as the stone of the Hall; the Mothers of the Cities neither moved nor seemed so much as to breathe.

The Mother spoke in the fluting tongue of the Sarn. "The Given Law is the Law of the Mother; by it I have promised to abide, save in time of emergency. This, Grayth, is such a time. You, this woman, and perhaps certain others have sought to plot against the Sarn and the Sarn Mother. That is the accusation; I am the accuser. What answer do you make?"

"If one be brought before the Mother, and faced with his accuser, he has then twenty-four hours to consider his reply. The accusation must have evidence enough to make it seem just in the Mother's eyes that an answer be made, and complete enough that the accused know why this thing is charged.

"The Mother is the accuser, but I may ask—by the Given Law—what reasoned facts bring forth this accusation?"

The Mother's eyes sparkled. Almost, a smile touched her tiny lips as she looked at Grayth's keen, gray eyes. The Sarn were proud that never in the millenniums of man's enslavement had cruelty been applied, nor intentional injustice. Where the Law of the Sarn could apply logically to humans, both races worked under the same law; where—as in the nature of two races such things must be—the laws could not apply identically, justice had been applied.

The Sarn were just; no human could say otherwise. The Sarn Mother's age covered six-score generations of mankind, and to some extent her immortality removed her alike from human and Sarn. Wherefore, it was easier for her, who had known man's greatness, to appreciate the keenness and strength that lay in Grayth's stubborn face. And, knowing mankind, to appreciate the steadfastness with which he would fight by every law or trick of law to win freedom back for Deya.

And—she appreciated the searching quickness with which Grayth had forced her once again on the defensive. Her case was true and solid—but made of ten thousand thousand little things, of things that had not happened as well as of things that had. Of subtle, reasoned psychology—and not half a dozen solid facts. Of those few, three were ruled out of this consideration, because they had been dealt with in that earlier trial, when Grayth was released.

She had no time to argue now with a mind that she knew was fully as keen as that of her own City Mothers. There were other, more important things afoot, as that gray-eyed man well knew. And he knew as well as she that her case was not a thing to be stated and in a dozen sentences. And also that it was a perfectly just, though unprovable, accusation.

"This is a time of emergency, Grayth," said the Mother softly. "I will give you the twenty-four hours you demand, however. And your companion, Deya.

"Decalon, let these two be taken to the fifteenth cell in the House of the Rocks."

The Decalon and her squad of ten moved forward. Grayth turned to Deya, a slight smile on his lips, as the Ten surrounded them. Back toward the great pillared corridor leading off into unseen distances, lighted by dwindling atom flames, the guards led them.

"The House of the Rocks. This, then, is the rumored prison of the Sarn. Ware . . . Ware—" Grayth called mentally.

"I am coming, Grayth. I will join you in an hour. You need not call continuously as I have made rapport with you and can follow your normal thoughts. The sky, as I suggested, is becoming overcast. It will be a very dark night."

"We could not leave unaided," sighed Deya.

"I do not believe it would be probable." Grayth laughed uneasily.

Grayth moved about the cell restlessly. The Decalon and her squadron were gone, down that tube that had brought them. The single huge old Sarn that served as warden, turnkey and guard had set the tumblers on the steel door, and left with soft, shuffling toe pads.

Grayth stopped in the center of the room, his head high and tense, furrows of concentration on his forehead. Deya, in her chair, sat motionless, her deep-blue eyes clouded in sudden thought. She rose slowly, a magnificent throwback to a race five thousand years forgotten, a viking's daughter, bearing a golden tan of the more southern sun of this region, but golden haired and blue eyed, tall and powerful.

Slowly her eyes cleared, and a slight frown of understanding met Grayth's eyes. "There are Sarn close by. At least a dozen. And if those Sarn are prisoners here, then all the Mother's laboratories have been stripped of talent," she said softly.

"Echoes," thought Grayth sharply. "Do not use voice."

Deya smiled. "They do, and yet no intelligible word is audible. The echoes do not carry words; they carry sounds, confusing, blended, intermingled sound. And concentration on telepaths might make impressions on instruments, where normal thought did not. Perhaps speech is better."

Grayth nodded. "There are a dozen Sarn, at least, all scientists. They are in the cell above, the cell below, the cells on each side. And the only clear things of their thoughts that I can make is—Aesir—and instruments."

"I've found that shaft," came Ware's thoughts. "I haven't traced every circuit of the palace for nothing, and as the palace electrotechnician, I've found many that were not on my charts. The sky is becoming heavily overcast. It will be very dark indeed. I will join you shortly."

The Mother pointed silently. Across the room, a section of rock had swung aside, and a broad signal board was revealed. A green light blinked irregularly, then went out. A blue bulb winked for a moment, and died in turn, as a yellow bulb glowed steadily. "By the shaft, then. The air is not open to him."

The Mothers of the Cities stirred restlessly. A second yel-

CLOAK OF AESIR

low light flashed. "If he goes below the sixth level—" suggested the Mother of Durban.

"The cage will remain down there, but probably he will not. He walked through a solid wall once; he may walk through solid rock." A third and fourth bulb flashed. The Mother watched quietly. The Mothers of Cities tensed as the fifth lighted. Abruptly it was out, and in sudden succession the blue and green bulbs winked.

"He knew," said the Mother, almost approvingly. "The car did not fall. Go."

A section of rock wall swung open. Silently the Mothers of Cities vanished behind it, and with them went the tall figures of the guards. The rock swung to. The Mother, alone on her tall throne, saw a darkening of the farther lights of the long corridor.

Aesir stood again before the Mother, a blackness, a thing that was not black, but was blackness incarnate. A thing some seven feet in height, vaguely manlike in form.

The Mother's thin lips smiled. "You have shrunk, Aesir. Have some of those billions of wills you mentioned left you, then?"

A voice stirred in her mind, a respecting, yet laughing voice. "Perhaps that may be it; a few wills more of cold metal than warm human flesh. But for the good of my race, two wills you hold captive must be freed. For this I have come again. And—perhaps that you and those who wait in five adjoining cells may know me somewhat better.

"I am the crystallization of a billion, and more than a billion wills, Mother of the Sarn."

"There are no humans here; the Sarn need no such tales." The Mother moved annoyedly.

"It is no tale; it is pure fact. This blackness is their product, not as, perhaps, I might explain to humans, but still their product." The voice that stirred soundless in the Mother's mind smiled.

The Mother nodded slowly in comprehension. "Wills and knowledge. That may be. We seek a new balance, you and I."

"We seek a new balance, your race and mine," corrected that blackness. "You and I might reach a balance in this minute, if it were we two alone. The balance would be—that your plan went down to a depth that none, neither Sarn nor human, knows, while I remained."

"Yes," acknowledged the Mother. "I might be wiped out,

and you remain. But your race would go, and mine remain, save that you alone continued."

"There is no need to exchange these thoughts; each knows the other to that extent. Man has one great advantage over Sarn; that, as a race, man is more nearly developed to universal telepathy. A few of my people can already talk among themselves; I have learned the different pattern that is Sarn telepathy. I can speak with you as Grayth cannot."

"Though he appears aware of Sarn thoughts when near us," sighed the Mother, "I had not thought of that."

"We make an exchange now," Aesir's thoughts laughed. "You wanted observations of my . . . my body stuff. I will give you that, and in exchange—"

Aesir stepped forward, and swept from the long table the silver case that contained the cloaks of the Mother and the goggles. Simultaneously, the Mother's finger moved, and a carven bit of her high throne sank under it. From unseen projectors, a shrieking hell of flame screamed out, intolerable—blasting— The rocky floor of the great chamber screamed and puffed out in incandescent fury. The great table boomed dully in the corridors, a sudden, expanding blot of livid gas. The mad shrieking screamed and thundered down the corridors, the floor of the vast cavern slumped in annihilation that speared down through a hundred feet of rock in a single second of cosmic fury—

And died in silence. The Mother dropped three curled arms before her face, blinking tear-blurred eyes. Aesir stood, blackness against fiery incandescence of the cooling rocks, unsupported in the air. His form was altered, a clumsy thing with a strange, angular belly. An almost rectangular protuberance. But the thing was not rectangular; one corner was twisted and bitten away.

"I never knew," said Aesir softly, "but I am certain now; the world of the Sarn was not so heavy as Earth. You move slowly, Mother."

Silently the blackness glided down the corridor, dwindling from the Mother's sight. Furious golden eyes glittered after the hunched, disfigured mass. Slowly the glitter faded from her eyes, and a concentration of thought appeared, perhaps even a mischievous twinkle of approbation.

The Mother's finger touched another button, and instantly a score of tense-faced guards leaped through the door, clumsy seeming, funnel mouthed, hand weapons ready. They stopped at the door, staring at the fiery incandescence in the floor.

CLOAK OF AESIR

The Mothers of Cities crowded through their ranks, a slow, dawning smile of satisfaction on their thin lips as they looked into the glow. The Mother of Targlan took her seat slowly. "Then the revolution is ended," she said with soft satisfaction.

The Mother turned angry eyes on her. "Daughter," she asked bitterly, "do you think I mount here weapons of the power I have in the Hall of Judgment? I did not turn that weapon on him—but on the cloaks. No more than a corner of them did I get; he moved too swiftly. My thoughts have been disturbed in this emergency, and I have not rested in fifty hours, or I would never have left that case where he might reach it.

"Aesir must win on this exchange, for he *will* know what makes the Cloak of the Mother, while I *may* know what makes the Cloak of Aesir." The Mother looked calmly down the long corridor, where a figure of hunched blackness turned into a narrow cleft in the great wall of the rocky tunnel.

The old Sarn warder of the House of Rocks had been instructed. The Sarn Mother had no desire to lose Sarn lives—and she wanted Aesir in that grim citadel. The warder, as Aesir appeared, turned away and left the passages open to him. The invisible guards at the narrow cleft that led into the impregnable citadel remained inactive, wrapped in invisibility.

Up the stairways carved in the glinting rock the Blackness strode. Down the corridor to the gray steel door behind which Grayth's and Deya's minds acted as directive calls.

And—between ranks and files of recording instruments set in every wall, in every doorway he passed. Tiny atom flames finer than the slimmest wire reached out to touch and feel at the black texture of his cloak. Unseen force fields caressed delicately at the fringes of blackness. Bolometers and thermometers felt and sampled the chill that poured from the blackness. Frigid air, like chilled puddles, flowed from that blackness and trickled across the stone floor behind him. White of frost coated the corridor pavement as he, in his dead blackness, passed.

"Grayth—Deya—stand back from the door. The door will fade to a vague transparency. Step through it instantly." Through the impenetrable blackness, the subtle mystery of thought reached out to contact and explain to the imprisoned humans.

The formless blackness of Aesir's hand waved stubbily over the gray metal of the door. As though that hand were a wet cloth, the door a chalked picture on slate, it vanished. Where the hand had passed in quick circles, the grim metal roiled and twisted—and vanished.

Deya's hand reached out uncertainly, touched the space where the door had been to feel a vague opposition, as though a thick and incredibly viscous gassy stuff remained. It was utterly without temperature sensation. She lunged through it sharply, overcome by an instant's strangling suffocation, then stood beside Aesir in the corridor. Grayth joined them silently.

"The cloaks?" he asked.

"They are useless save for information. The Mother's rays cut through the corner of the case, and cut strange patterns in them, no doubt. You could not use them. We'll have to go out as we are. Now come, and stay close behind me. We must put walls behind us, and that won't be easy."

"Can we go into the rock—or would that be impossible?" Deya asked.

Aesir's misshapen hand pointed. Behind them, the door of the cell was blackness similar to Aesir's own, a blackness rapidly congealing about two bent shadows overlapping on the surface. Two shadows were Deya and Grayth had passed through. A deadly chill was radiating from the door, a growing chill that sucked the light of the atom-flame lamps in the ceiling, and ice from the air.

"You felt that momentary suffocation. You can't breathe inside that steel, or inside rock. And that condition of interpenetrability is both temporary and frightfully treacherous. We'll have to go."

Ware went ahead, and now, as he passed the hair-fine atom flames that had probed for his cloak, a finger pointed and shape cracklings of lightning snapped where the jet beam of blackness struck the probing beams. Harmless to Aesir's blackness, they were hairlines of death to unshielded humans.

The flames ahead on their course abruptly sputtered and went out. The Sarn saw no reason to lose good instruments.

Down the stair, and out into the glare of the great atom flames lighting the House of Rocks. "There are invisible guards," said Aesir. "The Mother, I take it, warned them to let me pass in unhindered. They may seek to stop you—"

It was against the Mother's orders. But those Sarn guards, in their eight-foot power, in their contempt for humans, in the pride they held that never had any being imprisoned in the

House of the Rocks escaped, raised unseen weapons toward Grayth and Deya.

A long, stretching finger of jet shot out from Aesir's stubby hand. Something cracked in the air, darting lightnings and a wild, many-toned shriek of agony chopped off abruptly. A Sarn figure black as Aesir's jet stumbled from nothingness and faded behind a swiftly formed white curtain of frost crystals. The black finger swept around, and the Sarn guards died in blue lightnings and blackness.

"Run," commanded Ware. The three started down the straight narrow cleft that led to the outer corridor. Aesir turned right, then right again, into a low-roofed tunnel. Another elevator bank, the cars undamaged. The heavy, locked metal door faded under his hand to disclose a black shaft leading down and up in emptiness to unseen depths and heights. Another door—and another—

Then a car was found, and the three hastened through. Behind them in the main corridor a heavy pounding of running feet and clanking accouterments sounded. The blunt, dull-glossed nose of a war-blast swerved clumsily round the corridor with half a dozen giant Sarn tugging at it. Degravitized, it floated free, but its tons of mass were clumsy and hard to manage there in narrow rock corridors. Shouting, musical commands twisted it into place, settled it, and it thudded to the floor as the degravitizer was cut. Two Sarn swung the trajectory controls, and a third held the lanyard ready.

Aesir reached for the controls of the elevator cab as the blast roared in throaty fury at dissolving, flaming walls. The rock walls to the left and right flared into deadly flame of dying atoms. And the view was lost as the translucency of the metal door snapped instantly into blackness, a blackness that licked up the furious energy greedily and pulled with freezing fingers at the heat of the two human bodies within.

"That button, Grayth. Quickly. I cannot touch it through this cloak," Ware snapped.

Grayth pushed the thing, one among a bank of hundreds. The floor of the cab pushed against them momentarily, then a sense of weightless falling gripped them as Ware's black finger pointed at something in the control mechanism. Blackness and frightful cold drained every trace of warmth from a resistor in the controls, and the full current drove through the degravitator control. The car shot madly upward.

"The Mother has many of these cars wired with power cut-offs. If this is one—as it probably is—and she learns in time which car we took, she may cut out our circuit. If so—we still have one chance, though I have never dared try it."

"Better cut that resistance back in," said Grayth quietly. "Listen to the howl of the air above."

The shriek was mounting. Far above in the closed tube, compressed by the upward plunge of the tube-fitting car, the air was howling through some vent. It was a vast organ pipe that changed its tune upward, upward—more and more swiftly as the tube length shortened and the pressure mounted—

"I can't." Ware's hidden head shook. "The air pressure must stop us. But not until we reach the top of the building and the automatic safeguards go into action. They'll cut the current in the car and apply brakes as we pass the topmost floor. If the Mother hasn't already—"

The shriek mounted. Abruptly the drive of the car vanished. Grayth, already firmly gripping the carved cage walls, flung a protecting arm about Deya and gripped more tightly. Aesir tumbled upward toward the roof of the cab, inverted himself somehow in midflight, and hung poised.

"Don't touch me," snapped Ware's thoughts in their minds. "It would be death—"

A new sibilant hiss cut through the roar of the air in the tube above, and Ware sighed in relief. "The Mother was too late. She cut the power—but not before we had come so high, and so fast that the automatic safeguards tripped. The emergency brakes have gone on."

The deceleration died, and Ware floated back to the floor. The car was stopped, was sinking slowly. It clicked again, and a ratchet locked somewhere beneath their feet. The door of the car opened with a rumble, and an outer door slipped aside. The three stepped out into a corridor, a corridor lighted by the atom-flame lamps of the Sarn, lamps carved in alabaster and golden amber stone. They were in the uppermost floor of the Palace of the Sarn.

Far below, the Sarn Mother looked thoughtfully at the little lighted column of signal lamps. The City Mothers followed her gaze, furious as they saw the double red bulbs of the safety guard signals go on. "I am curious," said the Sarn Mother softly. "He froze the resistor in the degravitizer circuit with his blackness, surely, to get any such mad climb rate. But I have a thought that Aesir does nothing that he does not know some remedy for, nor attempt anything that he does not have some second, saving escape. What would he have done had I been able to cut his power before he could reach the safety trips?"

The City Mothers were not curious. They waited impatiently as the Mother let seconds slip away without flinging a rank of guards about that upper floor.

The Mother made no move. She saw no gain in throwing her guards against the blackness, that, so far as she could see, had no weakness. She saw, rather, that her best policy was to wait the report of her scientists. Knowledge was the power she needed now. That, and the power she already had; control over all sources of the materials whose lack rendered Aesir harmless—so far as revolution went.

Aesir stood in the entranceway of the Hall of Judgment. Behind, through the ever-open doors, the Gardens of the Sarn were visible. Aesir—Ware—smiled. "I said it might be an overcast night," his thought whispered softly.

Grayth and Deya shivered. The gardens knelt before a wind that howled in maniac fury. In the reflected light that shone against the low-pressed sky, a wrack of storm boiled overhead. And it was cold. The wind that shrieked across the gardens was a breath of savage winter cutting through this summer night.

"I think," said Ware, "that it will rain."

As he spoke the sky burst into flame. Vast tongues of lightning ripped across the sky, stabbing down to Earth in a mighty network of electric fire. The air exploded with a blast of thunder that rattled the mighty fabric of the Sarn Palace to its bones. Instantly the floodgates opened. The clouds split up and tumbled down in liquid streams. The shouting wind lashed the water droplets before it in a horizontal spray that was half falling water, half water slashed from the ground that was suddenly a pond. The twinkling lights of the human city beyond the Sarn City walls were suddenly gone.

"Perhaps," said Ware pleasedly, "I used too much."

"You?" gasped Grayth. "*You* did this?"

"The Sarn hate cold, and they hate the wet more than any cat ever did. You'll find no Sarn loose in the gardens tonight. Our way should be clear to the gates."

Deya shuddered and looked at Aesir's blackness. "That wind is cold; that rain must be near sleet. And I am dressed for June—not a February night."

"I used too much power," Ware shrugged. "I never did this thing before. Put it down to inexperience."

"Experimental error," Grayth sighed. "Gods, man, you've washed the city away. Come, let's start before we have to swim."

"Not yet," said Ware. "I've something else to do. The Mother wanted to study this blackness of mine. Well, by all the gods there are, I'll give her all she wants. I'll make her think again before she summons Aesir for her pleasure!"

He turned about and faced into the great Hall of Judgment. It was magnificent beneath the dim light of a few big lamps. It was jet stone and chrome, gold and sparkling, inlaid crystal. Aesir's arm became a funnel of blackness that pointed in slow circles around the room. Where that arm passed, the sparkle of polished stone and shining metal or gem vanished. It became a dead blackness. The walls ceased to have the appearance of walls, but became empty spaces that stretched off to some eternity of night.

The glint and whisper of the atom flames died away; their strong light dulled to something somber and depressing.

And cold—cold welled out of the place in a tangible flood. The humans shivered violently and fled from the doorway that dripped, suddenly, with frozen mist. Puddled air, chilled near its freezing point, it seemed, flowed down the walls and out the door. A breeze sprang up, a throaty gurgle of air rushing into the room at the top of the great door to rush out at the bottom in a freezing, unseen torrent.

Grayth and Deya hurried aside, shivering in unbearable chill. The torrent of air poured out, across the vestibule to the entranceway of the palace. It flowed down the steps, and as they watched, the howling rain turned to snow and froze as sleet on the stone.

"Yes," said Ware in satisfaction, "the Sarn hate cold. It will be a month before that room is habitable again. Now come."

He walked through the flood, and down the steps toward the windlashed gardens. The wind howled by him, swirled around his cloak of blackness, and the figure was outlined in white that swirled and glinted in the faint light radiated from the building. Behind him, Grayth and Deya made their way, white figures against the blackness. In a moment they were lost behind driving, glistening curtains of rain.

They were soaked and freezing in an instant. In his arms Grayth felt Deya shivering violently. "Ware," he called abruptly. "Ware—go on; we will meet you. We can follow that blackness only by the snow that forms around you, and on a night like this, may I be cursed if I follow a walking snowstorm. I'm freezing now, and Deya, too."

"Frozen," the girl chattered.

"I can't cut off this shield," Ware answered. "The instruments aren't insulated well enough. If water touches them—there'll be neither Sārn nor human city to squabble over. Meet me at my house. You can find your way?"

"I think so," nodded Grayth, shivering.

"Strike for the road. It will glow tonight, as usual. And there will be no Sarn upon it, with this liquid blizzard howling."

"Good." Grayth and Deya set out half-running. Black wind and water thundered through the gardens. The sky exploded once more in blinding light, the waves of sound rocking the ground beneath their feet so that even half-frozen as they were, they felt its shaking.

In the rock of that wild night, no eyes saw Grayth and Deya reach their goal. Rain in solid, blinding sheets hid them as they slipped between wind-bowed trees to Ware's small stone cottage, into its unlighted doorway. Ware's hand found Grayth's, and led the shivering, dripping pair through the tiny room, abruptly brilliant in the explosion of another lightning flash. At the far wall, Ware fumbled at a stone that grated and moved. Silently he led them down to a yet smaller room lined with rough granite. The stone above them swung back, and a light sprang up. But again Ware was fumbling, and again he led them down, down to a musty cavernous place, walled with age-rusted steel, supported by rusted columns of steel hidden at the heart of thicker columns—stalagmites and stalactites formed about and buttressing the corroded metal.

"The old subway," Ware explained. "It goes for a quarter of a mile in that direction and nearly a mile in the other before cave-ins block it. All, you see, beneath the human city—and most at a depth of more than one hundred and twenty feet. My lab's over here." It was set up on the concrete platform of a forgotten station.

"But here—strip off those wet things and stand before these heaters." Ware turned to a crude control panel, and a network of iron bars grew warm, hot, then faintly red as a welcome heat poured out.

"Do we hide," asked Deya softly, "or frankly return?"

"If," said Ware sadly, "I knew how much longer this queer status of half-revealed half-concealed revolt was going to continue before I could get somewhere, we might be in a better position to know what to do."

"Which makes me wonder, Ware. Half-concealed half-revealed, I mean. The Mother's Cloaks have the goggles to make vision possible. I don't know what that blackness of yours is—beyond that it is infernally cold; I'm still congealed—but if no ray can pierce it, pray tell me how you see where you are going."

Ware looked up, laughing. "I don't. Yet I found my way across that swamp called the Garden of the Sarn more easily than you, tonight. The telepath is the answer—I see through others' eyes. The Mother told me where the cloaks were hidden." He nodded toward the truncated case. "Without her eyes—I'd never have seen to reach them."

"Perhaps," said Deya, "if we knew better what you have, and what you lack, we could help more efficiently."

"Perhaps," suggested Grayth grimly, "you can wash the blasted Sarn out of their city. Another such 'overcast night' and you may do it."

"The Sarn City's higher than we are." Ware smiled. "But our people do stand cold and wet better than theirs."

"But," said Deya, "it isn't practical—nor fast enough. What have you there? My slowly thawing bones give me a very personal interest in that cloak of yours."

Ware sighed gustily, "It's hard to explain. About ninety percent of it isn't in words, or explainable in words. It's a mathematical concept that has reality.

"Wherefore I will now give you a typical pre-Sarn analogy, because neither you nor Grayth can get pictures from mathematics. It's a language, you know—as much a language as the one we normally speak, or the Sarn language. Some terms you can translate, and some can't be. For instance $x^2+y^2=c^2$ is mathematics language for 'circle.' I will give you analogies which I guarantee are not sound, and nearly conceal the truth. But I can't do any better.

"Dirac, a physicist of the pre-Sarn days, explained the positron as a whole in a continuum of electrons in negative energy states. Space, he said, was completely filled with electrons possessed of negative energies. It was full to the brim, and overflowed into the electrons we can detect—ordinary matter electrons.

"Shortly before the Sarn came, men were developing hints that there might be more to that. There was. Electrons in positive energy states, when vibrated, gave off radiation—

light, heat, and so on. If you use energy concentrated enough, you can vibrate electrons in negative energy states. You might say they give off negative energy radiation. They produce photons of energy in negative energy states.

"As I said, it's an analogy that I can't honestly describe, but the effect is radiated negative energy. Radiant cold or radiant darkness or radiant lack-of-X-rays—whatever you want.

"Energy being conserved, of course, the result is that the source of that radiation, instead of consuming energy, gives it off. My pack does not radiate negative energy; it sets up a condition in the air about me that makes the air atoms radiate negative energy.

"The atomic flame the Mother turned on me satisfied, to some extent, the ravening demand for energy that negative energy setup caused. The force that makes the air atoms radiate in that way makes them unstable—sort of splits them into two parts, two half-formed atoms of matter. In that state, neither half is real, but each has a terrible demand for sufficient mass—in the form of energy—to raise it to reality. In that median state, matter is interpenetrable. We walk through steel doors and stone floors, for instance. It will hang on that unstable point of half-and-half momentarily, before re-forming to matter. It's as dependable as a rattlesnake or a 'tame' tiger. While we're interpenetrating, it may fall off that delicate balance and consume our mass-energy in re-forming. When Sarn guards send atomic flames after us, the unstable matter greedily drinks in the energy, and starts definitely toward re-forming with the air of that energy. If left alone, one-half of the semiatoms absorbs the other half, and it's normal again. In the meantime, it's black. And cold—like the Mother's Hall of Judgment right now.

"When the Mother's beams were tearing at me, the energy was actively making extra atoms of air. It didn't make any difference what kind of beam she used—the energy was consumed. Her atomic flame had lots of power—and made a lot of air. Her curious atom-disruption beam didn't carry much energy, but the particular form of the beam was most deadly. The form passed through my shield quite unchanged, theoretically. But the energy had been removed from it.

"Naturally, the Mother's physicists are badly puzzled now by a completely unanimous report of 'nothing' on the part of their instruments. None of them, of course, read below absolute zero. That shield has a temperature of —55,000 Absolute—or thereabouts.

"I could wipe out the Sarn very readily. But"—Ware shrugged his shoulders—"they'd wipe out all humans while I was at it."

"What do you need?"

"An hour," Ware sighed. "One hour—in the Sarn workshops. A few pounds of molybdenum, some wire-drawing apparatus, a few ounces of scandium and special glass-blowing machinery. Then I'd have a duplicate of this toy of mine that would protect this whole city for fifty miles about."

"In other words," said Grayth, smiling slightly, "if you could drive the Sarn out, you could drive them away."

"Precisely," acknowledged Ware. "Which is comforting, if useless."

Deya rubbed her left arm with her right hand thoughtfully, and turned sideways to the heater. "How far," she asked, "will your present apparatus reach?"

"That, too, is helpful." Ware grinned. "Just about far enough to blanket completely the Sarn City. I could protect that against any attack. But not, by any means, the human city."

"That might help, though." Deya nodded. "I have something in mind. My dress is dry, if somewhat crumpled. Could you get us something to eat, Ware? My chill had left me hungry."

"What's your thought?" asked Ware eagerly, half annoyedly. The telepaths did not carry thoughts the wearer wished to conceal.

"I . . . I'd rather talk with Grayth first." Deya shook her head slowly. "I may be wrong."

Resignedly, Ware went up the crude stairway, up to the kitchen of his cottage one hundred and fifty feet above. Deya looked at Grayth as each in turn pulled off the telepath.

Deya pulled on her dress, smoothing the still slightly damp crinkles down. "How is Simons, Grayth?"

Grayth looked at her in slight puzzlement, his shirt half on. "Hopeless, as you know—but why do you ask now? He could not help us, anyway."

Deya's lips set in a slight, tight smile, her eyes bright and thoughtful. "I'm not so sure, Grayth. Not . . . so . . . sure. Ware has said that anything that he can run through an amplifier can be recorded, hasn't he? And if it can be recorded, it could be rebroadcast on a different wavelength, perhaps—"

Grayth started, went rigid. "By Aesir and all the gods of Earth! *Deya!* What fantastic idea have you now? That man is mad, horribly, loathsomely mad—"

"Negative energy," said Deya shortly, deft fingers arranging her hair. "If we could make the Sarn give up without fighting—in despair and hopelessness— And there are energies other than those purely physical ones that the Sarn are so thoroughly equipped to resist."

Grayth stood silent for a moment, his swift-working mind forgetting for the moment the task of driving his tired body. "You've talked with Dr. Wesson?" he asked intently.

Deya nodded slowly, "Yes—just this morning," then thought a moment before going on. "Or rather yesterday. It will be drawn in about three hours, if the storm has stopped. We should bring him here before then. You see what I have in mind?"

"Yes! I'll have Carron—"

Ware came down the steps, slowly, bearing two trays with bread and cheese and cold meat, some cups, cream and coffee. "If you will use those beakers for the water, the laboratory hot plates for a stove, Deya, I'd prefer your coffee to mine."

"Ware," asked Grayth tensely, "can you record a thought—a telepath thought?"

Ware stopped, brows suddenly furrowed. "Record it? Why? I've never tried—it's easier to think it again."

"Could it be done?"

"Hm-m-m . . . yes. I think so."

"How long to make the apparatus?" Grayth asked anxiously.

Ware hesitated. Shrugged. "A few hours. I can make that. Telepath apparatus, because of its very nature, has to be tiny. A few grains of the hard-to-get elements go a long way when the whole apparatus is less than a cubic millimeter in volume. But it takes time. A recorder and reproducer—say, two days, once I get the design. I think . . . yes, I know I can do it."

Grayth swept the telepath back to his head. Rapidly his thoughts drove out. "Carron—Carron—"

"Yes?" Sleepily Carron responded to the call.

"It's three hours to dawn. Carron—this must be done before the first people stir. Get Ohrman, the instrument maker, to Ware's at once. There are telepaths to be made. Get Dr. Wesson and tell him to call at Ware's. Then rouse one of the other men to receive and transmit my orders and get some sleep yourself.

"Now, Ware, draw out the plans for the parts you'll need for that apparatus, so Ohrman can start while you get some sleep. Oh . . . you can, I assume, make some translator arrangement that will twist human thought to Sarn telepath levels?"

"Eh? Human to Sarn levels—I don't know about that. I've been working on that problem on and off for weeks."

"Good—it'll be on, and not off, now. If you can do that, Ware, we win Earth again!"

The thing was incredibly tiny. It lay in Ware's palm, two small, inclosed reels connected by a bridge of bulging metal, the size, perhaps of a half peanut, between two slices of inch-thick steel rod. But the workmanship was wonderfully fine.

"This is only the reproducer," Ware sighed. His eyes were red and weary. "The recorder is there. You said that needn't be portable. And it records, as you wanted, in Sarn-type bands from the human thoughts, on a silver ribbon. The ribbon is endless, and repeats as long as this little spring is wound.

"Now, may I ask what you want of it? I've concentrated so on this that no question could enter my mind, I think. How is recorded thought to dislodge the Sarn? By repeating, 'Go away—go away.' Endlessly? Telepathic commands have no more force than words, you know."

"Not if they are resisted," Deya acknowledged. "But they can enter below conscious strength level. Do you want to see who—why—"

The stone above moved. Grayth and Deya and Ware looked up. Only the heavily sleeping, exhausted Ohrman remained unconscious of the intruder.

"Down, Simons," said Dr. Wesson's voice. There was a gentle urgency in it, a pitying yet firm tenderness. A pair of feet appeared, slowly, wearily, with an air of terrible, unending exhaustion—tired beyond all rest, misery and hopelessness subtly expressed in the dull, shambling descent of those heavy feet.

Loosely, miserably they came down the long flight, their mechanical, rhythmic drumming a muffled beat of defeat. The man came into view. His figure was lax, powerfully muscled arms and shoulders bent under a soul-deadening weight of overwhelming despair. Down—down—

"Down, Simons." The doctor's voice was weary with a queer despair caught somehow from that doom-weighted figure.

Ware turned slowly to look at Deya, at Grayth. "Who is he—Simons?"

They did not answer, and he turned back to look at the figure that stood unmoving now beneath the powerful lights of this buried laboratory. His face was pale and lined, powerful with the strength drained from it, set in a dead mask of uncaring despair. His eyes were black, black pits that looked without hope, or hope of hope, into the keen gray eyes of Aesir.

Ware felt something within him chill under the gaze of those eyes that no longer cared or hoped. The soul beyond them was not dead and longed for death. The lights of the bright room seemed cold and drear. Fatigue and hopelessness of the endless struggle against the overwhelming Sarn surged up in Ware, hopelessness and despair so deep he did not mind that the cause was lost before—

He tore his eyes away. "Deya—in the name of the gods, what—who—what is this thing!" he gasped.

"That is negative energy, Ware. That is the negative energy of the mind, the blackness of Aesir applied to all hope, all ambition. He is mad; he is a manic depressive. He has no hope, no thought of escape from that negative hell of despair that is beyond despair. He is mad, for no sane mind could conceive that awful blackness, the hopelessness that is a positive, devouring force that infests his being.

"If ever his mind should start to mend, he will become a suicidal maniac, driven to kill himself in any way he can, at any horrible expense. He cannot think of that escape now. That is struggle, that is in itself a hope—and he has none. To conceive of death as an escape is to hope, to believe that something better can be.

"That is beyond him now, for hope—struggle—effort to escape—all involve a will that mind has lost.

"He is mad, Ware, because no mind can hold the terrible despair his thoughts now know and remain sane.

"Record his thoughts. Record them there on that silver ribbon. Record that hopelessness that knows no resistance, no will to struggle. Record it, and broadcast that through the Sarn City!"

The Sarn Mother sat motionless at the high window of her tower, dull eyes looking out over the Gardens of the Sarn. Rich cloaks and heavy blankets wrapped her—useless things. The cold seeped through to her bones and drank her warmth. The great chamber, windowed on every side, was darkened by a heavy gloom, chilled by a cold that had grown slowly through the hours and the days she had sat here, almost unmoving. The bleak, cold stone of the walls was damp with a cold sweat of moisture. Great heaters in the walls ran at red heat and the dark air drank their warmth. Magnificent atom-flame lamps rustled softly in the high ceiling; their faint, silken whisper mumbled meaningless in her ears, and their strong light had lost its sparkle. Some subtle change in the air made it seem gray and very cold.

The sun did not shine here. A cold, steady rain beat down on the gardens below, ran endlessly over the clear windowpanes, stirring under vague, listless winds. The sun did not shine here. Through the fog of slowly dripping rain, beyond the limits of her gardens, the sun shone. It was brilliant there, she knew, a bright, hot sun sparkling in the bright clean air. It was June out there. The year was dead here, dead in a creeping, growing chill that burdened the land. The creeping, growing chill of—

That hellish thing of blackness. Almost, she felt angered at it, squatting there, dejected, black, unutterably woeful in the center of her gardens. Or what had been her gardens. It was a ravaged place now, plowed and harrowed by howling beams of atomic death, a shrieking incandescent effort to move that crouched thing of blackness. It had meant only the destruction of one slight spot of beauty in a dreary, cold world.

But that meant little, for there was no beauty now, or ever would be again. Only the chill that stole the heat from the air, the walls, her tired old body and the subtle darkness that cut through the brilliance of the atom flames and left light without sparkle, colors that all tinged gray.

A finger stirred listlessly and pressed a control. No, it was over. Full heat. She had known that; what sense to try again what she had tried a thousand times before during these endless, sleepless days that changed only from one shade of gray to a deeper black.

Dull eyes looked at the sweating walls. Cold, stone walls. When had it ever been that she had ordered stone? Warm marbles of rose and green. Warm? The rose of dying day before night's chill. The green of endless arctic ice. It mocked her and drove its chill to her age-old body.

Age-old. Unending years that had wheeled and rolled while she waited, useless. Waited for the coming of her people, or when she might again seek in space. Useless years of fruitless attempts to learn that one, lost secret of speed bettering

CLOAK OF AESIR

light's swift flight. Lost—lost with the ten trained Sarn that died those four thousand years gone in the blasting of this city once called New York. Too much else she'd had to do then to learn that secret.

Time she had now; four thousand wheeling years. But now she could not learn; it eluded her dulled mind, and the weakened minds of the decadent race.

As Aesir eluded her, and squatted miserable in the midst of misery his works had brought.

She stirred. The cold worked through. Hot food, hot drinks—they warmed a moment, then added dead, cold mass to the chill within her. A deadness that, she knew now, had been within her before this glooming chill had made her more aware. Her Sarn were weak; the soft product of an easy world, too sanely organized to require of them sharp, sharpening competition in endeavor.

And she was old. Immortality she had, and everlasting youth of tissue. But the mind grew old and dull, the courses of its thoughts narrowed and chilled with years and millenniums that passed. She was never to recall that exact age—but what matter? A stupid thing. What mattered that she thought of it or not; the years had passed, they'd graved their mark and narrowing on her. And on her race.

They had weakened. Humankind had strengthened, grown with the years that sapped the Sarn. Now, in her gardens, that hunched figure of dejection squatted, chilling all her city, defying the minds of all the Sarn. It had been a matter of time, inevitable as the fated motion of the planets. And the time had come. The humans were the stronger.

The door behind her opened slowly, but her brooding eyes remained fixed on the far wall till the intruder moved before her gaze. Barken Thil. Once, the Mother had thought her brilliant, hoped this physicist might find the forgotten secret of the speed drive. Now her eight-foot figure was shrunken, dimmed by the fog and gloom that curdled the air about them. "Yes?" The Mother spoke wearily.

"Nothing." The physicist shook her head. "It's useless, Mother of the Sarn. The blackness is there. No screen, no substance shuts it off. It registers no more than the cold we feel on our instruments; they tell us only what we know, that the air transmits less light, less heat. It is absorbed somehow, and yet does not warm thereby. A vacuum transmits energy as before—but we cannot live in vacua.

"Thard Nilo has gone mad. She sits on her stool and stares

at the wall, saying: 'The sun is warm . . . the sun is bright. The sun is warm . . . the sun is bright!' She will not move save when we lead her. She does not resist—but she does not act."

"The sun—is warm," the Mother said softly. "The sun—is bright. The sun—never shines here now. But the sun is bright and hot and the air is clean and dry in Bish-Waln."

The tired eyes looked up slowly toward the lax figure of the physicist. "I . . . I think I will visit. Bish-Waln. Where the sun is hot and bright and the air—

"I have never been there; never in all the time Earth became ours, four thousand years ago, have I left Sarn City. I have never seen Targlan of the ever-blue skies and the ever-white mountains. I have never seen Bish-Waln in the golden sands . . . the hot sands.

"I think that now, before humanity rises finally, I should like to see it. I think . . . yes, perhaps I will go."

Two hours later, she roused herself to give orders, vaguely, and hours later to enter her ship. The chill leaked out of metal and crystal as from the cold, green stone. She stared blankly through the rain-washed windows as the gloom-crowned gardens and the Sarn City dropped behind. One more ship rose slowly, listlessly behind her. Vaguely, she wondered that so few Sarn had been still there that these two ships could carry all.

For the first time in four thousand years she was leaving her city. For the first time in four thousand years no Sarn remained in Sarn City.

The clouds and gloom were suddenly below, a dull grayness that heaved and writhed like a living dome over Sarn City. June sunlight angled from the setting redness in the west across the human city stirring vaguely there below. A warmth she had not known in six unending days shot through her ancient body, and a blissfulness of sleep lapped her as the ship accelerated strongly, confidently, toward the sparkling waters beyond, toward Bish-Waln, bright and hot in the golden Sahara.

Her eyes closed, and she did not see through the dissolving clouds to the black figure that slowly rose erect, nor to the ordered division of the legion of peace that marched toward the blank, silent windows of the Sarn Palace. Behind them came a loose group of work-clad men to disperse among the dead, lightless shops of this, the city that had marked the landing of the Sarn.

THE DAY IS DONE

Astounding Science Fiction, May

by Lester del Rey (1915–)

Lester del Rey is important in the history of science fiction as an editor, critic, and writer. Best known for his stories "Helen O'Loy" (1938) and "Nerves" (1942), his 1962 novel THE ELEVENTH COMMANDMENT is one of the most interesting treatments of organized religion in sf.

"The Day Is Done" is a superb example of "prehistoric" science fiction, a category that is extremely difficult to write convincingly. That del Rey succeeds is obvious—what is not so obvious are the important things this story has to say about social relationships and the nature of evolutionary change in a revolutionary world.

(Lester is very fond of reminding me—at least once a month—that this story made me cry when I read it in the subway on the way to my classes at Columbia. Naturally, I always explain that I wept in agony over the excruciatingly bad writing, but it isn't true. Of all of Lester's stories this one is my favorite. IA)

Hwoogh scratched the hair on his stomach and watched the sun climb up over the hill. He beat listlessly on his chest and yelled at it timidly, then grumbled and stopped. In his youth, he had roared and stumped around to help the god up, but now it wasn't worth the effort. Nothing was. He found a fine flake of sweaty salt under his hair, licked it off his fingers, and turned over to sleep again.

But sleep wouldn't come. On the other side of the hill there was a hue and cry, and somebody was beating a drum in a throbbing chant. The old Neanderthaler grunted and held his hands over his ears, but the Sun-Warmer's chant couldn't be silence. More ideas of the Talkers.

In his day, it had been a lovely world, full of hairy grumbling people; people a man could understand. There had been game on all sides, and the caves about had been filled with the smoke of cooking fires. He had played with the few young that were born—though each year fewer children had come into the tribe—and had grown to young manhood with the pride of achievement. But that was before the Talkers had made this valley one of their hunting grounds.

Old traditions, half told, half understood, spoke of the land in the days of old, when only his people roamed over the broad tundra. They had filled the caves and gone out in packs too large for any animal to withstand. And the animals swarmed into the land, driven south by the Fourth Glaciation. Then the great cold had come again, and times had been hard. Many of his people had died.

But many had lived, and with the coming of the warmer, drier climate again, they had begun to expand before the Talkers arrived. After that—Hwoogh stirred uneasily—for no good reason he could see, the Talkers took more and more of the land, and his people retreated and diminished before them. Hwoogh's father had made it understood that their little band in the valley were all that were left, and that this was the only place on the great flat earth where Talkers seldom came.

Hwoogh had been twenty when he first saw them, great long-legged men, swift of foot and eye, stalking along as if they owned the earth, with their incessant mouth noises. In the summer that year, they pitched their skin-and-wattle tents at the back of the hill, away from the caves, and made magic to their gods. There was magic on their weapons, and the beasts fell their prey. Hwoogh's people had settled back, watching fearfully, hating numbly, finally resorting to begging and stealing. Once a young buck had killed the child of a Talker, and been flayed and sent out to die for it. Thereafter, there had been a truce between Cro-Magnon and Neanderthaler.

Now the last of Hwoogh's people were gone, save only

himself, leaving no children. Seven years it had been since Hwoogh's brother had curled up in the cave and sent his breath forth on the long journey to his ancestors. He had always been dispirited and weak of will, but he had been the only friend left to Hwoogh.

The old man tossed about and wished that Keyoda would return. Maybe she would bring food from the Talkers. There was no use hunting now, when the Talkers had already been up and killed all the easy game. Better that a man should sleep all the time, for sleep was the only satisfying thing left in the topsy-turvy world; even the drink the tall Cro-Magnons made from mashed roots left a headache the next day.

He twisted and turned in his bed of leaves at the edge of the cave, grunting surlily. A fly buzzed over his head provocatively, and he lunged at it. Surprise lighted his features as his fingers closed on the insect, and he swallowed it with a momentary flash of pleasure. It wasn't as good as the grub in the forest, but it made a tasty appetizer.

The sleep god had left, and no amount of lying still and snoring would lure him back. Hwoogh gave up and squatted down on his haunches. He had been meaning to make a new head for his crude spear for weeks, and he rummaged around in the cave for materials. But the idea grew farther away the closer he approached work, and he let his eyes roam idly over the little creek below him and the fleecy clouds in the sky. It was a warm spring, and the sun made idleness pleasant.

The sun god was growing stronger again, chasing the old fog and mist away. For years, he had worshiped the sun god as his, and now it seemed to grow strong again only for the Talkers. While the god was weak, Hwoogh's people had been mighty; now that its long sickness was over, the Cro-Magnons spread out over the country like the fleas on his belly.

Hwoogh could not understand it. Perhaps the god was mad at him, since gods are utterly unpredictable. He grunted, wishing again for his brother, who had understood such things better.

Keyoda crept around the boulder in front of the cave, interrupting his brooding. She brought scraps of food from the tent village and the half-chewed leg of a horse, which Hwoogh seized on and ripped at with his strong teeth. Evidently the Talkers had made a big kill the day before, for they were lavish with their gifts. He grunted at Keyoda, who sat under the cave entrance in the sun, rubbing her back.

Keyoda was as hideous as most of the Talkers were to Hwoogh, with her long dangling legs and short arms, and the ungainly straightness of her carriage. Hwoogh remembered the young girls of his own day with a sigh; they had been beautiful, short and squat, with forward-jutting necks and nice low foreheads. How the flat-faced Cro-Magnon women could get mates had been a puzzle to Hwoogh, but they seemed to succeed.

Keyoda had failed, however, and in her he felt justified in his judgment. There were times when he felt almost in sympathy with her, and in his own way he was fond of her. As a child, she had been injured, her back made useless for the work of a mate. Kicked around by the others of her tribe, she had gradually drifted away from them, and when she stumbled on Hwoogh, his hospitality had been welcome to her. The Talkers were nomads who followed the herds north in the summer, south in the winter, coming and going with the seasons, but Keyoda stayed with Hwoogh in his cave and did the few desultory tasks that were necessary. Even such a half-man as the Neanderthaler was preferable to the scornful pity of her own people, and Hwoogh was not unkind.

"Hwunkh?" asked Hwoogh. With his stomach partly filled, he felt more kindly toward the world.

"Oh, they come out and let me pick up their scraps—me, who was once a chief's daughter!—same as they always do." Her voice had been shrewish, but the weariness of failure and age had taken the edge from it. " 'Poor, poor Keyoda' thinks they, 'let her have what she wants, just so it don't mean nothin' we like.' Here." She handed him a roughly made spear, flaked on both sides of the point, but with only a rudimentary barb, unevenly made. "One of 'em give me this—it ain't the like of what they'd use, I guess, but it's good as you could make. One of the kids is practicing."

Hwoogh examined it; good, he admitted, very good, and the point was fixed nicely in the shaft. Even the boys, with their long limber thumbs that could twist any which way, made better weapons than he; yet once he had been famous among his small tribe for the nicety of his flint work.

Making a horse gesture, he got slowly to his feet. The shape of his jaw and the attachment of his tongue, together with a poorly developed left frontal lobe of his brain, made speech rudimentary, and he supplemented his glottals and labials with motions that Keyoda understood well enough. She shrugged and waved him out, gnawing on one of the bones.

Hwoogh wandered about without much spirit, conscious that he was growing old. And vaguely, he knew that age should not have fallen upon him for many snows; it was not the number of seasons, but something else, something that he could feel but not understand. He struck out for the hunting fields, hoping that he might find some game for himself that would require little effort to kill. The scornful gifts of the Talkers had become bitter in his mouth.

But the sun god climbed up to the top of the blue cave without Hwoogh's stumbling on anything. He swung about to return, and ran into a party of Cro-Magnons returning with the carcass of a reindeer strapped to a pole on their shoulders. They stopped to yell at him.

"No use, Hairy One!" they boasted, their voices light and gay. "We caught all the game this way. Turn back to your cave and sleep."

Hwoogh dropped his shoulders and veered away, his spear dragging limply on the ground. One of the party trotted over to him lightly. Sometimes Legoda, the tribal magic man and artist, seemed almost friendly, and this was one of the times.

"It was my kill, Hairy One," he said tolerantly. "Last night I drew strong reindeer magic, and the beast fell with my first throw. Come to my tent and I'll save a leg for you. Keyoda taught me a new song that she got from her father, and I would repay her."

Legs, ribs, bones! Hwoogh was tired of the outer meat. His body demanded the finer food of the entrails and liver. Already his skin was itching with a rash, and he felt that he must have the succulent inner parts to make him well; always, before, that had cured him. He grunted, between appreciation and annoyance, and turned off. Legoda pulled him back.

"Nay, stay, Hairy One. Sometimes you bring good fortune to me, as when I found the bright ocher for my drawing. There is meat enough in the camp for all. Why hunt today?" As Hwoogh still hesitated, he grew more insistent, not from kindness, but more from a wish to have his own way. "The wolves are running near today, and one is not enough against them. We carve the reindeer at the camp as soon as it comes from the poles. I'll give you first choice of the meat!"

Hwoogh grunted a surly acquiescence and waddled after the party. The dole of the Talkers has become gall to him, but liver was liver—if Legoda kept his bargain. They were chanting a rough marching song, trotting easily under the load of the reindeer, and he lumbered along behind, breathing hard at the pace they set.

As they neared the village of the nomads, its rough skin tents and burning fires threw out a pungent odor that irritated Hwoogh's nostrils. The smell of the long-limbed Cro-Magnons was bad enough without the dirty smell of a camp and the stink of their dung-fed fires. He preferred the accustomed moldy stench of his own musty cave.

Youths came swarming out at them, yelling with disgust at being left behind on this easy hunt. Catching sight of the Neanderthaler, they set up a howl of glee and charged at him, throwing sticks and rocks and jumping at him with play fury. Hwoogh shivered and crouched over, menacing them with his spear, and giving voice to throaty growls. Legoda laughed.

"In truth, O Hairy Chokanga, your voice should drive them from you. But see, they fear it not. Kuck, you two-legged pests! Out and away! Kuck, I say!" They leaped back at his voice and dropped behind, still yelling. Hwoogh eyed them warily, but so long as it suited the pleasure of Legoda, he was safe from their pranks.

Legoda was in a good mood, laughing and joking, tossing his quips at the women until his young wife came out and silenced it. She sprang at the reindeer with her flint knife, and the other women joined her.

"Heyo," called Legoda. "First choice goes to Chokanga, the Hairy One. By my word, it is his."

"Oh, fool!" There was scorn in her voice and in the look she gave Hwoogh. "Since when do we feed the beasts of the caves and the fish of the river? Art mad, Legoda. Let him hunt for himself."

Legoda tweaked her back with the point of his spear, grinning. "Aye, I knew thou'dst cry at that. But then, we owe his kind some pay—this was his hunting ground when we were but pups, straggling into this far land. What harm to give to an old man?" He swung to Hwoogh and gestured. "See, Chokanga, my word is good. Take what you want, but see that it is not more than your belly and that of Keyoda can hold this night."

Hwoogh darted in and came out with the liver and the fine sweet fat from the entrails. With a shrill cry of rage, Legoda's mate sprang for him, but the magic man pushed her back.

"Nay, he did right! Only a fool would choose the haunch when the heart of the meat was at hand. By the gods of my father, and I expected to eat of that myself! O Hairy One,

THE DAY IS DONE

you steal the meat from my mouth, and I like you for it. Go, before Heya gets free."

Tomorrow, Hwoogh knew, Legoda might set the brats on him for this day's act, but tomorrow was in another cave of the sun. He drew his legs under him and scuttled off to the left and around the hill, while the shrill yells of Heya and the lazy good humor of Legoda followed. A piece of liver dangled loose, and Hwoogh sucked on it as he went. Keyoda would be pleased, since she usually had to do the begging for both of them.

And a little of Hwoogh's self-respect returned. Hadn't he outsmarted Legoda and escaped with the choicest meat? And had Keyoda ever done as well when she went to the village of the Talkers? Ayeee, they had a thing yet to learn from the cunning brain of old Hwoogh!

Of course the Talkers were crazy; only fools would act as Legoda had done. But that was none of his business. He patted the liver and fat fondly and grinned with a slight return of good humor. Hwoogh was not one to look a gift horse in the mouth.

The fire had shrunk to a red bed of coals when he reached the cave, and Keyoda was curled up on his bed, snoring loudly, her face flushed. Hwoogh smelled her breath, and his suspicions were confirmed. Somehow, she had drunk of the devil brew of the Talkers, and her sleep was dulled with its stupor. He prodded her with his toe, and she sat up bleary-eyed.

"Oh, so you're back. Ayeee, and with liver and fat! But that never came from your spear throw; you been to the village and stole it. Oh, but you'll catch it!" She grabbed at the meat greedily and stirred up the fire, spitting the liver over it.

Hwoogh explained as best he could, and she got the drift of it. "So? Eh, that Legoda, what a prankster he is, and my own nephew, too." She tore the liver away, half raw, and they fell to eagerly, while she chuckled and cursed by turns. Hwoogh touched her nose and wrinkled his face up.

"Well, so what if I did?" Liquor had sharpened her tongue. "That no-good son of the chief come here, after me to be telling him stories. And to make my old tongue free, he brings me the root brew. Ah, what stories I'm telling—and some of 'em true, too!" She gestured toward a crude pot. "I reckon he steals it, but what's that to us? Help yourself, Hairy One. It ain't ever' day we're getting the brew."

Hwoogh remembered the headaches of former experiments, but he smelled it curiously and the lure of the magic water caught at him. It was the very essence of youth, the fire that brought life to his legs and memories to his mind. He held it up to his mouth, gasping as the beery liquid ran down his throat. Keyoda caught it before he could finish and drained the last quart.

"Ah, it strengthens my back and puts the blood a-running hot through me again." She swayed on her feet and sputtered out the fragments of an old skin-scraping song. "Now, there you go—can't you never learn not to drink it all to once? That way, it don't last as long, and you're out before you get to feeling good."

Hwoogh staggered as the brew took hold of him, and his knees bent even farther under him. The bed came up in his face, his head was full of bees buzzing merrily, and the cave spun around him. He roared at the cave, while Keyoda laughed.

"Heh! To hear you a-yelling, a body might think you was the only Chokanga left on earth. But you ain't—no, you ain't!"

"Hwunkh?" That struck home. To the best of Hwoogh's knowledge, there were no others of his kind left on earth. He grabbed at her and missed, but she fell and rolled against him, her breath against his face.

"So? Well, it's the truth. The kid up and told me. Legoda found three of 'em, just like you, he says, up the land to the east, three springs ago. You'll have to ask him—I dunno nothing about it." She rolled over against him, grunting half-formed words, and he tried to think of this new information. But the brew was too strong for his head, and he was soon snoring beside her.

Keyoda was gone to the village when he awoke, and the sun was a spear length high on the horizon. He rummaged around for a piece of the liver, but the flavor was not as good as it had been, and his stomach protested lustily at going to work again. He leaned back until his head got control of itself, then swung down to the creek to quench a thirst devil that had seized on him in the night.

But there was something he should do, something he half remembered from last night. Hadn't Keyoda said something about others of his people? Yes, three of them, and Legoda knew. Hwoogh hesitated, remembering that he had bested Legoda the day before; the young man might resent it today.

But he was filled with an overwhelming curiosity, and there was a strange yearning in his heart. Legoda must tell him.

Reluctantly, he went back to the cave and fished around in a hole that was a secret even from Keyoda. He drew out his treasures, fingering them reverently, and selecting the best. There were bright shells and colored pebbles, a roughly drilled necklace that had belonged to his father, a sign of completed manhood, bits of this and that with which he had intended to make himself ornaments. But the quest for knowledge was stronger than the pride of possession; he dumped them out into his fist and struck out for the village.

Keyoda was talking with the women, whining the stock formula that she had developed, and Hwoogh skirted around the camp, looking for the young artist. Finally he spotted the Talker out behind the camp, making odd motions with two sticks. He drew near cautiously, and Legoda heard him coming.

"Come near, Chokanga, and see my new magic." The young man's voice was filled with pride, and there was no threat to it. Hwoogh sighed with relief, but sidled up slowly. "Come nearer, don't fear me. Do you think I'm sorry of the gift I made? Nay, that was my own stupidity. See."

He held out the sticks and Hwoogh fingered them carefully. One was long and springy, tied end to end with a leather thong, and the other was a little spear with a tuft of feather on the blunt end. He grunted a question.

"A magic spear, Hairy One, that flies from the hand with wings, and kills beyond the reach of other spears."

Hwoogh snorted. The spear was too tiny to kill more than rodents, and the big stick had not even a point. But he watched as the young man placed the sharp stick to the tied one, and drew back on it. There was a sharp twang, and the little spear sailed out and away, burying its point in the soft bark of a tree more than two spear throws away. Hwoogh was impressed.

"Aye, Chokanga, a new magic that I learned in the south last year. There are many there who use it, and with it they can throw the point farther and better than a full-sized spear. One man may kill as much as three!"

Hwoogh grumbled: already they killed all the good game, and yet they must find new magic to increase their power. He held out his hand curiously, and Legoda gave him the long stick and another spear, showing him how it was held. Again there was a twang, and the leather thong struck at his wrist, but the weapon sailed off erratically, missing the tree by yards. Hwoogh handed it back glumly—such magic was not for his kind. His thumbs made the handling of it even more difficult.

Now, while the magic man was pleased with his superiority, was a good time to show the treasure. Hwoogh spread it out on the bare earth and gestured at Legoda, who looked down thoughtfully.

"Yes," the Talker conceded. "Some of it is good, and some would make nice trinkets for the women. What is it you want—more meat, or one of the new weapons? Your belly was filled yesterday; and with my beer, which was stolen, I think, though for that I blame you not. The boy has been punished already. And this weapon is not for you."

Hwoogh snorted, wriggled and fought for expression, while the young man stared. Little by little, his wants were made known, partly by the questions of the Cro-Magnon. Legoda laughed.

"So, there is a call of the kind in you, Old Man?" He pushed the treasure back to Hwoogh, except one gleaming bauble. "I would not cheat you, Chokanga, but this I take for the love I bear you, as a sign of our friendship." His grin was mocking as he stuck the valuable in a flap of his clout.

Hwoogh squatted down on his heels, and Legoda sat on a rock as he began. "There is but little to tell you, Hairy One. Three years ago I did run onto a family of your kind—a male and his mate, with one child. They ran from us, but we were near their cave, and they had to return. We harmed them not, and sometimes gave them food, letting them accompany us on the chase. But they were thin and scrawny, too lazy to hunt. When we returned next year, they were dead, and so far as I know, you are the last of your kind."

He scratched his head thoughtfully. "Your people die too easily, Chokanga; no sooner do we find them and try to help them than they cease hunting and become beggars. And then they lose interest in life, sicken and die. I think your gods must be killed off by our stronger ones."

Hwoogh grunted a half assent, and Legoda gathered up his bow and arrows, turning back toward camp. But there was a strange look on the Neanderthaler's face that did not escape the young man's eyes. Recognizing the misery in Hwoogh's expression, he laid a hand on the old man's shoulder and spoke more kindly.

"That is why I would see to your well-being, Hairy One. When you are gone, there will be no more, and my children will laugh at me and say I lie when I spin the tale of your race at the feast fire. Each time that I kill, you shall not lack for food."

He swung down the single street toward the tent of his family, and Hwoogh turned slowly back toward his cave. The assurance of food should have cheered him, but it only added to his gloom. Dully, he realized that Legoda treated him as a small child, or as one whom the sun god had touched with madness.

Hwoogh heard the cries and laughter of children as he rounded the hill, and for a minute he hesitated before going on. But the sense of property was well developed in him, and he leaped forward grimly. They had no business near his cave.

They were of all ages and sizes, shouting and chasing each other about in a crazy disorder. Having been forbidden to come on Hwoogh's side of the hill, and having broken the rule in a bunch, they were making the most of their revolt. Hwoogh's fire was scattered down the side of the hill into the creek, and they were busily sorting through the small store of his skins and weapons.

Hwoogh let out a savage yell and ran forward, his spear held out in jabbing position. Hearing him, they turned and jumped back from the cave entrance, clustering up into a tight group. "Go on away, Ugly Face," one yelled. "Go scare the wolves! Ugly Face. Ugly Face, waaaah!"

He dashed in among them, brandishing his spear, but they darted back on their nimble legs, slipping easily from in front of him. One of the older boys thrust out a leg and caught him, tripping him down on the rocky ground. Another dashed in madly and caught his spear away, hitting him roughly with it. From the time of the first primate, the innate cruelty of thoughtlessness had changed little in children.

Hwoogh let out a whooping bellow, scrambled up clumsily and was in among them. But they slipped nimbly out of his clutching hands. The little girls were dancing around gleefully, chanting, "Ugly Face ain't got no mother, Ugly Face ain't got no wife, waaaaah on Ugly Face!" Frantically he caught at one of the boys, swung him about savagely, and tossed him on the ground, where the youth lay white and silent. Hwoogh felt a momentary glow of elation at his strength. Then somebody threw a rock.

The old Neanderthaler was tied down crudely when he swam back to consciousness, and three of the boys sat on his chest, beating the ground with their heels in time to a victory chant. There was a dull ache in his head, and bruises were swelling on his arms and chest where they had handled him roughly. He growled savagely, heaving up, and tumbled them off, but the cords were too strong for him. As surely as if grown men had done it, he was captured.

For years they had been his enemies, ever since they had found that Hwoogh-baiting was one of the pleasant occupations that might relieve the tedium of camp life. Now that the old feud was about finished, they went at the business of subduing him with method and ingenuity.

While the girls rubbed his face with soft mud from the creek, the boys ransacked the cave and tore at his clothes. The rough bag in which he had put his valuables came away in their hands, and they paused to distribute this new wealth. Hwoogh howled madly.

But a measure of sanity was returning to them, now that the first fury of the flight was over, and Kechaka, the chief's eldest son, stared at Hwoogh doubtfully. "If the elders hear of this," he muttered unhappily, "there will be trouble. They'd not like our bothering Ugly Face."

Another grinned. "Why tell them? He isn't a man, anyway, but an animal; see the hair on his body! Toss old Ugly Face in the river, clean up his cave, and hide these treasures. Who's to know?"

There were half-hearted protests, but the thought of the beating waiting for them added weight to the idea. Kechaka nodded finally and set them to straightening up the mess they had made. With broken branches, they eliminated the marks of their feet, leaving only the trail to the creek.

Hwoogh tossed and pitched in their arms as four of them picked him up; the bindings loosened somewhat, but not enough to free him. With some satisfaction, he noted that the boy he had caught was still retching and moaning, but that was no help to his present position. They waded relentlessly into the water, laid him on it belly down, and gave him a strong push that sent him gliding out through the rushing stream. Foaming and gasping, he fought the current, struggling against his bonds. His lungs ached for air, and the current buffeted him about; blackness was creeping up on his mind.

With a last desperate effort he tore loose the bonds and pushed up madly for the surface, gulping in air greedily. Water was unpleasant to him, but he could swim, and he struck out for the bank. The children were disappearing down the trail and were out of sight as he climbed from the water, bemoaning his lost fire that would have warmed him. He lumbered back to his cave and sank soddenly on the bed.

He, who had been a mighty warrior, bested by a snarling pack of Cro-Magnon brats! He clenched his fists savagely and growled, but there was nothing he could do. Nothing! The futility of his own effort struck down on him like a burning knife. Hwoogh was an old man, and the tears that ran from his eyes were the bitter, aching tears that only age can shed.

Keyoda returned late, cursing when she found the fire gone, but her voice softened as she spied him huddled in his bed, staring dully at the wall of the cave. Her old eyes spotted the few footprints the boys had missed, and she swore with a vigor that was almost youthful before she turned back to Hwoogh.

"Come, Hairy One, get out of that cold, wet fur!" Her hands were gentle on the straps, but Hwoogh shook her aside. "You'll be sick, lying there on them few leaves, all wet like that. Get off the fur, and I'll go back to the village for fire. Them kids! Wait'll I tell Legoda!"

Seeing there was nothing he would let her do for him, she turned away down the trail. Hwoogh sat up to change his furs, then lay back. What was the use? He grumbled a little when Keyoda returned with fire, but refused the delicacies she had wheedled at the village, and tumbled over into a fitful sleep.

The sun was long up when he awoke to find Legoda and Keyoda fussing over him. There was an unhappy feeling in his head, and he coughed. Legoda patted his back. "Rest, Hairy One. You have the sickness devil that burns the throat and runs at the nose, but that a man can overcome. Ayeee, how the boys were whipped! I, personally, attended to that, and this morning not one is less sore than you. Before they bother you again, the moon will eat up the sun."

Keyoda pushed a stew of boiled liver and kidneys at him, but he shoved it away. Though the ache in his head had gone down, a dull weight seemed to rest on his stomach, and he could not eat. It felt as though all the boys he had fought were sitting on his chest and choking him.

Legoda drew out a small painted drum and made heavy magic for his recovery, dancing before the old man and shaking the magic gourd that drove out all sickness devils. But this was a stronger devil. Finally the young man stopped and left for the village, while Keyoda perched on a stone to watch over the sick man. Hwoogh's mind was heavy and numb, and his heart was leaden in his breast. She fanned the flies away, covering his eyes with a bit of skin, singing him some song that the mothers lulled their children with.

He slept again, stirring about in a nightmare of Talker mockery, with a fever flushing his face. But when Legoda came back at night, the magic man swore he should be well in three days. "Let him sleep and feed him. The devil will leave him soon. See, there is scarce a mark where the stone hit."

Keyoda fed him, as best she could, forcing the food that she begged at the village down his throat. She lugged water from the creek as often as he cried for it, and bathed his head and chest when he slept. But the three days came and went, and still he was not well. The fever was little higher, and the cold little worse, than he had gone though many times before. But he did not throw it off as he should have done.

Legoda came again, bringing his magic and food, but they were of little help. As the day drew to a close, he shook his head and spoke low words to Keyoda. Hwoogh came out of a half stupor and listened dully.

"He tires of life, Keyoda, my father's sister." The young man shrugged. "See, he lies there not fighting. When a man will not try to live, he cannot."

"Ayyeah!" Her voice shrilled dolefully. "What man will not live if he can? Thou art foolish, Legoda."

"Nay. His people tire easily of life, O Keyoda. Why, I know not. But it takes little to make them die." Seeing that Hwoogh had heard, he drew closer to the Neanderthaler. "O Chokanga, put away your troubles and take another bite out of life. It can still be good, if you choose. I have taken your gift as a sign of friendship, and I would keep my word. Come to my fire, and hunt no more; I will tend you as I would my father."

Hwoogh grunted. Follow the camps, eat from Legoda's hunting, be paraded as a freak and a half-man! Legoda was kind, sudden and warm in his sympathy, but the others were scornful. And if Hwoogh should die, who was to mourn him? Keyoda would go back to her people, Legoda would forget him, and not one Chokanga would be there to show them the ritual for burial.

Hwoogh's old friends had come back to him in his dreams, visiting him and showing the hunting grounds of his youth. He had heard the grunts and grumblings of the girls of his race, and they were awaiting him. That world was still empty of the Talkers, where a man could do great things and make his own kills, without hearing the laughter of the Cro-Magnons. Hwoogh sighed softly. He was tired, too tired to care what happened.

The sun sank low, and the clouds were painted a harsh red. Keyoda was wailing somewhere, far off, and Legoda beat on his drum and muttered his magic. But life was empty, barren of pride.

The sun dropped from sight, and Hwoogh sighed again, sending his last breath out to join the ghosts of his people.

THE ULTIMATE CATALYST

Thrilling Wonder Stories, June

by John Taine (1902-1960)

One of a number of professional scientists in this book, "John Taine" (Eric Temple Bell) was a famous mathematician at the California Institute of Technology and a former President of the Mathematics Association of America. However, most of his sf did not reflect his professional training (an exception is his novel THE TIME STREAM, 1946), and he employed a wide variety of themes in his fiction. Two of his most memorable works are THE IRON STAR (1930) and THE CRYSTAL HORDE (1952, magazine appearance, 1930).

"The Ultimate Catalyst" is about a subject that Taine knew well—the problems of the working scientist. It is unlikely, however, that any of his colleagues at Cal Tech (especially the chemists) ever faced a problem quite like this one.

(Whatever mark "John Taine" may make in the history of science fiction, and I am not as fond of his stories as some people are, there is no question but that his major work is "Men of Mathematics," a classic series of short biographies of great mathematicians. It is unlikely even to be surpassed in its field and if you want true pathos read his biography of Evariste Galois. IA)

The Dictator shoved his plate aside with a petulant gesture. The plate, like the rest of the official banquet service, was solid gold with the Dictator's monogram, K. I.—Kadir Imperator, or Emperor Kadir—embossed in a design of machine guns round the edge. And, like every other plate on the long banquet table, Kadir's was piled high with a colorful assortment of raw fruits.

This was the dessert. The guests had just finished the main course, a huge plateful apiece of steamed vegetables. For an appetizer they had tried to enjoy an iced tumblerful of mixed fruit juices.

There had been nothing else at the feast but fruit juice, steamed vegetables, and raw fruit. Such a meal might have sustained a scholarly vegetarian, but for soldiers of a domineering race it was about as satisfying as a bucketful of cold water.

"Vegetables and fruit," Kadir complained. "Always vegetables and fruit. Why can't we get some red beef with blood in it for a change? I'm sick of vegetables. And I hate fruit. Blood and iron—that's what we need."

The guests stopped eating and eyed the Dictator apprehensively. They recognized the first symptoms of an imperial rage. Always when Kadir was about to explode and lose control of his evil temper, he had a preliminary attack of the blues, usually over some trifle.

They sat silently waiting for the storm to break, not daring to eat while their Leader abstained.

Presently a middle-aged man, halfway down the table on Kadir's right, calmly selected a banana, skinned it, and took a bite. Kadir watched the daring man in amazed silence. The last of the banana was about to disappear when the Dictator found his voice.

"Americano!" he bellowed like an outraged bull. "Mister Beetle!"

"*Doctor* Beetle, if you don't mind, Senhor Kadir," the offender corrected. "So long as every other white man in Amazonia insists on being addressed by his title, I insist on being addressed by mine. It's genuine, too. Don't forget that."

"Beetle!" The Dictator began roaring again.

But Beetle quietly cut him short. " 'Doctor' Beetle, please. I insist."

Purple in the face, Kadir subsided. He had forgotten what he intended to say. Beetle chose a juicy papaya for himself and a huge, greenish plum for his daughter, who sat on his left. Ignoring Kadir's impotent rage, Beetle addressed him as if there had been no unpleasantness. Of all the company, Beetle was the one man with nerve enough to face the Dictator as an equal.

"You say we need blood and iron," he began. "Do you mean that literally?" the scientist said slowly.

"How else should I mean it?" Kadir blustered, glowering at Beetle. "I always say what I mean. I am no theorist. I am a man of action, not words!"

"All right, all right," Beetle soothed him. "But I thought perhaps your 'blood and iron' was like old Bismarck's—blood and sabres. Since you mean just ordinary blood, like the blood in a raw beefsteak, and iron not hammered into sabres, I think Amazonia can supply all we need or want."

"But beef, red beef—" Kadir expostulated.

"I'm coming to that in a moment." Beetle turned to his daughter. "Consuelo, how did you like that greenbeefo?"

"That *what?*" Consuelo asked in genuine astonishment.

Although as her father's laboratory assistant she had learned to expect only the unexpected from him, each new creation of his filled her with childlike wonderment and joy. Every new biological creation her father made demanded a new scientific name. But, instead of manufacturing new scientific names out of Latin and Greek, as many reputable biologists do, Beetle used English, with an occasional lapse into Portuguese, the commonest language of Amazonia. He had even tried to have his daughter baptized Buglette, as the correct technical term of the immature female offspring of a Beetle. But his wife, a Portuguese lady of irreproachable family, had objected, and the infant was named Consuelo.

"I asked how you liked the greenbeefo," Beetle repeated. "That seedless green plum you just ate."

"Oh, so that's what you call it." Consuelo considered carefully, like a good scientist, before passing judgment on the delicacy. "Frankly, I didn't like it a little bit. It smelt like underdone pork. There was a distinct flavor of raw blood. And it all had a rather slithery wet taste, if you get what I mean."

"I get you exactly," Beetle exclaimed. "An excellent de-

THE ULTIMATE CATALYST 121

scription." He turned to Kadir. "There! You see we've already done it."

"Done what?" Kadir asked suspiciously.

"Try a greenbeefo and see."

Somewhat doubtfully, Kadir selected one of the huge greenish plums from the golden platter beside him, and slowly ate it. Etiquette demanded that the guests follow their Leader's example.

While they were eating the greenbeefos, Beetle watched their faces. The women of the party seemed to find the juicy flesh of the plums unpalatable. Yet they kept on eating and several, after finishing one, reached for another.

The men ate greedily. Kadir himself disposed of the four greenbeefos on his platter and hungrily looked about for more. His neighbors on either side, after a grudging look at their own diminishing supplies, offered him two of theirs. Without a word of thanks, Kadir devoured the offerings.

As Beetle sat calmly watching their greed, he had difficulty in keeping his face impassive and not betraying his disgust. Yet these people were starving for flesh. Possibly they were to be pardoned for looking more like hungry animals than representatives of the conquering race at their first taste in two years of something that smelt like flesh and blood.

All their lives, until the disaster which had quarantined them in Amazonia, these people had been voracious eaters of flesh in all its forms from poultry to pork. Now they could get nothing of the sort.

The dense forests and jungles of Amazonia harbored only a multitude of insects, poisonous reptiles, gaudy birds, spotted cats, and occasional colonies of small monkeys. The cats and the monkeys eluded capture on a large scale, and after a few half-hearted attempts at trapping, Kadir's hardy followers had abandoned the forests to the snakes and the stinging insects.

The chocolate-colored waters of the great river skirting Amazonia on the north swarmed with fish, but they were inedible. Even the natives could not stomach the pulpy flesh of these bloated mud-suckers. It tasted like the water of the river, a foul soup of decomposed vegetation and rotting wood. Nothing remained for Kadir and his heroic followers to eat but the tropical fruits and vegetables.

Luckily for the invaders, the original white settlers from the United States had cleared enough of the jungle and forest to make intensive agriculture possible. When Kadir arrived, all of these settlers, with the exception of Beetle and his daughter, had fled. Beetle remained, partly on his own initiative, partly because Kadir insisted that he stay and "carry on" against the snakes. The others traded Kadir their gold mines in exchange for their lives.

The luscious greenbeefos had disappeared. Beetle suppressed a smile as he noted the flushed and happy faces of the guests. He remembered the parting words of the last of the mining engineers.

"So long, Beetle. You're a brave man and may be able to handle Kadir. If you do, we'll be back. Use your head, and make a monkey of this dictating brute. Remember, we're counting on you."

Beetle had promised to keep his friends in mind. "Give me three years. If you don't see me again by then, shed a tear and forget me."

"Senhorina Beetle!" It was Kadir roaring again. The surfeit of greenbeefos restored his old bluster.

"Yes?" Consuelo replied politely.

"I know now why your cheeks are always so red," Kadir shouted.

For a moment neither Consuelo nor her father got the drift of Kadir's accusation. They understood just as Kadir started to enlighten them.

"You and your traitorous father are eating while we starve."

Beetle kept his head. His conscience was clear, so far as the greenbeefos were concerned, and he could say truthfully that they were not the secret of Consuelo's rosy cheeks and his own robust health. He quickly forestalled his daughter's reply.

"The meat-fruit, as you call it, is not responsible for Consuelo's complexion. Hard work as my assistant keeps her fit. As for the greenbeefos, this is the first time anyone but myself has tasted one. You saw how my daughter reacted. Only a great actress could have feigned such inexperienced distaste. My daughter is a biological chemist, not an actress."

Kadir was still suspicious. "Then why did you not share these meatfruits with us before?"

"For a very simple reason. I created them by hybridization only a year ago, and the first crop of my fifty experimental plants ripened this week. As I picked the ripe fruit, I put it aside for this banquet. I thought it would be a welcome treat after two years of vegetables and fruit. And," Beetle continued, warming to his invention, "I imagined a taste of beef—

even if it is only green beef, 'greenbeefo'—would be a very suitable way of celebrating the second anniversary of the New Freedom in Amazonia."

The scientist's sarcasm anent the "new freedom" was lost upon Kadir, nor did Kadir remark the secret bitterness in Beetle's eyes. What an inferior human being a dictator was, the scientist thought! What stupidity, what brutality! So long as a single one remained—and Kadir was the last—the Earth could not be clean.

"Have you any more?" Kadir demanded.

"Sorry. That's all for the present. But I'll have tons in a month or less. You see," he explained, "I'm using hydroponics to increase production and hasten ripening."

Kadir looked puzzled but interested. Confessing that he was merely a simple soldier, ignorant of science, he deigned to ask for particulars. Beetle was only too glad to oblige.

"It all began a year ago. You remember asking me when you took over the country to stay and go on with my work at the antivenin laboratory? Well, I did. But what was I to do with all the snake venom we collected? There was no way of getting it out of the country now that the rest of the continent has quarantined us. We can't send anything down the river, our only way out to civilization—"

"Yes, yes," Kadir interrupted impatiently. "You need not remind anyone here that the mountains and the jungles are the strongest allies of our enemies. What has all this to do with the meat-fruit?"

"Everything. Not being able to export any venom, I went on with my research in biochemistry. I saw how you people were starving for flesh, and I decided to help you out. You had slaughtered and eaten all the horses at the antivenin laboratory within a month of your arrival. There was nothing left, for this is not a cattle country, and it never will be. There was nothing to do but try chemistry. I already had the greenhouses left by the engineers. They used to grow tomatoes and cucumbers before you came."

"So you made these meat-fruits chemically?"

Beetle repressed a smile at the Dictator's scientific innocence.

"Not exactly. But really it was almost as simple. There was nothing startlingly new about my idea. To see how simple it was, ask yourself what are the main differences between the higher forms of plant life and the lower forms of animal life.

"Both are living things. But the plants cannot move about

from place to place at will, whereas, the animals can. A plant is, literally, 'rooted to the spot.'

"There are apparent exceptions, of course, like water hyacinths, yeast spores, and others that are transported by water or the atmosphere, but they do not transport themselves as the living animal does. Animals have a 'dimension' of freedom that plants do not have."

"But the beef—"

"In a moment. I mentioned the difference between the freedoms of plants and animals because I anticipate that it will be of the utmost importance in the experiments I am now doing. However, this freedom was not, as you have guessed, responsible for the greenbeefos. It was another, less profound, difference between plants and animals that suggested the 'meat-fruits.'"

Kadir seemed to suspect Beetle of hidden and unflattering meanings, with all this talk of freedom in a country dedicated to the "New Freedom" of Kadir's dictatorship. But he could do nothing about it, so he merely nodded as if he understood.

"Plants and animals," Beetle continued, "both have a 'blood' of a sort. The most important constituents in the 'blood' of both differ principally in the metals combined chemically in each.

"The 'blood' of a plant contains chlorophyll. The blood of an animal contains haemoglobin. Chemically, chlorophyll and haemoglobin are strangely alike. The metal in chlorophyll is magnesium; in haemoglobin, it is iron.

"Well, it occurred to chemists that if the magnesium could be 'replaced' chemically by iron, the chlorophyll could be converted into haemoglobin! And similarly for the other way about: replace the iron in haemoglobin by magnesium, and get chlorophyll!

"Of course it is not all as simple or as complete as I have made it sound. Between haemoglobin and chlorophyll is a long chain of intermediate compounds. Many of them have been formed in the laboratory, and they are definite links in the chain from plant blood to animal blood."

"I see," Kadir exclaimed, his face aglow with enthusiasm at the prospect of unlimited beef from green vegetables. He leaned over the table to question Beetle.

"It is the blood that gives flesh its appetizing taste and nourishing strength. You have succeeded in changing the plant blood to animal blood?"

Beetle did not contradict him. In fact, he evaded the question.

"I expect," he confided, "to have tons of greenbeefos in a month, and thereafter a constant supply as great as you will need. Tray-culture—hydroponics—will enable us to grow hundreds of tons in a space no larger than this banquet hall."

The "banquet hall" was only a ramshackle dining room that had been used by the miners before Kadir arrived. Nevertheless, it could be called anything that suited the Dictator's ambition.

"Fortunately," Beetle continued, "the necessary chemicals for tray-culture are abundant in Amazonia. My native staff has been extracting them on a large scale for the past four months, and we will have ample for our needs."

"Why don't you grow the greenbeefos in the open ground?" one of Kadir's officers inquired a trifle suspiciously.

"Too inefficient. By feeding the plants only the chemicals they need directly, we can increase production several hundredfold and cut down the time between successive crops to a few weeks. By properly spacing the propagation of the plants, we can have a constant supply. The seasons cut no figure."

They seemed satisfied, and discussion of the glorious future in store for Amazonia became general and animated. Presently Beetle and Consuelo asked the Dictator's permission to retire. They had work to do at the laboratory.

"Hydroponics?" Kadir enquired jovially. Beetle nodded, and they bowed themselves out of the banquet hall.

Consuelo withheld her attack until they were safe from possible eavesdroppers.

"Kadir is a lout," she began, "but that is no excuse for your filling him up with a lot of impossible rubbish."

"But it *isn't* impossible, and it *isn't* rubbish," Beetle protested. "You know as well as I do—"

"Of course I know about the work on chlorophyll and haemoglobin. But you didn't make those filthy green plums taste like raw pork by changing the chlorophyll of the plants into haemoglobin or anything like it. How did you do it, by the way?"

"Listen, Buglette. If I tell you, it will only make you sick. You ate one, you know."

"I would rather be sick than ignorant. Go on, you may as well tell me."

"Very well. It's a long story, but I'll cut it short. Amazonia is the last refuge of the last important dictator on earth. When Kadir's own people came to their senses a little over two years ago and kicked him out, he and his top men and their women came over here with their 'new freedom.' But the people of this continent didn't want Kadir's brand of freedom. Of course a few thousand crackpots in the larger cities welcomed him and his gang as their 'liberators,' but for once in history the mass of the people knew what they did not want. They combined forces and chased Kadir and his cronies up here.

"I never have been able to see why they did not exterminate Kadir and company as they would any other pests. But the presidents of the United Republics agreed that to do so would only be using dictatorial tactics, the very thing they had united to fight. So they let Kadir and his crew live—more or less—in strict quarantine. The temporary loss of a few rich gold mines was a small price to pay, they said, for world security against dictatorships.

"So here we are, prisoners in the last plague spot of civilization. And here is Kadir. He can dictate to his heart's content, but he can't start another war. He is as powerless as Napoleon was on his island.

"Well, when the last of our boys left, I promised to keep them in mind. And you heard my promise to help Kadir *out*. I am going to keep that promise, if it costs me my last snake."

They had reached the laboratory. Juan, the night-nurse for the reptiles, was going his rounds.

"Everything all right, Juan?" Beetle asked cordially.

He liked the phlegmatic Portuguese who always did his job with a minimum of talk. Consuelo, for her part, heartily disliked the man and distrusted him profoundly. She had long suspected him of being a stool-pigeon for Kadir.

"Yes, Dr. Beetle. Good night."

"Good night, Juan."

When Juan had departed, Consuelo returned to her attack.

"You haven't told me yet how you made these things taste like raw pork."

She strolled over to the tank by the north window where a luxuriant greenbeefo, like an overdeveloped tomato vine, grew rankly up its trellis to the ceiling. About half a dozen of the huge greenish "plums" still hung on the vine.

Consuelo plucked one and was thoughtfully sampling its quality.

"This one tastes all right," she said. "What did you do to the others?"

"Since you really want to know, I'll tell you. I took a hypodermic needle and shot them full of snake blood. My pet constrictor had enough juice in him to do the whole job without discomfort to himself or danger to his health."

Consuelo hurled her half-eaten fruit at her father's head, but missed. She stood wiping her lips with the back of her hand.

"So you can't change the chlorophyll in a growing plant into anything like haemoglobin? You almost had me believing you could."

"I never said I could. Nor can anybody else, so far as I know. But it made a good story to tell Kadir."

"But why?"

"If you care to analyze one of these greenbeefos in your spare time, you will find their magnesium content extraordinarily high. That is not accident, as you will discover if you analyze the chemicals in the tanks. I shall be satisfied if I can get Kadir and his friends to gorge themselves on greenbeefos when the new crop comes in. Now, did I sell Kadir the greenbeefo diet, or didn't I? You saw how they all fell for it. And they will keep on falling as long as the supply of snake blood holds out."

"There's certainly no scarcity of snakes in this charming country," Consuelo remarked. "I'm going to get the taste of one of them out of my mouth right now. Then you can tell me what you want me to do in this new culture of greenbeefos you've gone in for."

So father and daughter passed their days under the last dictatorship. Beetle announced that in another week the lush crop of greenbeefos would be ripe. Kadir proclaimed the following Thursday "Festal Thursday" as the feast day inaugurating "the reign of plenty" in Amazonia.

As a special favor, Beetle had requested Kadir to forbid any sightseeing or other interference with his work.

Kadir had readily agreed, and for three weeks Beetle had worked twenty hours a day, preparing the coming banquet with his own hands.

"You keep out of this," he had ordered Consuelo. "If there is any dirty work to be done, I'll do it myself. Your job is to keep the staff busy as usual, and see that nobody steals any of the fruit. I have given strict orders that nobody is to taste a greenbeefo till next Thursday, and Kadir has issued a proclamation to that effect. So if you catch anyone thieving, report to me at once."

The work of the native staff consisted in catching snakes. The workers could see but little sense in their job, as they knew that no venom was being exported. Moreover, the eccentric Doctor Beetle had urged them to bring in every reptile they found, harmless as well as poisonous, and he was constantly riding them to bestir themselves and collect more.

More extraordinary still, he insisted every morning that they carry away the preceding day's catch and dump it in the river. The discarded snakes, they noticed, seemed half dead. Even the naturally most vicious put up no fight when they were taken from the pens.

Between ten and eleven every morning Beetle absented himself from the laboratory, and forbade anyone to accompany him. When Consuelo asked him what he had in the small black satchel he carried with him on these mysterious trips, he replied briefly:

"A snake. I'm going to turn the poor brute loose."

And once, to prove his assertion, he opened the satchel and showed her the torpid snake.

"I must get some exercise, and I need to be alone," he explained, "or my nerves will snap. Please don't pester me."

She had not pestered him, although she doubted his explanation. Left alone for an hour, she methodically continued her daily inspection of the plants till her father returned, when she had her lunch and he resumed his private business.

On the Tuesday before Kadir's Festal Thursday, Consuelo did not see her father leave for his walk, as she was already busy with her inspection when he left. He had been gone about forty minutes when she discovered the first evidence of treachery.

The foliage of one vine had obviously been disturbed since the last inspection. Seeking the cause, Consuelo found that two of the ripening fruits had been carefully removed from their stems. Further search disclosed the theft of three dozen in all. Not more than two had been stolen from any plant.

Suspecting Juan, whom she had always distrusted, Consuelo hastened back to her father's laboratory to await his return and report. There she was met with an unpleasant surprise.

She opened the door to find Kadir seated at Beetle's desk, his face heavy with anger and suspicion.

"Where is your father?"

"I don't know."

"Come, come. I have made women talk before this when they were inclined to be obstinate. Where is he?"

"Again I tell you I don't know. He always takes his exercise at this time, and he goes alone. Besides," she flashed, "what business is it of yours where he is?"

"As to that," Kadir replied carelessly, "everything in Amazonia is my business."

"My father and I are not citizens—or subjects—of Amazonia."

"No. But your own country is several thousand miles away, Senhorina Beetle. In case of impertinent questions I can always report—with regrets, of course—that you both died by one of the accidents so common in Amazonia. Of snakebite, for instance."

"I see. But may I ask the reason for this sudden outburst?"

"So you have decided to talk? You will do as well as your father, perhaps better."

His eyes roved to one of the wire pens.

In it were half a dozen small red snakes.

"What do you need those for, now that you are no longer exporting venom?"

"Nothing much. Just pets, I suppose."

"Pets? Rather an unusual kind of pet, I should say." His face suddenly contorted in fear and rage. "Why is your father injecting snake blood into the unripe meat-fruit?" he shouted.

Consuelo kept her head. "Who told you that absurdity?"

"Answer me!" he bellowed.

"How can I? If your question is nonsense, how can anybody answer it?"

"So you refuse. I know a way to make you talk. Unlock that pen."

"I haven't the key. My father trusts nobody but himself with the keys to the pens."

"No? Well, this will do." He picked up a heavy ruler and lurched over to the pen. In a few moments he had sprung the lock.

"Now you answer my question or I force your arm into that pen. When your father returns I shall tell him that someone had broken the lock, and that you had evidently been trying to repair it when you got bitten. He will have to believe me. You will be capable of speech for just about three minutes after one of those red beauties strike. Once more, why did your father inject snake blood into the green meat-fruits?"

"And once more I repeat that you are asking nonsensical questions. Don't you dare—"

But he did dare. Ripping the sleeve of her smock from her arm, he gripped her bare wrist in his huge fist and began dragging her toward the pen. Her frantic resistance was no match for his brutal strength. Instinctively she resorted to the only defense left her. She let out a yell that must have carried half a mile.

Startled in spite of himself, Kadir paused, but only for an instant. She yelled again.

This time Kadir did not pause. Her hand was already in the pen when the door burst open. Punctual as usual, Beetle had returned exactly at eleven o'clock to resume his daily routine.

The black satchel dropped from his hand.

"What the hell—" A well-aimed laboratory stool finished the sentence. It caught the Dictator squarely in the chest. Consuelo fell with him, but quickly disengaged herself and stood panting.

"You crazy fool," Beetle spat at the prostrate man. "What do you think you are doing? Don't you know that those snakes are the deadliest of the whole lot?"

Kadir got to his feet without replying and sat down heavily on Beetle's desk. Beetle stood eying him in disgust.

"Come on, let's have it. What were you trying to do to my daughter?"

"Make her talk," Kadir muttered thickly. "She wouldn't—"

"Oh, she wouldn't talk. I get it, Consuelo! You keep out of this. I'll take care of our friend. Now, Kadir, just what did you want her to talk about?"

Still dazed, Kadir blurted out the truth.

"Why are you injecting snake blood into the unripe meat-fruit?"

Beetle eyed him curiously. With great deliberation he placed a chair in front of the Dictator and sat down.

"Let us get this straight. You ask why I am injecting snake blood into the greenbeefos. Who told you I was?"

"Juan. He brought three dozen of the unripe fruit to show me."

"To show you what?" Beetle asked in deadly calm. Had that fool Juan brains enough to look for the puncture-marks made by the hypodermic needle?

"To show me that you are poisoning the fruit."

"And did he show you?"

"How should I know? He was still alive when I came over here. I forced him to eat all three dozen."

"You had to use force?"

"Naturally. Juan said the snake blood would poison him."

"Which just shows how ignorant Juan is." Beetle sighed his relief. "Snake blood is about as poisonous as cow's milk."

"Why are you injecting—"

"You believed what that ignorant fool told you? He must have been drinking again and seeing things. I've warned him before. This time he goes. That is, if he hasn't come to his senses and gone already of his own free will."

"Gone? But where could he go from here?"

"Into the forest, or the jungle," Beetle answered indifferently. "He might even try to drape his worthless hide over a raft of rotten logs and float down the river. Anyhow, he will disappear after having made such a fool of himself. Take my word for it, we shan't see Juan again in a month of Sundays."

"On the contrary," Kadir retorted with a crafty smile, "I think we shall see him again in a very few minutes." He glanced at the clock. It showed ten minutes past eleven. "I have been here a little over half an hour. Juan promised to meet me here. He found it rather difficult to walk after his meal. When he comes, we can go into the question of those injections more fully."

For an instant Beetle looked startled, but quickly recovered his composure.

"I suppose as you say, Juan is slow because he has three dozen of those unripe greenbeefos under his belt. In fact I shouldn't wonder if he were feeling rather unwell at this very moment."

"So there is a poison in the fruits?" Kadir snapped.

"A poison? Rubbish! How would you or anyone feel if you had been forced to eat three dozen enormous green apples, to say nothing of unripe greenbeefos? I'll stake my reputation against yours that Juan is hiding in the forest and being very sick right now. And I'll bet anything you like that nobody ever sees him again. By the way, do you know which road he was to follow you by? The one through the clearing, or the cut-off through the forest?"

"I told him to take the cut-off, so as to get here quicker."

"Fine. Let's go and meet him—only we shan't. As for what I saw when I opened that door, I'll forget it if you will. I know Consuelo has already forgotten it. We are all quarantined here together in Amazonia, and there's no sense in harboring grudges. We've got to live together."

Relieved at being able to save his face, Kadir responded with a generous promise.

"If we fail to find Juan, I will admit that you are right, and that Juan has been drinking."

"Nothing could be fairer. Come on, let's go."

Their way to the Dictator's "palace"—formerly the residence of the superintendent of the gold mines—lay through the tropical forest.

The road was already beginning to choke up in the gloomier stretches with a rank web of trailing plants feeling their way to the trees on either side, to swarm up their trunks and ultimately choke the life out of them. Kadir's followers, soldiers all and new to the tropics, were letting nature take its course. Another two years of incompetence would see the painstaking labor of the American engineers smothered in rank jungle.

Frequently the three were compelled to abandon the road and follow more open trails through the forest till they again emerged on the road. Dazzling patches of yellow sunlight all but blinded them temporarily as they crossed the occasional barren spots that seem to blight all tropical forests like a leprosy. Coming out suddenly into one of these blinding patches, Kadir, who happened to be leading, let out a curdling oath and halted as if he had been shot.

"What's the matter?" Consuelo asked breathlessly, hurrying to overtake him. Blinded by the glare she could not see what had stopped the Dictator.

"I stepped on it." Kadir's voice was hoarse with disgust and fear.

"Stepped on what?" Beetle demanded. "I can't see in this infernal light. Was it a snake?"

"I don't know," Kadir began hoarsely. "It moved under my foot. Ugh! I see it now. Look."

They peered at the spot Kadir indicated, but could see nothing. Then, as their eyes became accustomed to the glare, they saw the thing that Kadir had stepped on.

A foul red fungus, as thick as a man's arm and over a yard long, lay directly in the Dictator's path.

"A bladder full of blood and soft flesh," Kadir muttered, shaking with fright and revulsion. "And I stepped on it."

"Rot!" Beetle exclaimed contemptuously, but there was a

bitter glint in his eyes. "Pull yourself together, man. That's nothing but a fungus. If there's a drop of blood in it, I'll eat the whole thing."

"But it moved," Kadir expostulated.

"Nonsense. You stepped on it, and naturally it gave beneath your weight. Come on. You will never find Juan at this rate."

But Kadir refused to budge. Fascinated by the disgusting object at his feet, the Dictator stood staring down at it with fear and loathing in every line of his face.

Then, as if to prove the truth of his assertion, the thing did move, slowly, like a wounded eel. But, unlike an eel, it did not move in the direction of its length. It began to roll slowly over.

Beetle squatted, the better to follow the strange motion. If it was not the first time he had seen such a freak of nature, he succeeded in giving a very good imitation of a scientist observing a novel and totally unexpected phenomenon. Consuelo joined her father in his researches. Kadir remained standing.

"Is it going to roll completely over?" Consuelo asked with evident interest.

"I think not," Beetle hazarded. "In fact, I'll bet three to one it only gets halfway over. There—I told you so. Look, Kadir, your fungus is rooted to the spot, just like any other plant."

In spite of himself, Kadir stooped down and looked. As the fungus reached the halfway mark in its attempted roll, it shuddered along its entire length and seemed to tug at the decayed vegetation. But shuddering and tugging got it nowhere. A thick band of fleshy rootlets, like coarse green hair, held it firmly to the ground. The sight of that futile struggle to move like a fully conscious thing was too much for Kadir's nerves.

"I am going to kill it," he muttered, leaping to his feet.

"How?" Beetle asked with a trace of contempt. "Fire is the only thing I know of to put a mess like that out of its misery—if it is in misery. For all I know, it may enjoy life. You can't kill it by smashing it or chopping it into mincemeat. Quite the contrary, in fact. Every piece of it will start a new fungus, and instead of one helpless blob rooted to the spot, you will have a whole colony. Better leave it alone, Kadir, to get what it can out of existence in its own way. Why must men like you always be killing something?"

"It is hideous and—"

"And you are afraid of it? How would you like someone to treat you as you propose treating this harmless fungus?"

"If I were like that," Kadir burst out," I should want somebody to put a torch to me."

"What if nobody knew that was what you wanted? Or if nobody cared? You have done some pretty foul things to a great many people in your time, I believe."

"But never anything like this!"

"Of course not. Nobody has ever done anything like this to anybody. So you didn't know how. What were you trying to do to my daughter an hour ago?"

"We agreed to forget all that," Consuelo reminded him sharply.

"Sorry. My mistake. I apologize, Kadir. As a matter of scientific interest, this fungus is not at all uncommon."

"I never saw one like it before," Consuelo objected.

"That is only because you don't go walking in the forest as I do," he reminded her. "Just to prove I'm right, I'll undertake to find a dozen rolling fungi within a hundred yards of here. What do you say?"

Before they could protest, he was hustling them out of the blinding glare into a black tunnel of the forest. Beetle seemed to know where he was going, for it was certain that his eyes were as dazed as theirs.

"Follow closely when you find your eyes," he called. "I'll go ahead. Look out for snakes. Ah, here's the first beauty! Blue and magenta, not red like Kadir's friend. Don't be prejudiced by its shape. Its color is all the beauty this poor thing has."

If anything, the shapeless mass of opalescent fungus blocking their path was more repulsive than the monstrosity that had stopped Kadir. This one was enormous, fully a yard in breadth and over five feet long. It lay sprawled over the rotting trunk of a fallen tree like a decomposing squid.

Yet, as Beetle insisted, its color was beautiful with an unnatural beauty. However, neither Consuelo nor Kadir could overcome their nausea at their living death. They fled precipitately back to the patch of sunlight. The fleshy magenta roots of the thing, straining impotently at the decaying wood which nourished them, were too suggestive of helpless suffering for endurance. Beetle followed at his leisure, chuckling to himself. His amusement drew a sharp reprimand from Consuelo.

"How can you be amused? That thing was in misery."

"Aren't we all?" he retored lightly, and for the first time in her life Consuelo doubted the goodness of her father's heart.

They found no trace of Juan. By the time they reached the Dictator's palace, Kadir was ready to agree to anything. He was a badly frightened man.

"You were right," he admitted to Beetle. "Juan was lying, and has cleared out. I apologize."

"No need to apologize," Beetle reassured him cordially. "I knew Juan was lying."

"Please honor me by staying to lunch," Kadir begged. "You cannot? Then I shall go and lie down."

They left him to recover his nerve, and walked back to the laboratory by the long road, not through the forest. They had gone over halfway before either spoke. When Beetle broke the long silence, he was more serious than Consuelo ever remembered his having been.

"Have you ever noticed," he began, "what arrant cowards all brutal men are?" She made no reply, and he continued, "Take Kadir, for instance. He and his gang have tortured and killed thousands. You saw how that harmless fungus upset him. Frightened half to death of nothing."

"Are you sure it was nothing?"

He gave her a strange look, and she walked rapidly ahead. "Wait," he called, slightly out of breath.

Breaking into a trot, he overtook her.

"I have something to say that I want you to remember. If anything should ever happen to me—I'm always handling those poisonous snakes—I want you to do at once what I tell you now. You can trust Felipe."

Felipe was the Portuguese foreman of the native workers.

"Go to him and tell him you are ready. He will understand. I prepared for this two years ago, when Kadir moved in. Before they left, the engineers built a navigable raft. Felipe knows where it is hidden. It is fully provisioned. A crew of six native river men is ready to put off at a moment's notice. They will be under Felipe's orders. The journey down the river will be long and dangerous, but with that crew you will make it. Anyhow, you will not be turned back by the quarantine officers when you do sight civilization. There is a flag with the provisions. Hoist it when you see any signs of civilization, and you will not be blown out of the water. That's all."

"Why are you telling me this now?"

"Because dictators never take their own medicine before they make someone else taste it for them."

"What do you mean?" she asked in sudden panic.

"Only that I suspect Kadir of planning to give me a dose of his peculiar brand of medicine the moment he is through with me. When he and his crew find out how to propagate the greenbeefos, I may be bitten by a snake. He was trying something like that on you, wasn't he?"

She gave him a long doubtful look. "Perhaps," she admitted. She was sure that there was more in his mind than he had told her.

They entered the laboratory and went about their business without another word. To recover lost time, Consuelo worked later than usual. Her task was the preparation of the liquid made up by Beetle's formula, in which the greenbeefos were grown.

She was just adding a minute trace of chloride of gold to the last batch when a timid rap on the door of the chemical laboratory startled her unreasonably. She had been worrying about her father.

"Come in," she called.

Felipe entered. The sight of his serious face gave her a sickening shock. What had happened? Felipe was carrying the familiar black satchel which Beetle always took with him on his solitary walks in the forest.

"What is it?" she stammered.

For answer Felipe opened his free hand and showed her a cheap watch. It was tarnished greenish blue with what looked like dried fungus.

"Juan's," he said. "When Juan did not report for work this afternoon, I went to look for him."

"And you found his watch? Where?"

"On the cut-off through the forest."

"Did you find anything else?"

"Nothing belonging to Juan."

"But you found something else?"

"Yes. I had never seen anything like them before."

He placed the satchel on the table and opened it.

"Look. Dozens like that one, all colors, in the forest. Doctor Beetle forgot to empty his bag when he went into the forest this morning."

She stared in speechless horror at the swollen monstrosity filling the satchel. The thing was like the one that Kadir had stepped on, except that it was not red but blue and magenta. The obvious explanation flashed through her mind, and she struggled to convince herself that it was true.

"You are mistaken," she said slowly. "Doctor Beetle threw the snake away as usual and brought this specimen back to study."

Felipe shook his head.

"No, Senhorina Beetle. As I always do when the Doctor comes back from his walk, I laid out everything ready for tomorrow. The snake was in the bag at twelve o'clock this morning. He came back at his regular time. I was busy then, and did not get to his laboratory till noon. The bag had been dropped by the door. I opened it, to see if everything was all right. The snake was still there. All its underside had turned to hard blue jelly. The back was still a snake's back, covered with scales. The head had turned green, but it was still a snake's head. I took the bag into my room and watched the snake till I went to look for Juan. The snake turned into this. I thought I should tell you."

"Thank you, Felipe. It is all right; just one of my father's scientific experiments. I understand. Goodnight, and thank you again for telling me. Please don't tell anyone else. Throw that thing away and put the bag in its usual place."

Left to herself, Consuelo tried not to credit her reason and the evidence of her senses. The inconsequential remarks her father had dropped in the past two years, added to the remark of today that dictators were never the first to take their own medicine, stole into her memory to cause her acute uneasiness.

What was the meaning of this new technique of his, the addition of a slight trace of chloride of gold to the solution? He had talked excitedly of some organic compound of gold being the catalyst he had sought for months to speed up the chemical change in the ripening fruit.

"What might have taken months the old way," he had exclaimed, "can now be done in hours. I've got it at last!"

What, exactly, had he got? He had not confided in her. All he asked of her was to see that the exact amount of chloride of gold which he prescribed was added to the solutions. Everything she remembered now fitted into its sinister place in one sombre pattern.

"This must be stopped," she thought.

It must be stopped, yes. But how?

The next day the banquet took place.

"Festal Thursday" slipped into the past, as the long shadows crept over the banquet tables—crude boards on trestles—spread in the open air. For one happy, gluttonous hour the bearers of the "New Freedom" to a benighted continent had stuffed themselves with a food that looked like green fruit but tasted like raw pork. Now they were replete and somewhat dazed.

A few were furtively mopping the perspiration from their foreheads, and all were beginning to show the sickly pallor of the gourmand who had overestimated his capacity for food. The eyes of some were beginning to wander strangely. These obviously unhappy guests appeared to be slightly drunk.

Kadir's speech eulogizing Beetle and his work was unexpectedly short. The Dictator's famous gift for oratory seemed to desert him, and he sat down somewhat suddenly, as if he were feeling unwell. Beetle rose to reply.

"Senhor Kadir! Guests and bearers to Amazonia of the New Freedom, I salute you! In the name of a freedom you have never known, I salute you, as the gladiators of ancient Rome saluted their tyrant before marching into the arena where they were to be butchered for his entertainment."

Their eyes stared up at him, only half-seeing. What was he saying? It all sounded like the beginning of a dream.

"With my own hands I prepared your feast, and my hands alone spread the banquet tables with the meat-fruits you have eaten. Only one human being here has eaten the fruit as nature made it, and not as I remade it. My daughter has not eaten what you have eaten. The cold, wet taste of the snake blood which you have mistaken for the flavor of swine-flesh, and which you have enjoyed, would have nauseated her. So I gave her uncontaminated fruit for her share of our feast."

Kadir and Consuelo were on their feet together, Kadir cursing incoherently, Consuelo speechless with fear. What insane thing had her father done? Had he too eaten of— But he must have, else Kadir would not have touched the fruit!

Beetle's voice rose above the Dictator's, shouting him down.

"Yes, you were right when you accused me of injecting snake blood into the fruit. Juan did not lie to you. But the snake blood is not what is making you begin to feel like a vegetable. I injected the blood into the fruit only to delude all you fools into mistaking it for flesh. I anticipated months of

THE ULTIMATE CATALYST 139

feeding before I could make of you what *should* be made of you.

"A month ago I was relying on the slow processes of nature to destroy you with my help. Light alone, that regulates the chemistry of the growing plant and to a lesser degree the chemistry of animals, would have done what must be done to rid Amazonia and the world of the threat of your New Freedom, and to make you expiate your brutal past.

"But light would have taken months to bring about the necessary *replacement of the iron in your blood by magnesium*. It would have been a slow transformation—almost, I might say, a lingering death. By feeding you greenbeefo I could keep your bodies full at all times with magnesium in chemically available form *to replace every atom of iron in your blood!*

"Under the slow action of photosynthesis—the chemical transformations induced by exposure to light—you would have suffered a lingering illness. You would not have died. No! You would have lived, but not as animals. Perhaps not even as degenerated vegetables, but as some new form of life between plant and the animal. You might even have retained your memories.

"But I have spared you this—so far as I can prophesy. You will live, but you will not remember—much. Instead of walking forward like human beings, you will roll. That will be your memory.

"Three weeks ago I discovered the organic catalyst to hasten the replacement of the iron in your blood by magnesium and thus to change your animal blood to plant blood, chlorophyll. The catalyst is merely a chemical compound which accelerates chemical reactions without itself being changed.

"By injecting a minute trace of chloride of gold into the fruits, I—and the living plant—produced the necessary catalyst. I have not yet had time to analyze it and determine its exact composition. Nor do I expect to have time. For I have, perforce, taken the same medicine that I prescribed for you!

"Not so much, but enough. I shall remain a thinking animal a little longer than the rest of you. That is the only unfair advantage I have taken. Before the sun sets we shall all have ceased to be human beings, or even animals."

Consuelo was tugging frantically at his arm, but he brushed her aside. He spoke to her in hurried jerks as if racing against time.

"I did not lie to you when I told you I could *not* change

the chlorophyll in a living plant into haemoglobin. Nobody has done that. But did I ever say I could not change *the haemoglobin in a living animal into chlorophyll?* If I have not done that, I have done something very close to it. Look at Kadir, and see for yourself. Let go my arm—I must finish."

Wrenching himself free, he began shouting against time.

"Kadir! I salute you. Raise your right hand and return the salute."

Kadir's right hand was resting on the bare boards of the table. If he understood what Beetle said, he refused to salute. But possibly understanding was already beyond him. The blood seemed to have ebbed from the blue flesh, and the coarse hairs on the back of the hand had lengthened perceptibly even while Beetle was demanding a salute.

"Rooted to the spot, Kadir! You are taking root already. And so are the rest of you. Try to stand up like human beings! Kadir! Do you hear me? Remember that blue fungus we saw in the forest? I have good reason for believing that was your friend Juan. In less than an hour you and I and all these fools will be exactly like him, except that some of us will be blue, others green, and still others red—like the thing you stepped on.

"It rolled. Remember, Kadir? That red abomination was one of my pet fungus snakes—shot full of salts of magnesium and the catalyst I extracted from the fruits. A triumph of science. I am the greatest biochemist that ever lived! But I shan't roll farther than the rest of you. We shall all roll together—or try to. 'Merrily we roll along, roll along'—I can see already you are going to be a blue and magenta mess like your friend Juan."

Beetle laughed harshly and bared his right arm. "I'm going to be red, like the thing you stepped on, Kadir. But I've stepped on the lot of you!"

He collapsed across the table and lay still. No sane human being could have stayed to witness the end. Half mad herself, Consuelo ran from the place of living death.

"Felipe, Felipe! Boards, wood—bring dry boards, quick, quick! Tear down the buildings and pile them up over the tables. Get all the men, get them all!"

Four hours later she was racing down the river through the night with Felipe and his crew. Only once did she glance back. The flames which she herself had kindled flapped against the black sky.

THE GNARLY MAN   *Unknown*, June

by L. Sprague de Camp (1907–   )

Sprague de Camp is without doubt the most distinguished looking member of the science fiction community. The body of work he has produced since the late thirties is equally distinguished, and covers a wide variety of forms and themes—science fiction, fantasy, heroic fantasy, the popularization of science, research into myths and legends, and scholarship. He has written the so-far definitive biography of H. P. Lovecraft, and his LITERARY SWORDSMEN AND SORCERERS is a trail-blazing study of heroic fantasy authors. His SCIENCE-FICTION HANDBOOK (1953, revised 1975) remained the best single guide to writing sf for many years.

It is very tempting to use the word "classic" to describe the stories in this book. This one deserves the term.

(I first met Sprague just about the time this story appeared and in the forty years that has passed he seems to have scarcely aged. He can still pass for half his age—at least in my dazzled and envious eyes—and so can his wife, the beautiful Catherine. IA.)

Dr. Matilda Saddler first saw the gnarly man on the evening of June 14, 1946, at Coney Island.

The spring meeting of the Eastern Section of the American Anthropological Association had broken up, and Dr. Saddler had had dinner with two of her professional colleagues, Blue of Columbia and Jeffcott of Yale. She mentioned that she had never visited Coney, and meant to go there that evening. She urged Blue and Jeffcott to come along, but they begged off.

Watching Dr. Saddler's retreating back, Blue of Columbia cackled: "The Wild Woman from Wichita. Wonder if she's hunting another husband?" He was a thin man with a small gray beard and a who-the-hell-are-you-sir expression.

"How many has she had?" asked Jeffcott of Yale.

"Two to date. Don't know why anthropologists lead the most disorderly private lives of any scientists. Must be that they study the customs and morals of all these different peoples, and ask themselves, 'If the Eskimos can do it, why can't we?' I'm old enough to be safe, thank God."

"I'm not afraid of her," said Jeffcott. He was in his early forties and looked like a farmer uneasy in store clothes. "I'm so very thoroughly married."

"Yeah? Ought to have been at Stanford a few years ago, when she was there. Wasn't safe to walk across the campus, with Tuthill chasing all the females and Saddler all the males."

Dr. Saddler had to fight her way off the subway train, as the adolescents who infest the platform of the B. M. T.'s Stillwell Avenue station are probably the worst-mannered people on earth, possibly excepting the Dobu Islanders, of the western Pacific. She didn't much mind. She was a tall, strongly built woman in her late thirties, who had been kept in trim by the outdoor rigors of her profession. Besides, some of the inane remarks in Swift's paper on acculturation among the Arapaho Indians had gotten her fighting blood up.

Walking down Surf Avenue toward Brighton Beach, she looked at the concessions without trying them, preferring to watch the human types that did and the other human types that took their money. She did try a shooting gallery, but found knocking tin owls off their perch with a .22 too easy to be much fun. Long-range work with an army rifle was her idea of shooting.

The concession next to the shooting gallery would have been called a side show if there had been a main show for it to be a side show to. The usual lurid banner proclaimed the uniqueness of the two-headed calf, the bearded woman, Arachne the spider girl, and other marvels. The pièce de résistance was Ungo-Bungo, the ferocious ape-man, captured in the Congo at a cost of twenty-seven lives. The picture showed an enormous Ungo-Bungo squeezing a hapless Negro in each hand, while others sought to throw a net over him.

Dr. Saddler knew perfectly well that the ferocious ape-man would turn out to be an ordinary Caucasian with false hair on his chest. But a streak of whimsicality impelled her to go in. Perhaps, she thought, she could have some fun with her colleagues about it.

The spieler went through his leather-lunged harangue. Dr. Saddler guessed from his expression that his feet hurt. The tattooed lady didn't interest her, as her decorations obviously had no cultural significance, as they have among the Polynesians. As for the ancient Mayan, Dr. Saddler thought it in questionable taste to exhibit a poor microcephalic idiot that way. Professor Yoki's legerdemain and fire eating weren't bad.

There was a curtain in front of Ungo-Bungo's cage. At the appropriate moment there were growls and the sound of a length of chain being slapped against a metal plate. The spieler wound up on a high note: "—ladies and gentlemen, the one and only UNGO-BUNGO!" The curtain dropped.

The ape-man was squatting at the back of his cage. He dropped his chain, got up, and shuffled forward. He grasped two of the bars and shook them. They were appropriately loose and rattled alarmingly. Ungo-Bungo snarled at the patrons, showing his even, yellow teeth.

Dr. Saddler stared hard. This was something new in the ape-man line. Ungo-Bungo was about five feet three, but very massive, with enormous hunched shoulders. Above and below his blue swimming trunks thick, grizzled hair covered him from crown to ankle. His short, stout-muscled arms ended in big hands with thick, gnarled fingers. His neck projected slightly forward, so that from the front he seemed to have but little neck at all.

His face—well, thought Dr. Saddler, she knew all the living races of men, and all the types of freak brought about by glandular maladjustment, and none of them had a face like *that*. It was deeply lined. The forehead between the short scalp hair and the brows on the huge supraorbital ridges receded sharply. The nose, although wide, was not apelike; it was a shortened version of the thick, hooked Armenoid nose, so often miscalled Jewish. The face ended in a long upper lip and a retreating chin. And the yellowish skin apparently belonged to Ungo-Bungo.

The curtain was whisked up again.

Dr. Saddler went out with the others, but paid another dime, and soon was back inside. She paid no attention to the spieler, but got a good position in front of Ungo-Bungo's cage before the rest of the crowd arrived.

Ungo-Bungo repeated his performance with mechanical precision. Dr. Saddler noticed that he limped a little as he came forward to rattle the bars, and that the skin under his mat of hair bore several big whitish scars. The last joint of his left ring finger was missing. She noted certain things about the proportions of his shin and thigh, of his forearm and upper arm, and his big splay feet.

Dr. Saddler paid a third dime. An idea was knocking at her mind somewhere. If she let it in, either she was crazy or physical anthropology was haywire or—something. But she knew that if she did the sensible thing, which was to go home, the idea would plague her from now on.

After the third performance she spoke to the spieler. "I think your Mr. Ungo-Bungo used to be a friend of mine. Could you arrange for me to see him after he finishes?"

The spieler checked his sarcasm. His questioner was so obviously not a—not the sort of dame who asks to see guys after they finish.

"Oh, him," he said. "Calls himself Gaffney—Clarence Aloysius Gaffney. That the guy you want?"

"Why, yes."

"I guess you can." He looked at his watch. "He's got four more turns to do before we close. I'll have to ask the boss." He popped through a curtain and called, "Hey, Morrie!" Then he was back. "It's O. K. Morrie says you can wait in his office. Foist door to the right."

Morrie was stout, bald, and hospitable. "Sure, sure," he said, waving his cigar. "Glad to be of soivace, Miss Saddler. Chust a min while I talk to Gaffney's manager." He stuck his head out. "Hey, Pappas! Lady wants to talk to your ape-man later. I meant *lady*, O. K." He returned to orate on the difficulties besetting the freak business. "You take this Gaffney, now. He's the best damn ape-man in the business; all that hair rilly grows outa him. And the poor guy rilly has a face like that. But do people believe it? No! I hear 'em going out, saying about how the hair is pasted on, and the whole thing is a fake. It's mawtifying." He cocked his head, listening. "That rumble wasn't no rolly-coaster; it's gonna rain. Hope it's over by tomorrow. You wouldn't believe the way a rain can knock ya receipts off. If you drew a coive, it would be like this." He drew his finger horizontally through space, jerking it down sharply to indicate the effect of rain. "But as I said, people don't appreciate what you try to do for 'em. It's not just the money; I think of myself as an ottist. A creative ottist. A show like this got to have balance and propawtion, like any other ott—"

It must have been an hour later when a slow, deep voice at the door said: "Did somebody want to see me?"

The gnarly man was in the doorway. In street clothes, with the collar of his raincoat turned up and his hat brim pulled down, he looked more or less human, though the coat fitted his great, sloping shoulders badly. He had a thick, knobby walking stick with a leather loop near the top end. A small, dark man fidgeted behind him.

"Yeah," said Morrie, interrupting his lecture. "Clarence, this is Miss Saddler. Miss Saddler, this is Mr. Gaffney, one of our outstanding creative ottists."

"Pleased to meetcha," said the gnarly man. "This is my manager, Mr. Pappas."

Dr. Saddler explained, and said she'd like to talk to Mr. Gaffney if she might. She was tactful; you had to be to pry into the private affairs of Naga headhunters, for instance. The gnarly man said he'd be glad to have a cup of coffee with Miss Saddler; there was a place around the corner that they could reach without getting wet.

As they started out, Pappas followed, fidgeting more and more. The gnarly man said: "Oh, go home to bed, John. Don't worry about me." He grinned at Dr. Saddler. The effect would have been unnerving to anyone but an anthropologist. "Every time he sees me talking to anybody, he thinks it's some other manager trying to steal me." He spoke general American, with a suggestion of Irish brogue in the lowering of the vowels in words like "man" and "talk." "I made the lawyer who drew up our contract fix it so it can be ended on short notice."

Pappas departed, still looking suspicious. The rain had practically ceased. The gnarly man stepped along smartly despite his limp.

A woman passed with a fox terrier on a leash. The dog sniffed in the direction of the gnarly man, and then to all appearances went crazy, yelping and slavering. The gnarly man shifted his grip on the massive stick and said quietly, "Better hang onto him, ma'am." The woman departed hastily. "They just don't like me," commented Gaffney. "Dogs, that is."

They found a table and ordered their coffee. When the gnarly man took off his raincoat, Dr. Saddler became aware of a strong smell of cheap perfume. He got out a pipe with a big knobby bowl. It suited him, just as the walking stick did. Dr. Saddler noticed that the deep-sunk eyes under the beetling arches were light hazel.

"Well?" he said in his rumbling drawl.

She began her questions.

"My parents were Irish," he answered. "But I was born in South Boston . . . let's see . . . forty-six years ago. I can get you a copy of my birth certificate. Clarence Aloysius Gaffney, May 2, 1900." He seemed to get some secret amusement out of that statement.

"Were either of your parents of your somewhat unusual physical type?"

He paused before answering. He always did, it seemed. "Uh-huh. Both of 'em. Glands, I suppose."

"Were they both born in Ireland?"

"Yep. County Sligo." Again that mysterious twinkle.

She thought. "Mr. Gaffney, you wouldn't mind having some photographs and measurements made, would you? You could use the photographs in your business."

"Maybe." He took a sip. "Ouch! Gazooks, that's hot!"

"What?"

"I said the coffee's hot."

"I mean, before that."

The gnarly man looked a little embarrassed. "Oh, you mean the 'gazooks'? Well, I . . . uh . . . once knew a man who used to say that."

"Mr. Gaffney, I'm a scientist, and I'm not trying to get anything out of you for my own sake. You can be frank with me."

There was something remote and impersonal in his stare that gave her a slight spinal chill. "Meaning that I haven't been so far?"

"Yes. When I saw you I decided that there was something extraordinary in your background. I still think there is. Now, if you think I'm crazy, say so and we'll drop the subject. But I want to get to the bottom of this."

He took his time about answering. "That would depend." There was another pause. Then he said: "With your connections, do you know any really first-class surgeons?"

"But . . . yes, I know Dunbar."

"The guy who wears a purple gown when he operates? The guy who wrote a book on 'God, Man, and the Universe'?"

"Yes. He's a good man, in spite of his theatrical mannerisms. Why? What would you want of him?"

"Not what you're thinking. I'm satisfied with my . . . uh . . . unusual physical type. But I have some old injuries—broken bones that didn't knit properly—that I want fixed up. He'd have to be a good man, though. I have a couple of thousand dollars in the savings bank, but I know the sort of fees those guys charge. If you could make the necessary arrangements—"

"Why, yes, I'm sure I could. In fact, I could guarantee it. Then I *was* right? And you'll—" She hesitated.

"Come clean? Uh-huh. But remember, I can still prove I'm Clarence Aloysius if I have to."

"Who *are* you, then?"

Again there was a long pause. Then the gnarly man said: "Might as well tell you. As soon as you repeat any of it, you'll have put your professional reputation in my hands, remember.

"First off, I wasn't born in Massachusetts. I was born on the upper Rhine, near Mommenheim. And I was born, as nearly as I can figure out, about the year 50,000 B. C."

Matilda Saddler wondered whether she'd stumbled on the biggest thing in anthropology, or whether this bizarre personality was making Baron Munchausen look like a piker.

He seemed to guess her thoughts. "I can't prove that, of course. But so long as you arrange about that operation, I don't care whether you believe me or not."

"But . . . but . . . *how?*"

"I think the lightning did it. We were out trying to drive some bison into a pit. Well, this big thunderstorm came up, and the bison bolted in the wrong direction. So we gave up and tried to find shelter. And the next thing I knew I was lying on the ground with the rain running over me, and the rest of the clan standing around wailing about what had they done to get the storm god sore at them, so he made a bull's-eye on one of their best hunters. They'd never said *that* about me before. It's funny how you're never appreciated while you're alive.

"But I was alive, all right. My nerves were pretty well shot for a few weeks, but otherwise I was O. K., except for some burns on the soles of my feet. I don't know just what happened, except I was reading a couple of years ago that scientists had located the machinery that controls the replacement of tissue in the medulla oblongata. I think maybe the lightning did something to my medulla to speed it up. Anyway, I never got any older after that. Physically, that is. I was thirty-three at the time, more or less. We didn't keep track of ages. I look older now, because the lines in your face are bound to get sort of set after a few thousand years, and because our hair was always gray at the ends. But I can still tie an ordinary *Homo sapiens* in a knot if I want to."

"Then you're . . . you mean to say you're . . . you're trying to tell me you're—"

"A Neanderthal man? *Homo neanderthalensis?* That's right."

Matilda Saddler's hotel room was a bit crowded, with the gnarly man, the frosty Blue, the rustic Jeffcott, Dr. Saddler herself, and Harold McGannon, the historian. This McGannon was a small man, very neat and pink-skinned. He looked more like a New York Central director than a professor. Just now his expression was one of fascination. Dr. Saddler looked full of pride; Professor Jeffcott looked interested but puzzled; Dr. Blue looked bored—he hadn't wanted to come in the first place. The gnarly man, stretched out in the most comfortable chair and puffing his overgrown pipe, seemed to be enjoying himself.

McGannon was formulating a question. "Well, Mr.— Gaffney? I suppose that's your name as much as any."

"You might say so," said the gnarly man. "My original name meant something like Shining Hawk. But I've gone under hundreds of names since then. If you register in a hotel as 'Shining Hawk,' it's apt to attract attention. And I try to avoid that."

"Why?" asked McGannon.

The gnarly man looked at his audience as one might look at willfully stupid children. "I don't like trouble. The best way to keep out of trouble is not to attract attention. That's why I have to pull up stakes and move every ten or fifteen years. People might get curious as to why I never get any older."

"Pathological liar," murmured Blue. The words were barely audible, but the gnarly man heard them.

"You're entitled to your opinion, Dr. Blue," he said affably. "Dr. Saddler's doing me a favor, so in return I'm letting you all shoot questions at me. And I'm answering. I don't give a damn whether you believe me or not."

McGannon hastily threw in another question. "How is it that you have a birth certificate, as you say you have?"

"Oh, I knew a man named Clarence Gaffney once. He got killed by an automobile, and I took his name."

"Was there any reason for picking this Irish background?"

"Are you Irish, Dr. McGannon?"

"Not enough to matter."

"O. K. I didn't want to hurt any feelings. It's my best bet. There are real Irishmen with upper lips like mine."

Dr. Saddler broke in. "I meant to ask you, Clarence." She put a lot of warmth into his name. "There's an argument as to whether your people interbred with mine, when mine overran Europe at the end of the Mousterian. Some scientists have thought that some modern Europeans, especially along the west coast of Ireland, might have a little Neanderthal blood."

He grinned slightly. "Well—yes and no. There never was any back in the stone age, as far as I know. But these long-lipped Irish are my fault."

"How?"

"Believe it or not, but in the last fifty centuries there have been some women of your species that didn't find me too repulsive. Usually there was no offspring. But in the sixteenth century I went to Ireland to live. They were burning too many people for witchcraft in the rest of Europe to suit me at that time. And there was a woman. The result this time was a flock of hybrids—cute little devils, they were. So the Irishmen who look like me are my descendants."

"What did happen to your people?" asked McGannon. "Were they killed off?"

The gnarly man shrugged. "Some of them. We weren't at all warlike. But then the tall ones, as we called them, weren't either. Some of the tribes of the tall ones looked on us as legitimate prey, but most of them let us severely alone. I guess they were almost as scared of us as we were of them. Savages as primitive as that are really pretty peaceable people. You have to work so hard to keep fed, and there are so few of you, that there's no object in fighting wars. That comes later, when you get agriculture and livestock, so you have something worth stealing.

"I remember that a hundred years after the tall ones had come, there were still Neanderthalers living in my part of the country. But they died out. I think it was that they lost their ambition. The tall ones were pretty crude, but they were so far ahead of us that our things and our customs seemed silly. Finally we just sat around and lived on the scraps we could beg from the tall ones' camps. You might say we died of an inferiority complex."

"What happened to you?" aksed McGannon.

"Oh, I was a god among my own people by then, and naturally I represented them in their dealings with the tall ones. I got to know the tall ones pretty well, and they were willing to put up with me after all my own clan were dead. Then in a couple of hundred years they'd forgotten all about my people, and took me for a hunchback or something. I got to be pretty good at flint working, so I could earn my keep. When metal came in, I went into that, and finally into blacksmithing. If you'd put all the horseshoes I've made in a pile, they'd—well, you'd have a damn big pile of horseshoes, anyway."

"Did you . . . ah . . . limp at that time?" asked McGannon.

"Uh-huh. I busted my leg back in the Neolithic. Fell out of a tree, and had to set it myself, because there wasn't anybody around. Why?"

"Vulcan," said McGannon softly.

"Vulcan?" repeated the gnarly man. "Wasn't he a Greek god or something?"

"Yes. He was the lame blacksmith of the gods."

"You mean you think that maybe somebody got the idea from me? That's an interesting theory. Little late to check up on it, though."

Blue leaned forward and said crisply: "Mr. Gaffney, no real Neanderthal man could talk so fluently and entertainingly as you do. That's shown by the poor development of the frontal lobes of the brain and the attachments of the tongue muscles."

The gnarly man shrugged again. "You can believe what you like. My own clan considered me pretty smart, and then you're bound to learn something in fifty thousand years."

Dr. Saddler beamed. "Tell them about your teeth, Clarence."

The gnarly man grinned. "They're false, of course. My own lasted a long time, but they still wore out somewhere back in the Paleolithic. I grew a third set, and they wore out, too. So I had to invent soup."

THE GNARLY MAN

"You *what?*" It was the usually taciturn Jeffcott.

"I had to invent soup, to keep alive. You know, the bark-dish-and-hot-stones method. My gums got pretty tough after a while, but they still weren't much good for chewing hard stuff. So after a few thousand years I got pretty sick of soup and mushy foods generally. And when metal came in I began experimenting with false teeth. Bone teeth in copper plates. You might say I invented them, too. I tried often to sell them, but they never really caught on until around 1750 A. D. I was living in Paris then, and I built up quite a little business before I moved on." He pulled the handkerchief out of his breast pocket to wipe his forehead; Blue made a face as the wave of perfume reached him.

"Well, Mr. Shining Hawk," snapped Blue with a trace of sarcasm, "how do you like our machine age?"

The gnarly man ignored the tone of the question. "It's not bad. Lots of interesting things happen. The main trouble is the shirts."

"Shirts?"

"Uh-huh. Just try to buy a shirt with a twenty neck and a twenty-nine sleeve. I have to order 'em special. It's almost as bad with hats and shoes. I wear an eight and one half hat and a thirteen shoe." He looked at his watch. "I've got to get back to Coney to work."

McGannon jumped up. "Where can I get in touch with you again, Mr. Gaffney? There's lots of things I'd like to ask you."

The gnarly man told him. "I'm free mornings. My working hours are two to midnight on weekdays, with a couple of hours off for dinner. Union rules, you know."

"You mean there's a union for you show people?"

"Sure. Only they call it a guild. They think they're artists, you know. Artists don't have unions; they have guilds. But it amounts to the same thing."

Blue and Jeffcott saw the gnarly man and the historian walking slowly toward the subway together. Blue said: "Poor old Mac! Always thought he had sense. Looks like he's swallowed this Gaffney's ravings, hook, line, and sinker."

"I'm not so sure," said Jeffcott, frowning. "There's something funny about the business."

"What?" barked Blue. "Don't tell me that *you* believe this story of being alive fifty thousand years? A caveman who uses perfume! Good God!"

"N-no," said Jeffcott. "Not the fifty thousand part. But I don't think it's a simple case of paranoia or plain lying, either. And the perfume's quite logical, if he were telling the truth."

"Huh?"

"Body odor. Saddler told us how dogs hate him. He'd have a smell different from ours. We're so used to ours that we don't even know we have one, unless somebody goes without a bath for a month. But we might notice his if he didn't disguise it."

Blue snorted. "You'll be believing him yourself in a minute. It's an obvious glandular case, and he's made up this story to fit. All that talk about not caring whether we believe him or not is just bluff. Come on, let's get some lunch. Say, see the way Saddler looked at him every time she said 'Clarence'? Like a hungry wolf. Wonder what she thinks she's going to do with him?"

Jeffcott thought. "I can guess. And if he *is* telling the truth, I think there's something in Deuteronomy against it."

The great surgeon made a point of looking like a great surgeon, to pince-nez and Vandyke. He waved the X-ray negatives at the gnarly man, pointing out this and that.

"We'd better take the leg first," he said. "Suppose we do that next Thursday. When you've recovered from that we can tackle the shoulder. It'll all take time, you know."

The gnarly man agreed, and shuffled out of the little private hospital to where McGannon awaited him in his car. The gnarly man described the tentative schedule of operations, and mentioned that he had made arrangements to quit his job. "Those two are the main thing," he said. "I'd like to try professional wrestling again some day, and I can't unless I get this shoulder fixed so I can raise my left arm over my head."

"What happened to it?" asked McGannon.

The gnarly man closed his eyes, thinking. "Let me see. I get things mixed up sometimes. People do when they're only fifty years old, so you can imagine what it's like for me.

"In 42 B. C. I was living with the Bituriges in Gaul. You remember that Cæsar shut up Werkinghetorich—Vercingetorix to you—in Alesia, and the confederacy raised an army of relief under Coswollon."

"Coswollon?"

The gnarly man laughed shortly. "I meant Warcaswollon.

Caswollon was a Briton, wasn't he? I'm always getting those two mixed up.

"Anyhow, I got drafted. That's all you can call it; I didn't want to go. It wasn't exactly *my* war. But they wanted me because I could pull twice as heavy a bow as anybody else.

"When the final attack on Cæsar's ring fortifications came, they sent me forward with some other archers to provide a covering fire for their infantry. At least, that was the plan. Actually, I never saw such a hopeless muddle in my life. And before I even got within bowshot, I fell into one of the Romans' covered pits. I didn't land on the point of the stake, but I fetched up against the side of it and busted my shoulder. There wasn't any help, because the Gauls were too busy running away from Cæsar's German cavalry to bother about wounded men."

The author of "God, Man, and the Universe" gazed after his departing patient. He spoke to his head assistant: "What do you think of him?"

"I think it's so," said the assistant. "I looked over those X rays pretty closely. That skeleton never belonged to a human being. And it has more healed fractures than you'd think possible."

"Hm-m-m," said Dunbar. "That's right, he wouldn't be human, would he? Hm-m-m. You know, if anything happened to him—"

The assistant grinned understandingly. "Of course, there's the S. P. C. A."

"We needn't worry about *them*. Hm-m-m." He thought, you've been slipping; nothing big in the papers for a year. But if you published a complete anatomical description of a Neanderthal man—or if you found out why his medulla functions the way it does—Hm-m-m. Of course, it would have to be managed properly—

"Let's have lunch at the Natural History Museum," said McGannon. "Some of the people there ought to know you."

"O. K.," drawled the gnarly man. "Only I've still got to get back to Coney afterward. This is my last day. Tomorrow, Pappas and I are going up to see our lawyer about ending our contract. Guy named Robinette. It's a dirty trick on poor old John, but I warned him at the start that this might happen."

"I suppose we can come up to interview you while you're

". . . ah . . . convalescing? Fine. Have you ever been to the museum, by the way?"

"Sure," said the gnarly man. "I get around."

"What did you . . . ah . . . think of their stuff in the Hall of the Age of Man?"

"Pretty good. There's a little mistake in one of those big wall paintings. The second horn on the woolly rhinoceros ought to slant forward more. I thought of writing them a letter. But you know how it is. They'd say: 'Were you there?' and I'd say, 'Uh-huh,' and they'd say, 'Another nut.'"

"How about the pictures and busts of Paleolithic men?"

"Pretty good. But they have some funny ideas. They always show us with skins wrapped around our middles. In summer we didn't wear skins, and in winter we hung them around our shoulders, where they'd do some good.

"And then they show those tall ones that you call Cro-Magnon men clean-shaven. As I remember, they all had whiskers. What would they shave with?"

"I think," said McGannon, "that they leave the beards off the busts to . . . ah . . . show the shape of the chins. With the beards they'd all look too much alike."

"Is that the reason? They might say so on the labels." The gnarly man rubbed his own chin, such as it was. "I wish beards would come back into style. I look much more human with a beard. I got along fine in the sixteenth century when everybody had whiskers.

"That's one of the ways I remember when things happened, by the haircuts and whiskers that people had. I remember when a wagon I was driving in Milan lost a wheel and spilled flour bags from hell to breakfast. That must have been in the sixteenth century, before I went to Ireland, because I remember that most of the men in the crowd that collected had beards. Now—wait a minute—maybe that was the fourteenth. There were a lot of beards then, too."

"Why, why didn't you keep a diary?" asked McGannon with a groan of exasperation.

The gnarly man shrugged characteristically. "And pack around six trunks full of paper every time I moved? No, thanks."

"I . . . ah . . . don't suppose you could give me the real story of Richard III and the princes in the tower?"

"Why should I? I was just a poor blacksmith, or farmer, or something most of the time. I didn't go around with the big shots. I gave up all my ideas of ambition a long time before that. I had to, being so different from other people. As far as I can remember, the only real king I ever got a good look at was Charlemagne, when he made a speech in Paris one day. He was just a big, tall man with Santa Claus whiskers and a squeaky voice."

Next morning McGannon and the gnarly man had a session with Svedberg at the museum. Then McGannon drove Gaffney around to the lawyer's office, on the third floor of a seedy office building in the West Fifties. James Robinette looked something like a movie actor and something like a chipmunk. He looked at his watch and said to McGannon: "This won't take long. If you'd like to stick around, I'd be glad to have lunch with you." The fact was that he was feeling just a trifle queasy about being left with this damn queer client, this circus freak or whatever he was, with his barrel body and his funny slow drawl.

When the business had been completed, and the gnarly man had gone off with his manager to wind up his affairs at Coney, Robinette said: "Whew! I thought he was a half-wit, from his looks. But there was nothing half-witted about the way he went over those clauses. You'd have thought the damn contract was for building a subway system. What is he, anyhow?"

McGannon told him what he knew.

The lawyer's eyebrows went up. "Do you *believe* his yarn? Oh, I'll take tomato juice and filet of sole with tartar sauce—only without the tartar sauce—on the lunch, please."

"The same for me. Answering your question, Robinette, I do. So does Saddler. So does Svedberg up at the museum. They're both topnotchers in their respective fields. Saddler and I have interviewed him, and Svedberg's examined him physically. But it's just opinion. Fred Blue still swears it's a hoax or . . . ah . . . some sort of dementia. Neither of us can prove anything."

"Why not?"

"Well . . . ah . . . how are you going to prove that he was, or was not, alive a hundred years ago? Take one case: Clarence says he ran a sawmill in Fairbanks, Alaska, in 1906 and '07, under the name of Michael Shawn. How are you going to find out whether there was a sawmill operator in Fairbanks at that time? And if you did stumble on a record of a Michael Shawn, how would you know whether he and Clarence were the same? There's not a chance in a thousand that there'd be a photograph or a detailed description that you could check with. And you'd have an awful time trying to find anybody who remembered him at this late date.

"Then, Svedberg poked around Clarence's face, yesterday, and said that no *Homo sapiens* ever had a pair of zygomatic arches like that. But when I told Blue that, he offered to produce photographs of a human skull that did. I know what'll happen. Blue will say that the arches are practically the same, and Svedberg will say that they're obviously different. So there we'll be."

Robinette mused, "He does seem damned intelligent for an ape-man."

"He's not an ape-man, really. The Neanderthal race was a separate branch of the human stock; they were more primitive in some ways and more advanced in others than we are. Clarence may be slow, but he usually grinds out the right answer. I imagine that he was . . . ah . . . brilliant, for one of his kind, to begin with. And he's had the benefit of so much experience. He knows an incredible lot. He knows us; he sees through us and our motives."

The little pink man puckered up his forehead. "I do hope nothing happens to him. He's carrying around a lot of priceless information in that big head of his. Simply priceless. Not much about war and politics; he kept clear of those as a matter of self-preservation. But little things, about how people lived and how they thought thousands of years ago. He gets his periods mixed up sometimes, but he gets them straightened out if you give him time.

"I'll have to get hold of Pell, the linguist. Clarence knows dozens of ancient languages, such as Gothic and Gaulish. I was able to check him on one of them, like vulgar Latin; that was one of the things that convinced me. And there are archeologists and psychologists—

"If only something doesn't happen to scare him off. We'd never find him. I don't know. Between a man-crazy female scientist and a publicity-mad surgeon—I wonder how it'll work out—"

The gnarly man innocently entered the waiting room of Dunbar's hospital. He, as usual, spotted the most comfortable chair and settled luxuriously into it.

Dunbar stood before him. His keen eyes gleamed with anticipation behind their pince-nez. "There'll be a wait of about half an hour, Mr. Gaffney," he said. "We're all tied up now, you know. I'll send Mahler in; he'll see that you have anything you want." Dunbar's eyes ran lovingly over the gnarly man's stumpy frame. What fascinating secrets mightn't he discover once he got inside it?

Mahler appeared, a healthy-looking youngster. Was there anything Mr. Gaffney would like? The gnarly man paused as usual to let his massive mental machinery grind. A vagrant impulse moved him to ask to see the instruments that were to be used on him.

Mahler had his orders, but this seemed a harmless enough request. He went and returned with a tray full of gleaming steel. "You see," he said, "these are called scalpels."

Presently the gnarly man asked: "What's this?" He picked up a peculiar-looking instrument.

"Oh, that's the boss's own invention. For getting at the mid-brain."

"Mid-brain? What's that doing here?"

"Why, that's for getting at your—— That must be there by mistake——"

Little lines tightened around the queer hazel eyes. "Yeah?" He remembered the look Dunbar had given him, and Dunbar's general reputation. "Say, could I use your phone a minute?"

"Why . . . I suppose . . . what do you want to phone for?"

"I want to call my lawyer. Any objections?"

"No, of course not. But there isn't any phone here."

"What do you call that?" The gnarly man got up and walked toward the instrument in plain sight on a table. But Mahler was there before him, standing in front of it.

"This one doesn't work. It's being fixed."

"Can't I try it?"

"No, not till it's fixed. It doesn't work, I tell you."

The gnarly man studied the young physician for a few seconds. "O. K., then I'll find one that does." He started for the door.

"Hey, you can't go out now!" cried Mahler.

"Can't I? Just watch me!"

"Hey!" It was a full-throated yell. Like magic more men in white coats appeared.

Behind them was the great surgeon. "Be reasonable, Mr. Gaffney," he said. "There's no reason why you should go out now, you know. We'll be ready for you in a little while."

"Any reason why I shouldn't?" The gnarly man's big face

swung on his thick neck, and his hazel eyes swiveled. All the exits were blocked. "I'm going."

"Grab him!" said Dunbar.

The white coats moved. The gnarly man got his hands on the back of a chair. The chair whirled, and became a dissolving blur as the men closed on him. Pieces of chair flew about the room, to fall with the dry, sharp *ping* of short lengths of wood. When the gnarly man stopped swinging, having only a short piece of the chair back left in each fist, one assistant was out cold. Another leaned whitely against the wall and nursed a broken arm.

"Go on!" shouted Dunbar when he could make himself heard. The white wave closed over the gnarly man, then broke. The gnarly man was on his feet, and held young Mahler by the ankles. He spread his feet and swung the shrieking Mahler like a club, clearing the way to the door. He turned, whirled Mahler around his head like a hammer thrower, and let the now mercifully unconscious body fly. His assailants went down in a yammering tangle.

One was still up. Under Dunbar's urging he sprang after the gnarly man. The latter had gotten his stick out of the umbrella stand in the vestibule. The knobby upper end went *whoosh* past the assistant's nose. The assistant jumped back and fell over one of the casualties. The front door slammed, and there was a deep roar of "Taxi!"

"Come on!" shrieked Dunbar. "Get the ambulance out!"

James Robinette was sitting in his office, thinking the thoughts that lawyers do in moments of relaxation, when there was a pounding of large feet in the corridor, a startled protest from Miss Spevak in the outer office, and the strange client of the day before was at Robinette's desk, breathing hard.

"I'm Gaffney," he growled between gasps. "Remember me? I think they followed me down here. They'll be up any minute. I want your help."

"They? Who's they?" Robinette winced at the impact of that damn perfume.

The gnarly man launched into his misfortunes. He was going well when there were more protests from Miss Spevak, and Dr. Dunbar and four assistants burst into the office.

"He's ours," said Dunbar, his glasses agleam.

"He's an ape-man," said the assistant with the black eye.

"He's a dangerous lunatic," said the assistant with the cut lip.

"We've come to take him away," said the assistant with the torn coat.

The gnarly man spread his feet and gripped his stick like a baseball bat by the small end.

Robinette opened a desk drawer and got out a large pistol. "One move toward him and I'll use this. The use of extreme violence is justified to prevent commission of a felony, to wit: kidnaping."

The five men backed up a little. Dunbar said: "This isn't kidnaping. You can only kidnap a person, you know. He isn't a human being, and I can prove it."

The assistant with the black eye snickered. "If he wants protection, he better see a game warden instead of a lawyer."

"Maybe that's what *you* think," said Robinette. "You aren't a lawyer. According to the law, he's human. Even corporations, idiots, and unborn children are legally persons, and he's a damn sight more human they they are."

"Then he's a dangerous lunatic," said Dunbar.

"Yeah? Where's your commitment order? The only persons who can apply for one are: (a) close relatives and (b) public officials charged with the maintenance of order. You're neither."

Dunbar continued stubbornly: "He ran amuck in my hospital and nearly killed a couple of my men, you know. I guess that gives us some rights."

"Sure," said Robinette. "You can step down to the nearest station and swear out a warrant." He turned to the gnarly man. "Shall we throw the book at 'em, Gaffney?"

"I'm all right," said that individual, his speech returning to its normal slowness. "I just want to make sure these guys don't pester me any more."

"O. K. Now listen, Dunbar. One hostile move out of you and we'll have a warrant out for you for false arrest, assault and battery, attempted kidnaping, criminal conspiracy, and disorderly conduct. *And* we'll slap on a civil suit for damages for sundry torts, to wit: assault, deprivation of civil rights, placing in jeopardy of life and limb, menace, and a few more I may think of later."

"You'll never make that stick," snarled Dunbar. "We have all the witnesses."

"Yeah? And wouldn't the great Evan Dunbar look sweet defending such actions? Some of the ladies who gush over your books might suspect that maybe you weren't such a damn knight in shining armor. We can make a prize monkey of you, and you know it."

"You're destroying the possibility of a great scientific discovery, you know, Robinette."

"To hell with that. My duty is to protect my client. Now beat it, all of you, before I call a cop." His left hand moved suggestively to the telephone.

Dunbar grasped at a last straw. "Hm-m-m. Have you got a permit for that gun?"

"Damn right. Want to see it?"

Dunbar sighed. "Never mind. You *would* have." His greatest opportunity for fame was slipping out of his fingers. He drooped toward the door.

The gnarly man spoke up. "If you don't mind, Dr. Dunbar, I left my hat at your place. I wish you'd send it to Mr. Robinette here. I have a hard time getting hats to fit me."

Dunbar looked at him silently and left with his cohorts.

The gnarly man was giving the lawyer further details when the telephone rang. Robinette answered: "Yes. . . . Saddler? Yes, he's here. . . . Your Dr. Dunbar was going to murder him so he could dissect him. . . . O. K." He turned to the gnarly man. "Your friend Dr. Saddler is looking for you. She's on her way up here."

"Zounds!" said Gaffney. "I'm going."

"Don't you want to see her? She was phoning from around the corner. If you go out now you'll run into her. How did she knew where to call?"

"I gave her your number. I suppose she called the hospital and my boardinghouse, and tried you as a last resort. This door goes into the hall, doesn't it? Well, when she comes in the regular door I'm going out this one. And I don't want you saying where I've gone. It's nice to have known you, Mr. Robinette."

"Why? What's the matter? You're not going to run out now, are you? Dunbar's harmless, and you've got friends. I'm your friend."

"You're durn tootin' I'm going to run out. There's too much trouble. I've kept alive all these centuries by staying away from trouble. I let down my guard with Dr. Saddler, and went to the surgeon she recommended. First he plots to take me apart to see what makes me tick. If that brain instrument hadn't made me suspicious, I'd have been on my way to the alcohol jars by now. Then there's a fight, and it's just pure luck I didn't kill a couple of those internes, or whatever they are, and get sent up for manslaughter. Now Matilda's after me with a more-than-friendly interest. I know what it means when a woman looks at you that way and calls you 'dear.' I wouldn't mind if she weren't a prominent person of the kind that's always in some sort of garboil. That would mean more trouble, sooner or later. You don't suppose I *like* trouble, do you?"

"But look here, Gaffney, you're getting steamed up over a lot of damn—"

"*Ssst!*" The gnarly man took his stick and tiptoed over to the private entrance. As Dr. Saddler's clear voice sounded in the outer office, he sneaked out. He was closing the door behind him when the scientist entered the inner office.

Matilda Saddler was a quick thinker. Robinette hardly had time to open his mouth when she flung herself at and through the private door with a cry of "Clarence!"

Robinette heard the clatter of feet on the stairs. Neither the pursued nor the pursuer had waited for the creaky elevator. Looking out the window, he saw Gaffney leap into a taxi. Matilda Saddler sprinted after the cab, calling: "Clarence! Come back!" But the traffic was light and the chase correspondingly hopeless.

They did hear from the gnarly man once more. Three months later Robinette got a letter whose envelope contained, to his vast astonishment, ten ten-dollar bills. The single sheet was typed, even to the signature.

DEAR MR. ROBINETTE:

I do not know what your regular fees are, but I hope that the inclosed will cover your services to me of last June.

Since leaving New York I have had several jobs. I pushed a hack—as we say—in Chicago, and I tried out as pitcher on a bush league baseball team. Once I made my living by knocking over rabbits and things with stones, and I can still throw fairly well. Nor am I bad at swinging a club, such as a baseball bat. But my lameness makes me too slow for a baseball career, and it will be some time before I try any remedial operations again.

I now have a job whose nature I cannot disclose because I do not wish to be traced. You need pay no attention to the postmark; I am not living in Kansas City, but had a friend post this letter there.

Ambition would be foolish for one in my peculiar position. I am satisfied with a job that furnishes me with the essentials, and allows me to go to an occasional movie, and a few friends with whom I can drink beer and talk.

I was sorry to leave New York without saying good-by to Dr. Harold McGannon, who treated me very nicely. I wish you would explain to him why I had to leave as I did. You can get in touch with him through Columbia University.

If Dunbar sent you my hat as I requested, pleased mail it to me: General Delivery, Kansas City, Mo. My friend will pick it up. There is not a hat store in this town where I live that can fit me. With best wishes, I remain,

Yours sincerely,
SHINING HAWK
Alias CLARENCE ALOYSIUS GAFFNEY

BLACK DESTROYER

Astounding Science Fiction, July

by A. E. van Vogt (1912–)

"Black Destroyer" was the Canadian born van Vogt's first published story, and it propelled him to the top of the science fiction world. His was to be an important and contentious career, characterized by controversy, a long hiatus from sf (with the loss of what many felt were his potentially most creative years), and the production of many works of lasting interest.

There had been hundreds of stories about "space monsters" and BEMS before "Black Destroyer," the vast majority relying on the appearance of the creatures to frighten and amaze the reader. However, here it is not tentacles that provide the chills and frights, but Coeurl's insatiable hunger. Van Vogt would return to the theme of the menacing alien numerous times, and this story forms part of his popular "novel" THE VOYAGE OF THE SPACE BEAGLE (1950).

(The July, 1939, Astounding is sometimes taken as the opening of the two decades of science fiction's "Golden Age" when John Campbell, at the height of his powers, was undisputed Emperor of Science Fiction. Why this issue? Very largely because of Black Destroyer which had the wallop of a pile driver to those reading it then for the first time. I know, because I remember. IA)

On and on Coeurl prowled! The black, moonless, almost starless night yielded reluctantly before a grim reddish dawn that crept up from his left. A vague, dull light, it was, that gave no sense of approaching warmth, no comfort, nothing but a cold, diffuse lightness, slowly revealing a nightmare landscape.

Black, jagged rock and black, unliving plain took form around him, as a pale-red sun peered at last above the grotesque horizon. It was then Coeurl recognized suddenly that he was on familiar ground.

He stopped short. Tenseness flamed along his nerves. His muscles pressed with sudden, unrelenting strength against his bones. His great forelegs—twice as long as his hindlegs—twitched with a shuddering movement that arched every razor-sharp claw. The thick tentacles that sprouted from his shoulders ceased their weaving undulation, and grew taut with anxious alertness.

Utterly appalled, he twisted his great cat head from side to side, while the little hairlike tendrils that formed each ear vibrated frantically, testing every vagrant breeze, every throb in the ether.

But there was no response, no swift tingling along his intricate nervous system, not the faintest suggestion anywhere of the presence of the all-necessary id. Hopelessly, Coeurl crouched, an enormous catlike figure silhouetted against the dim reddish skyline, like a distorted etching of a black tiger resting on a black rock in a shadow world.

He had known this day would come. Through all the centuries of restless search, this day had loomed ever nearer, blacker, more frightening—this inevitable hour when he must return to the point where he began his systematic hunt in a world almost depleted of id-creatures.

The truth struck in waves like an endless, rhythmic ache at the seat of his ego. When he had started, there had been a few id-creatures in every hundred square miles, to be mercilessly rooted out. Only too well Coeurl knew in this ultimate hour that he had missed none. There were no id-creatures left to eat. In all the hundreds of thousands of square miles that he had made his own by right of ruthless conquest—until no neighboring coeurl dared to question his sovereignty—there was no id to feed the otherwise immortal engine that was his body.

Square foot by square foot he had gone over it. And now—he recognized the knoll of rock just ahead, and the black rock bridge that formed a queer, curling tunnel to his right. It was in that tunnel he had lain for days, waiting for the simple-minded, snakelike id-creature to come forth from its hole in the rock to bask in the sun—his first kill after he had realized the absolute necessity of organized extermination.

He licked his lips in brief gloating memory of the moment his slavering jaws tore the victim into precious toothsome bits. But the dark fear of an idless universe swept the sweet remembrance from his consciousness, leaving only certainty of death.

He snarled audibly, a defiant, devilish sound that quavered on the air, echoed and re-echoed among the rocks, and shuddered back along his nerves—instinctive and hellish expression of his will to live.

And then—abruptly—it came.

He saw it emerge out of the distance on a long downward slant, a tiny glowing spot that grew enormously into a metal ball. The great shining globe hissed by above Coeurl, slowing visibly in quick deceleration. It sped over a black line of hills to the right, hovered almost motionless for a second, then sank down out of sight.

Coeurl exploded from his startled immobility. With tiger speed, he flowed down among the rocks. His round, black eyes burned with the horrible desire that was an agony within him. His ear tendrils vibrated a message of id in such tremendous quantities that his body felt sick with the pangs of his abnormal hunger.

The little red sun was a crimson ball in the purple-black heavens when he crept up from behind a mass of rock and gazed from its shadows at the crumbling, gigantic ruins of the city that sprawled below him. The silvery globe, in spite of its great size, looked strangely inconspicuous against that vast, fairylike reach of ruins. Yet about it was a leashed aliveness, a dynamic quiescence that, after a moment, made it stand out, dominating the foreground. A massive, rock-crushing thing of metal, it rested on a cradle made by its own weight in the harsh, resisting plain which began abruptly at the outskirts of the dead metropolis.

Coeurl gazed at the strange, two-legged creatures who stood in little groups near the brilliantly lighted opening that yawned at the base of the ship. His throat thickened with the immediacy of his need; and his brain grew dark with the first wild impulse to burst forth in furious charge and smash these flimsy, helpless-looking creatures whose bodies emitted the id-vibrations.

Mists of memory stopped that mad rush when it was still only electricity surging through his muscles. Memory that brought fear in an acid stream of weakness, pouring along his nerves, poisoning the reservoirs of his strength. He had time to see that the creatures wore things over their real bodies, shimmering transparent material that glittered in strange, burning flashes in the rays of the sun.

Other memories came suddenly. Of dim days when the city that spread below was the living, breathing heart of an age of glory that dissolved in a single century before flaming guns whose wielders knew only that for the survivors there would be an ever-narrowing supply of id.

It was the remembrance of those guns that held him there, cringing in a wave of terror that blurred his reason. He saw himself smashed by balls of metal and burned by searing flame.

Came cunning—understanding of the presence of these creatures. This, Coeurl reasoned for the first time, was a scientific expedition from another star. In the older days, the coeurls had thought of space travel, but disaster came too swiftly for it ever to be more than a thought.

Scientist meant investigation, not destruction. Scientists in their way were fools. Bold with his knowledge, he emerged into the open. He saw the creatures become aware of him. They turned and stared. One, the smallest of the group, detached a shining metal rod from a sheath, and held it casually in one hand. Coeurl loped on, shaken to his core by the action; but it was too late to turn back.

Commander Hal Morton heard little Gregory Kent, the chemist, laugh with the embarrassed half gurgle with which he invariably announced inner uncertainty. He saw Kent fingering the spindly metalite weapon.

Kent said: "I'll take no chances with anything as big as that."

Commander Morton allowed his own deep chuckle to echo along the communicators. "That," he grunted finally, "is one of the reasons why you're on this expedition, Kent—because you never leave anything to chance."

His chuckle trailed off into silence. Instinctively, as he watched the monster approach them across that black rock plain, he moved forward until he stood a little in advance of the others, his huge form bulking the transparent metalite suit. The comments of the men pattered through the radio communicator into his ears:

"I'd hate to meet that baby on a dark night in an alley."

"Don't be silly. This is obviously an intelligent creature. Probably a member of the ruling race."

"It looks like nothing else than a big cat, if you forget those tentacles sticking out from its shoulders, and making allowances for those monster forelegs."

"Its physical development," said a voice, which Morton recognized as that of Siedel, the psychologist, "presupposes an animal-like adaptation to surroundings, not an intellectual one. On the other hand, its coming to us like this is not the act of an animal but of a creature possessing a mental awareness of our possible identity. You will notice that its movements are stiff, denoting caution, which suggests fear and consciousness of our weapons. I'd like to get a good look at the end of its tentacles. If they taper into handlike appendages that can really grip objects, then the conclusion would be inescapable that it is a descendant of the inhabitants of this city. It would be a great help if we could establish communication with it, even though appearances indicate that it has degenerated into a historyless primitive."

Coeurl stopped when he was still ten feet from the foremost creature. The sense of id was so overwhelming that his brain drifted to the ultimate verge of chaos. He felt as if his limbs were bathed in molten liquid; his very vision was not quite clear, as the sheer sensuality of his desire thundered through his being.

The men—all except the little one with the shining metal rod in his fingers—came closer. Coeurl saw that they were frankly and curiously examining him. Their lips were moving, and their voices beat in a monotonous, meaningless rhythm on his ear tendrils. At the same time he had the sense of waves of a much higher frequency—his own communication level—only it was a machinelike clicking that jarred his brain. With a distinct effort to appear friendly, he broadcast his name from his ear tendrils, at the same time pointing at himself with one curving tentacle.

Gourlay, chief of communications, drawled: "I got a sort of static in my radio when he wiggled those hairs, Morton. Do you think——"

"Looks very much like it," the leader answered the unfinished question. "That means a job for you, Gourlay. If it speaks by means of radio waves, it might not be altogether impossible that you can create some sort of television picture of its vibrations, or teach him the Morse code."

"Ah," said Siedel. "I was right. The tentacles each develop into seven strong fingers. Provided the nervous system is complicated enough, those fingers could, with training, operate any machine."

Morton said: "I think we'd better go in and have some lunch. Afterward, we've got to get busy. The material men can set up their machines and start gathering data on the planet's metal possibilities, and so on. The others can do a little careful exploring. I'd like some notes on architecture and on scientific development of this race, and particularly what happened to wreck the civilization. On earth civilization after civilization crumbled, but always a new one sprang up in its dust. Why didn't that happen here? Any questions?"

"Yes. What about pussy? Look, he wants to come in with us."

Commander Morton frowned, an action that emphasized the deep-space pallor of his face. "I wish there was some way we could take it in with us, without forcibly capturing it. Kent, what do you think?"

"I think we should first decide whether it's an it or a him, and call it one or the other. I'm in favor of him. As for taking him in with us——" The little chemist shook his head decisively. "Impossible. This atmosphere is twenty-eight percent chlorine. Our oxygen would be pure dynamite to his lungs."

The commander chuckled. "He doesn't believe that, apparently." He watched the catlike monster follow the first two men through the great door. The men kept an anxious distance from him, then glanced at Morton questioningly. Morton waved his hand. "O.K. Open the second lock and let him get a whiff of the oxygen. That'll cure him."

A moment later, he cursed his amazement. "By Heaven, he doesn't even notice the difference! That means he hasn't any lungs, or else the chlorine is not what his lungs use. Let him in! You bet he can go in! Smith, here's a treasure house for a biologist—harmless enough if we're careful. We can always handle him. But what a metabolism!"

Smith, a tall, thin, bony chap with a long, mournful face, said in an oddly forceful voice: "In all our travels, we've found only two higher forms of life. Those dependent on chlorine, and those who need oxygen—the two elements that support combustion. I'm prepared to stake my reputation that no complicated organism could ever adapt itself to both gases in a natural way. At first thought I should say here is an extremely advanced form of life. This race long ago discovered truths of biology that we are just beginning to suspect. Morton, we mustn't let this creature get away if we can help it."

"If his anxiety to get inside is any criterion," Commander Morton laughed, "then our difficulty will be to get rid of him."

He moved into the lock with Coeurl and the two men. The automatic machinery hummed; and in a few minutes they were standing at the bottom of a series of elevators that led up to the living quarters.

"Does that go up?" One of the men flicked a thumb in the direction of the monster.

"Better send him up alone, if he'll go in."

Coeurl offered no objection, until he heard the door slam behind him; and the closed cage shot upward. He whirled with a savage snarl, his reason swirling into chaos. With one leap, he pounced at the door. The metal bent under his plunge, and the desperate pain maddened him. Now, he was all trapped animal. He smashed at the metal with his paws, bending it like so much tin. He tore great bars loose with his thick tentacles. The machinery screeched; there were horrible jerks as the limitless power pulled the cage along in spite of projecting pieces of metal that scraped the outside walls. And then the cage stopped, and he snatched off the rest of the door and hurtled into the corridor.

He waited there until Morton and the men came up with drawn weapons. "We're fools," Morton said. "We should have shown him how it works. He thought we'd double-crossed him."

He motioned to the monster, and saw the savage glow fade from the coal-black eyes as he opened and closed the door with elaborate gestures to show the operation.

Coeurl ended the lesson by trotting into the large room to his right. He lay down on the rugged floor, and fought down the electric tautness of his nerves and muscles. A very fury of rage against himself for his fright consumed him. It seemed to his burning brain that he had lost the advantage of appearing a mild and harmless creature. His strength must have startled and dismayed them.

It meant greater danger in the task which he now knew he must accomplish: To kill everything in the ship, and take the machine back to their world in search of unlimited id.

With unwinking eyes, Coeurl lay and watched the two men clearing away the loose rubble from the metal doorway of the huge old building. His whole body ached with the hunger of his cells for id. The craving tore through his palpitant muscles, and throbbed like a living thing in his brain. His every nerve quivered to be off after the men who had wandered into the city. One of them, he knew, had gone—alone.

The dragging minutes fled; and still he restrained himself, still he lay there watching, aware that the men knew he watched. They floated a metal machine from the ship to the rock mass that blocked the great half-open door, under the direction of a third man. No flicker of their fingers escaped his fierce stare, and slowly, as the simplicity of the machinery became apparent to him, contempt grew upon him.

He knew what to expect finally, when the flame flared in incandescent violence and ate ravenously at the hard rock beneath. But in spite of his preknowledge, he deliberately jumped and snarled as if in fear, as that white heat burst forth. His ear tendrils caught the laughter of the men, their curious pleasure at his simulated dismay.

The door was released, and Morton came over and went inside with the third man. The latter shook his head.

"It's a shambles. You can catch the drift of the stuff. Obviously, they used atomic energy, but . . . but it's in wheel form. That's a peculiar development. In our science, atomic energy brought in the nonwheel machine. It's possible that here they've progressed—*further* to a new type of wheel mechanics. I hope their libraries are better preserved than this, or we'll never know. What could have happened to a civilization to make it vanish like this?"

A third voice broke through the communicators: "This is Siedel. I heard your question, Pennons. Psychologically and sociologically speaking, the only reason why a territory becomes uninhabited is lack of food."

"But they're so advanced scientifically, why didn't they develop space flying and go elsewhere for their food?"

"Ask Gunlie Lester," interjected Morton. "I heard him expounding some theory even before we landed."

The astronomer answered the first call. "I've still got to verify all my facts, but this desolate world is the only planet revolving around that miserable red sun. There's nothing else. No moon, not even a planetoid. And the nearest star system is *nine hundred light-years* away.

"So tremendous would have been the problem of the ruling race of this world, that in one jump they would not only have had to solve interplanetary but interstellar space traveling. When you consider how slow our own development was— first the moon, then Venus—each success leading to the next, and after centuries to the nearest stars; and last of all to the anti-accelerators that permitted galactic travel. Considering all this, I maintain it would be impossible for any race to create such machines without practical experience. And, with the nearest star so far away, they had no incentive for the space adventuring that makes for experience."

Coeurl was trotting briskly over to another group. But now, in the driving appetite that consumed him, and in the frenzy of his high scorn, he paid no attention to what they were doing. Memories of past knowledge, jarred into activity by what he had seen, flowed into his consciousness in an ever developing and more vivid stream.

From group to group he sped, a nervous dynamo—jumpy, sick with his awful hunger. A little car rolled up, stopping in front of him, and a formidable camera whirred as it took a picture of him. Over on a mound of rock, a gigantic telescope was rearing up toward the sky. Nearby, a disintegrating machine drilled its searing fire into an ever-deepening hole, down and down, straight down.

Coeurl's mind became a blur of things he watched with half attention. And ever more imminent grew the moment when he knew he could no longer carry on the torture of acting. His brain strained with an irresistible impatience; his body burned with the fury of his eagerness to be off after the man who had gone alone into the city.

He could stand it no longer. A green foam misted his mouth, maddening him, he saw that, for the bare moment, nobody was looking.

Like a shot from a gun, he was off. He floated along in great, gliding leaps, a shadow among the shadows of the rocks. In a minute, the harsh terrain hid the spaceship and the two-legged beings.

Coeurl forgot the ship, forgot everything but his purpose, as if his brain had been wiped clear by a magic, memory-erasing brush. He circled widely, then raced into the city, along deserted streets, taking short cuts with the ease of familiarity, through gaping holes in time-weakened walls, through long corridors of moldering buildings. He slowed to a crouching lope as his ear tendrils caught the id vibrations.

Suddenly, he stopped and peered from a scatter of fallen rock. The man was standing at what must once have been a window, sending the glaring rays of his flashlight into the gloomy interior. The flashlight clicked off. The man, a heavy-set, powerful fellow, walked off with quick, alert steps. Coeurl didn't like that alertness. It presaged trouble; it meant lightning reaction to danger.

Coeurl waited till the human being had vanished around a corner, then he padded into the open. He was running now, tremendously faster than a man could walk, because his plan was clear in his brain. Like a wraith, he slipped down the next street, past a long block of buildings. He turned the first corner at top speed; and then, with dragging belly, crept into the hall-darkness between the building and a huge chunk of débris. The street ahead was barred by a solid line of loose rubble that made it like a valley, ending in a narrow, bottle-like neck. The neck had its outlet just below Coeurl.

His ear tendrils caught the log-frequency waves of whistling. The sound throbbed through his being; and suddenly terror caught with icy fingers at his brain. The man would have a gun. Suppose he leveled one burst of atomic energy—*one burst*—before his own muscles would whip out in murder fury.

A little shower of rocks streamed past. And then the man was beneath him. Coeurl reached out and struck a single crushing blow at the shimmering transparent headpiece of the spacesuit. There was a tearing sound of metal and a gushing of blood. The man doubled up as if part of him had been telescoped. For a moment, his bones and legs and muscles combined miraculously to keep him standing. Then he crumpled with a metallic clank of his space armor.

Fear completely evaporated, Coeurl leaped out of hiding. With ravenous speed, he smashed the metal and the body within it to bits. Great chunks of metal, torn piecemeal from the suit, sprayed the ground. Bones cracked. Flesh crunched.

It was simple to tune in on the virbrations of the id, and to create the violent chemical disorganization that freed it from the crushed bone. The id was, Coeurl discovered, mostly in the bone.

He felt revived, almost reborn. Here was more food than he had had in the whole past year.

Three minutes, and it was over, and Coeurl was off like a thing fleeing dire danger. Cautiously, he approached the glistening globe from the opposite side to that by which he had left. The men were all busy at their tasks. Gliding noiselessly, Coeurl slipped unnoticed up to a group of men.

Morton stared down at the horror of tattered flesh, metal and blood on the rock at his feet, and felt a tightening in his throat that prevented speech. He heard Kent say:

"He *would* go alone, damn him!" The little chemist's voice held a sob imprisoned; and Morton remembered that Kent and Jarvey had chummed together for years in the way only two men can.

"The worst part of it is," shuddered one of the men, "it looks like a senseless murder. His body is spread out like little lumps of flattened jelly, but it seems to be all there. I'd almost wager that if we weighed everything here, there'd still be one hundred and seventy-five pounds by earth gravity. That'd be about one hundred and seventy pounds here."

Smith broke in, his mournful face lined with gloom: "The killer attacked Jarvey, and then discovered his flesh was alien—uneatable. Just like our big cat. Wouldn't eat anything we set before him—" His words died out in sudden, queer silence. Then he said slowly: "Say, what about that creature? He's big enough and strong enough to have done this with his own little paws."

Morton frowned. "It's a thought. After all, he's the only living thing we've seen. We can't just execute him on suspicion, of course—"

"Besides," said one of the men, "he was never out of my sight."

Before Morton could speak, Siedel, the psychologist, snapped, "Positive about that?"

The man hesitated. "Maybe he was for a few minutes. He was wandering around so much, looking at everything."

"Exactly," said Siedel with satisfaction. He turned to Morton. "You see, commander, I, too, had the impression that he was always around; and yet, thinking back over it, I find gaps. There were moments—probably long minutes—when he was completely out of sight."

Morton's face was dark with thought, as Kent broke in fiercely: "I say, take no chances. Kill the brute on suspicion before he does any more damage."

Morton said slowly: "Korita, you've been wandering around with Cranessy and Van Horne. Do you think pussy is a descendant of the ruling class of this planet?"

The tall Japanese archeologist stared at the sky as if collecting his mind. "Commander Morton," he said finally, respectfully, "there is a mystery here. Take a look, all of you, at that majestic skyline. Notice the almost Gothic outline of the architecture. In spite of the magalopolis which they created, these people were close to the soil. The buildings are not simply ornamented. They are ornamental in themselves. Here is the equivalent of the Doric column, the Egyptian pyramid, the Gothic cathedral, growing out of the ground, earnest, big with destiny. If this lonely, desolate world can be regarded as a mother earth, then the land had a warm, a spiritual place in the hearts of the race.

"The effect is emphasized by the winding streets. Their machines prove they were mathematicians, but they were artists first; and so they did not create the geometrically designed cities of the ultra-sophisticated world metropolis. There is a genuine artistic abandon, a deep joyous emotion written in the curving and unmathematical arrangements of houses, buildings and avenues; a sense of intensity, of divine belief in an inner certainty. This is not a decadent, hoary-with-age civilization, but a young and vigorous culture, confident, strong with purpose.

"There it ended. Abruptly, as if at this point culture had its Battle of Tours, and began to collapse like the ancient Mohammedan civilization. Or as if in one leap it spanned the centuries and entered the period of contending states. In the Chinese civilization that period occupied 480–230 B.C., at the end of which the State of Tsin saw the beginning of the Chinese Empire. This phase Egypt experienced between 1780–1580 B.C., of which the last century was the 'Hyksos'—unmentionable—time. The classical experienced it from Chæronea—338—and, at the pitch of horror, from the Gracchi—133—to Actium—31 B.C. The West European Americans were devastated by it in the nineteenth and twentieth centuries, and modern historians agree that, nominally, we entered the same phase fifty years ago; though, of course, we have solved the problem.

"You may ask, commander, what has all this to do with

your question? My answer is: there is no record of a culture entering abruptly into the period of contending states. It is always a slow development; and the first step is a merciless questioning of all that was once held sacred. Inner certainties cease to exist, are dissolved before the ruthless probings of scientific and analytic minds. The skeptic becomes the highest type of being.

"I say that this culture ended abruptly in its most flourishing age. The sociological effects of such a catastrophe would be a sudden vanishing of morals, a reversion to almost bestial criminality, unleavened by any sense of ideal, a callous indifference to death. If this . . . this pussy is a descendant of such a race, then he will be a cunning creature, a thief in the night, a cold-blooded murderer, who would cut his own brother's throat for gain."

"That's enough!" It was Kent's clipped voice. "Commander, I'm willing to act the rôle of executioner."

Smith interrupted sharply: "Listen, Morton, you're not going to kill that cat yet, even if he is guilty. He's a biological treasure house."

Kent and Smith were glaring angrily at each other. Morton frowned at them thoughtfully, then said: "Korita, I'm inclined to accept your theory as a working basis. But one question: Pussy comes from a period earlier than our own? That is, we are entering the highly civilized era of our culture, while he became suddenly historyless in the most vigorous period of his. *But* is it possible that his culture is a later one on this planet than ours is in the galactic-wide system we have civilized?"

"Exactly. His may be the middle of the tenth civilization of his world; while ours is the end of the eighth sprung from earth, each of the ten, of course, having been builded on the the ruins of the one before it."

"In that case, pussy would not know anything about the skepticism that made it possible for us to find him out so positively as a criminal and murderer?"

"No; it would be literally magic to him."

Morton was smiling grimly. "Then I think you'll get your wish, Smith. We'll let pussy live; and if there are any fatalities, now that we know him, it will be due to rank carelessness. There's just the chance, of course, that we're wrong. Like Siedel, I also have the impression that he was always around. But now—we can't leave poor Jarvey here like this. We'll put him in a coffin and bury him."

"No, we won't!" Kent barked. He flushed. "I beg your pardon, commander. I didn't mean it that way. I maintain pussy wanted something from that body. It looks to be all there, but something must be missing. I'm going to find out what, and pin this murder on him so that you'll have to believe it beyond the shadow of a doubt."

It was late night when Morton looked up from the book and saw Kent emerge through the door that led from the laboratories below.

Kent carried a large, flat bowl in his hands; his tired eyes flashed across at Morton, and he said in a weary, yet harsh, voice: "Now watch!"

He started toward Coeurl, who lay sprawled on the great rug, pretending to be asleep.

Morton stopped him. "Wait a minute, Kent. Any other time, I wouldn't question your actions, but you look ill; you're overwrought. What have you got there?"

Kent turned, and Morton saw that his first impression had been but a flashing glimpse of the truth. There were dark pouches under the little chemist's gray eyes—eyes that gazed feverishly from sunken cheeks in an ascetic face.

"I've found the missing element," Kent said. "It's phosphorus. There wasn't so much as a square millimeter of phosphorus left in Jarvey's bones. Every bit of it had been drained out—by what superchemistry I don't know. There are ways of getting phosphorus out of the human body. For instance, a quick way was what happened to the workman who helped build this ship. Remember, he fell into fifteen tons of molten metalite—at least, so his relatives claimed—but the company wouldn't pay compensation until the metalite, on analysis, was found to contain a high percentage of phosphorus—"

"What about the bowl of food?" somebody interrupted. Men were putting away magazines and books, looking up with interest.

"It's got organic phosphorus in it. He'll get the scent, or whatever it is that he uses instead of scent—"

"I think he gets vibrations of things," Gourlay interjected lazily. "Sometimes, when he wiggles those tendrils, I get a distinct static on the radio. And then, again, there's no reaction, just as if he's moved higher or lower on the wave scale. He seems to control the vibrations at will."

Kent waited with obvious impatience until Gourlay's last

word, then abruptly went on: "All right, then, when he gets the vibration of the phosphorus and reacts to it like an animal, then—well, we can decide what we've proved by his reaction. Can I go ahead, Morton?"

"There are three things wrong with your plan," Morton said. "In the first place, you seem to assume that he is only animal; you seem to have forgotten he may not be hungry after Jarvey; you seem to think that he will not be suspicious. But set the bowl down. His reaction may tell us something."

Coeurl stared with unblinking black eyes as the man set the bowl before him. His ear tendrils instantly caught the id-vibrations from the contents of the bowl—and he gave it not even a second glance.

He recognized this two-legged being as the one who had held the weapon that morning. Danger! With a snarl, he floated to his feet. He caught the bowl with the fingerlike appendages at the end of one looping tentacle, and emptied its contents into the face of Kent, who shrank back with a yell.

Explosively, Coeurl flung the bowl aside and snapped a hawser-thick tentacle around the cursing man's waist. He didn't bother with the gun that hung from Kent's belt. It was only a vibration gun, he sensed—atomic powered, but not an atomic disintegrator. He tossed the kicking Kent onto the nearest couch—and realized with a hiss of dismay that he should have disarmed the man.

Not that the gun was dangerous—but, as the man furiously wiped the gruel from his face with one hand, he reached with the other for his weapon. Coeurl crouched back as the gun was raised slowly and a white beam of flame was discharged at his massive head.

His ear tendrils hummed as they canceled the efforts of the vibration gun. His round, black eyes narrowed as he caught the movement of men reaching for their metalite guns. Morton's voice lashed across the silence.

"Stop!"

Kent clicked off his weapon; and Coeurl crouched down, quivering with fury at this man who had forced him to reveal something of his power.

"Kent," said Morton coldly, "you're not the type to lose your head. You deliberately tried to kill pussy, knowing that the majority of us are in favor of keeping him alive. You know what our rule is: If anyone objects to my decisions, he must say so *at the time*. If the majority object, my decisions are overruled. In this case, no one but you objected, and, therefore, your action in taking the law into your own hands is most reprehensible, and automatically debars you from voting for a year."

Kent stared grimly at the circle of faces. "Korita was right when he said ours was a highly civilized age. It's decadent." Passion flamed harshly in his voice. "My God, isn't there a man here who can see the horror of the situation? Jarvey dead only a few hours, and this creature, whom we all know to be guilty, lying there unchained, planning his next murder; and the victim is right here in this room. What kind of men are we—fools, cynics, ghouls—or is it that our civilization is so steeped in reason that we can contemplate a murderer sympathetically?"

He fixed brooding eyes on Coeurl. "You were right, Morton, that's no animal. That's a devil from the deepest hell of this forgotten planet, whirling its solitary way around a dying sun."

"Don't go melodramatic on us," Morton said. "Your analysis is all wrong, so far as I am concerned. We're not ghouls or cynics; we're simply scientists, and pussy here is going to be studied. Now that we suspect him, we doubt his ability to trap any of us. One against a hundred hasn't a chance." He glanced around. "Do I speak for all of us?"

"Not for me, commander!" It was Smith who spoke, and, as Morton stared in amazement, he continued: "In the excitement and momentary confusion, no one seems to have noticed that when Kent fired his vibration gun, the beam hit this creature squarely on his cat head—and didn't hurt him."

Morton's amazed glance went from Smith to Coeurl, and back to Smith again. "Are you certain it hit him? As you say, it all happened so swiftly—when pussy wasn't hurt I simply assumed that Kent had missed him."

"He hit him in the face," Smith said positively. "A vibration gun, of course, can't even kill a man right away—but it can injure him. There's no sign of injury on pussy, though, not even a singed hair."

"Perhaps his skin is a good insulation against heat of any kind."

"Perhaps. But in view of our uncertainty, I think we should lock him up in the cage."

While Morton frowned darkly in thought, Kent spoke up. "Now you're talking sense, Smith."

Morton asked: "Then you would be satisfied, Kent, if we put him in the cage?"

Kent considered, finally: "Yes. If four inches of microsteel can't hold him, we'd better give him the ship."

Coeurl followed the men as they went out into the corridor. He trotted docilely along as Morton unmistakably motioned him through a door he had not hitherto seen. He found himself in a square, solid metal room. The door clanged metallically behind him; he felt the flow of power as the electric lock clicked home.

His lips parted in a grimace of hate, as he realized the trap, but he gave no other outward reaction. It occurred to him that he had progressed a long way from the sunk-into-primitiveness creature who, a few hours before, had gone incoherent with fear in an elevator cage. Now, a thousand memories of his powers were reawakened in his brain; ten thousand cunnings were, after ages of disuse, once again part of his very being.

He sat quite still for a moment on the short, heavy haunches into which his body tapered, his ear tendrils examining his surroundings. Finally, he lay down, his eyes glowing with contemptuous fire. The fools! The poor fools!

It was about an hour later when he heard the man—Smith—fumbling overhead. Vibrations poured upon him, and for just an instant he was startled. He leaped to his feet in pure terror—and then realized that the vibrations *were* vibrations, not atomic explosions. Somebody was taking pictures of the inside of his body.

He crouched down again, but his ear tendrils vibrated, and he thought contemptuously: the silly fool would be surprised when he tried to develop those pictures.

After a while the man went away, and for a long time there were noises of men doing things far away. That, too, died away slowly.

Coeurl lay waiting, as he felt the silence creep over the ship. In the long ago, before the dawn of immortality, the coeurls, too, had slept at night; and the memory of it had been revived the day before when he saw some of the men dozing. At last, the vibration of two pairs of feet, pacing, pacing endlessly, was the only human-made frequency that throbbed on his ear tendrils.

Tensely, he listened to the two watchmen. The first one walked slowly past the cage door. Then about thirty feet behind him came the second. Coeurl sensed the alertness of these men; knew that he could never surprise either while they walked separately. It meant—he must be doubly careful!

Fifteen minutes, and they came again. The moment they were past, he switched his senses from their vibrations to a vastly higher range. The pulsating violence of the atomic engines stammered its soft story to his brain. The electric dynamos hummed their muffled song of pure power. He felt the whisper of that flow through the wires in the walls of his cage, and through the electric lock of his door. He forced his quivering body into straining immobility, his senses seeking, searching to tune in on that sibilant tempest of energy. Suddenly, his ear tendrils vibrated in harmony—he caught the surging change into shrillness of that rippling force wave.

There was a sharp click of metal on metal. With a gentle touch of one tentacle, Coeurl pushed open the door, and glided out into the dully gleaming corridor. For just a moment, he felt contempt, a glow of superiority, as he thought of the stupid creatures who dared to match their wit against a coeurl. And in that moment, he suddenly thought of other coeurls. A queer, exultant sense of race pounded through his being; the driving hate of centuries of ruthless competition yielded reluctantly before pride of kinship with the future rulers of all space.

Suddenly, he felt weighed down by his limitations, his need for other coeurls, his aloneness—one against a hundred, with the stake all eternity; the starry universe itself beckoned his rapacious, vaulting ambition. If he failed, there would never be a second chance—no time to revive long-rotted machinery, and attempt to solve the secret of space travel.

He padded along on tensed paws—through the salon—into the next corridor—and came to the first bedroom door. It stood half open. One swift flow of synchronized muscles, one swiftly lashing tentacle that caught the unresisting throat of the sleeping man, crushing it; and the lifeless head rolled crazily, the body twitched once.

Seven bedrooms; seven dead men. It was the seventh taste of murder that brought a sudden return of lust, a pure, unbounded desire to kill, return of a millennium-old habit of destroying everything containing the precious id.

As the twelfth man slipped convulsively into death, Coeurl emerged abruptly from the sensuous joy of the kill to the sound of footsteps.

They were not near—that was what brought wave after wave of fright swirling into the chaos that suddenly became his brain.

The watchmen were coming slowly along the corridor

toward the door of the cage where he had been imprisoned. In a moment, the first man would see the open door—and sound the alarm.

Coeurl caught at the vanishing remnants of his reason. With frantic speed, careless now of accidental sounds, he raced—along the corridor with its bedroom doors—through the salon. He emerged into the next corridor, cringing in awful anticipation of the atomic flame he expected would stab into his face.

The two men were together, standing side by side. For one single instant, Coeurl could scarcely believe his tremendous good luck. Like a fool the second had come running when he saw the other stop before the open door. They looked up, paralyzed, before the nightmare of claws and tentacles, the ferocious cat head and hate-filled eyes.

The first man went for his gun, but the second, physically frozen before the doom he saw, uttered a shriek, a shrill cry of horror that floated along the corridors—and ended in a curious gurgle, as Coeurl flung the two corpses with one irresistible motion the full length of the corridor. He didn't want the dead bodies found near the cage. That was his one hope.

Shaking in every nerve and muscle, conscious of the terrible error he had made, unable to think coherently, he plunged into the cage. The door clicked softly shut behind him. Power flowed once more through the electric lock.

He crouched tensely, simulating sleep, as he heard the rush of many feet, caught the vibration of excited voices. He knew when somebody actuated the cage audioscope and looked in. A few moments now, and the other bodies would be discovered.

"Siedel gone!" Morton said numbly. "What are we going to do without Siedel? And Breckenridge! And Coulter and—Horrible!"

He covered his face with his hands, but only for an instant. He looked up grimly, his heavy chin outthrust as he stared into the stern faces that surrounded him. "If anybody's got so much as a germ of an idea, bring it out."

"Space madness!"

"I've thought of that. But there hasn't been a case of a man going mad for fifty years. Dr. Eggert will test everybody, of course, and right now he's looking at the bodies with that possibility in mind."

As he finished, he saw the doctor coming through the door. Men crowded aside to make way for him.

"I heard you, commander," Dr. Eggert said, "and I think I can say right now that the space-madness theory is out. The throats of these men have been squeezed to a jelly. No human being could have exerted such enormous strength without using a machine."

Morton saw that the doctor's eyes kept looking down the corridor, and he shook his head and groaned:

"It's no use suspecting pussy, doctor. He's in his cage, pacing up and down. Obviously heard the racket and—Man alive! You can't suspect him. That cage was built to hold literally *anything*—four inches of micro-steel—and there's not a scratch on the door. Kent, even you won't say, 'Kill him on suspicion,' because there can't be any suspicion, unless there's a new science here. Beyond anything we can imagine—"

"On the contrary," said Smith flatly, "we have all the evidence we need. I used the telefluor on him—you know the arrangement we have on top of the cage—and tried to take some pictures. They just blurred. Pussy jumped when the telefluor was turned on, as if he felt the vibrations.

"You all know what Gourlay said before? This beast can apparently receive and send vibrations of any lengths. The way he dominated the power of Kent's gun is final proof of his special ability to interfere with energy."

"What in the name of all the hells have you got here?" One of the men groaned. "Why, if he can control that power, and send it out in any vibrations, there's nothing to stop him killing all of us."

"Which proves," snapped Morton, "that he isn't invincible, or he would have done it long ago."

Very deliberately, he walked over to the mechanism that controlled the prison cage.

"You're not going to open the door!" Ken gasped, reaching for his gun.

"No, but if I pull this switch, electricity will flow through the floor, and electrocute whatever's inside. We've never had to use this before, so you had probably forgotten about it."

He jerked the switch hard over. Blue fire flashed from the metal, and a bank of fuses above his head exploded with a single bang.

Morton frowned. "That's funny. Those fuses shouldn't have blown! Well, we can't even look in, now. That wrecked the audios, too."

Smith said: "If he could interfere with the electric lock, enough to open the door, then he probably probed every possible danger and was ready to interfere when you threw that switch."

"At least, it proves he's vulnerable to our energies!" Morton smiled grimly. "Because he rendered them harmless. The important thing is, we've got him behind four inches of the toughest of metal. At the worst we can open the door and ray him to death. But first, I think we'll try to use the telefluor power cable—"

A commotion from inside the cage interrupted his words. A heavy body crushed against a wall, followed by a dull thump.

"He knows what we were trying to do!" Smith grunted to Morton. "And I'll bet it's a very sick pussy in there. What a fool he was to go back into the cage and does he realize it!"

The tension was relaxing; men were smiling nervously, and there was even a ripple of humorless laughter at the picture Smith drew of the monster's discomfiture.

"What I'd like to know," said Pennons, the engineer, "is, why did the telefluor meter dial jump and waver at full power when pussy made that noise? It's right under my nose here, and the dial jumped like a house afire!"

There was silence both without and within the cage, then Morton said: "It may mean he's coming out. Back, everybody, and keep your guns ready. Pussy was a fool to think he could conquer a hundred men, but he's by far the most formidable creature in the galactic system. He may come out of that door, rather than die like a rat in a trap. And he's just tough enough to take some of us with him—if we're not careful."

The men backed slowly in a solid body; and somebody said: "That's funny. I thought I heard the elevator."

"Elevator!" Morton echoed. "Are you sure, man?"

"Just for a moment I was!" The man, a member of the crew, hesitated. "We were all shuffling our feet—"

"Take somebody with you, and go look. Bring whoever dared to run off back here—"

There was a jar, a horrible jerk, as the whole gigantic body of the ship careened under them. Morton was flung to the floor with a violence that stunned him. He fought back to consciousness, aware of the other men lying all around him. He shouted: "Who the devil started those engines!"

The agonizing acceleration continued; his feet dragged with awful exertion, as he fumbled with the nearest audioscope, and punched the engine-room number. The picture that flooded onto the screen brought a deep bellow to his lips:

"It's pussy! He's in the engine room—and we're heading straight out into space."

The screen went black even as he spoke, and he could see no more.

It was Morton who first staggered across the salon floor to the supply room where the spacesuits were kept. After fumbling almost blindly into his own suit, he cut the effects of the body-torturing acceleration, and brought suits to the semiconscious men on the floor. In a few moments, other men were assisting him; and then it was only a matter of minutes before everybody was clad in metalite, with antiacceleration motors running at half power.

It was Morton then who, after first looking into the cage, opened the door and stood, silent as the others crowded about him, to stare at the gaping hole in the real wall. The hole was a frightful thing of jagged edges and horribly bent metal, and it opened upon another corridor.

"I'll swear," whispered Pennons, "that it's impossible. The ten-ton hammer in the machine shops couldn't more than dent four inches of micro with one blow—and we only heard one. It would take at least a minute for an atomic disintegrator to do the job. Morton, this is a super-being."

Morton saw that Smith was examining the break in the wall. The biologist looked up. "If only Breckenridge weren't dead! We need a metallurgist to explain this. Look!"

He touched the broken edge of the metal. A piece crumbled in his finger and slithered away in a fine shower of dust to the floor. Morton noticed for the first time that there was a little pile of metallic débris and dust.

"You've hit it." Morton nodded. "No miracle of strength here. The monster merely used his special powers to interfere with the electronic tensions holding the metal together. That would account, too, for the drain on the telefluor power cable that Pennons noticed. The thing used the power with his body as a transforming medium, smashed through the wall, ran down the corridor to the elevator shaft, and so down to the engine room."

"In the meantime, commander," Kent said quietly, "we are faced with a super-being in control of the ship, completely dominating the engine room, and its almost unlimited power, and in possession of the best part of the machine shops."

Morton felt the silence, while the men pondered the chemist's words. Their anxiety was a tangible thing that lay heavily upon their faces; in every expression was the growing realization that here was the ultimate situation in their lives; their very existence was at stake, and perhaps much more. Morton voiced the thought in everybody's mind:

"Suppose he wins. He's utterly ruthless, and he probably sees galactic power within his grasp."

"Kent is wrong," barked the chief navigator. "The thing doesn't dominate the engine room. We've still got the control room, and that gives us, *first* control of all the machines. You fellows may not know the mechanical set-up we have; but though he can eventually disconnect us, we can cut off all the switches in the engine room *now*. Commander, why didn't you just shut off the power instead of putting us into spacesuits? At the very least you could have adjusted the ship to the acceleration."

"For two reasons," Morton answered. "Individually, we're safer within the force fields of our spacesuits. And we can't afford to give up our advantages in panicky moves."

"Advantages. What other advantages have we got?"

"We know things about him," Morton replied. "And right now, we're going to make a test. Pennons, detail five men to each of the four approaches to the engine room. Take atomic disintegrators to blast through the big doors. They're all shut, I noticed. He's locked himself in.

"Selenski, you go up to the control room and shut off everything except the drive engines. Gear them to the master switch, and shut them off all at once. One thing though—leave the acceleration on full blast. No anti-acceleration must be applied to the ship. Understand?"

"Aye, sir!" The pilot saluted.

"And report to me through the communicators if any of the machines start to run again." He faced the men. "I'm going to lead the main approach. Kent, you take No. 2; Smith, No. 3, and Pennons, No. 4. We're going to find out right now if we're dealing with unlimited science, or a creature limited like the rest of us. I'll bet on the last possibility."

Morton had an empty sense of walking endlessly, as he moved, a giant of a man in his transparent space armor, along the glistening metal tube that was the main corridor of the engine-room floor. Reason told him the creature had already shown feet of clay, yet the feeling that here was an invincible being persisted.

He spoke into the communicator: "It's no use trying to sneak up on him. He can probably hear a pin drop. So just wheel up your units. He hasn't been in that engine room long enough to do anything."

"As I've said, this is largely a test attack. In the first place, we could never forgive ourselves if we didn't try to conquer him now, before he's had time to prepare against us. But, aside from the possibility that we can destroy him immediately, I have a theory.

"The idea goes something like this: Those doors are built to withstand accidental atomic explosions, and it will take fifteen minutes for the atomic disintegrators to smash them. During that period the monster will have no power. True, the drive will be on, but that's straight atomic explosion. My theory is, he can't touch stuff like that; and in a few minutes you'll see what I mean—I hope."

His voice was suddenly crisp: "Ready, Selenski?"

"Aye, ready."

"Then cut the master switch."

The corridor—the whole ship, Morton knew—was abruptly plunged into darkness. Morton clicked on the dazzling light of his spacesuit; the other men did the same, their faces pale and drawn.

"Blast!" Morton barked into his communicator.

The mobile units throbbed; and then pure atomic flame ravened out and poured upon the hard metal of the door. The first molten droplet rolled reluctantly, not down, but up the door. The second was more normal. It followed a shaky downward course. The third rolled sideways—for this was pure force, not subject to gravitation. Other drops followed until a dozen streams trickled sedately yet unevenly in every direction—streams of hellish, sparkling fire, bright as fairy gems, alive with the coruscating fury of atoms suddenly tortured, and running blindly, crazy with pain.

The minutes ate at time like a slow acid. At last Morton asked huskily:

"Selenski?"

"Nothing yet, commander."

Morton half whispered: "But he must be doing something. He can't be just waiting in there like a cornered rat. Selenski?"

"Nothing, commander."

Seven minutes, eight minutes, then twelve.

"Commander!" It was Selenski's voice, taut. "He's got the electric dynamo running."

Morton drew a deep breath, and heard one of his men say:

"That's funny. We can't get any deeper. Boss, take a look at this."

Morton looked. The little scintillating streams had frozen rigid. The ferocity of the disintegrators vented in vain against metal grown suddenly invulnerable.

Morton sighed. "Our test is over. Leave two men guarding every corridor. The others come up to the control room."

He seated himself a few minutes later before the massive control keyboard. "So far as I'm concerned the test was a success. We know that of all the machines in the engine room, the most important to the monster was the electric dynamo. He must have worked in a frenzy of terror while we were at the doors."

"Of course, it's easy to see what he did," Pennons said. "Once he had the power he increased the electronic tensions of the door to their ultimate."

"The main thing is this," Smith chimed in. "He works with vibrations only so far as his special powers are concerned, and the energy must come from outside himself. Atomic energy in its pure form, not being vibration, he can't handle any differently than we can."

Kent said glumly: "The main point in my opinion is that he stopped us cold. What's the good of knowing that his control over vibrations did it? If we can't break through those doors with our atomic disintegrators, we're finished."

Morton shook his head. "Not finished—but we'll have to do some planning. First, though, I'll start these engines. It'll be harder for him to get control of them when they're running."

He pulled the master switch back into place with a jerk. There was a hum, as scores of machines leaped into violent life in the engine room a hundred feet below. The noises sank to a steady vibration of throbbing power.

Three hours later, Morton paced up and down before the men gathered in the salon. His dark hair was uncombed; the space pallor of his strong face emphasized rather than detracted from the outthrust aggressiveness of his jaw. When he spoke, his deep voice was crisp to the point of sharpness:

"To make sure that our plans are fully co-ordinated, I'm going to ask each expert in turn to outline his part in the overpowering of this creature. Pennons first!"

Pennons stood up briskly. He was not a big man, Morton thought, yet he looked big, perhaps because of his air of authority. This man knew engines, and the history of engines. Morton had heard him trace a machine through its evolution from a simple toy to the highly complicated modern instrument. He had studied machine development on a hundred planets; and there was literally nothing fundamental that he didn't know about mechanics. It was almost weird to hear Pennons, who could have spoken for a thousand hours and still only have touched upon his subject, say with absurd brevity:

"We've set up a relay in the control room to start and stop every engine rhythmically. The trip lever will work a hundred times a second, and the effect will be to create vibrations of every description. There is just a possibility that one or more of the machines will burst, on the principle of soldiers crossing a bridge in step—you've heard that old story, no doubt—but in my opinion there is no real danger of a break of that tough metal. The main purpose is simply to interfere with the interference of the creature, and smash through the doors."

"Gourlay next!" barked Morton.

Gourlay climbed lazily to his feet. He looked sleepy, as if he was somewhat bored by the whole proceedings, yet Morton knew he loved people to think him lazy, a good-for-nothing slouch, who spent his days in slumber and his nights catching forty winks. His title was chief communication engineer, but his knowledge extended to every vibration field; and he was probably, with the possible exception of Kent, the fastest thinker on the ship. His voice drawled out, and—Morton noted—the very deliberate assurance of it had a soothing effect on the men—anxious faces relaxed, bodies leaned back more restfully:

"Once inside," Gourlay said, "we've rigged up vibration screens of pure force that should stop nearly everything he's got on the ball. They work on the principle of reflection, so that everything he sends will be reflected back to him. In addition, we've got plenty of spare electric energy that we'll just feed him from mobile copper cups. There must be a limit to his capacity for handling power with those insulated nerves of his."

"Selenski!" called Morton.

The chief pilot was already standing, as he had anticipated Morton's call. And that, Morton reflected, was the man. His nerves had that rocklike steadiness which is the first requirement of the master controller of a great ship's movements; yet that very steadiness seemed to rest on dynamite ready to explode at its owner's volition. He was not a man of great learning, but he "reacted" to stimuli so fast that he always seemed to be anticipating.

"The impression I've received of the plan is that it must be cumulative. Just when the creature thinks that he can't stand any more, another thing happens to add to his trouble and confusion. When the uproar's at its height, I'm supposed to cut in the anti-accelerators. The commander thinks with Gunlie Lester that these creatures will know nothing about anti-acceleration. It's a development, pure and simple, of the science of interstellar flight, and couldn't have been developed in any other way. We think when the creature feels the first effects of the anti-acceleration—you all remember the caved-in feeling you had the first month—it won't know what to think or do."

"Korita next."

"I can only offer you encouragement," said the archeologist, "on the basis of my theory that the monster has all the characteristics of a criminal of the early ages of any civilization, complicated by an apparent reversion to primitiveness. The suggestion has been made by Smith that his knowledge of science is puzzling, and could only mean that we are dealing with an actual inhabitant, not a descendant of the inhabitants of the dead city we visited. This would ascribe a virtual immortality to our enemy, a possibility which is borne out by his ability to breathe both oxygen and chlorine—or neither—but even that makes no difference. He comes from a certain age in his civilization; and he has sunk so low that his ideas are mostly memories of that age.

"In spite of all the powers of his body, he lost his head in the elevator the first morning, until he remembered. He placed himself in such a position that he was forced to reveal his special powers against vibrations. He bungled the mass murders a few hours ago. In fact, his whole record is one of the low cunning of the primitive, egotistical mind which has little or no conception of the vast organization with which it is confronted.

"He is like the ancient German soldier who felt superior to the elderly Roman scholar, yet the latter was part of a mighty civilization of which the Germans of that day stood in awe.

"You may suggest that the sack of Rome by the Germans

in later years defeats my argument; however, modern historians agree that the 'sack' was an historical accident, and not history in the true sense of the word. The movement of the 'Sea-peoples' which set in against the Egyptian civilization from 1400 B.C. succeeded only as regards the Cretan island-realm—their mighty expeditions against the Libyan and Phœnician coasts, with the accompaniment of Viking fleets, failed as those of the Huns failed against the Chinese Empire. Rome would have been abandoned in any event. Ancient, glorious Samarra was desolate by the tenth century; Pataliputra, Asoka's great capital, was an immense and completely uninhabited waste of houses when the Chinese traveler Hsinan-tang visited it about A.D. 635.

"We have, then, a primitive, and that primitive is now far out in space, completely outside of his natural habitat. I say, let's go in and win."

One of the men grumbled, as Korita finished: "You can talk about the sack of Rome being an accident, and about this fellow being a primitive, but the facts are facts. It looks to me as if Rome is about to fall again; and it won't be no primitive that did it, either. This guy's got plenty of what it takes."

Morton smiled grimly at the man, a member of the crew. "We'll see about that—right now!"

In the blazing brilliance of the gigantic machine shop, Coeurl slaved. The forty-foot, cigar-shaped spaceship was nearly finished. With a grunt of effort, he completed the laborious installation of the drive engines, and paused to survey his craft.

Its interior, visible through the one aperture in the outer wall, was pitifully small. There was literally room for nothing but the engines—and a narrow space for himself.

He plunged frantically back to work as he heard the approach of the men, and the sudden change in the tempest-like thunder of the engines—a rhythmical off-and-on hum, shriller in tone, sharper, more nerve-racking than the deep-throated, steady throb that had preceded it. Suddenly, there were the atomic disintegrators again at the massive outer doors.

He fought them off, but never wavered from his task. Every mighty muscle of his powerful body strained as he carried great loads of tools, machines and instruments, and dumped them into the bottom of his makeshift ship. There was no time to fit anything into place, no time for anything—no time—no time.

The thought pounded at his reason. He felt strangely weary for the first time in his long and vigorous existence. With a last, tortured heave, he jerked the gigantic sheet of metal into the gaping aperture of the ship—and stood there for a terrible minute, balancing it precariously.

He knew the doors were going down. Half a dozen disintegrators concentrating on one point were irresistibly, though slowly, eating away the remaining inches. With a gasp, he released his mind from the doors and concentrated every ounce of his mind on the yard-thick outer wall, toward which the blunt nose of his ship was pointing.

His body cringed from the surging power that flowed from the electric dynamo through his ear tendrils into that resisting wall. The whole inside of him felt on fire, and he knew that he was dangerously close to carrying his ultimate load.

And still he stood there, shuddering with the awful pain, holding the unfastened metal plate with hard-clenched tentacles. His massive head pointed as in dread fascination at that bitterly hard wall.

He heard one of the engine-room doors crash inward. Men shouted; disintegrators rolled forward, their raging power unchecked. Coeurl heard the floor of the engine room hiss in protest, as those beams of atomic energy tore everything in their path to bits. The machines rolled closer; cautious footsteps sounded behind them. In a minute they would be at the flimsy doors separating the engine room from the machine shop.

Suddenly, Coeurl was satisfied. With a snarl of hate, a vindictive glow of feral eyes, he ducked into his little craft, and pulled the metal plate down into place as if it were a hatchway.

His ear tendrils hummed, as he softened the edges of the surrounding metal. In an instant, the plate was more than welded—it was part of his ship, a seamless, rivetless part of a whole that was solid opaque metal except for two transparent areas, one in the front, one in the rear.

His tentacle embraced the power drive with almost sensuous tenderness. There was a forward surge of his fragile machine, straight at the great outer wall of the machine shops. The nose of the forty-foot craft touched—and the wall dissolved in a glittering shower of dust.

Coeurl felt the barest retarding movement; and then he

kicked the nose of the machine out into the cold of space, twisted it about, and headed back in the direction from which the big ship had been coming all these hours.

Men in space armor stood in the jagged hole that yawned in the lower reaches of the gigantic globe. The men and the great ship grew smaller. Then the men were gone; and there was only the ship with its blaze of a thousand blurring portholes. The ball shrank incredibly, too small now for individual portholes to be visible.

Almost straight ahead, Coeurl saw a tiny, dim, reddish ball—his own sun, he realized. He headed toward it at full speed. There were caves where he would hide and with other coeurls build secretly a spaceship in which they could reach other planets safely—now that he knew how.

His body ached from the agony of acceleration, yet he dared not let up for a single instant. He glanced back, half in terror. The globe was still there, a tiny dot of light in the immense blackness of space. Suddenly it twinkled and was gone.

For a brief moment, he had the empty, frightened impression that just before it disappeared, it moved. But he could see nothing. He could not escape the belief that they had shut off all their lights, and were sneaking up on him in the darkness. Worried and uncertain, he looked through the forward transparent plate.

A tremor of dismay shot through him. The dim red sun toward which he was heading was not growing larger. *It was becoming smaller* by the instant, and it grew visibly tinier during the next five minutes, became a pale-red dot in the sky—and vanished like the ship.

Fear came then, a blinding surge of it, that swept through his being and left him chilled with the sense of the unknown. For minutes, he stared frantically into the space ahead, searching for some landmark. But only the remote stars glimmered there, unwinking points against a velvet background of unfathomable distance.

Wait! One of the points was growing larger. With every muscle and nerve tense, Coeurl watched the point becoming a dot, a round ball of light—red light. Bigger, bigger, it grew. Suddenly, the red light shimmered and turned white—and there, before him, was the great globe of the spaceship, lights glaring from every porthole, the very ship which a few minutes before he had watched vanish behind him.

Something happened to Coeurl in that moment. His brain was spinning like a flywheel, faster, faster, more incoherently.

Suddenly, the wheel flew apart into a million aching fragments. His eyes almost started from their sockets as, like a maddened animal, he raged in his small quarters.

His tentacles clutched at precious instruments and flung them insensately; his paws smashed in fury at the very walls of his ship. Finally, in a brief flash of sanity, he knew that he couldn't face the inevitable fire of atomic disintegrators.

It was a simple thing to create the violent disorganization that freed every drop of id from his vital organs.

They found him lying dead in a little pool of phosphorus.

"Poor pussy," said Morton. "I wonder what he thought when he saw us appear ahead of him, after his own sun disappeared. Knowing nothing of anti-accelerators, he couldn't know that we could stop short in space, whereas it would take him more than three hours to decelerate; and in the meantime he'd be drawing farther and farther away from where he wanted to go. He couldn't know that by stopping, we flashed past him at millions of miles a second. Of course, he didn't have a chance once he left our ship. The whole world must have seemed topsy-turvy."

"Never mind the sympathy," he heard Kent say behind him. "We've got a job—to kill every cat in that miserable world."

Korita murmured softly: "That should be simple. They are but primitives; and we have merely to sit down, and they will come to us, cunningly expecting to delude us."

Smith snapped: "You fellows make me sick! Pussy was the toughest nut we ever had to crack. He had everything he needed to defeat us—"

Morton smiled as Korita interrupted blandly: "Exactly, my dear Smith, except that he reacted according to the biological impulses of his type. His defeat was already foreshadowed when we unerringly analyzed him as a criminal from a certain era of his civilization.

"It was history, honorable Mr. Smith, our knowledge of history that defeated him," said the Japanese archeologist, reverting to the ancient politeness of his race.

GREATER THAN GODS

Astounding Science Fiction, July

by C. L. Moore (1911–   )

One of the pioneer women science fiction writers, Catherine (the C. L. is dramatic evidence of the then status of women in the field) Moore wrote in collaboration with Henry Kuttner after their marriage in 1940. Previously, she was best known for her female fantasy character "Jirel of Jory" who appeared in a series of stories in Weird Tales, *and the "Northwest Smith" stories in the sf magazines of the thirties. Both series were outstanding, and very popular.*

"Greater Than Gods" is a non-series story about an alternate future. It is also about choosing, one of the most difficult of all human activities.

(Science fiction in the Self-conscious Seventies is as much a female activity, both in the reading and writing, as it is a male activity, but it wasn't always thus. Right through the Golden Age, it was almost entirely masculine. But even in the depth of the male-chauvinist Thirties there were women who dared, successfully, to compete. C. L. Moore was perhaps the best of these, but Leslie F. Stone and A. R. Long were two others. Notice the use of initials and epicene given names to hide the fatal feminism of the writers. IA)

The desk was glass-clear steel, the mirror above it a window that opened upon distance and sight and sound whenever the televisor buzzer rang. The two crystal cubes on the desk were three-dimensional photographs of a sort undreamed of before the Twenty-third Century dawned. But between them on the desk lay a letter whose message was older than the history of writing itself.

"*My darling*—" it began in a man's strongly slanting handwriting. But there Bill Cory had laid down his pen and run despairing fingers through his hair, looking from one crystal-cubed photograph to the other and swearing a little under his breath. It was fine stuff, he told himself savagely, when a man couldn't even make up his mind which of two girls he wanted to marry. Biology House of Science City, that trusted so faithfully the keenness and clarity of Dr. William Cory's decisions, would have shuddered to see him now.

For the hundredth time that afternoon he looked from one girl's face to the other, smiling at him from the crystal cubes, and chewed his lip unhappily. On his left, in the translucent block that had captured an immortal moment when dark Marta Mayhew smiled, the three-dimensional picture looked out at him with a flash of violet eyes. Dr. Marta Mayhew of Chemistry House, ivory whiteness and satin blackness. Not at all the sort of picture the mind conjures up of a leading chemist in Science City which houses the greatest scientists in the world.

Bill Cory wrinkled his forehead and looked at the other girl. Sallie Carlisle dimpled at him out of the crystal, as real as life itself to the last flying tendril of fair curls that seemed to float on a breeze frozen eternally into glass. Bill reached out to turn the cube a little, bringing the delicate line of her profile into view, and it was as if time stood still in the crystalline deeps and pretty Sallie in the breathing flesh paused for an eternal moment with her profile turned away.

After a long moment Bill Cory sighed and picked up his pen. After the *"darling"* of the letter he wrote firmly, *"Sallie."*

"Dr. Cory," hesitated a voice at the door. Bill looked up, frowning. Miss Brown blinked at him nervously behind her glasses. "Dr. Ashley's—"

"Don't announce me, Brownie," interrupted a languid voice behind her. " I want to catch him loafing. Ah, Bill, writing love letters? May I come in?"

"Could I stop you?" Bill's grin erased the frown from his forehead. The tall and tousled young man in the doorway was Charles Ashley, head of Telepathy House, and though their acquaintance had long been on terms of good-natured insult, behind it lay Bill's deep recognition of a quality of genius in Ashley that few men ever attain. No one could have risen to the leadership of Telepathy House whose mind did not encompass many more levels of infinite understanding than the ordinary mind even recognizes.

"I've worked myself into a stupor," announced the head of Telepathy House, yawning. "Come on up to the Gardens for a swim, huh?"

"Can't." Bill laid down his pen. "I've got to see the pups—"

"Damn the pups! You think Science City quivers every time those little mutts yap! Let Miss Brown look after 'em. She knows more than you do about genetics, anyhow. Some day the Council's going to find it out and you'll go back to working for a living."

"Shut up," requested Bill with a grin. "How are the pups, Miss Brown?"

"Perfectly normal, doctor. I just gave them their three o'clock feeding and they're asleep now."

"Do they seem happy?" inquired Ashley solicitously.

"That's right, scoff," sighed Bill. "Those pups and I will go ringing down the corridors of time, you mark my words."

Ashley nodded, half seriously. He knew it might well be true. The pups were the living proof of Bill's success in prenatal sex determination—six litters of squirming maleness with no female among them. They represented the fruit of long, painstaking experiments in the X-ray bombardment of chromosomes to separate and identify the genes carrying the factors of sex determination, of countless failures and immeasurable patience. If the pups grew into normal dogs—well, it would be one long, sure stride nearer the day when, through Bill's own handiwork, the world would be perfectly balanced between male and female in exact proportion to the changing need.

Miss Brown vanished with a shy, self-effacing smile. As the door closed behind her, Ashley, who had been regarding the two photograph cubes on Bill's desk with a lifted eyebrow, arranged his long length on the couch against the wall and was heard to murmur: "Eenie-meenie-minie-mo. Which is it going to be, Will-yum?"

They were on terms too intimate for Bill to misunderstand, or pretend to.

GREATER THAN GODS

"I don't know," he admitted miserably, glancing down in some hesitation at the letter beginning, *"My darling Sallie—"*

Ashley yawned again and fumbled for a cigarette. "You know," he murmured comfortably, "it's interesting to speculate on your possible futures. With Marta or Sallie, I mean. Maybe some day somebody will find a way to look ahead down the branching paths of the future and deliberately select the turning points that will carry him toward the goal he chooses. Now if you could know beforehand where life with Sallie would lead, or life with Marta, you might alter the whole course of human history. That is, if you're half as important as you think you are."

"Huh-uh," grunted Bill. "If you predicate a fixed future, then it's fixed already, isn't it? And you'd have no real choice."

Ashley scratched a match deliberately and set his cigarette aglow before he said: "I think of the future as an infinite reservoir of an infinite number of futures, each of them fixed, yet malleable as clay. Do you see what I mean? At every point along our way we confront crossroads at which we make choices among the many possible things we may do the next moment. Each crossroad leads to a different future, all of them possible, all of them fixed, waiting for our choice to give them reality. Perhaps there's a—call it a Plane of Probability—where all these possible results of our possible choices exist simultaneously. Blueprints of things to come. When the physical time of matter catches up with, and fills in, any one particular plan, it becomes fixed in the present.

"But before time has caught up with it, while our choice at the crossroads is still unmade, an infinite number of possible futures must exist as it were in suspension, waiting for us in some unimaginable, dimensionless infinity. Can you imagine what it would be like to open a window upon that Probability Plane, look out into the infinities of the future, trace the consequences of future actions *before* we make them? We could mold the destiny of mankind! We could do what the gods must do, Bill! We'd be greater than gods! We could look into the Cosmic Mind—the very brain that planned us—and of our own will choose among those plans!"

"Wake up, Ash," said Bill softly.

"You think I'm dreaming? It's not a new idea, really. The old philosopher, Berkeley, had a glimpse of it when he taught his theories of subjective idealism, that we're aware of the cosmos only through a greater awareness all around us, an infinite mind—

"Listen, Bill. If you vision these . . . these blueprints of possible futures, you've got to picture countless generations, finite as ourselves, existing simultaneously and completely in all the circumstances of their entire lives—yet all of them still unborn, still even uncertain of birth if the course of the present is diverted from their particular path. To themselves, they must seem as real as we to each other.

"Somewhere on the Plane of Probability, Bill, there may be two diverging lines of your descendants, unborn generations whose very existence hinges on your choice here at the crossroads. Projections of yourself, really, their lives and deaths trembling in the balance. Think well before you choose!"

Bill grinned. "Suppose you go back to the Slum and dope out a way for me to look into the Cosmic Plan," he suggested.

Ashley shook his head.

"Wish I could. Boy, would you eat that word 'Slum' then! Telepathy House wouldn't be the orphan child around the City any longer if I could really open a window onto the Probability Plane. I wouldn't bother with you and your pint-sized problems. I'd look ahead into the future of the City. It's the heart of the world, now. Some day it may rule the world. And we're biased, you know. We can't help being. With all the sciences housed here under one city-wide roof, wielding powers that kings never dreamed of— No, it may go to our heads. We may overbalance into . . . into . . . well, I'd like to look ahead and prevent it. And if this be treason—" He shrugged and got up. "Sure you won't join me?"

"Go on—get out. I'm a busy man."

"So I see." Ashley twitched an eyebrow at the two crystal cubes. "Maybe it's good you can't look ahead. The responsibility of choosing might be heavier than you could bear. After all, we aren't gods and it must be dangerous to usurp a god's prerogative. Well, see you later."

Bill leaned in the doorway watching the lounging figure down the hall toward the landing platform where crystal cars waited to go flashing along the great tubes which artery Science City. Beyond, at the platform's edge, the great central plaza of the City dropped away in a breath-taking void a hundred stories deep. He stood looking out blind-eyed, wondering if Sallie or Marta would walk this hall in years to come.

Life would be more truly companionship with Marta, perhaps. But did a family need two scientists! A man wanted relaxation at home, and who could make life gayer than pretty Sallie with her genius for entertainment, her bubbling laughter? Yes, let it be Sallie. If there were indeed a Probability Plane where other possible futures hung suspended, halfway between waking and oblivion, let them wink out into nothingness.

He shut the door with a little slam to wake himself out of the dream, greeting the crystal-shrined girl on his desk with a smile. She was so real—the breeze blowing those curls was a breeze in motion. The lashes should flutter against the soft fullness of her lids—

Bill squeezed his eyes shut and shook his head to clear it. There was something wrong—the crystal was clouding—

A ringing in his ears grew louder in company with that curious blurring of vision. From infinitely far away, yet strangely in his own ears, a tiny voice came crying. A child's voice calling, "Daddy. . . . daddy!" A girl's voice, coming nearer, "Father—" A woman's voice saying over and over in a smooth, sweet monotone, "Dr. Cory. . . . Dr. William Cory—"

Upon the darkness behind his closed lids a streaked and shifting light moved blurrily. He thought he saw towers in the sun, forests, robed people walking leisurely—and it all seemed to rush away from his closed eyes so bewilderingly—he lifted his lids to stare at—

To stare at the cube where Sallie smiled. Only this was not Sallie. He gaped with the blankness of a man confronting impossibilities. It was not wholly Sallie now, but there was a look of Sallie upon the lovely, sun-touched features in the cube. All of her sweetness and softness, but with it—something more. Something familiar. What upon this living, lovely face, with its level brown eyes and courageous mouth, reminded Bill of—himself?

His hands began to shake a little. He thrust them into his pockets and sat down without once taking his eyes from the living stare in the cube. There was amazement in that other stare, too, and a half-incredulous delight that brightened as he gazed.

Then the sweet curved lips moved—lips with the softness of Sallie's closing on the firm, strong line of Bill's. They said distinctly, in a sound that might have come from the cube itself or from somewhere deep within his own brain: "Dr. Cory . . . Dr. Cory, do you hear me?"

"I hear you," he heard himself saying hoarsely, like a man talking in a dream. "But—"

The face that was Sallie's and his blended blazed into joyful recognition, dimples denting the smooth cheeks with delicious mirth. "Oh, thank Heaven it *is* you! I've reached through at last. I've tried so hard, so long—"

"But who . . . what—" Bill choked a little on his own amazement and fell silent, marveling at the strange warm tenderness that was flooding up in him as he watched this familiar face he had never seen before. A tenderness more melting and protective and passionately selfless than he had ever imagined a man could feel. Dizzy with complete bewilderment, too confused to wonder if he dreamed, he tried again. "Who are you? What are you doing here? How did—"

"But I'm not there—not really." The sweet face smiled again, and Bill's heart swelled until his throat almost closed with a warmth of pride and tenderness he was too dizzy to analyze now. "I'm here—here at home in Eden, talking to you across the millennium! Look—"

Somehow, until then he had not seen beyond her. Sallie's face had smiled out of a mist of tulle, beyond which the cube had been crystal-clear. But behind the face which was no longer wholly Sallie's, a green hillside filled the cube. And, very strangely, it had no look of smallness. Though the cube's dimensions confined it, here was no miniature scene he gazed upon. He looked through the cube as through a window, out into a forest glade where upon a bank of green myrtle at the foot of a white garden wall a little group of tanned men and women reclined in a circle with closed eyes, lying almost like corpses on the dark, glossy leaves. But there was no relaxation in them. Tensity more of the spirit than the body knit the group into a whole, focused somehow upon the woman in the circle's center—this fair-haired woman who leaned forward with her elbows on her knees, chin in hand, staring brown-eyed and tensely into space—into Bill Cory's eyes. Dimly he realized that his perception had expanded as he stared. Awareness now of a whole countryside beyond her, just over the garden wall, made this cube that had housed Sallie's careless smile a window indeed, opening upon distance in space and time far outside his imagining.

GREATER THAN GODS

He knew he was dreaming. He was sure of it, though the memory of what Ashley had been saying hovered uneasily in the back of his mind, too elusive now to be brought consciously into view. But in this impossible dream he clenched his hands hard in his pockets, taking a firm hold upon reality.

"Just who are you, and what do you want? And how did you—"

She chose to answer the last question first, breaking into it as if she could read his thoughts as she knelt staring on the myrtle leaves.

"I speak to you along an unbroken cord between us—father. Thousands of times removed, but—father. A cord that runs back through the lives that have parted us, yet which unite us. With the help of these people around me, their full mental strength supplementing mine, we've established contact at last, after so many failures, so much groping in mysteries which even I understand only partly, though my family for generations has been trained in the secrets of heredity and telepathy."

"But why—"

"Isn't the fact of achievement an end in itself? Success in establishing a two-way contact with the past, in talking to one's own ancestors—do I need more reason for attempting that than the pure joy of achieving it? You wonder why you were chosen. Is that it? Because you are the last man in a direct line of males to be born into my family before the blessed accident that saved the world from itself.

"Don't look so bewildered!" Laughter bubbled from the cube—or was it a sound in his own brain? "You aren't dreaming! Is it so incredible that along the unbroken cord of memories which links your mind to mine the current might run backward against the time flow?"

"But who are you? Your face—it's like—"

"My face is the face of the daughter that Sallie Cory bore you, thousands of years ago. That resemblance is a miracle and a mystery beyond all understanding—the mystery of heredity which is a stranger thing than the fact of our communication. We have wondered among ourselves if immortality itself—but no, I'll have mercy on you!"

This bewilderingly beloved face that had darkened with mystical brooding, flashed suddenly alive again with swift laughter, and hearing it, catching a lift of the brows that was his and a quirk of the soft lips that was Sallie's own, Bill made no effort to stem the tide of warm affection rising higher and higher in him. It was himself looking out of this cube through Sallie's brown eyes—himself exultant in achievement for the simple sake of achieving. She had called him father. Was this a father's love, selfless, unfathomable, for a lovely and beloved daughter?

"Don't wonder any more," laughed the voice in his ears. "Look—here's the past that lies between us. I want you to understand what parts your world from mine."

Softly the myrtle glade and the lovely smiling face that blended Sallie and Bill melted into the depths of a cloud forming inside the three dimensions of the cube. For a moment—nothing. Then motion was lifting behind the mist, shouldering the veils aside. Three-dimensional space seemed to open up all around him—

He saw a wedding procession coming down a church aisle toward him, Sallie smiling mistily through a cloud of silver tulle. And he knew at the sight of her that though it was only chance which had chosen her instead of dark Marta Mayhew, he could come to love Sallie Carlisle Cory with an intensity almost frightening.

He saw time go by with a swiftness like thought itself, events telescoping together with no sense of confusion, moving like memories through his mind, clear, yet condensed into split seconds. He was watching his own future, seeing a life that revolved around Sallie as the center of existence. He saw her flashing in and out of his laboratory as he worked, and whenever she entered, the whole room seemed to light up; whenever she left, he could scarcely work for the longing to follow.

He saw their first quarrel. Sallie, spinning in a shimmer of bright glass-silk as soft as gossamer, dimpled at the self which in this waking dream was more vividly Bill Cory than the Bill who watched. "See, darling, aren't I heavenly?" And he heard himself answering, "Edible, darling! But isn't that stuff expensive?"

Sallie's laughter was light. "Only fifteen hundred credits. That's dirt-cheap for a Skiparelle model."

He gasped. "Why Sallie, that's more than we're allowed for living expenses! I can't—"

"Oh, daddy'll pay for it if you're going to be stingy. I only wanted—"

"I'll buy my wife's clothes." Bill was grim. "But I can't afford Paris fashions, darling."

Sallie's pretty underlip pouted alarmingly. Tears sparkled

in the soft brown eyes she lifted to his, and his heart melted almost painfully in one hopeless rush.

"Don't cry, sweetheart! You can keep it, just this once. But we'll have to make it up next month. Never again, Sallie, understand?"

Her nod was bright and oblivious as a child's.

But they didn't make it up. Sallie loved partying, and Bill loved Sallie, and nowadays there was much more hilarity than work going on behind the door in Biology House marked "Dr. William Vincent Cory." The television's panels were tuned to orchestras playing strong rhythm now, not to lectures and laboratory demonstrations as of old.

No man can do two jobs well. The work on sex determination began to strike snags in the path that had seemed almost clear to success, and Bill had so little time any more to smooth them out. Always Sallie was in the back of his mind, sweet, smiling, adorable.

Sallie wanted the baby to be born in her father's home. It was a lovely place, white-walled on low green hills above the Pacific. Sallie loved it. Even when little Sue was big enough to travel she hated to think of leaving. And the climate was so wonderful for the baby there—

Anyhow, by then the Council had begun to frown over Bill Cory's work. After all, perhaps he wasn't really cut out to be a scientist—Sallie's happiness was more important than any man's job, and Sallie could never be really happy in Science City.

The second baby was a girl, too. There were a lot of girls being born nowadays. The telenews broadcasters joked about it. A good sign, they said. When a preponderance of boys was born, it had always meant war. Girls should bring peace and plenty for the new generation.

Peace and plenty—that was what mattered most to Bill and Sallie Cory now. That and their two exquisite daughters and their home on the green Pacific hills. Young Susan was growing up into a girlhood so enchanting that Bill suffused with pride and tenderness every time he thought of her. She had Sallie's beauty and blondeness, but there was a resolution in her that had been Bill's once, long ago. He liked to think of her, in daydreams, carrying on the work that he would never finish now.

Time ran on, years telescoping pleasantly into uneventful years. Presently the Cory girls were growing up . . . were married . . . were mothers. The grandchildren were girls, too. When Gandfather Cory joined his wife in the little graveyard on the sea-turned hill beyond the house, the Cory name died with him, though there was in his daughter's level eyes and in her daughter's look of serene resolution something more intrinsically Bill Cory than his name. The name might die, but something of the man who had borne it lived on in his descendants.

Girls continued to outnumber boys in the birth records as the generations passed. It was happening all over the world, for no reason that anyone could understand. It didn't matter much, really. Women in public offices were proving very efficient; certainly they governed more peacefully than men. The first woman president won her office on a platform that promised no war so long as a woman dwelt in the White House.

Of course, some things suffered under the matriarchy. Women as a sex are not scientists, not inventors, not mechanics or engineers or architects. There were men enough to keep these essentially masculine arts alive—that is, as much of them as the new world needed. There were many changes. Science City, for instance. Important, of course, but not to the extent of draining the country dry to maintain it. Life went on very nicely without too much machinery.

The tendency was away from centralized living in these new days. Cities spread out instead of up. Skyscrapers were hopelessly old-fashioned. Now parklands and gardens stretched between low-roofed houses where the children played all day. And war was a barbarous memory from those nightmare years when men still ruled the world.

Old Dr. Phillips, head of the dwindling and outmoded Science City, provoked President Wiliston into a really inspiring fury when he criticized the modern tendency toward a non-mechanized rural civilization. It happened on the telenews, so that half the world heard it.

"But Madam President," he said, "don't you realize where we're heading? The world's going backward! It's no longer worth-while for our best minds to attempt bettering living conditions. We're throwing genius away! Do you realize that your cabinet yesterday flatly rejected the brilliant work of one of our most promising young men?"

"I do!" Alice Wiliston's voice rang with sudden violence over half the world. "That 'brilliant work,' as you call it, was a device that might have led to war! Do you think we want that? Remember the promise that the first woman president made the world, Dr. Phillips! So long as we sit in the White House there will be no need for war!"

And Elizabeth of England nodded in London; Julianna VII smiled into her Amsterdam telenews screen. While women ruled, war was outlawed. Peace and ease, and plenty would dominate civilization, leisure for cultivation of the arts, humankind coming into its own at last, after so many ages of pain and blood and heartbreak.

Years telescoped into centuries of peace and plenty in a garden world. Science had turned its genius to the stabilization of the climate so that nowhere was shelter necessary from cold or storms; food was freely abundant for all. The Garden that Adam and Eve forfeited in the world's beginning had returned again to their remotest descendants, and the whole earth was Eden.

And in this world that no longer demanded the slightest physical effort, mankind was turning to the cultivation of the mind. In these white, low-roofed houses set among garden parks, men and women increasingly adventured into the realms beyond the flesh, exploring the mysteries of the mind.

Bill Cory, leaning forward in his chair, had lost all identity with himself. He was simply a consciousness watching time unfold before him. The gravestone that bore his name on the California hillside had long since sunk into the sod, but if there is immortality at all, Bill Cory watched himself move forward through the centuries, down the long, expanding line of his descendants. Now and again, startlingly, his own face looked briefly at him from some faraway child of his remote grandchildren. His face, and Sallie's.

He saw pretty Sue come and go like reflections in a mirror. Not always Sue unmistakably and completely—sometimes only her brown eyes lighted the face of a many-times-great-granddaughter; sometimes the lift of her smile or the tilt of her pretty nose alone was familiar to him in a strange face. But sometimes Sue herself, perfect to the last detail, moved through the remote future. And every time he saw those familiar features, his heart contracted with an ache of tenderness for the daughter he yet might never have.

It was for these beloved Susans that he was becoming uneasy as he watched time go by in this lazy paradise world. People were slowing mentally and physically. What need any more for haste or trouble? Why worry because certain unimportant knowledge was being lost as time went on? The weather machines, the food machines were eternal; what else really mattered? Let the birth rate decline, let the dwindling race of the inventive and the ambitious fade like the anachronism it was. The body had taken mankind as far as it could; the mind was the vehicle for the future. In the vast reaches of infinity were fields aplenty for the adventurous spirit. Or one could simply drowse the days away—

Clouds thickened softly across the dreamy vistas of Eden. Bill Cory leaned back in his chair and rubbed his eyes with both hands. The hands were shaking, and he stared at them a little stupidly, still half lost in the wonder of what he had seen, in the strange welter of emotions that still warred in him—the memory of Sallie and his strong love for her, the memory of Sue's sweetness, the memory of pride in them both. And in the queer feeling that it had been himself in those many daughters of his through the ages, striving so hard for world peace to the ultimate end that mankind might achieve—*ruin*.

For it was wrong—it was bad. The whole world. The race of man was too splendid, too capable of working miracles, to end on a myrtle bank dreaming about abstractions. He had just seen a decadent, indolent, civilization going down the last incline into oblivion as a result—yes, as a direct result—of his own action. He'd seen himself sinking into a fat, idle old age, without honor of achievement.

Suddenly and desperately he hoped that Ashley had been right—that this was not the inevitable and changeless future. If he tore up the letter lying on his desk now, if he never married Sallie, would not his work be finished successfully some day, and the catastrophe of unbalanced births avoided? Or could a man change his ordained future?

Almost fearfully he reached for the letter lying beside that clouded cube in which the years had mirrored themselves. Would he be able to take the letter up and rip it across—like this? The sound of tearing paper reassured him. So far, at least, he was still a free agent.

And knowing that, suddenly he was sorry. Not to marry Sallie, with her bubbling laugh. Never to see young Sue growing into beauty and courage and sweetness. Old age without achievement, had he said to himself a moment ago? Sue herself was achievement enough for any man. Sue and those other Susans down the long line of his descendants, incarnating again and again all that was finest in him, eternal as life itself through millenniums.

He did not want to meet again the brown eyes of this latest Susan who had come to him in the depths of the cube. While he looked, his reason was lost in his love for her, and not even against reason could he believe the world which had produced her to be anything but perfect, simply because this beloved daughter moved and breathed in it.

But the letter was torn. He would never marry Sallie if he could help himself. The cost was too high, even for such a reward as Sue. And an almost tremulous awe broke over him in a sudden tide as he realized what he was doing. This was what Ashley had dreamed of—opening a window into the Plane of Probability and learning enough to force the Cosmic Mind out of its course. Changing the shape of his own future and that of all mankind. Greater than gods—but he was no god. And Ashley had warned him that it might be dangerous to usurp a god's prerogative. Suddenly he was afraid.

He looked away from that cube which held his future, and across from it on his desk the violet eyes of Marta Mayhew caught his, fixed in their changeless smile. She was a girl, he thought, he remembered from half a lifetime ago, so much had happened since he glanced last into her face. Dark and lovely she was, her eyes meeting his almost as if there were vision behind their deep, long stare. Almost as if—

Light flared out in one white, blinding sheet that blotted out the cube and the violet-eyed face and the room around him. Involuntarily Bill clapped his hands to his eyes, seeing behind the darkness of his lids a dazzle of blurring colors. It had happened too quickly for wonder—he was not even thinking as he opened his eyes and looked into the cube where Marta's gaze had met him a moment before.

And then a great tide of awe and wonder came washing up into his consciousness, and he knew that Ashley had been right. There was an alternative future. There comes a point beyond which bewilderment and shock no longer affect the human brain, and Bill was outside wondering now, or groping for logical explanations. He only knew that he stood here staring into the cube from which Marta's eyes had smiled at him so short an instant ago—

They were still Marta's eyes, deep-colored in a boy face almost Bill's own, feature for feature, under a cap of blue steel. Somehow that other future had come to him, too. He was aware of a sudden urgent wonder *why* they had come so nearly together, though neither could be conscious of the other— But things were moving in the depths of the cube.

Behind the boy's face, three-dimensional perspective had started vividly back from the crystal surfaces, as if the cube were a wide window flung suddenly open upon a new world. In that world, a place of glass and shining chromium, faces crowded as if indeed at an open window, peering into his room. Steel-helmed faces with staring eyes. And foremost among them, leaning almost through the opened window into his own past, the steel-capped boy whose features were Bill's looked eagerly out, the sound of quickened breath through his lips a soft, clear sound in the room. They were Bill's lips, Bill's features—but Marta's gentle courage had somehow grown masculine in the lines of the boy's face, and her eyes met Bill's in his.

In the instant before those parted lips spoke, Bill knew him, and his throat closed on an unuttered cry of recognition—recognition of this face he had never seen before, yet could not mistake. The deep welling of love and pride in his heart would have told him the boy's identity, he thought, had he not known at sight who he was—would be—might one day be—

He heard his own voice saying doubtfully, "Son—?"

But if the boy heard he must not have understood. He was handicapped by no such emotion as stirred Bill. His clipped, metallic voice spoke as clearly as if indeed through an opened window: "Greetings from the United World, William Vincent Cory! Greetings from the Fifteenth Leader in the Fifth New Century, A.G."

Behind the disciplined, stern-featured young face others crowded, men with steel-hard features under steel caps. As the boy's voice paused, a dozen right arms slanted high, a dozen open palms turned forward in a salute that was old when Caesar took it in ancient Rome. A dozen voices rolled out in clipped accents, "Greetings, William Vincent Cory!"

Bill's bewildered stammer was incoherent, and the boy's face relaxed a little into a smile. He said: "We must explain, of course. For generations our scientists have been groping in the past, Dr. Cory. This is our first successful two-way contact, and for its demonstration to our Council, connection with you was selected as the most appropriate and fitting contact possible. Because your name is holy among us; we know all there is to know of your life and work, but we have wished to look upon your face and speak to you of our gratitude for molding mankind into the patterns of the United World.

"As a matter of record, I have been instructed to ask first at what point we have intersected the past. What date is it in your calendar?"

"Why, it's July 7, 2240," Bill heard his own voice stammer a little as he answered, and he was conscious of a broad and rather foolish grin overspreading his face. He couldn't help it. This was his boy—the child who wouldn't be born for years yet, who might, really, never be born. Yet he knew him, and he couldn't help smiling with pride, and warm, delighted amusement. So stern-faced, so conscious of his own responsibility! Marta's son and his—only of course it couldn't be, exactly. This scene he looked into must be far ahead in time—

"Twenty-two forty!" exclaimed the boy who was not his son. "Why, the Great Work isn't even finished yet then! We're earlier than we knew!"

"Who are you, son?" Bill couldn't keep the question back any longer.

"I'm John Williams Cory IV, sir," said the boy proudly. "Your direct descendant through the Williams line, and—first in the Candidates Class." He said it proudly, a look of almost worshiping awe lighting his resolute young face. "That means, of course, that I shall be the Sixteenth Leader when the great Dunn retires, and the sixth Cory—the sixth, sir!—to be called to that highest of all human stations, the Leadership!" The violet eyes so incongruous in that disciplined young face blazed with almost fanatic exaltation.

Behind him, a heavy-faced man moved forward, lifting the Roman salute, smiling wintrily beneath his steel helmet.

"I am Dunn, sir," he said in a voice as heavy as his features. "We've let Candidate Cory contact you because of the relationship, but it's my turn now to extend greetings from the System you made possible. I want to show it to you, but first let me thank you for founding the greatest family the United World has ever known. No other name has appeared more than twice on the great rôle of Leaders, but we have had five Corys—and the finest of them all is yet to come!"

Bill saw a wave of clear red mount his boy's proud, exalted face, and his own heart quickened with love and pride. For this was his son, by whatever name he went here. The memory of his lovely daughter had been drowned out momentarily in the deep uprushing of pride in this tall, blue-eyed boy with his disciplined face and his look of leashed eagerness. There was drive and strength and power of will in that young face now.

He scarcely heard Dunn's heavy voice from the room beyond the cube, so eagerly was he scanning the face of his son he yet might never have, learning almost hungrily the already familiar features, at once hard and eager and exultant. That mouth was his, tight and straight, and the cheeks that creased with deep hollows when he smiled, but the violet eyes were his mother's eyes, and the gentle inflexibility of Marta's courage at once strengthened and softened the features that were Bill's own. The best of them both was here, shining now with something more than either had ever known—an almost fanatic devotion to some stern purpose as exalting as worship, as inflexible as duty—

"Your own future, sir," Dunn was saying. "But our past, of course. Would you like to see it, Dr. Cory, so that you may understand just how directly we owe to you all that our world is today?"

"Yes—v-very much." Bill grinned at his own stammer, suddenly light-hearted and incredulous. All this was a dream. He knew that, of course. Why, the very coincidences in it proved that. Or—were they coincidences? Desperately he tried to clarify the thought taking form in his own mind, a terrifyingly vast thought, terrifyingly without explanation. And yet it must be a dream— If it were real, then there was more than chance here. It could be no accident that these two children of his, groping blindly in the dark for contact with him, had succeeded at so nearly the same moment. There would be reason behind it, reason too vast for comprehension. He parted his lips to speak, but Dunn was already speaking.

"Look then, William Vincent Cory! Watch your own greatness unfolding in the years that lie ahead."

Hazily the scene in the cube blurred. The beloved, blue-eyed face of the boy he might never have, faded as a dream fads—a dream fading in a dream, he thought dimly—

This time it was Marta coming down the church aisle toward him, looking like a violet-eyed madonna coifed and veiled in white lace. He knew that he did not love her, now. His heart was still sore with the memory of Sallie. But love would come; with a woman like this it could not but come. There was tenderness and humor and passion on that raptly lifted face, and a strength that would call out the strength in him, not a weakness such as dimpled in Sallie's face to evoke

GREATER THAN GODS

an underlying weakness in himself. For weakness was in him. He knew it. It would depend upon the woman who shared his life which quality overcame the other.

Life would be good with Marta. He saw it unfolding before him in a long succession of days, work and play and companionship that brought out the best in both. And the memory of the strange vision in which he thought he loved Sallie faded. This was the woman he loved. Her courage and humor, her violet eyes bright with pride of him—

Life went by—clear, condensed, swift. He saw his own work moving steadily toward success, Marta's eager encouragement tiding him over the low ebbs when difficulties threatened. She was so full of pride in her brilliant young husband that her enthusiasm almost ran away with her. It was she who insisted upon making the discovery public.

"I want to flaunt you before the world!" she urged. "Let's report to the Council now, darling. Aw, please, Bill!"

"We're not ready yet," he protested feebly. "Let's wait—"

"What for? Look." She shook a record sheet under his nose. "A hundred per cent success in the last dozen experiments! What more do you want? It's time to make an official report—anounce what you're doing to the world! You've been all the way from fruit flies to monkeys. You'll have to make a report to the Council anyhow before you can take the next step. And remember, darling, when you come to that, I'm first in line as a candidate."

He seized her shoulders in a heavy grip, frowning down into the eagerness of her lifted face. "There'll be no guinea pigs in this family! When Junior Cory comes into the world he—or she—will do it without benefit of X-rays. Understand?"

"But darling, I thought the whole idea was to give parents their choice of boys or girls in the family."

"The thing's not perfected yet to the point where I'd want to risk my own wife. And anyhow . . . anyhow, I've got a funny notion I'd rather just take what comes. Don't know why, exactly, but—"

"Bill, I do believe you're superstitious! Well, we'll fight that out later. But right now, you're going to make a full report of your success to the Council, and I'm going to be the proudest wife in the City. And that's final!"

So the report was made public. It created a tremendous furor; the world clamored for the magical stuff that would put the molding of the future into their hands. Bill Cory blushed and grinned for a delighted public in the telenews screens, promising the great gift soon, and Marta glowed with vicarious pride.

By the time he had made his first experiment with a human subject, the puppies which were the result of his first successful mammalian experiment were beginning to worry him a little. Miss Brown was the first to notice it. She came in from the kennels one day with a frown behind her steel-rimmed spectacles.

"Dr. Cory, has someone been training those dogs?"

"Training them?" Bill looked up, puzzled. "Of course not. Why?"

"Well, they've got the makings of the finest trained dogs on Earth. Either the whole lot of them is exceptionally intelligent or . . . or . . . something. They just fall over each other obeying every command you can make clear to them."

Bill straightened from his microscope. "Um-m-m . . . funny. Usually one or two dogs in a litter are more intelligent and obedient than the rest. But to have every one in six litters a canine genius is something pretty queer. What do you make of it?"

"I wouldn't call it genius, exactly. As I say, I'm not sure if it's unusual intelligence or . . . well, maybe a strong strain of obedience, or lack of initiative, or . . . it's too soon to say. But they're not normal dogs, Dr. Cory."

It was too soon to say. Tests simply showed the pups to be extraordinarily amenable to training, but what quality in them made this so was difficult to determine. Bill was not sure just what it implied, but an uneasiness in him woke and would not be quieted.

The first "X-ray" babies began to be born. Without exception they were fine, strong, healthy infants, and without exception of the predetermined sex. The Council was delighted; the parents were delighted; everyone was delighted except Bill. The memory of those oddly obedient pups haunted him—

Within three years the Cory System was available to the public. The experimental babies had made such an excellent showing that, in the end, Bill gave in to the insistent world, though something in the recesses of his mind urged delay. Yet he couldn't explain it. The babies were all healthy, normal, intelligent children. Unusually amenable to authority, yes, but that was an asset, not a liability.

GREATER THAN GODS

Presently all over the world the first crops of Cory System babies began to appear, and gradually Bill's misgivings faded. By then Bill Junior had arrived to take his mind off other people's children, but even now he was obscurely glad that little Bill was a boy on his own initiative, not because his parents had forced masculinity upon him. There was no rhyme or reason to Bill's queer obsession that his own child should not be a product of the X-ray system, but he had been firm about it.

And in later years he had reason to be glad. Bill Jr. grew up fast. He had Marta's violet eyes and his father's darkly blond hair, and a laughing resolution all his own. He was going to be an architect, and neither his mother's shocked protest at this treason to the family profession, nor Bill's not wholly concealed disappointment could swerve him. But he was a good lad. Between school terms he and his father had entirely marvelous vacations together, and for Bill the world revolved about this beloved, talented, headstrong youngster whose presence upon Earth seemed reason enough for Bill's whole existence.

He was glad, even, that the boy *was* stubborn. For there could be no question now about a weakness in the children of the Cory System births. In all ways but one they were quite normal, it was true, but initiative seemed to have been left out of them. It was as if the act of predetermining their sex had robbed them of all ability to make any decisions of their own. Excellent followers they were—but no leaders sprang up among them.

And it was dangerous to fill with unquestioning followers of the strongest man a world in which General George Hamilton controlled the United States. He was in his fourth term as president as the first great group of Cory System children came to maturity. Fiercely and sincerely he believed in the subjugation of the many to the State, and this new generation found in him an almost divinely inspired leader.

General George dreamed of a United World in which all races lived in blind obedience and willing sacrifice for the common good. And he was a man to make his dreams come true. Of course, he admitted, there would be opposition at first. There might be bloody wars, but in his magnificent dreams he believed sincerely that no price could be too high, that the end justified any means necessary to achieve it. And it seemed like the coöperation of Heaven itself to find almost an entire generation coming into adulthood ready to accept his leadership implicitly.

He understood why. It was no secret now what effect the Cory System had upon the children it produced. They would follow the strongest leader with blind faith. But upon this one generation of followers General George knew he could build a future that would live after him in the magnificent fulfillment of his most magnificent dreams. For a war lord needs a nation of soldiers, a great crop of boy babies to grow into armies, and surprisingly few saw the real motive behind General George's constant cry for boys, boys, boys—huge families of them. Fathers of many sons were feted and rewarded. Everybody knew there was the certainty of war behind this constant appeal for families of sons, but comparatively few realized that since the best way to be sure of boys was the use of the Cory System, the whole new generation would be blind followers of the strongest leader, just as their fathers were. Perhaps the Cory System might have died of its own great weakness, its one flaw, had not General George so purposefully demanded sons of his followers.

General George died before the first great war was over. His last words, gasped in the bursting tumult of a bomb raid over Washington were, "Carry on—unite the world!" And his vice-president and second in command, Phillip Spaulding, was ready to snatch up the falling torch and light the world to union.

Half the United States lay in smoking ruins before the Great War ended. But General George had built well upon that most enduring of all foundations—the faith of men. "Be fruitful and multiply," was a command his followers had obeyed implicitly, and Spaulding had mighty resources of human brawn and human obedience to draw upon.

The great general had died gladly for his dream, and he had not died in vain. Half the world was united under his starry banners within a decade after his death; the United World of his vision came into being less than fifty years later.

With peace and blind faith and prosperity, Science City indeed came into its own. And because a taste of power had made the Leaders hungry, the eyes of the City turned upward toward starry space. During the command of the Fourth Leader after the immortal General George, the first successful space voyage was achieved. The first living man stood knee-deep in the dead pumice dust of the moon and a mighty forward stride for mankind was recorded.

It was only a step. Mars came next, three generations later. After a brief and bloody war, its decadent inhabitants surrendered and the Seventh Leader began to have giddily intoxicating dreams of a United Solar System—

Time telescoped by. Generation melted into generation in changing tides over a world population that seemed unaltering in its by now age-old uniforms of George Blue. And in a sense they were unaltering. Mankind was fixed in a mold—a good enough mold for the military life of the U. W.—the United World. The Cory System had long ago become compulsory, and men and women were produced exactly in the ratio that the Leaders decreed. But it was significant that the Leader class came into the world in the old haphazard fashion of the days before the legendary Dr. Cory's discovery.

The name of Cory was a proud one. It had long been a tradition in that famous family that the founder's great System should not be used among themselves. They were high among the Leader class. Several of the Leaders had borne the surname of Cory, though the office of course was not hereditary, but passed after rigid training and strict examination to the most eligible of the Candidates Class when an old Leader passed his prime.

And among the mighty Corys, family resemblance was strong. Generations saw the inevitable dilution of the original strain, but stubbornly through the years the Cory features came and went. Sometimes only the darkly blond hair of the first great Bill, sometimes the violet eyes which his pretty Marta had bequeathed her son, sometimes the very face of young Bill Jr. himself, that had roused an ache of pride and love in his father's heart whenever he saw those beloved features.

The Cory eyes looked now upon two worlds, triumphantly regimented to the last tiny detail. Mankind was proving his supremacy over himself—over his weaknesses and his sentimental, selfish desires for personal happiness as opposed to the great common good. Few succumbed to such shameful yearnings, but when they did, every man was a spy against his neighbor, as stern as the Leader himself in crushing these threats to the U. W.'s strength. It should be the individual's holiest and most mystically passionate dream to sacrifice his happiness for the Leader and the U. W., and the Leader and the United World lived for the sole purpose of seeing that he did.

Marvelous was the progress of mankind. The elements had long since been conquered; the atom had yielded up its incalculable power in the harness of the machines, space itself was a highway for the vehicles of the U. W.

Under the blue-black skies of Mars, mankind's checkerboard cities patterned the hot red soil; under the soft gray clouds of Venus, those roofed and checkered cities spread from a common center through jungles steaming in more than tropic heat. Many-mooned Jupiter was drawing the covetous eyes of the Leaders in their sky-high cities of glass and steel.

And moving through these patterned cities upon three worlds, the followers of the Leader went about their ways, resolute, unfaltering, their faces set in one pattern of determination.

It was not a happy pattern. There was little laughter here; the only emotion upon the serious faces, aside from the shadow of that same exaltation that blazed in the Leader's eyes, was a subtle furtiveness, a sidelong quality that by intuition seemed to distrust its neighbors. Bill recognized it. Every man's duty was to sacrifice for the Cause not only his personal desires and happiness, but his personal honor as well; he must keep relentlessly alert for traitorous weakness in his friends, his associates, his own family.

Mistily the panorama of the centuries began to melt into itself, to fade, while behind it a blue-eyed face, helmed in blue steel, took form to smile straight into Bill's eyes. A tense, expectant smile, supremely confident.

Bill sat back and breathed deeply, avoiding for a moment the proudly smiling face of his son. "I'm—there!" he was thinking. "That was me being born again and again, working with all my heart to crush out human happiness— But there was Sue, too, generations of her—yes, and of me—working just as sincerely toward an opposite goal, a world without war. Either way they've got me. If I don't finish my work, the world unbalances toward matriarchy; if I do, mankind turns into a machine. It's bad. Either way it's bad—"

"The doctor is almost overwhelmed at the realization of his own greatness," Dunn's voice murmured from the window into the future. Bill recognized it for a sort of apology, and sat up with an effort to meet the pride-bright eyes of the boy who one day might be his son. There was nothing but happy expectancy of praise on the boy's face, but Dunn must have read a little doubt in Bill's, for he said heavily, as if to overwhelm that doubt:

"We build toward one common end, all of us—we have no thought for any smaller purpose than the conquest of the Solar System for the mighty race of man! And this great purpose is yours no less than ours, Dr. Cory."

"Manpower is what counts, you know, sir." Young Billy's voice took up the tale as Dunn's died. "We've got tremendous reserves, and we're piling up still more. Lots of room yet on Mars to fill up, and Venus is almost untouched yet. And after that, we'll breed men and women adapted to Jupiter's gravity, perhaps . . . oh, there'll be no end to our power, sir! We'll go on and on— Who knows? There may come a day when we're a United Universe!"

For an instant, hearing the young voice shake with eagerness, Bill doubted his own doubtfulness. The mighty race of man! And he was part of it, living in this far-off future no less than he lived now in the flesh, in the burning ardor of this iron-faced boy. For a moment he forgot to be amazed and incredulous that he stood in the Twenty-third Century and looked as if through a window into the Thirtieth, talking with the unborn descendant of his yet unconceived son. For this moment it was all accomplished reality, a very magnificent and blood-stirring present achieved directly through his own efforts.

"Father . . . father!" The voice was sweet and high in the core of his brain. And memory came back in an overwhelming rush that for an instant drowned out everything but a father's awareness of special love for a favorite daughter.

"Yes, Susan . . . yes, dear." He murmured it aloud, swinging around toward the cube that housed his other future. Sue leaned forward upon her knees among the myrtle leaves, her brown eyes wide and a little frightened upon his. There was a crease between her winged brows that dented Bill's own forehead as he faced her. For a moment it was almost as if each of them looked into a mirror which reflected the features of the other, identical in nearly every detail. Then Sallie's smile dimpled the cheeks of her far-descended daughter, and Sue laughed a small, uneasy laugh.

"What is it, father? Is something wrong?"

He opened his lips to speak—but what could he say? What could he possibly say to her, who did not even dream that her own time was anything but inevitable? How could he explain to a living, warmly breathing woman that she did not exist, might never exist?

He stared at her unhappily, groping for words he could not find. But before he spoke—

"Dr. Cory, sir— Is anything wrong?" He turned back to Billy with a harried crease between his brows and then stared wildly from one face to the other. How could they help hearing one another? But obviously Billy, from his window into the present, saw simply the cube that held Sallie's immortal smile, while Sue, from hers, looked upon Marta's changeless face. It seemed to Bill that the boy and the girl had spoken in voices almost identical, using words nearly the same, though neither was aware of the other. How could they be? They could not even exist simultaneously in the same world. He might have one of these beloved children or the other; not both. Equally beloved children, between whom he must choose—and how could he choose?

"Father—" said Sue on a rising inflection of alarm. "There *is* something wrong. I . . . feel it in your mind— Oh, what is it, father?"

Bill sat speechless, staring from one face to the other of these mutually exclusive children. Here they stood, with their worlds behind them, looking anxiously at him with the same little crease between the brows of each. And he could not even speak to either without convincing the other he was a madman talking to empty air. He wanted insanely to laugh. It was a deadlock beyond all solution. Yet he must answer them—he must make his choice—

As he sat there groping in vain for words, a curious awareness began to take shape in his mind. How strange it was that these two should have been the ones to reach him, out of all the generations behind each that had been searching the past. And why had they established contact at so nearly the same time, when they had all his life span to grope through, hunting him for such different reasons, in such different ways? There was more than accident here, if all this were not a dream—

Billy and Sue—so similar despite the wide divergence of their words, a wider divergence than the mind can well grasp, for how can one measure the distance between mutually incompatible things? Billy who was all of Bill Cory that was strong and resolute and proud; Sue, who incarnated his gentler qualities, the tenderness, the deep desire for peace. They were such poles apart—why, *they were the poles!* The positive and negative qualities that, together, made up all that was best in Bill Cory. Even their worlds were like two halves of a whole; one all that was strong and ruthless, the other the epitome of gentle, abstract idealism. And both were bad, as all extremes must be.

And if he could understand the purpose behind the fact that these two poles of human destiny had reached back in their own pasts to find him at the same moment—if he could understand why the two halves of his soul, split into positive and negative entities, stood here clothed almost in his own flesh to torture him with indecision, perhaps—

He could not choose between them, for there was no choice, but there was a deeper question here than the simple question of conduct. He groped for it blindly, wondering if the answer to everything might not lie in the answer to that question. For there was purpose here vaster than anything man has words for—something loomed behind it to shadowy heights that made his mind reel a little as he tried to understand.

He said inadequately to both his staring children: "But why . . . how did you . . . at this very moment out of all time—"

To Billy it was mere gibberish, but Sue must have understood the question in his mind, for after a moment, in a puzzled murmur, she said:

"I—don't know, exactly. There *is* something here beyond the simple fact of success. I . . . I feel it— I can sense something behind my own actions that . . . that frightens me. Something guiding and controlling my own mind—Oh, father, father, I'm afraid!"

Every protective instinct in him leaped ahead of reason in Bill's instant, "Don't be frightened, honey! I won't let anything happen to you!"

"*Dr. Cory!*" Young Billy's voice cracked a little in horror at what must have sounded to him like raving madness. Behind him, staring faces went tense with bewilderment. Above their rising murmurs Sue wailed, "Father!" in a frightened echo to Billy's, "Dr. Cory, are you ill, sir?"

"Oh, wait a minute, both of you!" said Bill wildly. And then in a stammer, to stop Billy's almost hysterical questions, "Your . . . your sister— Oh, Sue, honey, I hear you! I'll take care of you! Wait a minute!"

In the depths of the cube the boy's face seemed to freeze, the eyes that were Marta's going blank beneath the steel cap, Bill's very mouth moving stiffly with the stiffness of his lips.

"But you never had a daughter—"

"No, but I might have, if—I mean, if I'd married Sallie of course you'd never even— Oh, God!" Bill gave it up and pressed both hands over his eyes to shut out the sight of the boy's amazed incredulity, knowing he's said too much, yet too numbed and confused now for diplomacy. The only clear idea in his head was that he must somehow be fair to both of them, the boy and the girl. Each must understand why he—

"Is the doctor ill, Candidate Cory?" Dunn's voice was heavy from the cube.

Bill heard the boy's voice stammering: "No—that is, I don't—" And then, faltering, more softly: "Leader, was the great doctor ever—mad?"

"Good God, boy!"

"But—speak to him, Leader!"

Bill looked up haggardly as Dunn's voice rolled out with the sternness of a general addressing armies. "Pull yourself together, sir! You never had a daughter! Don't you remember?"

Bill laughed wildly. "Remember? I've never had a son yet! I'm not married—not even engaged! How can I remember what hasn't happened?"

"But you *will* marry Marta Mayhew! You did marry her! You founded the great line of Corys and gave the world your—"

"Father . . . father! What's wrong?" Sue's sweet wail was in his ears. He glanced toward her window momentarily, seeing the terror in the soft brown eyes that stared at him, but he could only murmur: "Hush, darling—wait, please!" before he faced the Leader and said with a strong effort at calmness, "None of all that has happened—yet."

"But it will—it must—it *did!*"

"Even if I never married Marta, never had a son?"

Dunn's dark face convulsed with a grimace of exasperated anger.

"But good Lord, man, look here!" He seized Billy's blue-uniformed shoulders with both hands, thrusting him forward. "You did have a son! This is his descendant, the living likeness of young Cory Junior! This world . . . I myself . . . all of us . . . we're the result of that marriage of yours! And you never had a daughter! Are you trying to tell us we don't exist? Is this a . . . a dream I'm showing you?" And he shook the boy's broad young shoulders between his hands. "You're looking at us, hearing us, talking to us! Can't you see that you must have married Marta Mayhew?"

"Father, I want you! Come back!" Sue's wail was insistent.

Bill groaned. "Wait a minute, Dunn." And then, turning, "Yes, honey, what is it?"

On her knees among the myrtle leaves Sue leaned forward among the sun-flecked shadows of her cool green glade, crying: "Father, you won't . . . you can't believe them? I heard . . . through your ears I heard them, and I can understand a little through your mind linked with mine. I can understand what you're thinking . . . but it can't be true! You're telling yourself that we're still on the Probability Plane . . . but that's just a theory! That's nothing but a speculation about the future! How could I be anything but real? Why, it's silly! Look at me! Listen to me! Here I am! Oh, don't let me go on thinking that maybe . . . maybe you're right, after all. But it *was* Sallie Carlisle you married, wasn't it, father? Please say it was!"

Bill gulped. "Wait, honey. Let me explain to them first." He knew he shouldn't have started the whole incredible argument. You can't convince a living human that he doesn't exist. They'd only think him mad. Well—Sue might understand. Her training in metaphysics and telepathy might make it possible. But Billy—

He turned with a deep breath and a mental squaring of shoulders, determined to try, anyhow. For he must be fair. He began: "Dunn, did you ever hear of the Plane of Probability?"

At the man's incredulous stare he knew a dizzy moment of wonder whether he, too, lived in an illusion as vivid as theirs, and in that instant the foundations of time itself rocked beneath his feet. But he had no time now for speculation. Young Billy must understand, no matter how mad Dunn believed him, and Sue must know why he did what he must do—though he didn't understand himself, yet, what that would be. His head was ringing with bewilderment.

"The . . . the Plane of Probability?" In Dunn's eyes upon his he saw a momentary conviction flare that, reality or not, and history be damned, this man was mad. And then, doubtfully, the Leader went on, "Hm-m-m . . . yes, somewhere I *have* heard— Oh, I remember. Some clap-trap jargon the old

Telepathy House fakers used to use before we cleared them out of Science City. But what's that nonsense got to—"

"It's not nonsense." Bill closed his eyes in a sudden, almost intolerable longing for peace, for time to think what he must do. But no, the thing must be settled now, without time for thinking. And perhaps that was the best way, after all. A man's brain would crack if he paused to think out this madness. Only he must say something to young Billy— And what could he say? How could he face either of these beloved children and, to their uncomprehending, pleading faces, refuse them life? If he could only break the connection that riveted them all into a sort of triple time balance— But he couldn't. He must make it clear to Billy—

"It's not nonsense," he heard his own voice repeating wildly. "The future—you and your world—is a probability only. I'm a free agent. If I never marry Marta, never perfect the sex-determination idea, the probable future shifts to . . . to another pattern. *And that as bad as yours, or worse!*" he finished to himself.

"Is he mad?" Billy's voice was a whisper in the screen.

The Leader said as if to himself, in an awed and stumbling voice, "I don't . . . I can't . . . the thing's preposterous! And yet he *is* unmarried, the Great Work's still unfinished. Suppose he never— But we're real! We're flesh and blood, aren't we?" He stamped a booted foot on the floor as if to test the foundations of his world. "We're descended in an unbroken line from this . . . this madman. Lord in heaven, are we all mad?"

"Father! Come back!" Sue's voice shrilled in Bill's ears. He turned desperately, glad of an excuse to escape the haunted stares from that other window even though he must face hers. She had risen to her feet among the myrtle leaves. The glade was cool and still about her in this lazy, sunlit world of her own future. She was crying desperately, "Don't listen, father! I can feel the confusion in your mind. I know what they're saying! But they aren't real, father—they can't be! You never had a son, don't you remember? All this you're saying is just . . . just talk, isn't it? That silly stuff about the Probability Plane—it's nothing but speculation! Oh, say it is, father! We've got such a lovely world, we love living so . . . I want to live, father! I *am* real! We've fought so hard, for so many centuries, for peace and happiness and our beautiful garden world. Don't let it snuff out into nothingness! But"—she laughed uncertainly—"how could you, when it's all around us, and has been for thousands of years? I . . . oh, father!" Her voice broke on a little quivering gulp that made Bill's heart quiver with it, and he ached intolerably with the rising of her tears. She was his to protect and cherish, forever. How could he—

"Dr. Cory—do you hear me? Oh, please listen!" Young Billy's familiar voice reached out to him from that other future. He glanced toward him once, and then put his hands to his ears and whirled from them both, the two voices mingling in an insane chaos of pleading.

Sue on her myrtle bank in a future immeasurably far ahead, child of a decadent world slipping easily down the slope of oblivion.

Billy's world might be as glorious as he believed, but the price was too high to pay for it. Bill remembered the set, unsmiling faces he had seen in the streets of that world. These were men his own work had robbed of the initiative that was their birthright. Happiness was their birthright, too, and the power to make the decisions that determined their own futures.

No, not even for such achievements as theirs must mankind be robbed of the inalienable right to choose for himself. If it lay in Bill Cory's power to outlaw a system which destroyed men's freedom and honor and joy, even for such an end as mankind's immortal progress, he had no choice to make. The price was too high. Confusedly he remembered something out of the dim past: "What shall it profit a man if he gain the whole world and lose his own soul. . .?"

But—the alternative. Bill groaned. Happiness, peace, freedom, honor—yes, Sue's world had all that Billy's lacked. And to what end? Indolence and decadence and extinction for the great race that Billy's civilization would spread gloriously among the stars.

"But I'm thinking of *choice*," groaned Bill to himself. "And, I haven't got any choice! If I marry Sallie and don't finish my work—one future follows. If I marry Marta and do finish it, the other comes. And both are bad—but what can I do? Man or mankind; which has the stronger claim? Happiness and extinction—or unhappiness and splendid immortality; which is better?"

"Cory—Dr. Cory!" It was Dunn's voice, heavy enough to break through the daze of bewilderment that shrouded Bill's brain. He turned. The Leader's iron-hard face under the steel helmet was settling into lines of fixed resolution. Bill saw that he had reached some decision, and knew a sudden, dazed admiration for the man. After all, he had not been chosen Leader for nothing.

"You're a fool to tell us all this, Cory. Mad, or a fool, or both. Don't you know what it means? Don't think we established this connection unprepared for trouble! The same force that carries the sight and sound of us from our age to yours can carry destruction, too! Nowhere in our past is there a record that William Cory was killed by a blast of atom-gun fire as he sat at his desk—but, by God, sir, if you can change that past, so can we!"

"It would mean wiping yourself out, you know," Bill reminded him as steadily as he could, searching the angry eyes of this man who must never have faced resolute opposition before, and wondering if the man had yet accepted a truth that must seem insanely impossible to him. He wanted overwhelmingly to laugh, and yet somewhere inside him a chilly conviction was growing that it might be possible for the children of his unborn son, in a future that would never exist, to blast him out of being. He said: "You and your whole world would vanish if I died."

"But not unavenged!" The Leader said it savagely, and then hesitated. "But what am I saying? You've driven me almost as mad as you! Look, man, try to be sensible! Can you imagine yourself dissolving into nothingness that never existed? Neither can I!"

"But if you could kill me, then how could your world ever have been born?"

"To hell with all that!" exploded Dunn. "I'm no metaphysician! I'm a fighting man! I'll take the chance!"

"Please, Dr. Cory—" Billy pressed forward against the very surface of the cube, as if he could thrust himself back into his own past and lay urgent hands upon this man so like him, staring white-faced and stubborn into the future. Perhaps it was more than the desire for peace that spoke in his shaken voice. If Bill Cory, looking into that young face so like his own, had felt affection and recognition for it, then must not the boy know a feeling akin to it as he saw himself in Cory's features? Perhaps it was that subtle, strange identification between the two that made the boy's voice tremble a little as if with the first weakening of belief. When he spoke he seemed to be acknowledging the possibility of doubt, almost without realizing it. He said in that shaken, ardent voice:

"Please, try to understand! It's not death we're afraid of. All of us would die now, willingly, if our deaths could further the common good. What we can't endure to face is the death of our civilization, this marvelous thing that makes mankind immortal. Think of that, sir! This is the only right thing possible for you to do! Would we feel so strongly if we weren't *sure?* Can you condemn your own race to eternity on one small planet, when you could give them the universe to expand in and every good thing science can offer?"

"Father . . . father!" It was Sue again, frantic and far away.

But before Bill could turn to her, Dunn's voice broke in heavily over both the others. "Wait—I've made up my mind!" Billy fell back a little, turning to his Leader with a blaze of sudden hope. Bill stared. "As I see it," went on Dunn, "the whole preposterous question hinges on the marriage you make. Naturally I can't concede even to myself that you could possibly marry anyone but the woman you *did* marry—but if you honestly feel that there's any question in your mind about it, I'll settle it for you."

He turned to nod toward a corner of the room in which he stood that was outside Bill's range, and in a moment the blue-uniformed, staring crowd about him parted and a low, rakish barrel of blue-gleaming steel glided noiselessly forward toward that surface of the cube which was a window into the past-future that parted Bill and themselves. Bill had never seen anything like it before, but he recognized its lethal quality. It crouched streamlined down upon its base as if for a lunge, and its mouth facing him was a dark doorway for death itself. Dunn bent behind it and laid his hand upon a half-visible lever in its base.

"Now," he said heavily. "William Cory, there seems to be a question in your mind as to whether we could reach you with our weapons. Let me assure you that the force-beam which connects us can carry more than sight and sound into your world! I hope I shan't have to demonstrate that. I hope you'll be sensible enough to turn to that televisor screen in the wall behind you and call Marta Mayhew."

"M—Marta?" Bill heard the quiver in his voice. "Why—"

"You will call her, and in our sight and hearing you are going to ask her to marry you. That much choice is yours, marriage or death. Do you hear me?"

Bill wanted insanely to laugh. Shotgun wedding from a mythical future—"You can't threaten me with that popgun forever," he said with a quaver of mirth he could not control. "How do you know I'll marry her once you're away?"

"You'll keep your word," said Dunn serenely. "Don't forget, Cory, we know you much better than you know yourself. We know your future far more completely than you saw it. We know how your character will develop with age. Yes, you're an honorable man. Once you've asked her to marry you, and heard her say yes—and she will—you won't try to back out. No, the promise given and received between you constitutes a marriage as surely as if we'd seen the ceremony performed. You see, we trust your honor, William Cory."

"But—" Bill got no further than that, for explosively in his brain a sweet, high voice was sobbing:

"Father, father, what are you doing? What's happened? Why don't you speak to me?"

In the tension Bill had nearly forgotten Sue, but the sound of that familiar voice tore at him with sudden, almost intolerable poignancy. Sue—the promise to protect her had risen to his lips involuntarily at the very mention of danger. It was answer to an urgency rooted race-deep, the instinct to protect the helpless and the loved. For a moment he forgot the gun trained on him from the other window; he forgot Billy and the world behind him. He was conscious only of his daughter crying in terror for help—for help from him and for protection against him at once, in a dizzy confusion that made his head swim.

"Sue—" he began uncertainly.

"Cory, we're waiting!" Dunn's voice had an ominous undernote.

But there was a solution. He never knew just when he first became aware of it. A long while ago, perhaps, subconsciously, the promise of it had begun to take shape in his mind. He did not know when he first realized that—but he thought he knew whence it came. There was a sureness and a vastness about it that did not originate in himself. It was the Cosmic Mind indeed in which his own small soul was floundering, and out of that unthinkably limitless Plan, along with the problem came at last the solution. (*There must be balance . . . the force that swings the worlds in their orbits can permit of no question without an answer—*)

There was no confusion here; there had never been. This was not chance. Purpose was behind it, and sudden confidence came flooding into him from outside. He turned with resolution so calm upon his face that Billy sighed and smiled, and Dunn's tense face relaxed.

"Thank God, sir," breathed Billy, "I knew you'd come to your senses. Believe me, sir, you won't be sorry."

"Wait," said Bill to them both, and laid his hand on the button beneath his desk that rang a bell in his laboratory. "Wait and see."

In three worlds and times, three people very nearly identical in more than the flesh alone—perhaps three facets of the same personality, who can say?—stood silent and tense and waiting. It seemed like a very long time before the door opened and Miss Brown came into the room, hesitating on the threshold with her calm, pleasant face questioning.

"You want me, Dr. Cory?"

Bill did not answer for a moment. He was pouring his whole soul into this last long stare that said good-by to the young son he would never know. For understanding from some vast and nameless source was flooding his mind now, and he knew what was coming and why it would be so. He looked across the desk and gazed his last upon Sue's familiar face so like his own, the fruit of a love he would never share with pretty Sallie. And then, drawing a deep breath, he gulped and said distinctly:

"Miss Brown, will you marry me?"

Dunn had given him the key—a promise given and received between this woman and himself would be irrevocable, would swing the path of the future into a channel that led to no world that either Billy or Sue could know.

Bill got his first glimmer of hope for that future from the way the quiet woman in the doorway accepted his question. She did not stare or giggle or stammer. After one long, deep look into his eyes—he saw for the first time that hers were gray and cool behind the lenses—she answered calmly.

"Thank you, Dr. Cory. I shall be very happy to marry you."

And then—it came. In the very core of his brain, heartbreak and despair exploded in a long, wailing scream of faith betrayed as pretty Sue, his beloved, his darling, winked out into the oblivion from which she would never now emerge. The lazy green Eden was gone forever; the sweet fair girl on her knees among the myrtle leaves had never been—would never be.

Upon that other window surface, in one last flash of unbearable clearness, young Billy's incredulous features stared at him. Behind that beloved, betrayed face he saw the face of the Leader twisting with fury. In the last flashing instant while the vanishing, never-to-exist future still lingered in the cube, Bill saw an explosion of white-hot violence glare blindingly from the gun mouth, a heat and violence that seared the very brain. Would it have reached him—could it have harmed him? He never knew, for it lasted scarcely a heartbeat before eternity closed over the vanishing world in a soundless, fathomless, all-swallowing tide.

Where that world had stretched so vividly a moment ago, now Marta's violet gaze looked out into the room through crystal. Across the desk Sallie's lovely, careless smile glowed changelessly. They had been gateways to the future—but the gates were closed. There would never be such futures now; there never had been. In the Cosmic Mind, the great Plan of Things, two half-formed ideas went out like blown candle flames.

And Bill turned to the gray-eyed woman in the doorway with a long, deep, shaken sigh. In his own mind as he faced her, thoughts too vast for formulation moved cloudily.

"I know now something no man was ever sure of before—our oneness with the Plan. There are many, many futures. I couldn't face the knowledge of another, but I think—yes, I believe, ours will be the best. She won't let me neglect the work we're doing, but neither will she force me to give it to the world unperfected. Maybe, between us, we can work out that kink that robs the embryo of determination, and then—who knows?

"Who knows why all this had to happen? There was Purpose behind it—all of it—but I'll never understand just why. I only know that the futures are infinite—and that I haven't lost Billy or Sue. I couldn't have done what I did without being sure of that. I couldn't lose them, because they're me—the best of me, going on forever. Perhaps I'll never die, really—not the real me—until these incarnations of the best that's in me, whatever form and face and name they wear, work out mankind's ultimate destiny in some future I'll never see. There was reason behind all this. Maybe, after all, I'll understand—some day."

He said nothing aloud, but he held out his hand to the woman in the door and smiled down confidently into her cool, gray eyes.

TRENDS *Astounding Science Fiction, July*

by Isaac Asimov (1920–   )

"Trends" was not my first published story, but my third. The first two, however, did not appear in Astounding and so I rarely count them. This was the very first story I sold to John Campbell, and I became the youngest member of the "stable" of writers he had already gathered around himself.

Though others still younger came his way later, I don't think that ever in his career did he have an acolyte less worldly and more naive than I was. I believe that amused him and that it pleased him to have so excellent an opportunity to do a bit of molding. At any rate, I have always thought that of all his writers I was his favorite and that he spent more time and effort on me than on anyone else. I believe it still shows.

I have always been proud that my first Astounding story appeared in the first issue of the Golden Age, but I know very well that there was no connection. In fact, in the blaze of Van Vogt's lead story Black Destroyer, *I doubt that anyone noticed the twinkle of my own presence.* IA

John Harman was sitting at his desk, brooding, when I entered the office that day. It had become a common sight, by then, to see him staring out at the Hudson, head in hand, a scowl contorting his face—all too common. It seemed unfair for the little bantam to be eating his heart out like that day after day, when by rights he should have been receiving the praise and adulation of the world.

I flopped down into a chair. "Did you see the editorial in today's *Clarion*, boss?"

He turned weary, bloodshot eyes toward me. "No, I haven't. What do they say? Are they calling the vengeance of God down upon me again?" His voice dripping with bitter sarcasm.

"They're going a little farther *now*, boss," I answered. "Listen to this:

" 'Tomorrow is the day of John Harman's attempt at profaning the heavens. Tomorrow, in defiance of world opinion and world conscience, this man will defy God.

" 'It is not given to man to go wheresoever ambition and desire lead him. There are things forever denied him, and aspiring to the stars is one of these. Like Eve, John Harman wishes to eat of the forbidden fruit, and like Eve he will suffer due punishment therefor.

" 'But it is not enough, this mere talk. If we allow him thus to brook the vengeance of God, the trespass is mankind's and not Harman's alone. In allowing him to carry out his evil designs, we make ourselves accessory to the crime, and Divine vengeance will fall on all alike.

" 'It is, therefore, essential that immediate steps be taken to prevent Harman from taking off in his so-called rocketship tomorrow. The government in refusing to take such steps may force violent action. If it will make no move to confiscate the rocketship, or to imprison Harman, our enraged citizenry may have to take matters into their own hands—' "

Harman sprang from his seat in a rage and, snatching the paper from my hands, threw it into the corner furiously. "It's an open call to a lynching," he raved. "Look at this!"

He cast five or six envelopes in my direction. One glance sufficed to tell what they were.

"More death threats?" I asked.

"Yes, exactly that. I've had to arrange for another increase in the police patrol outside the building and for a motorcycle police escort when I cross the river to the testing ground tomorrow."

He marched up and down the room with agitated stride. "I don't know what to do, Clifford. I've worked on the *Prometheus* almost ten years. I've slaved, spent a fortune of money, given up all that makes life worth while—and for what? So that a bunch of fool revivalists can whip up public sentiment against me until my very life isn't safe."

"You're in advance of the times, boss," I shrugged my shoulders in a resigned gesture which made him whirl upon me in a fury.

"What do you mean 'in advance of the times'? This is 1973. The world has been ready for space travel for half a century now. Fifty years ago, people were talking, dreaming of the day when man could free himself of Earth and plumb the depths of space. For fifty years, science has inched toward this goal, and now . . . now I finally have it, and behold! you say the world is not ready for me."

"The '20s and '30s were years of anarchy, decadence, and misrule, if you remember your history," I reminded him gently. "You cannot accept them as criteria."

"I know, I know. You're going to tell me of the First War of 1914, and the Second of 1940. It's an old story to me; my father fought in the Second and my grandfather in the First. Nevertheless, those were the days when science *flourished*. Men were not afraid then; somehow they dreamed and dared. There was no such thing as conversation when it came to matters mechanical and scientific. No theory was too radical to advance, no discovery too revolutionary to publish. Today, dry rot has seized the world when a great vision, such as space travel, is hailed as 'defiance of God.'"

His head sank slowly down, and he turned away to hide his trembling lips and the tears in his eyes. Then he suddenly straightened again, eyes blazing: "But I'll show them. I'm going through with it, in spite of Hell, Heaven and Earth. I've put too much into it to quit now."

"Take it easy, boss," I advised. "This isn't going to do you any good tomorrow, when you get into that ship. Your chances of coming out alive aren't too good now, so what will they be if you start out worn to pieces with excitement and worry?"

"You're right. Let's not think of it any more. Where's Shelton?"

"Over at the Institute arranging for the special photographic plates to be sent us."

"He's been gone a long time, hasn't he?"

"Not especially; but listen, boss, there's something wrong with him. I don't like him."

"Poppycock! He's been with me two years, and I have no complaints."

"All right." I spread my hands in resignation. "If you won't listen to me, you won't. Just the same I caught him reading one of those infernal pamphlets Otis Eldredge puts out. You know the kind: 'Beware, O mankind, for judgment draws near. Punishment for your sins is at hand. Repent and be saved.' And all the rest of the time-honored junk."

Harman snorted in disgust. "Cheap tub-thumping rivivalist! I suppose the world will never outgrow his type—not while sufficient morons exist. Still you can't condemn Shelton just because he reads it. I've read them myself on occasion."

"He *says* he picked it up on the sidewalk and read it in 'idle curiosity,' but I'm pretty sure I saw him take it out of his wallet. Besides, he goes to church every Sunday."

"Is *that* a crime? Everyone does, nowadays!"

"Yes, but not to the Twentieth Century Evangelical Society. That's Eldredge's."

That jolted Harman. Evidently, it was the first he had heard of it. "Say, that *is* something, isn't it? We'll have to keep an eye on him, then."

But after that, things started to happen, and we forgot all about Shelton—until it was too late.

There was nothing much left to do that last day before the test, and I wandered into the next room, where I went over Harman's final report to the Institute. It was my job to correct any errors or mistakes that crept in, but I'm afraid I wasn't very thorough. To tell the truth, I couldn't concentrate. Every few minutes, I'd fall into a brown study.

It seemed queer, all this fuss over space travel. When Harman had first announced the approaching perfection of the *Prometheus*, some six months before, scientific circles had been jubilant. Of course, they were cautious in their statements and qualified everything they said, but there was real enthusiasm.

However, the masses didn't take it that way. It seems strange, perhaps, to you of the twenty-first century, but perhaps we should have expected it in those days of '73. People weren't very progressive then. For years there had been a swing toward religion, and when the churches came out unanimously against Harman's rocket—well, there you were.

At first, the opposition confined itself *to* the churches and we thought it might play itself out. But it didn't. The papers got hold of it, and literally spread the gospel. Poor Harman became an anathema to the world in a remarkably short time, and then his troubles began.

He received death threats, and warnings of divine vengeance every day. He couldn't walk the streets in safety. Dozens of sects, to none of which he belonged—he was one of the very rare free-thinkers of the day, which was another count against him—excommunicated him and placed him under special interdict. And, worst of all, Otis Eldredge and his Evangelical Society began stirring up the populace.

Eldridge was a queer character—one of those geniuses, in their way, that arise every so often. Gifted with a golden tongue and a sulphurous vocabulary, he could fairly hypnotize a crowd. Twenty thousand people were so much putty in his hands, could he only bring them within earshot. And for four months, he thundered against Harman; for four months, a pouring stream of denunciation rolled forth in oratorical frenzy. And for four months, the temper of the world rose.

But Harman was not to be daunted. In his tiny, five-foot-two body, he had enough spirit for five six-footers. The more the wolves howled, the firmer he held his ground. With almost divine—his enemies said, diabolical—obstinacy, he refused to yield an inch. Yet his outward firmness was to me, who knew him, but an imperfect concealment of the great sorrow and bitter disappointment within.

The ring of the doorbell interrupted my thoughts at that point and brought me to my feet in surprise. Visitors were very few those days.

I looked out the window and saw a tall, portly figure talking with Police Sergeant Cassidy. I recognized him at once as Howard Winstead, head of the Institute. Harman was hurrying out to greet him, and after a short exchange of phrases, the two entered the office. I followed them in, being rather curious as to what could have brought Winstead, who was more politician than scientist, here.

Winstead didn't seem very comfortable, at first; not his usual suave self. He avoided Harman's eyes in an embarrassed manner and mumbled a few conventionalities concerning the weather. Then he came to the point with direct, undiplomatic bluntness.

"John," he said, "how about postponing the trial for a time?"

"You really mean abandoning it altogether, don't you? Well, I won't, and that's final."

Winstead lifted his hand. "Wait now, John, don't get excited. Let me state my case. I know the Institute agreed to give you a free hand, and I know that you paid at least half the expenses out of your own pocket, but—you can't go through with it."

"Oh, can't I, though?" Harman snorted derisively.

"Now listen, John, you know your science, but you don't know your human nature and I do. This is not the world of the 'Mad Decades,' whether you realize it or not. There have been profound changes since 1940." He swung into what was evidently a carefully prepared speech.

"After the First World War, you know, the world as a whole swung away from religion and toward freedom from convention. People were disgusted and disillusioned, cynical and sophisticated. Eldredge calls them 'wicked and sinful.' In spite of that, science flourished—some say it always fares best in such an unconventional period. From *its* standpoint it was a 'Golden Age.'

"However, you know the political and economic history of the period. It was a time of political chaos and international anarchy; a suicidal, brainless, insane period—and it culminated in the Second World War. And just as the First War led to a period of sophistication, so the Second initiated a return to religion.

"People were disgusted with the 'Mad Decades.' They had had enough of it, and feared, beyond all else, a return to it. To remove that possibility, they put the ways of those decades behind them. Their motives, you see, were understandable and laudable. All the freedom, all the sophistication, all the lack of convention were gone—swept away clean. We are living now in a second Victorian age; and naturally so, because human history goes by swings of the pendulum and this is the swing toward religion and convention.

"One thing only is left over since those days of half a century ago. That one thing is respect of humanity for science. We have prohibition; smoking for women is outlawed; cosmetics are forbidden; low dresses and short skirts are unheard of; divorce is frowned upon. But science has not been confined—*as yet*.

"It behooves science, then, to be circumspect, to refrain from arousing the people. It will be very easy to make them believe—and Otis Eldredge has come perilously close to doing it in some of his speeches—that it was science that brought about the horrors of the Second World War. Science outstripped culture, they will say, technology outstripped sociology, and it was that unbalance that came so near to destroying the world. Somehow, I am inclined to believe they are not so far wrong, at that.

"But do you know what would happen, if it ever *did* come to that? Scientific research may be forbidden or, if they don't go that far, it will certainly be so strictly regulated as to stifle in its own decay. It will be a calamity from which humanity would not recover for a millennium.

"And it is your trial flight that may precipitate all this. You are arousing the public to a stage where it will be difficult to calm them. I warn you, John. The consequences will be on your head."

There was absolute silence for a moment and then Harman forced a smile. "Come, Howard, you're letting yourself be frightened by shadows on the wall. Are you trying to tell me that it is your serious belief that the world as a whole is ready to plunge into a second Dark Ages? After all, the intelligent men are on the side of science, aren't they?"

"If they are, there aren't many of them left from what I see." Winstead drew a pipe from his pocket and filled it slowly with tobacco as he continued: "Eldridge formed a League of the Righteous two months ago—they call it the L. R.—and it has grown unbelievably. *Twenty million is its membership in the United States alone.* Eldredge boasts that after the next election Congress will be his; and there seems to be more truth than bluff in that. Already there has been strenuous lobbying in favor of a bill outlawing rocket experiments, and laws of that type have been enacted in Poland, Portugal, and Rumania. Yes, John, we are perilously close to open persecution of science." He was smoking now in rapid, nervous puffs.

"But if I succeed, Howard, if I succeed! What then?"

"Bah! You know the chances for that. Your own estimate gives you only one chance in ten of coming out alive."

"What does that signify? The next experimenter will learn by my mistakes, and the odds will improve. That's the scientific method."

"The mob doesn't know anything about the scientific method; and they don't want to know. Well, what do you say? Will you call it off?"

Harman sprang to his feet, his chair tumbling over with a crash. "Do you know what you ask? Do you want me to give up my life's work, my dream, just like that? Do you think I'm going to sit back and wait for your *dear* public to become benevolent? Do you think they'll change in *my* lifetime?

"Here's my answer: I have an inalienable right to pursue knowledge. Science has an inalienable right to progress and develop without interference. The world, in interfering with me, is wrong; I am right. And it shall go hard, but I *will not* abandon my rights."

Winstead shook his head sorrowfully. "You're wrong, John, when you speak of 'inalienable' rights. What you call a 'right' is merely a *privilege, generally agreed upon*. What society accepts, is right; what it does not, is wrong."

"Would your friend, Eldredge, agree to such a definition of his 'righteousness'?" questioned Harmon bitterly.

"No, he would not, but that's irrelevant. Take the case of those African tribes who used to be cannibals. They were brought up as cannibals, have the long tradition of cannibalism, and their society accepts the practice. To *them*, cannibalism is *right*, and why shouldn't it be? So you see how relative the whole notion is, and how inane your conception of 'inalienable' rights to perform experiments is."

"You know, Howard, you missed your calling when you didn't become a lawyer." Harman was really growing angry. "You've been bringing out every moth-eaten argument you can think of. For God's sake, man, are you trying to pretend that it is a crime to refuse to run with the crowd? Do you stand for absolute uniformity, ordinariness, orthodoxy, commonplaceness? Science would die far sooner under the program you outline than under governmental prohibition."

Harman stood up and pointed an accusing finger at the other. "You're betraying science and the tradition of those glorious rebels: Galileo, Darwin, Einstein and their kind. My rocket leaves tomorrow on schedule in spite of you and every other stuffed shirt in the United States. That's that, and I refuse to listen to you any longer. So you can just get out."

The head of the Institute, red in the face, turned to me. "You're my witness, young man, that I warned this obstinate nitwit, this . . . this hare-brained fanatic." He spluttered a bit, and then strode out, the picture of fiery indignation.

Harman turned to me when he had gone: "Well, what do *you* think? I suppose you agree with him."

There was only one possible answer and I made it:

"You're not paying me to do anything else but follow orders, boss. I'm sticking with you."

Just then Shelton came in and Harman packed us both off to go over the calculations of the orbit of flight for the umpteenth time, while he himself went off to bed.

The next day, July 15th, dawned in matchless splendor, and Harman, Shelton, and myself were in an almost gay mood as we crossed the Hudson to where the *Prometheus*—surrounded by an adequate police guard—lay in gleaming grandeur.

Around it, roped off at an apparently safe distance, rolled a crowd of gigantic proportions. Most of them were hostile, raucously so. In fact, for one fleeting moment, as our motorcycle police escort parted the crowds for us, the shouts and imprecations that reached our ears almost convinced me that we should have listened to Winstead.

But Harman paid no attention to them at all, after one supercilious sneer at a shout of: "There goes John Harman, son of Belial." Calmly, he directed us about our task of inspection. I tested the foot-thick outer walls and the air locks for leaks, then made sure the air purifier worked. Shelton checked up on the repellent screen and the fuel tanks. Finally, Harman tried on the clumsy spacesuit, found it suitable, and announced himself ready.

The crowd stirred. Upon a hastily erected platform of wooden planks piled in confusion by some in the mob, there rose up a striking figure. Tall and lean; with thin, ascetic countenance; deep-set, burning eyes, peering and half closed; a thick, white mane crowning all—it was Otis Eldredge. The crowd recognized him at once and many cheered. Enthusiasm waxed and soon the entire turbulent mass of people shouted themselves hoarse over him.

He raised a hand for silence, turned to Harman, who regarded him with surprise and distaste, and pointed a long, bony finger at him:

"John Harman, son of the devil, spawn of Satan, you are here for an evil purpose. You are about to set out upon a blasphemous attempt to pierce the veil beyond which man is forbidden to go. You are tasting of the forbidden fruit of Eden and beware that you taste not of the fruits of sin."

The crowd cheered him to the echo and he continued: "The finger of God is upon you, John Harman. He shall not allow His works to be defiled. You die today, John Harman."

His voice rose in intensity and his last words were uttered in truly prophetlike fervor.

Harman turned away in disdain. In a loud, clear voice, he addressed the police sergeant: "Is there any way, officer, of removing these spectators? The trial flight may be attended by some destruction because of the rocket blasts, and they're crowding too close."

The policeman answered in a crisp, unfriendly tone: "If you're afraid of being mobbed, say so, Mr. Harman. You don't have to worry, though, we'll hold them back. And as for danger—from *that* contraption—" He sniffed loudly in the direction of the *Prometheus,* evoking a torrent of jeers and yells.

Harman said nothing further, but climbed into the ship in silence. And when he did so, a queer sort of stillness fell over the mob; a palpable tension. There was no attempt at rushing the ship, an attempt I had thought inevitable. On the contrary, Otis Eldredge himself shouted to everyone to move back.

"Leave the sinner to his sins," he shouted. " 'Vengeance is mine,' saith the Lord."

As the moment approached, Shelton nudged me. "Let's get out of here," he whispered in a strained voice. "Those rocket blasts are poison." Saying this, he broke into a run, beckoning anxiously for me to follow.

We had not yet reached the fringes of the crowd when there was a terrific roar behind me. A wave of heated air swept over me. There was the frightening hiss of some speeding object past my ear, and I was thrown violently to the ground. For a few minutes I lay dazed, my ears ringing and my head reeling.

When I staggered drunkenly to my feet again, it was to view a dreadful sight. Evidently, the entire fuel supply of the *Prometheus* had exploded at once, and where it had lain a moment ago there was now only a yawning hole. The ground was strewn with wreckage. The cries of the hurt were heart-rending and the mangled bodies—but I won't try to describe those.

A weak groan at my feet attracted my attention. One look, and I gasped in horror, for it was Shelton, the back of his head a bloody mass.

"I did it." His voice was hoarse and triumphant but withal so low that I could scarcely hear it. "I did it. I broke open the liquid-oxygen compartments and when the spark went through the acetyline mixture the whole cursed thing exploded." He gasped a bit and tried to move but failed. "A piece of wreckage must have hit me, but I don't care. I'll die knowing that—"

His voice was nothing more than a rasping rattle, and on his face was the ecstatic look of a martyr. He died then, and I could not find it in my heart to condemn him.

It was then I first thought of Harman. Ambulances from Manhattan and from Jersey City were on the scene, and one had sped to a wooden patch some five hundred yards distant where, caught in the treetops, lay a splintered fragment of the *Prometheus*' forward compartment. I limped there as fast as I could, but they had dragged out Harman and clanged away long before I could reach them.

After that, I didn't stay. The disorganized crowd had no thought but for the dead and wounded *now*, but when they recovered, and bent their thoughts to revenge, my life would not be worth a straw. I followed the dictates of the better part of valor and quietly disappeared.

The next week was a hectic one for me. During that time, I lay in hiding at the home of a friend, for it would have been more than my life was worth to allow myself to be seen and recognized. Harman, himself, lay in a Jersey City hospital, with nothing more than superficial cuts and bruises— thanks to the backward force of the explosion and the saving clump of trees which cushioned the fall of the *Prometheus*. It was on him that the brunt of the world's wrath fell.

New York, and the rest of the world also, just about went crazy. Every last paper in the city came out with gigantic headlines, "28 Killed, 73 Wounded—the Price of Sin," printed in blood-red letters. The editorials howled for Harman's life, demanding he be arrested and tried for first-degree murder.

The dreaded cry of "Lynch him!" was raised throughout the five boroughs, and milling thousands crossed the river and converged on Jersey City. At their head was Otis Eldredge, both legs in splints, addressing the crowd from an open automobile as they marched. It was a veritable army.

Mayor Carson of Jersey City called out every available policeman and phoned frantically to Trenton for the State militia. New York clamped down on every bridge and tunnel leaving the city—but not till after many thousands had left.

There were pitched battles on the Jersey coast that sixteenth of July. The vastly outnumbered police clubbed indiscriminately but were gradually pushed back and back. Mounties rode down upon the mob relentlessly but were swallowed up and pulled down by sheer force of numbers. Not until tear gas was used, did the crowd halt—and even then they did not retreat.

The next day, martial law was declared, and the State militia entered Jersey City. That was the end for the lynchers. Eldredge was called to confer with the mayor, and after the conference ordered his followers to disperse.

In a statement to the newspapers, Mayor Carson said: "John Harman must needs suffer for his crime, but it is essential that he do so legally. Justice must take its course, and the State of New Jersey will take all necessary measures."

By the end of the week, normality of a sort had returned and Harman slipped out of the public spotlight. Two more weeks and there was scarcely a word about him in the newspapers, excepting such casual references to him in the discussion of the new Zittman antirocketry bill that had just passed both houses of Congress by unanimous votes.

Yet he remained in the hospital still. No legal action had been taken against him, but it began to appear that a sort of indefinite imprisonment "for his own protection" might be his eventual fate. Therefore, I bestirred myself to action.

Temple Hospital is situated in a lonely and outlying district of Jersey City, and on a dark, moonless night I experienced no difficulty at all in invading the grounds unobserved. With a facility that surprised me, I sneaked in through a basement window, slugged a sleepy interne into insensibility and proceeded to Room 15E, which was listed in the books as Harman's.

"Who's there?" Harman's surprised shout was music in my ears.

"Sh! Quiet! It's I, Cliff McKenny."

"You! What are you doing here?"

"Trying to get you out. If I don't, you're liable to stay here the rest of your life. Come on, let's go."

I was hustling him into his clothes while we were speaking, and in no time at all we were sneaking down the corridor. We were out safely and into my waiting car before Harman collected his scattered wits sufficiently to begin asking questions.

"What's happened since that day?" was the first question.

"I don't remember a thing after starting the rocket blasts until I woke up in the hospital."

"Didn't they tell you anything?"

"Not a damn thing," he swore. "I asked until I was hoarse."

So I told him the whole story from the explosion on. His eyes were wide with shocked surprise when I told of the dead and wounded, and filled with wild rage when he heard of Shelton's treachery. The story of the riots and attempted lynching evoked a muffled curse fom between set lips.

"Of course, the papers howled 'murder,'" I concluded, "but they couldn't pin *that* on you. They tried manslaughter, but there were too many eye-witnesses that had heard your request for the removal of the crowd and the police sergeant's absolute refusal to do so. That, of course, absolved you from all blame. The police sergeant himself died in the explosion, and they couldn't make him the goat.

"Still, with Eldredge yelling for your hide, you're never safe. It would be best to leave while able."

Harman nodded his head in agreement. "Eldredge survived the explosion, did he?"

"Yes, worse luck. He broke both legs, but it takes more than that to shut his mouth."

Another week had passed before I reached our future haven—my uncle's farm in Minnesota. There, in a lonely and out-of-the-way rural community, we stayed while the hullabaloo over Harman's disappearance gradually died down and the perfunctory search for us faded away. The search, by the way, was short indeed, for the authorities seemed more relieved than concerned over the disappearance.

Peace and quiet did wonders with Harman. In six months he seemed a new man—quite ready to consider a second attempt at space travel. Not all the misfortunes in the world could stop him, it seemed, once he had his heart set on something.

"My mistake the first time," he told me one winter's day, "lay in announcing the experiment. I should have taken the temper of the people into account, as Winstead said. This time, however"—he rubbed his hands and gazed thoughtfully into the distance—"I'll steal a march on them. The experiment will be performed in secrecy—absolute secrecy."

I laughed grimly. "It would have to be. Do you know that

all future experiments in rocketry, even entirely theoretical research, is a crime punishable by death?"

"Are you afraid, then?"

"Of course not, boss. I'm merely stating a fact. And here's another plain fact. We two can't build a ship all by ourselves, you know."

"I've thought of that and figured a way out, Cliff. What's more, I can take care of the money angle, too. You'll have to do some traveling, though.

"First, you'll have to go to Chicago and look up the firm of Roberts & Scranton and withdraw everything that's left of my father's inheritance, which," he added in a rueful aside, "is more than half gone on the first ship. Then, locate as many of the old crowd as you can: Harry Jenkins, Joe O'Brien, Neil Stanton—all of them. And get back as quickly as you can. I am tired of delay."

Two days later, I left for Chicago. Obtaining my uncle's consent to the entire business was a simple affair. "Might as well be strung up for a herd of sheep as for a lamb," he grunted, "so go ahead. I'm in enough of a mess now and can afford a bit more, I guess."

It took quite a bit of traveling and even more smooth talk and persuasion before I managed to get four men to come: the three mentioned by Harman and one other, a Saul Simonoff. With that skeleton force and with the half million still left Harman out of the reputed millions left him by his father, we began work.

The building of the *New Prometheus* is a story in itself—a long story of five years of discouragement and insecurity. Little by little, buying girders in Chicago, beryl-steel plates in New York, a vanadium cell in San Francisco, miscellaneous items in scattered corners of the nation, we constructed the sister ship to the ill-fated *Prometheus*.

The difficulties in the way were all but unsuperable. To prevent drawing suspicion down upon us, we had to spread our purchases over periods of time, and to see to it, as well, that the orders were made out to various places. For this we required the co-operation of various friends, who, to be sure, did not know at the time for exactly what purpose the purchases were being used.

We had to synthesize our own fuel, ten tons of it, and that was perhaps the hardest job of all; certainly it took the most time. And finally, as Harman's money dwindled, we came up against our biggest problem—the necessity of economizing.

From the beginning we had known that we could never make the *New Prometheus* as large or as elaborate as the first ship had been, but it soon developed that we would have to reduce its equipment to a point perilously close to the danger line. The repulsive screen was barely satisfactory and all attempts at radio communication were perforce abandoned.

And as we labored through the years, there in the backwoods of northern Minnesota, the world moved on, and Winstead's prophecies proved to have hit amazingly near the mark.

The events of those five years—from 1973 to 1978—are well known to the schoolboys of today, the period being the climax of what we now call the "Neo-Victorian Age." The happenings of those years seem well-nigh unbelievable as we look back upon them now.

The outlawing of all research on space travel came in the very beginning, but was a bare start compared to the antiscientific measures taken in the ensuing years. The next congressional elections, those of 1974, resulted in a Congress in which Eldredge controlled the House and held the balance of power in the Senate.

Hence, no time was lost. At the first session of the ninety-third Congress, the famous Stonely-Carter bill was passed. It established the Federal Scientific Research Investigatory Bureau—the FSRIB—which was given full power to pass on the legality of all research in the country. Every laboratory, industrial or scholastic, was required to file information, in advance, on all projected research before this new bureau, which could, and did, ban absolutely all such as it disapproved of.

The inevitable appeal to the supreme court came on November 9, 1974, in the case of Westly vs. Simmons, in which Joseph Westly of Stanford upheld his right to continue his investigations on atomic power on the grounds that the Stonely-Carter act was unconstitutional.

How we five, isolated amid the snowdrifts of the Middle West, followed that case! We had all the Minneapolis and St. Paul papers sent to us—always reaching us two days late—and devoured every word of print concerning it. For the two months of suspense work ceased entirely on the *New Prometheus*.

It was rumored at first that the court would declare the act unconstitutional, and monster parades were held in every large town against this eventuality. The League of the Righteous brought its powerful influence to bear—and even the supreme court submitted. It was five to four for constitutionality. *Science strangled by the vote of one man.*

And it was strangled beyond a doubt. The members of the bureau were Eldredge men, heart and soul, and nothing that would not have immediate industrial use was passed.

"Science has gone too far," said Eldredge in a famous speech at about that time. "We must halt it indefinitely, and allow the world to catch up. Only through that and trust in God may we hope to achieve universal and permanent prosperity."

But this was one of Eldredge's last statements. He had never fully recovered from the broken legs he received that fateful day in July of '73, and his strenuous life since then strained his constitution past the breaking point. On February 2, 1976, he passed away amid a burst of mourning unequaled since Lincoln's assassination.

His death had no immediate effect on the course of events. The rules of the FSRIB grew, in fact, in stringency as the years passed. So starved and choked did science become, that once more colleges found themselves forced to reinstate philosophy and the classics as the chief studies—and at that the student body fell to the lowest point since the beginning of the twentieth century.

These conditions prevailed more or less throughout the civilized world, reaching even lower depths in England, and perhaps least depressing in Germany, which was the last to fall under the "Neo-Victorian" influence.

The nadir of science came in the spring of 1978, a bare month before the completion of the *New Prometheus*, with the passing of the "Easter Edict"—it was issued the day before Easter. By it, *all* independent research or experimentation was absolutely forbidden. The FSRIB thereafter reserved the right to allow only such research as it *specifically requested*.

John Harman and I stood before the gleaming metal of the *New Prometheus* that Easter Sunday; I in the deepest gloom, and he in an almost jovial mood.

"Well, Clifford, my boy," said he, "the last ton of fuel, a few polishing touches, and I am ready for my second attempt. This time there will be no Sheltons among us." He hummed a hymn. That was all the radio played those days, and even we rebels sang them from sheer frequency of repetition.

I grunted sourly: "It's no use, boss. Ten to one, you end up somewhere in space, and even if you come back, you'll most likely be hung by the neck. We can't win." My head shook dolefully from side to side.

"Bah! This state of affairs can't last, Cliff."

"I think it will. Winstead was right that time. The pendulum swings, and since 1945 it's been swinging against us. We're ahead of the times—or behind them."

"Don't speak of that fool Winstead. You're making the same mistake he did. Trends are things of centuries and millenniums, not years or decades. For five hundred years we have been moving toward science. You can't reverse that in thirty years."

"Then what are we doing?" I asked sarcastically.

"We're going through a momentary reaction following a period of too-rapid advance in the Mad Decades. Just such a reaction took place in the Romantic Age—the first Victorian Period—following the too-rapid advance of the eighteenth-century Age of Reason."

"Do you really think so?" I was shaken by his evident self-assurance.

"Of course. This period has a perfect analogy in the spasmodic 'revivals' that used to hit the small towns in America's Bible Belt a century or so ago. For a week, perhaps, everyone would get religion and virtue would reign triumphant. Then, one by one, they would backslide and the Devil would resume his sway.

"In fact, there are symptoms of backsliding even now. The L. R. has indulged in one squabble after another since Eldredge's death. There have been half a dozen schisms already. The very extremities to which those in power are going are helping us, for the country is rapidly tiring of it."

And that ended the argument—I in total defeat, as usual.

A month later, the *New Prometheus* was complete. It was nowhere near as glittering and as beautiful as the original, and bore many a trace of makeshift workmanship, but we were proud of it—proud and triumphant.

"I'm going to try again, men"—Harman's voice was husky, and his little frame vibrant with happiness—"and I may not make it, but for that I don't care." His eyes shone in anticipation. "I'll be shooting through the void at last, and the dream of mankind will come true. Out around the Moon and back; the first to see the other side. It's worth the chance."

"You won't have fuel enough to land on the Moon, boss, which is a pity," I said.

"That doesn't matter. There'll be other flights after this, better prepared and better equipped."

At that a pessimistic whisper ran through the little group surrounding him, to which he paid no attention.

"Good-by," he said. "I'll be seeing you." And with a cheerful grin he climbed into the ship.

Fifteen minutes later, the five of us sat about the living-room table, frowning, lost in thought, eyes gazing out the building at the spot where a burned section of soil marked the spot where a few minutes earlier the *New Prometheus* had lain.

Simonoff voiced the thought that was in the mind of each one of us: "Maybe it would be better for him *not* to come back. He won't be treated very well if he does, I think." And we all nodded in gloomy assent.

How foolish that prediction seems to me now from the hindsight of three decades.

The rest of the story is really not mine, for I did not see Harman again until a month after his eventful trip ended in a safe landing.

It was almost thirty-six hours after the take-off that a screaming projectile shot its way over Washington and buried itself in the mud just across the Potomac.

Investigators were at the scene of the landing within fifteen minutes, and in another fifteen minutes the police were there, for it was found that the projectile was a *rocketship*. They stared in involuntary awe at the tired, disheveled man who staggered out in near-collapse.

There was utter silence while he shook his fist at the gawking spectators and shouted: "Go ahead, hang me, fools. But I've reached the Moon, and you can't hang *that*. Get the FSRIB. Maybe they'll declare the flight illegal and, therefore, nonexistent." He laughed weakly and suddenly collapsed.

Someone shouted: "Take him to a hospital. He's sick." In stiff unconsciousness Harman was bundled into a police car and carried away, while the police formed a guard about the rocketship.

Government officials arrived and investigated the ship, read the log, inspected the drawings and photographs he had taken of the Moon, and finally departed in silence. The crowd grew and the word spread that a man had reached the Moon.

Curiously enough, there was little resentment of the fact. Men were impressed and awed; the crowd whispered and cast inquisitive glances at the dim crescent of Luna, scarcely seen in the bright sunlight. Over all, an uneasy pall of silence, the silence of indecision, lay.

Then, at the hospital, Harman revealed his identity, and the fickle world went wild. Even Harman himself was stunned in surprise at the rapid change in the world's temper. It seemed almost incredible, and yet it was true. Secret discontent, combined with a heroic tale of man against overwhelming odds—the sort of tale that had stirred man's soul since the beginning of time—served to sweep everyone into an ever-swelling current of anti-Victorianism. And Eldredge was dead—no other could replace him.

I saw Harman at the hospital shortly after that. He was propped up and still half buried with papers, telegrams and letters. He grinned at me and nodded. "Well, Cliff," he whispered, "the pendulum swung back again."

THE BLUE GIRAFFE

Astounding Science Fiction, August

by L. Sprague de Camp

Sprague possesses a sharp wit and a fine sense of humor, never better expressed than in this delightful tale.

(The craft of the short story, by the way, is by no means identical with that of the novel. Many an excellent short-story writer writes novels with difficulty, if at all, and vice versa. Sprague, however, could do either with equal skill and, as a matter of fact, I think his novels are even more effective than his short stories. How I wish it were possible to include Divide and Rule *or* Lest Darkness Fall *or* The Roaring Trumpet, *but alas, we must stick to reasonably short stories. IA)*

Athelstan Cuff was, to put it very mildly, astonished that his son should be crying. It wasn't that he had exaggerated ideas about Peter's stoicism, but the fact was that Peter never cried. He was, for a twelve-year-old boy, self-possessed to the point of grimness. And now he was undeniably sniffling. It must be something jolly well awful.

Cuff pushed aside the pile of manuscript he had been reading. He was the editor of *Biological Review;* a stoutish Englishman with prematurely white hair, prominent blue eyes, and a complexion that could have been used for painting box cars. He looked a little like a lobster who had been boiled once and was determined not to repeat the experience.

"What's wrong, old man?" he asked.

Peter wiped his eyes and looked at his father calculatingly. Cuff sometimes wished that Peter wasn't so damned rational.

A spot of boyish unreasonableness would be welcome at times.

"Come on, old fella, out with it. What's the good of having a father if you can't tell him things?"

Peter finally got it out. "Some of the guys—" He stopped to blow his nose. Cuff winced slightly at the "guys." His one regret about coming to America was the language his son picked up. As he didn't believe in pestering Peter all the time, he had to suffer in silence.

"Some of the guys say you aren't really my father."

It had come, thought Cuff, as it was bound to sooner or later. He shouldn't have put off telling the boy for so long.

"What do you mean, old man?" he stalled.

"They say," *sniff*, "I'm just a 'dopted boy."

Cuff forced out, "So what?" The despised Americanism seemed to be the only thing that covered the situation.

"What do you mean, 'so what'?"

"I mean just that. What of it? It doesn't make a particle of difference to your mother or me, I assure you. So why should it to you?"

Peter thought. "Could you send me away some time, on account of I was only 'dopted?"

"Oh, so that's what's worrying you? The answer is no. Legally you're just as much our son as if . . . as anyone is anybody's son. But whatever gave you the idea we'd ever send you away? I'd like to see that chap who could get you away from us."

"Oh, I just wondered."

"Well, you can stop wondering. We don't want to, and we couldn't if we did. It's perfectly all right, I tell you. Lots of people start out as adopted children, and it doesn't make any difference to anybody. You wouldn't get upset if somebody tried to make fun of you because you had two eyes and a nose, would you?"

Peter had recovered his composure. "How did it happen?"

"It's quite a story. I'll tell you, if you like."

Peter only nodded.

"I've told you," said Athelstan Cuff, "about how before I came to America I worked for some years in South Africa. I've told you about how I used to work with elephants and lions and things, and about how I transplanted some white rhino from Swaziland to the Kruger Park. But I've never told you about the blue giraffe—"

In the 1940's the various South African governments were considering the problem of a park that would be not merely a game preserve available to tourists, but a completely wild area in which no people other than scientists and wardens would be allowed. They finally agreed on the Okvango River Delta in Ngamiland, as the only area that was sufficiently large and at the same time thinly populated.

The reasons for its sparse population were simple enough: nobody likes to settle down in a place when he is likely to find his house and farm under three feet of water some fine morning. And it is irritating to set out to fish in a well-known lake only to find that the lake has turned into a grassy plain, around the edges of which the mopane trees are already springing up.

So the Batawana, in whose reserve the Delta lay, were mostly willing to leave this capricious stretch of swamp and jumble to the elephant and the lion. The few Batawana who did live in and around the Delta were bought out and moved. The Crown Office of the Bechuanaland Protectorate got around its own rules against alienation of tribal lands by taking a perpetual lease on the Delta and surrounding territory from the Batawana, and named the whole area Jan Smuts Park.

When Athelstan Cuff got off the train at Francistown in September of 1976, a pelting spring rain was making the platform smoke. A tall black in khaki loomed out of the grayness, and said: "You are Mr. Cuff, from Cape Town? I'm George Mtengeni, the warden at Smuts. Mr. Opdyck wrote me you were coming. The Park's car is out this way."

Cuff followed. He'd heard of George Mtengeni. The man wasn't a Chwana at all, but a Zulu from near Durban. When the Park had been set up, the Batawana had thought that the warden ought to be a Tawana. But the Makoba, feeling chesty about their independence from their former masters, the Batawana, had insisted on his being one of their nation. Finally the Crown Office in disgust had hired an outsider. Mtengeni had the dark skin and narrow nose found in so many of the Kaffir Bantu. Cuff guessed that he probably had a low opinion of the Chwana people in general and the Batawana in particular.

They got into the car. Mtengeni said: "I hope you don't mind coming way out here like this. It's too bad that you couldn't come before the rains started; the pans they are all full by now."

"So?" said Cuff. "What's the Mababe this year?" He referred to the depression known variously as Mababe Lake, Swamp, or Pan, depending on whether at a given time it contained much, little, or no water.

"The Mababe, it is a lake, a fine lake full of drowned trees and hippo. I think the Okavango is shifting north again. That means Lake Ngami it will dry up again."

"So it will. But look here, what's all this business about a blue giraffe? Your letter was dashed uninformative."

Mtengeni showed his white teeth. "It appeared on the edge of the Mopane Forest seventeen months ago. That was just the beginning. There have been other things since. If I'd told you more, you would have written the Crown Office saying that their warden was having a nervous breakdown. Me, I'm sorry to drag you into this, but the Crown Office keeps saying they can't spare a man to investigate."

"Oh, quite all right, quite," answered Cuff. "I was glad to get away from Cape Town anyway. And we haven't had a mystery since old Hickey disappeared."

"Since who disappeared? You know me, I can't keep up with things out in the wilds."

"Oh, that was many years ago. Before your time, or mine for that matter. Hickey was a scientist who set out into the Kalahari with a truck and a Xosa assistant, and disappeared. Men flew all over the Kalahari looking for him, but never found a trace, and the sand had blown over his tire tracks. Jolly odd, it was."

The rain poured down steadily as they wallowed along the dirt road. Ahead, beyond the gray curtain, lay the vast plains of northern Bechuanaland with their great pans. And beyond the plains were, allegedly, a blue giraffe, and other things.

The spidery steelwork of the tower hummed as they climbed. At the top, Mtengeni said: "You can look over that way . . . west . . . to the other side of the forest. That's about twenty miles."

Cuff screwed up his eyes at the eyepieces. "Jolly good 'scope you've got here. But it's too hazy beyond the forest to see anything."

"It always is, unless we have a high wind. That's the edge of the swamps."

"Dashed if I see how you can patrol such a big area all by yourself."

"Oh, these Bechuana they don't give much trouble. They are honest. Even I have to admit that they have some good qualities. Anyway, you can't get far into the Delta without getting lost in the swamps. There are ways, but then, I only know them. I'll show them to you, but please don't tell these Bechuana about them. Look, Mr. Cuff, there's our blue giraffe."

Cuff started. Mtengeni was evidently the kind of man who would announce an earthquake as casually as the morning mail.

Several hundred yards from the tower half a dozen giraffes were moving slowly through the brush, feeding on the tops of the scrubby trees. Cuff swung the telescope on them. In the middle of the herd was the blue one. Cuff blinked and looked again. There was no doubt about it; the animal was as brilliant a blue as if somebody had gone over it with paint. Athelstan Cuff suspected that that was what somebody *had* done. He said as much to Mtengeni.

The warden shrugged. "That, it would be a peculiar kind of amusement. Not to say risky. Do you see anything funny about the others?"

Cuff looked again. "Yes . . . by Jove, one of 'em's got a beard like a goat; only it must be six feet long, at least, now look here, George, what's all this leading up to?"

"I don't know myself. Tomorrow, if you like, I'll show you one of those ways into the Delta. But that, it's quite a walk, so we'd better take supplies for two or three days."

As they drove toward the Tamalakane, they passed four Batawana, sad-looking reddish-brown men in a mixture of native and European clothes. Mtengeni slowed the car and looked at them suspiciously as they passed, but there was no evidence that they had been poaching.

He said: "Ever since their Makoba slaves were freed, they've been going on a . . . decline, I suppose you would call it. They are too dignified to work."

They got out at the river. "We can't drive across the ford this time of year," explained the warden, locking the car. "But there's a rapid a little way down, where we can wade."

They walked down the trail, adjusting their packs. There wasn't much to see. The view was shut off by the tall soft-bodied swamp plants. The only sound was the hum of insects.

THE BLUE GIRAFFE

The air was hot and steamy already, though the sun had been up only half an hour. The flies drew blood when they bit, but the men were used to that. They simply slapped and waited for the next bite.

Ahead there was a deep gurgling noise, like a foghorn with water in its works. Cuff said: "How are your hippo doing this year?"

"Pretty good. There are some in particular that I want you to see. Ah, here we are."

They had come in sight of a stretch of calm water. In the foreground a hippopotamus repeated its foghorn bellow. Cuff saw others, of which only the eyes, ears, and nostrils were visible. One of them was moving; Cuff could make out the little V-shaped wakes pointing back from its nearly submerged head. It reached the shallows and lumbered out, dripping noisily.

Cuff blinked. "Must be something wrong with my eyes."

"No," said Mtengeni. "That hippo she is one of those I wanted you to see."

The hippopotamus was green with pink spots.

She spied the men, grunted suspiciously, and slid back into the water.

"I still don't believe it," said Cuff. "Dash it, man, that's impossible."

"You will see many more things," said Mtengeni. "Shall we go on?"

They found the rapid and struggled across; then walked along what might, by some stretch of the imagination, be called a trail. There was little sound other than their sucking footfalls, the hum of insects, and the occasional screech of a bird or the crashing of a buck through the reeds.

They walked for some hours. Then Mtengeni said: "Be careful. There is a rhino near."

Cuff wondered how the devil the Zulu knew, but he was careful. Presently they came on a clear space in which the rhinoceros was browsing.

The animal couldn't see them at that distance, and there was no wind to carry their smell. It must have heard them, though, for it left off its feeding and snorted, once, like a locomotive. It had two heads.

It trotted toward them sniffing.

The men got out their rifles. "My God!" said Athelstan Cuff. "Hope we don't have to shoot him. My God!"

"I don't think so," said the warden. "That's Tweedle. I know him. If he gets too close, give him one at the base of the horn and he ... he will run."

"Tweedle?"

"Yes. The right head is Tweedledum and the left is Tweedledee," said Mtengeni solemnly. "The whole rhino I call Tweedle."

The rhinoceros kept coming. Mtengeni said: "Watch this." He waved his hat and shouted: "Go away! *Footsack!*"

Tweedle stopped and snorted again. Then he began to circle like a waltzing mouse. Round and round he spun.

"We might as well go on," said Mtengeni. "He will keep that up for hours. You see Tweedledum is fierce, but Tweedledee, he is peaceful, even cowardly. So when I yell at Tweedle, Tweedledum wants to charge us, but Tweedledee he wants to run away. So the right legs go forward and the left legs go back, and Tweedle, he goes in circles. It takes him some time to agree on a policy."

"*Whew!*" said Athelstan Cuff. "I say, have you got any more things like this in your zoo?"

"Oh, yes, lots. That's what I hope you'll do something about."

Do something about this! Cuff wondered whether this was touching evidence of the native's faith in the white omniscience, or whether Mtengeni had gotten him there for the cynical amusement of watching him run in useless circles. Mtengeni himself gave no sign of what he was thinking.

Cuff said: "I can't understand, George, why somebody hasn't looked into this before."

Mtengeni shrugged. "Me, I've tried to get somebody to, but the government won't send anybody, and the scientific expeditions, there haven't been any of them for years. I don't know why."

"I can guess," said Cuff. "In the old days people even in the so-called civilized countries expected travel to be a jolly rugged proposition, so they didn't mind putting up with a few extra hardships on trek. But now that you can ride or fly almost anywhere on soft cushions, people won't put themselves out to get to a really uncomfortable and out-of-the-way place like Ngamiland."

Over the swampy smell came another, of carrion. Mtengeni pointed to the carcass of a waterbuck fawn, which the scavengers had apparently not discovered yet.

THE BLUE GIRAFFE

"That's why I want you to stop this whatever-it-is," he said. There was real concern in his voice.

"What do you mean, George?"

"Do you see its legs?"

Cuff looked. The forelegs were only half as long as the hind ones.

"That buck," said the Zulu. "It naturally couldn't live long. All over the Park, freaks like this they are being born. Most of them don't live. In ten years more, maybe twenty, all my animals will have died out because of this. Then my job, where is it?"

They stopped at sunset. Cuff was glad to. It had been some time since he'd done fifteen miles in one day, and he dreaded the morrow's stiffness. He looked at his map and tried to figure out where he was. But the cartographers had never seriously tried to keep track of the changes in the Okavango's multifarious branches, and had simply plastered the whole Delta with little blue dashes with tufts of blue lines sticking up from them, meaning simply "swamp." In all directions the country was a monotonous alternation of land and water. The two elements were inextricably mixed.

The Zulu was looking for a dry spot free of snakes. Cuff heard him suddenly shout *"Footsack!"* and throw a clod at a log. The log opened a pair of jaws, hissed angrily, and slid into the water.

"We'll have to have a good fire," said Mtengeni, hunting for dry wood. "We don't want a croc or hippo wandering into our tent by mistake."

After supper they set the automatic bug sprayer going, inflated their mattresses, and tried to sleep. A lion roared somewhere in the west. That sound no African, native or Africander, likes to hear when he is on foot at night. But the men were not worried; lions avoided the swampy areas. The mosquitoes presented a more immediate problem.

Many hours later, Athelstan Cuff heard Mtengeni getting up.

The warden said: "I just remembered a high spot half a mile from here, where there's plenty of firewood. Me, I'm going out to get some."

Cuff listened to Mtengeni's retreating steps in the soft ground; then to his own breathing. Then he listened to something else. It sounded like a human yell.

He got up and pulled on his boots quickly. He fumbled around for the flashlight, but Mtengeni had taken it with him.

The yell came again.

Cuff found his rifle and cartridge belt in the dark and went out. There was enough starlight to walk by if you were careful. The fire was nearly out. The yells seemed to come from a direction opposite to that in which Mtengeni had gone. They were high-pitched, like a woman's screams.

He walked in their direction, stumbling over irregularities in the ground and now and then stepping up to his calves in unexpected water. The yells were plainer now. They weren't in English. Something was also snorting.

He found the place. There was a small tree, in the branches of which somebody was perched. Below the tree a noisy bulk moved around. Cuff caught the outline of a sweeping horn, and knew he had to deal with a buffalo.

He hated to shoot. For a Park official to kill one of his charges simply wasn't done. Besides, he couldn't see to aim for a vital spot, and he didn't care to try to dodge a wounded buffalo in the dark. They could move with race-horse speed through the heaviest growth.

On the other hand, he couldn't leave even a poor fool of a native woman treed. The buffalo, if it was really angry, would wait for days until its victim weakened and fell. Or it would butt the tree until the victim was shaken out. Or it would rear up and try to hook the victim out with its horns.

Athelstan Cuff shot the buffalo. The buffalo staggered about a bit and collapsed.

The victim climbed down swiftly, pouring out a flood of thanks in Xosa. It was very bad Xosa, even worse than the Englishman's. Cuff wondered what she was doing here, nearly a thousand miles from where the Maxosa lived. He assumed that she was a native, though it was too dark to see. He asked her if she spoke English, but she didn't seem to understand the question, so he made shift with the Bantu dialect.

"*Uveli phi na?*" he asked sternly. "Where do you come from? Don't you know that nobody is allowed in the Park without special permission?"

"*Izwe kamafene wabantu,*" she replied.

"What? Never heard of the place. Land of the baboon people, indeed! What are you?"

"*Ingwamza.*"

"You're a white stork? Are you trying to be funny?"

"I didn't say I was a white stork. Ingwamza's my name."

THE BLUE GIRAFFE

"I don't care about your name. I want to know what you *are*."

"*Umfene umfazi.*"

Cuff controlled his exasperation. "All right, all right, you're a baboon woman. I don't care what clan you belong to. What's your tribe? Batawana, Bamangwato, Bangwaketse, Barolong, Herero, or what? Don't try to tell me you're a Xosa; no Xosa ever used an accent like that."

"*Amafene abantu.*"

"What the devil are the baboon people?"

"People who live in the Park."

Cuff resisted the impulse to pull out two handfuls of hair by the roots. "But I tell you nobody lives in the Park! It isn't allowed! Come now, where do you really come from and what's your native language and why are you trying to talk Xosa?"

"I told you, I live in the Park. And I speak Xosa because all we *amafene abantu* speak it. That's the language Mqhavi taught us."

"Who is Mqhavi?"

"The man who taught us to speak Xosa."

Cuff gave up. "Come along, you're going to see the warden. Perhaps he can make some sense out of your gabble. And you'd better have a good reason for trespassing, my good woman, or it'll go hard with you. Especially as it resulted in the killing of a good buffalo." He started off toward the camp, making sure that Ingwamza followed him closely.

The first thing he discovered was that he couldn't see the light of any fire to guide him back. Either he'd come farther than he thought, or the fire had died altogether while Mtengeni was getting wood. He kept on for a quarter of an hour in what he thought was the right direction. Then he stopped. He had, he realized, not the vaguest idea of where he was.

He turned. "*Sibaphi na?*" he snapped. "Where are we?"

"In the Park."

Cuff began to wonder whether he'd ever succeed in delivering this native woman to Mtengeni before he strangled her with his bare hands. "I know we're in the Park," he snarled. "But *where* in the Park?"

"I don't know exactly. Somewhere near my people's land."

"That doesn't do me any good. Look: I left the warden's

camp when I heard you yell. I want to get back to it. Now how do I do it?"

"Where is the warden's camp?"

"I don't know, stupid. If I did I'd go there."

"If you don't know where it is, how do you expect me to guide you thither? I don't know either."

Cuff made strangled noises in his throat. Inwardly he had to admit that she had him there, which only made him madder. Finally he said: "Never mind, suppose you take me to your people. Maybe they have somebody with some sense."

"Very well," said the native woman, and she set off at a rapid pace, Cuff stumbling after her vague outline. He began to wonder if maybe she wasn't right about living in the Park. She seemed to know where she was going.

"Wait," he said. He ought to write a note to Mtengeni, explaining what he was up to, and stick it on a tree for the warden to find. But there was no pencil or paper in his pockets. He didn't even have a match safe or a cigarette lighter. He'd taken all those things out of his pockets when he'd lain down.

They went on a way, Cuff pondering on how to get in touch with Mtengeni. He didn't want himself and the warden to spend a week chasing each other around the Delta. Perhaps it would be better to stay where they were and build a fire—but again, he had no matches, and didn't see much prospect of making a fire by rubbing sticks in this damned damp country.

Ingwamza said: "Stop. There are buffalo ahead."

Cuff listened and heard faintly the sound of snapping grass stems as the animals fed.

She continued: "We'll have to wait until it gets light. Then maybe they'll go away. If they don't, we can circle around them, but I couldn't find the way around in the dark."

They found the highest point they could and settled down to wait. Something with legs had crawled inside Cuff's shirt. He mashed it with a slap.

He strained his eyes into the dark. It was impossible to tell how far away the buffalo were. Overhead a nightjar brought its wings together with a single startling clap. Cuff told his nerves to behave themselves. He wished he had a smoke.

The sky began to lighten. Gradually Cuff was able to make out the black bulks moving among the reeds. They were at least two hundred yards away. He'd have preferred that they

THE BLUE GIRAFFE 259

were at twice the distance, but it was better than stumbling right on them.

It became lighter and lighter. Cuff never took his eyes off the buffalo. There was something queer about the nearest one. It had six legs.

Cuff turned to Ingwamza and started to whisper: "What kind of buffalo do you call—" Then he gave a yell of pure horror and jumped back. His rifle went off, tearing a hole in his boot.

He had just gotten his first good look at the native woman in the rapidly waxing dawn. Ingwamza's head was that of an overgrown chacma baboon.

The buffalo stampeded through the feathery papyrus. Cuff and Ingwamza stood looking at each other. Then Cuff looked at his right foot. Blood was running out of the jagged hole in the leather.

"What's the matter? Why did you shoot yourself?" asked Ingwamza.

Cuff couldn't think of an answer to that one. He sat down and took off his boot. The foot felt numb, but there seemed to be no harm done aside from a piece of skin the size of a sixpence gouged out of the margin. Still, you never knew what sort of horrible infection might result from a trifling wound in these swamps. He tied his foot up with his handkerchief and put his boot back on.

"Just an accident," he said. "Keep going, Ingwamza."

Ingwamza went, Cuff limping behind. The sun would rise any minute now. It was light enough to make out colors. Cuff saw that Ingwamza, in describing herself as a baboon-woman, had been quite literal, despite the size, general proportions, and posture of a human being. Her body, but for the greenish-yellow hair and the short tail, might have passed for that of a human being, if you weren't too particular. But the astonishing head with its long bluish muzzle gave her the appearance of an Egyptian animal-headed god. Cuff wondered vaguely if the *'fene abantu* were a race of man-monkey hybrids. That was impossible, of course. But he'd seen so many impossible things in the last couple of days.

She looked back at him. "We shall arrive in an hour or two. I'm sleepy." She yawned. Cuff repressed a shudder at the sight of four canine teeth big enough for a leopard. Ingwamza could tear the throat out of a man with those fangs as easily as biting the end off a banana. And he'd been using his most hectoring colonial-administrator tone on her in the dark!

He made a resolve never to speak harshly to anybody he couldn't see.

Ingwamza pointed to a carroty baobab against the sky. "*Izew kamagene wabantu.*" They had to wade a little stream to get there. A six-foot monitor lizard walked across their path, saw them, and disappeared with a scuttle.

The *'fene abantu* lived in a village much like that of any Bantu people, but the circular thatched huts were smaller and cruder. Baboon people ran out to peer at Cuff and to feel his clothes. He gripped his rifle tightly. They didn't act hostile, but it gave you a dashed funny feeling. The males were larger than the females, with even longer muzzles and bigger tusks.

In the center of the village sat a big *umfene umntu* scratching himself in front of the biggest hut. Ingwamza said, "That is my father, the chief. His name is Indlovu." To the baboon-man she told of her rescue.

The chief was the only *umfene umntu* that Cuff had seen who wore anything. What he wore was a necktie. The necktie had been a gaudy thing once.

The chief got up and made a speech, the gist of which was that Cuff had done a great thing, and that Cuff would be their guest until his wound healed. Cuff had a chance to observe the difficulties that the *'fene abantu* had with the Xosa tongue. The clicks were blurred, and they stumbled badly over the lipsmack. With those mouths, he could see how they might.

But he was only mildly interested. His foot was hurting like the very devil. He was glad when they led him into a hut so he could take off his boot. The hut was practically unfurnished. Cuff asked the *'fene abantu* if he might have some of the straw used for thatching. They seemed puzzled by his request, but complied, and he made himself a bed of sorts. He hated sleeping on the ground, especially on ground infested with arthropodal life. He hated vermin, and knew he was in for an intimate acquaintance with them.

He had nothing to bandage his foot with, except the one handkerchief, which was now thoroughly blood-soaked. He'd have to wash and dry it before it would be fit to use again. And where in the Okavango Delta could he find water fit to wash the handkerchief in? Of course he could boil the water. In what? He was relieved and amazed when his questions brought forth the fact that there was a large iron pot in the village, obtained from God knew where.

The wound had clotted satisfactorily, and he dislodged the handkerchief with infinite care from the scab. While his water was boiling, the chief, Indlovu, came in and talked to him. The pain in his foot had subsided for the moment, and he was able to realize what an extraordinary thing he had come across, and to give Indlovu his full attention. He plied Indlovu with questions.

The chief explained what he knew about himself and his people. It seemed that he was the first of the race; all the others were his descendants. Not only Ingwamza but all the other *amafene abafazi* were his daughters. Ingwamza was merely the last. He was old now. He was hazy about dates, but Cuff got the impression that these beings had a shorter life span than human beings, and matured much more quickly. If they were in fact baboons, that was natural enough.

Indlovu didn't remember having had any parents. The earliest he remembered was being led around by Mqhavi. Stanley H. Mqhavi had been a black man, and worked for the machine man, who had been a pink man like Cuff. He had had a machine up on the edge of the Chobe Swamp. His name had been Heeky.

Of course, Hickey! thought Cuff. Now he was getting somewhere. Hickey had disappeared by simply running his truck up to Ngamiland without bothering to tell anybody where he was going. That had been before the Park had been established; before Cuff had come out from England. Mqhair must have been his Xosa assistant. His thoughts raced ahead of Indlovu's words.

Indlovu went on to tell about how Heeky had died, and how Mqhavi, not knowing how to run the machine, had taken him, Indlovu, and his now numerous progeny in an attempt to find his way back to civilization. He had gotten lost in the Delta. Then he had cut his foot somehow, and gotten sick, very sick. Cuff had come out from England. Mqhavi must have Mqhavi, had gotten well he had been very weak. So he had settled down with Indlovu and his family. They already walked upright and spoke Xosa, which Mqhavi had taught them. Cuff got the idea that the early family relationships among the *'fene abantu* had of necessity involved close inbreeding. Mqhavi had taught them all he knew, and then died, after warning them not to go within a mile of the machine, which, as far as they knew, was still up at the Chobe Swamp.

Cuff thought, that blasted machine is an electronic tube of some sort, built to throw short waves of the length to affect animal genes. Probably Indlovu represented one of Hickey's early experiments. Then Hickey had died, and—left the thing going. He didn't know how it got power; some solar system, perhaps.

Suppose Hickey had died while the thing was turned on. Mqhavi might have dragged his body out and left the door open. He might have been afraid to try to turn it off, or he might not have thought of it. So every animal that passed that doorway got a dose of the rays, and begat monstrous offspring. These super-baboons were one example; whether an accidental or a controlled mutation, might never be known.

For every useful mutation there were bound to be scores of useless or harmful ones. Mtengeni had been right: it had to be stopped while there was still normal stock left in the Park. He wondered again how to get in touch with the warden. He'd be damned if anything short of the threat of death would get him to walk on that foot, for a few days anyhow.

Ingwamza entered with a wooden dish full of a mess of some sort. Athelstan Cuff decided resignedly that he was expected to eat it. He couldn't tell by looking whether it was animal or vegetable in nature. After the first mouthful he was sure it was neither. Nothing in the animal and vegetable worlds could taste as awful as that. It was too bad Mqhavi hadn't been a Bamangwato; he'd have really known how to cook, and could have taught these monkeys. Still, he had to eat something to support life. He fell to with the wooden spoon they gave him, suppressing an occasional gag and watching the smaller solid particles closely. Sure enough, he had to smack two of them with the spoon to keep them from crawling out.

"How it is?" asked Ingwamza. Indlovu had gone out.

"Fine," lied Cuff. He was chasing a slimy piece of what he suspected was waterbuck tripe around the dish.

"I am glad. We'll feed you a lot of that. Do you like scorpions?"

"You mean to *eat?*"

"Of course. What else are they good for?"

He gulped. "No."

"I won't give you any then. You see I'm glad to know what my future husband likes."

"What?" He thought he had misunderstood her.

"I said, I am glad to know what you like, so I can please you after you are my husband."

Athelstan Cuff said nothing for sixty seconds. His naturally prominent eyes bulged even more as her words sank in. Finally he spoke.

"Gluk," he said.

"What's that?"

"Gug. Gah. My God. Let me out of here!" His voice jumped two octaves, and he tried to get up. Ingwamza caught his shoulders and pushed him gently, but firmly, back on his pallet. He struggled, but without visibly exerting herself the *'fene umfazi* held him as in a vise.

"You can't go," she said. "If you try to walk on that foot you will get sick."

His ruddy face was turning purple! "Let me up! Let me up, I say! I can't stand this!"

"Will you promise not to try to go out if I do? Father would be furious if I let you do anything unwise."

He promised, getting a grip on himself again. He already felt a bit foolish about his panic. He was in a nasty jam, certainly, but an official of His Majesty didn't act like a frightened schoolgirl at every crisis.

"What," he asked, "is this all about?"

"Father is so grateful to you for saving my life that he intends to bestow me on you in marriage, without even asking a bride price."

"But . . . but . . . I'm married already," he lied.

"What of it? I'm not afraid of your other wives. If they got fresh, I'd tear them in pieces like this." She bared her teeth and went through the motions of tearing several Mistresses Cuff in pieces. Athelstan Cuff shut his eyes at the horrid sight.

"Among my people," he said, "you're allowed only one wife."

"That's too bad," said Ingwamza. "That means that you couldn't go back to your people after you married me, doesn't it?"

Cuff sighed. These *'fene abantu* combined the mental outlook of uneducated Maxosa with physical equipment that would make a lion think twice before attacking one. He'd probably have to shoot his way out. He looked around the hut craftily. His rifle wasn't in sight. He didn't dare ask about it for fear of arousing suspicion.

"Is your father set on this plan?" he asked.

"Oh, yes, very. Father is a good *umntu*, but he gets set on ideas like this and nothing will make him change them. And he has a terrible temper. If you cross him when he has his heart set on something, he will tear you in pieces. *Small pieces.*" She seemed to relish the phrase.

"How do *you* feel about it, Ingwamza?"

"Oh, I do everything father says. He knows more than any of us."

"Yes, but I mean you personally. Forget about your father for the moment."

She didn't quite catch on for a moment, but after further explanation she said: "I wouldn't mind. It would be a great thing for my people if one of us was married to a man."

Cuff silently thought that that went double for him.

Indlovu came in with two other *amafene abantu*. "Run along, Ingwamza," he said. The three baboon-men squatted around Athelstan Cuff and began questioning him about men and the world outside the Delta.

When Cuff stumbled over a phrase, one of the questioners, a scarred fellow named Sondlo, asked why he had difficulty. Cuff explained that Xosa wasn't his native language.

"Men do speak other languages?" asked Indlovu. "I remember now, the great Mqhavi once told me something to that effect. But he never taught me any other languages. Perhaps he and Heeky spoke one of these other languages, but I was too young when Heeky died to remember."

Cuff explained something about linguistics. He was immediately pressed to "say something in English." Then they wanted to learn English, right then, that afternoon.

Cuff finished his evening meal and looked without enthusiasm at his pallet. No artificial light, so these people rose and set with the sun. He stretched out. The straw rustled. He jumped up, bringing his injured foot down hard. He yelped, swore, and felt the bandage. Yes, he'd started it bleeding again. Oh, to hell with it. He attacked the straw, chasing out a mouse, six cockroaches, and uncounted smaller bugs. Then he stretched out again. Looking up, he felt his scalp prickle. A ten-inch centipede was methodically hunting its prey over the underside of the roof. If it missed its footing when it was right over him—He unbuttoned his shirt and pulled it up over his face. Then the mosquitoes attacked his midriff. His foot throbbed.

A step brought him up; it was Ingwamza.

"What is it now?" he asked.

"Ndiya kuhlaha apha," she answered.

"Oh no, you're not going to stay here. We're not . . . well, anyway, it simply isn't done among my people."

"But Esselten, somebody must watch you in case you get sick. My father—"

"No, I'm sorry, but that's final. If you're going to marry me you'll have to learn how to behave among men. And we're beginning right now."

To his surprise and relief, she went without further objection, albeit sulkily. He'd never have dared to try to put her out by force.

When she had gone, he crawled over to the door of the hut. The sun had just set, and the moon would follow it in a couple of hours. Most of the *'fene abantu* had retired. But a couple of them squatted outside their huts, in sight of his place, watchfully.

Heigh ho, he thought, they aren't taking any chances. Perhaps the old boy *is* grateful and all that rot. But I think my fiancée let the cat out when she said that about the desirability of hitching one of the tribe to a human being. Of course the poor things don't know that it wouldn't have any legal standing at all. But that fact wouldn't save me from a jolly unpleasant experience in the meantime. Suppose I haven't escaped by the time of the ceremony. Would I go through with it? *Br-r-r!* Of course not. I'm an Englishman and an officer of the Crown. But if it meant my life . . . I don't know. I'm dashed if I do. Perhaps I can talk them out of it . . . being careful not to get them angry in the process—

He was tied to the straw, and enormous centipedes were dropping off the ceiling onto his face. Then he was running through the swamp, with Ingwamza and her irate pa after him. His feet stuck in the mud so he couldn't move, and there was a light in his face. Mtengeni—good old George!—was riding a two headed rhino. But instead of rescuing him, the warden said: "Mr. Cuff, you must do something about these Bechuana. Them, they are catching all my animals and painting them red with green stripes." Then he woke up.

It took him a second to realize that the light was from the

setting moon, not the rising sun, and that he therefore had been asleep less than two hours. It took him another second to realize what had wakened him. The straw of the hut wall had been wedged apart, and through the gap a *'fene umntu* was crawling. While Cuff was still wondering why one of his hosts, or captors, should use this peculiar method of getting in, the baboon-man stood up. He looked enormous in the faint light.

"What is it?" asked Cuff.

"If you make a noise," said the stranger, "I will kill you."

"What? What's the idea? Why should you want to kill me?"

"You have stolen my Ingwamza."

"But . . . but—" Cuff was at a loss. Here the gal's old man would tear him in pieces—*small* pieces—if he didn't marry her, and a rival or something would kill him if he did. "Let's talk it over first," he said, in what he hoped was a normal voice. "Who are you, by the way?"

"My name is Cukata. I was to have married Ingwamza next month. And then you came."

"What . . . what—"

"I won't kill you. Not if you make no noise. I will just fix you so you won't marry Ingwamza." He moved toward the pile of straw.

Cuff didn't waste time inquiring into the horrid details. "Wait a minute," he said, cold sweat bedewing not merely his brow, but his whole torso. "My dear fellow, this marriage wasn't my idea. It was Indlovu's, entirely. I don't want to steal your girl. They just informed me that I was going to marry her, without asking me about it at all. I don't *want* to marry her. In fact there's nothing I want to do less."

The *'fene umntu* stood still for a moment, thinking. Then he said softly: "You wouldn't marry my Ingwamza if you had the chance? You think she is ugly?"

"Well—"

"By u-Qamata, that's an insult! Nobody shall think such thoughts of my Ingwamza! Now I will kill you for sure!"

"Wait, wait!" Cuff's voice, normally a pleasant low baritone, became a squeak. "That isn't it at all! She's beautiful, intelligent, industrious, all that a *'ntu* could want. But I can never marry her." Inspiration! Cuff went on rapidly. Never had he spoken Xosa so fluently. "You know that if lion mates with leopard, there are no offspring." Cuff wasn't sure that was so, but he took a chance. "It is that way with my people and yours. We are too different. There would be no issue to our marriage. And Indlovu would not have grandchildren by us to gladden his old age."

Cukata, after some thought, saw, or thought he did. "But," he said, "how can I prevent this marriage without killing you?"

"You could help me escape."

"So. Now that's an idea. Where do you want to go?"

"Do you know where the Hickey machine is?"

"Yes, though I have never been close to it. That is forbidden. About fifteen miles north of here, on the edge of the Chobe Swamp, is a rock. By the rock are three baobab trees, close together. Between the trees and the swamp are two houses. The machine is in one of those houses."

He was silent again. "You can't travel fast with that wounded foot. They would overtake you. Perhaps Indlovu would tear you in pieces, or perhaps he would bring you back. If he brought you back, we should fail. If he tore you in pieces, I should be sorry, for I like you, even if you are a feeble little *isi-pham-pham*." Cuff wished that the simian brain would get around to the point. "I have it. In ten minutes I shall whistle. You will then crawl out through this hole in the wall, making no noise. You understand?"

When Athelstan Cuff crawled out, he found Cukata in the alley between two rows of huts. There was a strong reptilian stench in the air. Behind the baboon-man was something large and black. It walked with a swaying motion. It brushed against Cuff, and he almost cried out at the touch of cold, leathery hide.

"This is the largest," said Cukata. "We hope some day to have a whole herd of them. They are fine for traveling across the swamps, because they can swim as well as run. And they grow much faster than the ordinary crocodile."

The thing was a crocodile but such a crocodile! Though not much over fifteen feet in length, it had long, powerful legs that raised its body a good four feet off the ground, giving it a dinosaurian look. It rubbed against Cuff, and the thought occurred to him that it had taken an astonishing mutation indeed to give a brainless and voracious reptile an affection for human beings.

Cukata handed Cuff a knobkerry, and explained: "Whistle, loudly, when you want him to come. To start him, hit him on the tail with this. To stop him, hit him on the nose. To make him go to the left, hit him on the right side of the neck, not too hard. To make him go to the right, hit him—"

"On the left side of the neck, but not too hard," finished Cuff. "What does he eat?"

"Anything that is meat. But you needn't feed him for two or three days; he has been fed recently."

"Don't you use a saddle?"

"Saddle? What's that?"

"Never mind." Cuff climbed aboard, wincing as he settled onto the sharp dorsal ridges of the animal's hide.

"Wait," said Cukata. "The moon will be completely gone in a moment. Remember, I shall say that I know nothing about your escape, but that you go out and stole him yourself. His name Soga."

There were the baobab trees, and there were the houses. There were also a dozen elephants, facing the rider and his bizarre mount and spreading their immense ears. Athelstan Cuff was getting so blasé about freaks that he hardly noticed that two of the elephants had two trunks apiece; that another of them was colored a fair imitation of a Scotch tartan; that another of them had short legs like a hippopotamus, so that it looked like something out of a dachshund breeder's nightmare.

The elephants, for their part, seemed undecided whether to run or to attack, and finally compromised by doing nothing. Cuff realized when he was already past them that he had done a wickedly reckless thing in going so close to them unarmed except for the useless kerry. But somehow he couldn't get excited about mere elephants. His whole life for the past forty-eight hours had had a dreamlike quality. Maybe he was dreaming. Or maybe he had a charmed life. Or something. Though there was nothing dreamlike about the throb in his foot, or the acute soreness in his gluteus maximus.

Soga, being a crocodile, bowed his whole body at every stride. First the head and tail went to the right and the body to the left; then the process was reversed. Which was most unpleasant for his rider.

Cuff was willing to swear that he'd ridden at least fifty miles instead of the fifteen Cukata had mentioned. Actually he had done about thirty, not having been able to follow a straight line and having to steer by stars and, when it rose, the sun. A fair portion of the thirty had been hugging Soga's barrel while the croc's great tail drove them through the water like a racing shell. No hippo or other crocs had bothered them; evidently they knew when they were well off.

Athelstan Cuff slid—almost fell—off, and hobbled up to the entrance of one of the houses. His practiced eye took in the roof cistern, the solar boiler, the steam-electric plant, the batteries, and finally the tube inside. He went in. Yes, by Jove, the tube was in operation after all these years. Hickey must have had something jolly unusual. Cuff found the main switch easily enough and pulled it. All that happened was that the little orange glow in the tube died.

The house was so silent it made Cuff uncomfortable, except for the faint hum of the solar power plant. As he moved about, using the kerry for a crutch, he stirred up the dust which lay six inches deep on the floor. Maybe there were notebooks or something which ought to be collected. There had been, he soon discovered, but the termites had eaten every scrap of paper, and even the imitation-leather covers, leaving only the metal binding rings and their frames. It was the same with the books.

Something white caught his eye. It was paper, lying on a little metal-legged stand that the termites evidently hadn't thought well enough of to climb. He limped toward it eagerly. But it was only a newspaper, *Umlindi we Nyanga*—"The Monthly Watchman"—published in East London. Evidently, Stanley H. Mqhavi had subscribed to it. It crumbled at Cuff's touch.

Oh, well, he thought, can't expect much. We'll run along, and some of the bio-physicist chappies can come in and gather up the scientific apparatus.

He went out, called Soga, and started east. He figured that he could strike the old wagon road somewhere north of the Mababe, and get down to Mtengeni's main station that way.

Were those human voices? Cuff shifted uneasily on his Indian fakir's seat. He had gone about four miles after leaving Hickey's scientific station.

They were voices, but not human ones. They belonged to a dozen *'fene abantu*, who came loping through the grass with old Indlovu at their head.

Cuff reached back and thumped Soga's tail. If he could get the croc going all out, he might be able to run away from his late hosts. Soga wasn't as fast as a horse, but he could trot right along. Cuff was relieved to see that they hadn't brought his rifle along. They were armed with kerries and spears, like any of the more savage *abantu*. Perhaps the fear of injuring their pet would make them hesitate to throw things at him. At least he hoped so.

A familiar voice caught up with him in a piercing yell of "Soga!" The croc slackened his pace and tried to turn his head. Cuff whacked him unmercifully. Indlovu's yell came again, followed by a whistle. The croc was now definitely off his stride. Cuff's efforts to keep him headed away from his proper masters resulted in his zigzagging erratically. The contrary directions confused and irritated him. He opened his jaws and hissed. The baboon-men were gaining rapidly.

So, thought Cuff, this is the end. I hate like hell to go out before I've had a chance to write my report. But mustn't show it. Not an Englishman and an officer of the Crown. Wonder what poor Mtengeni'll think.

Something went *whick* past him; a fraction of a second later, the crash of an elephant rifle reached him. A big puff of dust ballooned up in front of the baboon-men. They skittered away from it as if the dust and not the bullet that made it were something deadly. George Mtengeni appeared from behind the nearest patch of thorn scrub, and yelled, "Hold still there, or me, I'll blow your heads off." If the *'fene abantu* couldn't understand his English, they got his tone.

Cuff thought vaguely, good old George, he could shoot their ears off at that distance, but he has more sense then to kill any of them before he finds out. Cuff slid off Soga and almost fell in a heap.

The warden came up. "What . . . what in the heavens has been happening to you, Mr. Cuff? What are these?" He indicated the baboon-men.

"Joke," giggled Cuff. "Good joke on you, George. Been living in your dashed Park for years, and you never knew— Wait, I've got to explain something to these chaps. I say, Indlovu . . . hell, he doesn't know English. Got to use Xosa. You know Xosa, don't you George?" He giggled again.

"Why, me, I . . . I can follow it. It's much like Zulu. But my God, what happened to the seat of your pants?"

Cuff pointed a wavering finger at Soga's sawtoothed back. "Good old Soga. Should have had a saddle. Dashed outrage, not providing a saddle for His Majesty's representative."

"But you look as if you'd been skinned! Me, I've got to get you to a hospital . . . and what about your foot?"

"T'hell with the foot. 'Nother joke, Can't stand up, can't sit down. Jolly, what? Have to sleep on my stomach. But, Ind-

THE BLUE GIRAFFE

lovu! I'm sorry I had to run away. I couldn't marry Ingwamza. Really. Because . . . because—" Athelstan Cuff swayed and collapsed in a small, ragged pile.

Peter Cuff's eyes were round. He asked the inevitable small-boy question: "What happened then?"

Athelstan Cuff was stuffing his pipe. "Oh, about what you'd expect. Indlovu was jolly vexed, I can tell you, but he didn't dare do anything with George standing there with the gun. He calmed down later after he understood what I had been driving at, and we became good friends. When he died, Cukata was elected chief in his place. I still get Christmas cards from him."

"Christmas cards from a baboon?"

"Certainly. If I get one next Christmas, I'll show it to you. It's the same card every year. He's an economical fella, and he bought a hundred cards of the same pattern because he could get them at a discount."

"Were you all right?"

"Yes, after a month in the hospital. I still don't know why I didn't get sixteen kinds of blood poisoning. Fool's luck, I suppose."

"But what's that got to do with me being a 'dopted boy?"

"Peter!" Cuff gave the clicks represented in the Bantu languages by *x* and in English by *tsk*. "Isn't it obvious? That tube of Hickey's was on when I approached his house. So I got a full dose of the radiations. Their effect was to produce violent mutations in the germ-plasm. You know what that is, don't you? Well, I never dared have any children of my own after that, for fear they'd turn out to be some sort of monster. That didn't occur to me until afterward. It fair bowled me over, I can tell you, when I did think of it. I went to pieces, rather, and lost my job in South Africa. But now that I have you and your mother, I realize that it wasn't so important after all."

"Father—" Peter hesitated.

"Go on, old man."

"If you'd thought of the rays before you went to the house, would you have been brave enough to go ahead anyway?"

Cuff lit his pipe and looked off at nothing. "I've often wondered about that myself. I'm dashed if I know. I wonder . . . just what would have happened—"

THE MISGUIDED HALO

Unknown, August

by Henry Kuttner (1915-1958)

The late Henry Kuttner accomplished much in his too-short life, but some of his accomplishments were unappreciated because most observers of science fiction felt "his" best work was that done in collaboration with his wife, the gifted C. L. Moore, under the name "Lewis Padgett." Although it was really impossible to separate out who did what in these collaborative efforts, it seemed to many that Moore was more responsible for their success than Kuttner. This is always a problem in collaborations, and it was a shame because Kuttner, although he turned out a number of stories for the pulps that even he was not proud of, was a very talented writer, especially of "science-fantasy."

His particular specialty was a most effective use of irony, a device as demanding and difficult for a writer as any in literature. "The Misguided Halo" is an excellent example.

(I met Henry Kuttner only once, in the mid-1940s, at a party which nearly drowned in the combined noise of Bob Heinlein, Sprague de Camp and myself. He sat through it all quietly, holding hands with his wife, and listening with patent amusement. He must have said something, but I don't remember what that might have been. IA.)

The youngest angel could scarcely be blamed for the error. They had given him a brand-new, shining halo and pointed down to the particular planet they meant. He had followed directions implicitly, feeling quite proud of the responsibility. This was the first time the youngest angel had ever been commissioned to bestow sainthood on a human.

So he swooped down to the earth, located Asia, and came to rest at the mouth of a cavern that gaped halfway up a Himalayan peak. He entered the cave, his heart beating wildly with excitement, preparing to materalize and give the holy lama his richly earned reward. For ten years the ascetic Tibetan Kai Yung had sat motionless, thinking holy thoughts. For ten more years he had dwelt on top of a pillar, acquiring additional merit. And for the last decade he had lived in this cave, a hermit, forsaking fleshly things.

The youngest angel crossed the threshold and stopped with a gasp of amazement. Obviously he was in the wrong place. An overpowering odor of fragrant *sake* assailed his nostrils, and he stared aghast at the wizened, drunken little man who squatted happily beside a fire, roasting a bit of goat flesh. A den of iniquity!

Naturally, the youngest angel, knowing little of the ways of the world, could not understand what had led to the lama's fall from grace. The great pot of *sake* that some misguidedly pious one had left at the cave mouth was an offering, and the lama had tasted, and tasted again. And by this time he was clearly not a suitable candidate for sainthood.

The youngest angel hesitated. The directions had been explicit. But surely this tippling reprobate could not be intended to wear a halo. The lama hiccuped loudly and reached for another cup of *sake* and thereby decided the angel, who unfurled his wings and departed with an air of outraged dignity.

Now, in a Midwestern State of North America there is a town called Tibbett. Who can blame the angel if he alighted there, and, after a brief search, discovered a man apparently ripe for sainthood, whose name, as stated on the door of his small suburban home, was K. Young?

"I may have got it wrong," the youngest angel thought. "They said it was Kai Yung. But this is Tibbett, all right. He must be the man. Looks holy enough, anyway.

"Well," said the youngest angel, "here goes. Now, where's that halo?"

Mr. Young sat on the edge of his bed, with head lowered, brooding. A depressing spectacle. At length he arose and donned various garments. This done, and shaved and washed and combed, he descended the stairway to breakfast.

Jill Young, his wife, sat examining the paper and sipping

orange juice. She was a small, scarcely middle-aged, and quite pretty woman who had long ago given up trying to understand life. It was, she decided, much too complicated. Strange things were continually happening. Much better to remain a bystander and simply let them happen. As a result of this attitude, she kept her charming face unwrinkled and added numerous gray hairs to her husband's head.

More will be said presently of Mr. Young's head. It had, of course, been transfigured during the night. But as yet he was unaware of this, and Jill drank orange juice and placidly approved a silly-looking hat in an advertisement.

"Hello, Filthy," said Young. "Morning."

He was not addressing his wife. A small and raffish Scotty had made its appearance, capering hysterically about its master's feet, and going into a fit of sheer madness when the man pulled its hairy ears. The raffish Scotty flung its head sidewise upon the carpet and skated about the room on its muzzle, uttering strangled squeaks of delight. Growing tired of this at last, the Scotty, whose name was Filthy McNasty, began thumping its head on the floor with the apparent intention of dashing out its brains, if any.

Young ignored the familiar sight. He sat down, unfolded his napkin, and examined his food. With a slight grunt of appreciation he began to eat.

He became aware that his wife was eying him with an odd and distrait expression. Hastily he dabbed at his lips with the napkin. But Jill still stared.

Young scrutinized his shirt front. It was, if not immaculate, at least free from stray shreds of bacon or egg. He looked at his wife, and realized that she was staring at a point slightly above his head. He looked up.

Jill started slightly. She whispered, "Kenneth, what *is* that?"

Young smoothed his hair. "Er . . . what, dear?"

"That thing on your head."

The man ran exploring fingers across his scalp. "My head? How do you mean?"

"It's shining," Jill explained. "What on earth have you been doing to yourself?"

Mr. Young felt slightly irritated. "I have been doing nothing to myself. A man grows bald eventually."

Jill frowned and drank orange juice. Her fascinated gaze crept up again. Finally she said, "Kenneth, I wish you'd—"

"What?"

She pointed to a mirror on the wall.

With a disgusted grunt Young arose and faced the image in the glass. At first he saw nothing unusual. It was the same face he had been seeing in mirrors for years. Not an extraordinary face—not one at which a man could point with pride and say: "Look. *My face.*" But, on the other hand, certainly not a countenance which would cause consternation. All in all, an ordinary, clean, well-shaved, and rosy face. Long association with it had given Mr. Young a feeling of tolerance, if not of actual admiration.

But topped by a halo it acquired a certain eeriness.

The halo hung unsuspended about five inches from the scalp. It measured perhaps seven inches in diameter, and seemed like a glowing, luminous ring of white light. It was impalpable, and Young passed his hand through it several times in a dazed manner.

"It's a . . . halo," he said at last, and turned to stare at Jill.

The Scotty, Filthy McNasty, noticed the luminous adornment for the first time. He was greatly interested. He did not, of course, know what it was, but there was always a chance that it might be edible. He was not a very bright dog.

Filthy sat up and whined. He was ignored. Barking loudly, he sprang forward and attempted to climb up his master's body in a mad attempt to reach and rend the halo. Since it had made no hostile move, it was evidently fair prey.

Young defended himself, clutched the Scotty by the nape of its neck, and carried the yelping dog into another room, where he left it. Then he returned and once more looked at Jill.

At length she observed, "Angels wear halos."

"Do I look like an angel?" Young asked. "It's a . . . a scientific manifestation. Like . . . like that girl whose bed kept bouncing around. You read about that."

Jill had. "She did it with her muscles."

"Well, I'm not," Young said definitely. "How could I? It's scientific. Lots of things shine by themselves."

"Oh, yes. Toadstools."

The man winced and rubbed his head. "Thank you, my dear. I suppose you know you're being no help at all."

"Angels have halos," Jill said with a sort of dreadful insistence.

Young was at the mirror again. "Darling, would you mind

keeping your trap shut for a while? I'm scared as hell, and you're far from encouraging."

Jill burst into tears, left the room, and was presently heard talking in a low voice to Filthy.

Young finished his coffee, but it was tasteless. He was not as frightened as he had indicated. The manifestation was strange, weird, but in no way terrible. Horns, perhaps, would have caused horror and consternation. But a halo— Mr. Young read the Sunday newspaper supplements, and had learned that everything odd could be attributed to the bizarre workings of science. Somewhere he had heard that all mythology had a basis in scientific fact. This comforted him, until he was ready to leave for the office.

He donned a derby. Unfortunately the halo was too large. The hat seemed to have two brims, the upper one whitely luminous.

"Damn!" said Young in a heartfelt manner. He searched the closet and tried on one hat after another. None would hide the halo. Certainly he could not enter a crowded bus in such a state.

A large furry object in a corner caught his gaze. He dragged it out and eyed the thing with loathing. It was a deformed, gigantic woolly headpiece, resembling a shako, which had once formed a part of a masquerade costume. The suit itself had long since vanished, but the hat remained to the comfort of Filthy, who sometimes slept on it.

Yet it would hide the halo. Gingerly Young drew the monstrosity on his head and crept toward the mirror. One glance was enough. Mouthing a brief prayer, he opened the door and fled.

Choosing between two evils is often difficult. More than once during that nightmare ride downtown Young decided he had made the wrong choice. Yet, somehow, he could not bring himself to tear off the hat and stamp it underfoot, though he was longing to do so. Huddled in a corner of the bus, he steadily contemplated his fingernails and wished he was dead. He heard titters and muffled laughter, and was conscious of probing glances riveted on his shrinking head.

A small child tore open the scar tissue on Young's heart and scrabbled about in the open wound with rosy, ruthless fingers.

"Mamma," said the small child piercingly, "look at the funny man."

"Yes, honey," came a woman's voice. "Be quiet."

THE MISGUIDED HALO

"What's that on his head?" the brat demanded.

There was a significant pause. Finally the woman said, "Well, I don't really know," in a baffled manner.

"What's he got it on for?"

No answer.

"Mamma!"

"Yes, honey."

"Is he crazy?"

"Be quiet," said the woman, dodging the issue.

"But what *is* it?"

Young could stand it no longer. He arose and made his way with dignity through the bus, his glazed eyes seeing nothing. Standing on the outer platform, he kept his face averted from the fascinated gaze of the conductor.

As the vehicle slowed down Young felt a hand laid on his arm. He turned. The small child's mother was standing there, frowning.

"Well?" Young inquired snappishly.

"It's Billy," the woman said. "I try to keep nothing from him. Would you mind telling me just what that is on your head?"

"It's Rasputin's beard," Young grated. "He willed it to me." The man leaped from the bus and, ignoring a half-heard question from the still-puzzled woman, tried to lose himself in the crowd.

This was difficult. Many were intrigued by the remarkable hat. But, luckily, Young was only a few blocks from his office, and at last, breathing hoarsely, he stepped into the elevator, glared murderously at the operator, and said, "Ninth floor."

"Excuse me, Mr. Young," the boy said mildly. "There's something on your head."

"I know," Young replied. "I put it there."

This seemed to settle the question. But after the passenger had left the elevator, the boy grinned widely. When he saw the janitor a few minutes later he said:

"You know Mr. Young? The guy—"

"I know him. So what?"

"Drunk as a lord."

"Him? You're screwy."

"Tighter'n a drum," declared the youth, "swelp me Gawd."

Meanwhile, the sainted Mr. Young made his way to the office of Dr. French, a physician whom he knew slightly, and who was conveniently located in the same building. He had not long to wait. The nurse, after one startled glance at the remarkable hat, vanished, and almost immediately reappeared to usher the patient into the inner sanctum.

Dr. French, a large, bland man with a waxed, yellow mustache, greeted Young almost effusively.

"Come in, come in. How are you today? Nothing wrong, I hope. Let me take your hat."

"Wait," Young said, fending off the physician. "First let me explain. There's something on my head."

"Cut, bruise or fracture?" the literal-minded doctor inquired. "I'll fix you up in a jiffy."

"I'm not *sick*," said Young. "At least, I hope not. I've got a ... um ... a halo."

"Ha, ha," Dr. French applauded. "A halo, eh? Surely you're not that good."

"Oh, the hell with it!" Young snapped, and snatched off his hat. The doctor retreated a step. Then, interested, he approached and tried to finger the halo. He failed.

"I'll be— This is odd," he said at last. "Does look rather like one, doesn't it?"

"What is it? That's what I want to know."

French hesitated. He plucked at his mustache. "Well, it's rather out of my line. A physicist might— No. Perhaps Mayo's. Does it come off?"

"Of course not. You can't even touch the thing."

"Ah. I see. Well, I should like some specialists' opinions. In the meantime, let me see—" There was orderly tumult. Young's heart, temperature, blood, saliva and epidermis were tested and approved.

At length French said: "You're fit as a fiddle. Come in tomorrow, at ten. I'll have some other specialists here then."

"You ... uh ... you can't get rid of this?"

"I'd rather not try just yet. It's obviously some form of radioactivity. A radium treatment may be necessary—"

Young left the man mumbling about alpha and gamma rays. Discouraged, he donned his strange hat and went down the hall to his own office.

The Atlas Advertising Agency was the most conservative of all advertising agencies. Two brothers with white whiskers had started the firm in 1820, and the company still seemed to wear dignified mental whiskers. Changes were frowned upon by the board of directors, who, in 1938, were finally convinced that radio had come to stay, and had accepted contracts for advertising broadcasts.

THE MISGUIDED HALO

Once a junior vice president had been discharged for wearing a red necktie.

Young slunk into his office. It was vacant. He slid into his chair behind the desk, removed his hat, and gazed at it with loathing. The headpiece seemed to have grown even more horrid than it had appeared at first. It was shedding, and, moreover, gave off a faint but unmistakable aroma of unbathed Scotties.

After investigating the halo, and realizing that it was still firmly fixed in its place, Young turned to his work. But the Norns were casting baleful glances in his direction, for presently the door opened and Edwin G. Kipp, president of Atlas, entered. Young barely had time to duck his head beneath the desk and hide the halo.

Kipp was a small, dapper, and dignified man who wore pince-nez and Vandyke with the air of a reserved fish. His blood had long since been metamorphosed into ammonia. He moved, if not in beauty, at least in an almost visible aura of grim conservatism.

"Good morning, Mr. Young," he said. "Er . . . is that you?"

"Yes," said the invisible Young. "Good morning. I'm tying my shoelace."

To this Kipp made no reply save for an almost inaudible cough. Time passed. The desk was silent.

"Er . . . Mr. Young?"

"I'm . . . still here," said the wretched Young. "It's knotted. The shoelace, I mean. Did you want me?"

"Yes."

Kipp waited with gradually increasing impatience. There were no signs of a forthcoming emergence. The president considered the advisability of his advancing to the desk and peering under it. But the mental picture of a conversation conducted in so grotesque a manner was harrowing. He simply gave up and told Young what he wanted.

"Mr. Devlin has just telephoned," Kipp observed. "He will arrive shortly. He wishes to . . . er . . . to be shown the town, as he put it."

The invisible Young nodded. Devlin was one of their best clients. Or, rather, he had been until last year, when he suddenly began to do business with another firm, to the discomfiture of Kipp and the board of directors.

The president went on. "He told me he is hesitating about his new contract. He had planned to give it to World, but I had some correspondence with him on the matter, and suggested that a personal discussion might be of value. So he is visiting our city and wishes to go . . . er . . . sightseeing."

Kipp grew confidential. "I may say that Mr. Devlin told me rather definitely that he prefers a less conservative firm. 'Stodgy,' his term was. He will dine with me tonight, and I shall endeavor to convince him that our service will be of value. Yet"—Kipp coughed again—"yet diplomacy is, of course, important. I should appreciate your entertaining Mr. Devlin today."

The desk had remained silent during this oration. Now it said convulsively: "I'm sick. I can't—"

"You are ill? Shall I summon a physician?"

Young hastily refused the offer, but remained in hiding. "No, I . . . but I mean—"

"You are behaving most strangely," Kipp said with commendable restraint. "There is something you should know, Mr. Young. I had not intended to tell you as yet, but . . . at any rate, the board has taken notice of you. There was a discussion at the last meeting. We have planned to offer you a vice presidency in the firm."

The desk was stricken dumb.

"You have upheld our standards for fifteen years," said Kipp. "There has been no hint of scandal attached to your name. I congratulate you, Mr. Young."

The president stepped forward, extending his hand. An arm emerged from beneath the desk, shook Kipp's, and quickly vanished.

Nothing further happened. Young tenaciously remained in his sanctuary. Kipp realized that, short of dragging the man out bodily, he could not hope to view an entire Kenneth Young for the present. With an admonitory cough he withdrew.

The miserable Young emerged, wincing as his cramped muscles relaxed. A pretty kettle of fish. How could he entertain Devlin while he wore a halo? And it was vitally necessary that Devlin be entertained, else the elusive vice presidency would be immediately withdrawn. Young knew only too well that employees of Atlas Advertising Agency trod a perilous pathway.

His reverie was interrupted by the sudden appearance of an angel atop the bookcase.

It was not a high bookcase, and the supernatural visitor sat there calmly enough, heels dangling and wings furled. A

THE MISGUIDED HALO

scanty robe of white samite made up the angel's wardrobe—that and a shining halo, at sight of which Young felt a wave of nausea sweep him.

"This," he said with rigid restraint, "is the end. A halo may be due to mass hypnotism. But when I start seeing angels—"

"Don't be afraid," said the other. "I'm real enough."

Young's eyes were wild. "How do I know? I'm obviously talking to empty air. It's schizo-something. Go away."

The angel wriggled his toes and looked embarrassed. "I can't, just yet. The fact is, I made a bad mistake. You may have noticed that you've a slight halo—"

Young gave a short, bitter laugh. "Oh, yes. I've *noticed* it."

Before the angel could reply the door opened. Kipp looked in, saw that Young was engaged, and murmured, "Excuse me," as he withdrew.

The angel scratched his golden curls. "Well, your halo was intended for somebody else—a Tibetan lama, in fact. But through a certain chain of circumstances I was led to believe that you were the candidate for sainthood. So—" The visitor made a comprehensive gesture.

Young was baffled. "I don't quite—"

"The lama . . . well, sinned. No sinner may wear a halo. And, as I say, I gave it to you through error."

"Then you can take it away again?" Amazed delight suffused Young's face. But the angel raised a benevolent hand.

"Fear not. I have checked with the recording angel. You have led a blameless life. As a reward, you will be permitted to keep the halo of sainthood."

The horrified man sprang to his feet, making feeble swimming motions with his arms. "But . . . but . . . but—"

"Peace and blessings be upon you," said the angel, and vanished.

Young fell back into his chair and massaged his aching brow. Simultaneously the door opened and Kipp stood on the threshold. Luckily Young's hands temporarily hid the halo.

"Mr. Devlin is here," the president said. "Er . . . who was that on the bookcase?"

Young was too crushed to lie plausibly. He muttered, "An angel."

Kipp nodded in satisfaction. "Yes, of course. . . . *What?* You say an angel . . . an angel? Oh, my gosh!" The man turned quite white and hastily took his departure.

Young contemplated his hat. The thing still lay on the desk, wincing slightly under the baleful stare directed at it.

To go through life wearing a halo was only less endurable than the thought of continually wearing the loathsome hat. Young brought his fist down viciously on the desk.

"I won't stand it! I . . . I don't have to—" He stopped abruptly. A dazed look grew in his eyes.

"I'll be . . . that's right! I don't *have* to stand it. If that lama got out of it . . . of course. 'No sinner may wear a halo.' " Young's round face twisted into a mask of sheer evil. "I'll be a sinner, then! I'll break all the Commandments—"

He pondered. At the moment he couldn't remember what they were. "Thou shalt not covet thy neighbor's wife." That was one.

Young thought of his neighbor's wife—a certain Mrs. Clay, a behemothic damsel of some fifty summers, with a face like a desiccated pudding. That was one Commandment he had no intention of breaking.

But probably one good, healthy sin would bring back the angel in a hurry to remove the halo. What crimes would result in the least inconvenience? Young furrowed his brow.

Nothing occurred to him. He decided to go for a walk. No doubt some sinful opportunity would present itself.

He forced himself to don the shako and had reached the elevator when a hoarse voice was heard hallooing after him. Racing along the hall was a fat man.

Young knew instinctively that this was Mr. Devlin.

The adjective "fat," as applied to Devlin, was a considerable understatement. The man bulged. His feet, strangled in biliously yellow shoes, burst out at the ankles like blossoming flowers. They merged into calves that seemed to gather momentum as they spread and mounted, flung themselves up with mad abandon, and revealed themselves in their complete, unrestrained glory at Devlin's middle. The man resembled, in silhouette, a pineapple with elephantiasis. A great mass of flesh poured out of his collar, forming a pale, sagging lump in which Young discerned some vague resemblance to a face.

Such was Devlin, and he charged along the hall, as mammoths thunder by, with earth-shaking tramplings of his crashing hoofs.

"You're Young!" he wheezed. "Almost missed me, eh? I was waiting in the office—" Devlin paused, his fascinated gaze upon the hat. Then, with an effort at politeness, he laughed falsely and glanced away. "Well, I'm all ready and r'aring to go."

THE MISGUIDED HALO

Young felt himself impaled painfully on the horns of a dilemma. Failure to entertain Devlin would mean the loss of that vice presidency. But the halo weighed like a flatiron on Young's throbbing head. One thought was foremost in his mind: he *had* to get rid of the blessed thing.

Once he had done that, he would trust to luck and diplomacy. Obviously, to take out his guest now would be fatal, insanity. The hat alone would be fatal.

"Sorry," Young grunted. "Got an important engagement. I'll be back for you as soon as I can."

Wheezing laughter, Devlin attached himself firmly to the other's arm. "No, you don't. You're showing me the town! Right now!" An unmistakable alcoholic odor was wafted to Young's nostrils. He thought quickly.

"All right," he said at last. "Come along. There's a bar downstairs. We'll have a drink, eh?"

"Now you're talking," said the jovial Devlin, almost incapacitating Young with a comradely slap on the back. "Here's the elevator."

They crowded into the cage. Young shut his eyes and suffered as interested stares were directed upon the hat. He fell into a state of coma, arousing only at the ground floor, where Devlin dragged him out and into the adjacent bar.

Now Young's plan was this: he would pour drink after drink down his companion's capacious gullet, and await his chance to slip away unobserved. It was a shrewd scheme, but it had one flaw—Devlin refused to drink alone.

"One for you and one for me," he said. "That's fair. Have another."

Young could not refuse, under the circumstances. The worst of it was that Devlin's liquor seemed to seep into every cell of his huge body, leaving him, finally, in the same state of glowing happiness which had been his originally. But poor Young was, to put it as charitably as possible, tight.

He sat quietly in a booth, glaring across at Devlin. Each time the waiter arrived, Young knew that the man's eyes were riveted upon the hat. And each round made the thought of that more irritating.

Also, Young worried about his halo. He brooded over sins. Arson, burglary, sabotage, and murder passed in quick review through his befuddled mind. Once he attempted to snatch the waiter's change, but the man was too alert. He laughed pleasantly and placed a fresh glass before Young.

The latter eyed it with distaste. Suddenly coming to a decision, he arose and wavered toward the door. Devlin overtook him on the sidewalk.

"What's the matter? Let's have another—"

"I have work to do," said Young with painful distinctness. He snatched a walking cane from a passing pedestrian and made threatening gestures with it until the remonstrating victim fled hurriedly. Hefting the stick in his hand, he brooded blackly.

"But why work?" Devlin inquired largely. "Show me the town."

"I have important matters to attend to." Young scrutinized a small child who had halted by the curb and was returning the stare with interest. The tot looked remarkably like the brat who had been so insulting on the bus.

"What's important?" Devlin demanded. "Important matters, eh? Such as what?"

"Beating small children," said Young, and rushed upon the startled child, brandishing his cane. The youngster uttered a shrill scream and fled. Young pursued for a few feet and then became entangled with a lamp-post. The lamp-post was impolite and dictatorial. It refused to allow Young to pass. The man remonstrated and, finally, argued, but to no avail.

The child had long since disappeared. Administering a brusque and snappy rebuke to the lamp-post, Young turned away.

"What in Pete's name are you trying to do?" Devlin inquired. "That cop's looking at us. Come along." He took the other's arm and led him along the crowded sidewalk.

"What am I trying to do?" Young sneered. "It's obvious, isn't it? I wish to sin."

"Er . . . sin?"

"Sin."

"Why?"

Young tapped his hat meaningly, but Devlin put an altogether wrong interpretation on the gesture. "You're nuts?"

"Oh, shut up," Young snapped in a sudden burst of rage, and thrust his cane between the legs of a passing bank president whom he knew slightly. The unfortunate man fell heavily to the cement, but arose without injury save to his dignity.

"I beg your pardon!" he barked.

Young was going through a strange series of gestures. He had fled to a show-window mirror and was doing fantastic things to his hat, apparently trying to lift it in order to catch a glimpse of the top of his head—a sight, it seemed, to be shielded jealously from profane eyes. At length he cursed loudly, turned, gave the bank president a contemptuous stare, and hurried away, trailing the puzzled Devlin like a captive balloon.

Young was muttering thickly to himself.

"Got to sin—really sin. Something big. Burn down an orphan asylum. Kill m' mother-in-law. Kill . . . anybody!" He looked quickly at Devlin, and the latter shrank back in sudden fear. But finally Young gave a disgusted grunt.

"Nrgh. Too much blubber. Couldn't use a gun or a knife. Have to blast—Look!" Young said, clutching Devlin's arm. "Stealing's a sin, isn't it?"

"Sure is," the diplomatic Devlin agreed. "But you're not—"

Young shook his head. "No. Too crowded here. No use going to jail. Come on!"

He plunged forward. Devlin followed. And Young fulfilled his promise to show his guest the town, though afterward neither of them could remember exactly what had happened. Presently Devlin paused in a liquor store for refueling, and emerged with bottles protruding here and there from his clothing.

Hours merged into an alcoholic haze. Life began to assume an air of foggy unreality to the unfortunate Devlin. He sank presently into a coma, dimly conscious of various events which marched with celerity through the afternoon and long into the night. Finally he roused himself sufficiently to realize that he was standing with Young confronting a wooden Indian which stood quietly outside a cigar store. It was, perhaps, the last of the wooden Indians. The outworn relic of a bygone day, it seemed to stare with faded glass eyes at the bundle of wooden cigars it held in an extended hand.

Young was no longer wearing a hat. And Devlin suddenly noticed something decidedly peculiar about his companion.

He said softly, "You've got a halo."

Young started slightly. "Yes," he replied, "I've got a halo. This Indian—" He paused.

Devlin eyed the image with disfavor. To his somewhat fuzzy brain the wooden Indian appeared even more horrid than the surprising halo. He shuddered and hastily averted his gaze.

"Stealing's a sin," Young said under his breath, and then, with an elated cry, stooped to lift the Indian. He fell immediately under its weight, emitting a string of smoking oaths as he attempted to dislodge the incubus.

"Heavy," he said, rising at last. "Give me a hand."

Devlin had long since given up any hope of finding sanity in this madman's actions. Young was obviously determined to sin, and the fact that he possessed a halo was somewhat disquieting, even to the drunken Devlin. As a result, the two men proceeded down the street, bearing with them the rigid body of a wooden Indian.

The proprietor of the cigar shop came out and looked after them, rubbing his hands. His eyes followed the departing statue with unmitigated joy.

"For ten years I've tried to get rid of that thing," he whispered gleefully. "And now . . . aha!"

He re-entered the store and lit a Corona to celebrate his emancipation.

Meanwhile, Young and Devlin found a taxi stand. One cab stood there; the driver sat puffing a cigarette and listening to his radio. Young hailed the man.

"Cab, sir?" The driver sprang to life, bounced out of the car, and flung open the door. Then he remained frozen in a half-crouching position, his eyes revolving wildly in their sockets.

He had never believed in ghosts. He was, in fact, somewhat of a cynic. But in the face of a bulbous ghoul and a decadent angel bearing the stiff corpse of an Indian, he felt with a sudden, blinding shock of realization that beyond life lies a black abyss teeming with horror unimaginable. Whining shrilly, the terrified man leaped back into his cab, got the thing into motion, and vanished as smoke before the gale.

Young and Devlin looked at one another ruefully.

"What now?" the latter asked.

"Well," said Young, "I don't live far from here. Only ten blocks or so. Come on!"

It was very late, and few pedestrians were abroad. These few, for the sake of their sanity, were quite willing to ignore the wanderers and go their separate ways. So eventually Young, Devlin, and the wooden Indian arrived at their destination.

The door of Young's home was locked, and he could not locate the key. He was curiously averse to arousing Jill. But, for some strange reason, he felt it vitally necessary that the wooden Indian be concealed. The cellar was the logical place. He dragged his two companions to a basement window,

THE MISGUIDED HALO

smashed it as quietly as possible, and slid the image through the gap.

"Do you really live here?" asked Devlin, who had his doubts.

"Hush!" Young said warningly. "Come on!"

He followed the wooden Indian, landing with a crash in a heap of coal. Devlin joined him after much wheezing and grunting. It was not dark. The halo provided about as much illumination as a twenty-five-watt globe.

Young left Devlin to nurse his bruises and began searching for the wooden Indian. It had unaccountably vanished. But he found it at last cowering beneath a washtub, dragged the object out, and set it up in a corner. Then he stepped back and faced it, swaying a little.

"That's a sin, all right," he chuckled. "Theft. It isn't the amount that matters. It's the principle of the thing. A wooden Indian is just as important as a million dollars, eh, Devlin?"

"I'd like to chop that Indian into fragments," said Devlin with passion. "You made me carry it for three miles." He paused, listening. "What in heaven's name is that?"

A small tumult was approaching. Filthy, having been instructed often in his duties as a watchdog, now faced opportunity. Noises were proceeding from the cellar. Burglars, no doubt. The raffish Scotty cascaded down the stairs in a babel of frightful threats and oaths. Loudly declaring his intention of eviscerating the intruders, he flung himself upon Young, who made hasty clucking sounds intended to soothe the Scotty's aroused passions.

Filthy had other ideas. He spun like a dervish, yelling bloody murder. Young wavered, made a vain snatch at the air, and fell prostrate to the ground. He remained face down, while Filthy, seeing the halo, rushed at it and trampled upon his master's head.

The wretched Young felt the ghosts of a dozen and more drinks rising to confront him. He clutched at the dog, missed, and gripped instead the feet of the wooden Indian. The image swayed perilously. Filthy cocked up an apprehensive eye and fled down the length of his master's body, pausing halfway as he remembered his duty. With a muffled curse he sank his teeth into the nearest portion of Young and attempted to yank off the miserable man's pants.

Meanwhile, Young remained face down, clutching the feet of the wooden Indian in a despairing grip.

There was a resounding clap of thunder. White light blazed through the cellar. The angel appeared.

Devlin's legs gave way. He sat down in a plump heap, shut his eyes, and began chattering quietly to himself. Filthy swore at the intruder, made an unsuccessful attempt to attain a firm grasp on one of the gently fanning wings, and went back to think it over, arguing throatily. The wing had an unsatisfying lack of substantiality.

The angel stood over Young with golden fires glowing in his eyes, and a benign look of pleasure molding his noble features. "This," he said quietly, "shall be taken as a symbol of your first successful good deed since your enhaloment." A wingtip brushed the dark and grimy visage of the Indian. Forthwith, there was no Indian. "You have lightened the heart of a fellow man—little, to be sure, but some, and at a cost of much labor on your part.

"For a day you have struggled with this sort to redeem him, but for this no success has rewarded you, albeit the morrow's pains will afflict you.

"Go forth, K. Young, rewarded and protected from all sin alike by your halo." The youngest angel faded quietly, for which alone Young was grateful. His head was beginning to ache and he'd feared a possible thunderous vanishment.

Filthy laughed nastily, and renewed his attack on the halo. Young found the unpleasant act of standing upright necessary. While it made the walls and tubs spin round like all the hosts of heaven, it made impossible Filthy's dervish dance on his face.

Some time later he awoke, cold sober and regretful of the fact. He lay between cool sheets, watching morning sunlight lance through the windows, his eyes, and feeling it splinter in jagged bits in his brain. His stomach was making spasmodic attempts to leap up and squeeze itself out through his burning throat.

Simultaneous with awakening came realization of three things: the pains of the morrow had indeed afflicted him; the halo mirrored still in the glass above the dressing table—and the parting words of the angel.

He groaned a heartfelt triple groan. The headache would pass, but the halo, he knew, would not. Only by sinning could one become unworthy of it, and—shining protector!—it made him unlike other men. His deeds must all be good, his works a help to men. He could not sin!

HEAVY PLANET

Astounding Science Fiction, August

by Milton A. Rothman (1919–   )

The pen name originally appearing on this was "Lee Gregory." Lee Gregory was really Milton Rothman, long-time Philadelphia sf fan and working scientist (Ph.D., Physics, University of Pennsylvania, 1952). "Heavy Planet" was probably the finest "hard" science fiction story of 1939—published when the author was all of twenty.

(Milt threatens to be something that is common in Hollywood but rare in science fiction, the founder of a dynasty. It is rare for a science fiction writer to have offspring who turn to science fiction—perhaps the force of the dreadful example makes it unlikely. Young Tony Rothman, who is as bright as his father (and taller) is now beginning to make it in the field. I.A.)

Ennis was completing his patrol of Sector EM, Division 426 of the Eastern Ocean. The weather had been unusually fine, the liquid-thick air roaring along in a continuous blast that propelled his craft with a rush as if it were flying, and lifting short, choppy waves that rose and fell with a startling suddenness. A short savage squall whirled about, pounding down on the ocean like a million hammers, flinging the little boat ahead madly.

Ennis tore at the controls, granite-hard muscles standing out in bas-relief over his short, immensely thick body, skin gleaming scalelike in the slashing spray. The heat from the sun that hung like a huge red lantern on the horizon was a tangible intensity, making an inferno of the gale.

The little craft, that Ennis maneuvered by sheer brawn, took a leap into the air and seemed to float for many seconds before burying its keel again in the sea. It often floated for long distances, the air was so dense. The boundary between air and water was sometimes scarcely defined at all—one merged into the other imperceptibly. The pressure did strange things.

Like a dust mote sparkling in a beam, a tiny speck of light above caught Ennis' eye. A glider, he thought, but he was puzzled. Why so far out here on the ocean? They were nasty things to handle in the violent wind.

The dust mote caught the light again. It was lower, tumbling down with a precipitancy that meant trouble. An upward blast caught it, checked its fall. Then it floated down gently for a space until struck by another howling wind that seemed to distort its very outlines.

Ennis turned the prow of his boat to meet the path of the falling vessel. Curious, he thought; where were its wings? Were they retracted, or broken off? It ballooned closer, and it wasn't a glider. Far larger than any glider ever made, it was of a ridiculous shape that would not stand up for an instant. And with the sharp splash the body made as it struck the water—a splash that fell in almost the same instant it rose—a thought seemed to leap up in his mind. A thought that was more important than anything else on that planet; or was to him, at least. For if it was what he thought it was—and it had to be that—it was what Shadden had been desperately seeking for many years. What a stroke of inconceivable luck, falling from the sky before his very eyes!

The silvery shape rode the ragged waters lightly. Ennis' craft came up with a rush; he skillfully checked its speed and the two came together with a slight jar. The metal of the strange vessel dented as if it were made of rubber. Ennis stared. He put out an arm and felt the curved surface of the strange ship. His finger prodded right through the metal. What manner of people were they who made vessels of such weak materials?

He moored his little boat to the side of the larger one and climbed to an opening. The wall sagged under him. He knew he must be careful; it was frightfully weak. It would not hold together very long; he must work fast if it were to be saved. The atmospheric pressure would have flattened it out long ago, had it not been for the jagged rent above which had allowed the pressure to be equalized.

He reached the opening and lowered himself carefully into the interior of the vessel. The rent was too small; he enlarged it by taking the two edges in his hands and pulling them apart. As he went down he looked askance at the insignificant plates and beams that were like tissue paper on his world. Inside was wreckage. Nothing was left in its original shape. Crushed, mutilated machinery, shattered vacuum tubes, sagging members, all ruined by the gravity and the pressure.

There was a pulpy mess on the floor that he did not examine closely. It was like red jelly, thin and stalky, pulped under a gravity a hundred times stronger and an atmosphere ten thousand times heavier than that it had been made for.

He was in a room with many knobs and dials on the walls, apparently a control room. A table in the center with a chart on it, the chart of a solar system. It had nine planets; his had but five.

Then he knew he was right. If they came from another system, what he wanted must be there. It could be nothing else.

He found a staircase, descended. Large machinery bulked there. There was no light, but he did not notice that. He could see well enough by infra red, and the amount of energy necessary to sustain his compact gianthood kept him constantly radiating.

Then he went through a door that was of a comfortable massiveness, even for his planet—and there it was. He recognized it at once. It was big, squat, strong. The metal was soft, but it was thick enough even to stand solidly under the enormous pull of this world. He had never seen anything quite like it. It was full of coils, magnets, and devices of shapes unknown to him. But Shadden would know. Shadden, and who knows how many other scientists before him, had tried to make something which would do what this could do, but they had all failed. And without the things this machine could perform, the race of men on Heavyplanet was doomed to stay down on the surface of the planet, chained there immovably by the crushing gravity.

It was atomic energy. That he had known as soon as he knew that the body was not a glider. For nothing else but atomic energy and the fierce winds was capable of lifting a body from the surface of Heavyplanet. Chemicals were impotent. There is no such thing as an explosion where the atmosphere pressed inward with more force than an explosion could press outward. Only atomic, of all the theoretically possible sources of energy, could supply the work necessary to lift a vessel away from the planet. Every other source of energy was simply too weak.

Yes, Shadden, all the scientists must see this. And quickly, because the forces of sea and storm would quickly tear the ship to shreds, and, even more vital, because the scientists of Bantin and Marak might obtain the secret if there was delay. And that would mean ruin—the loss of its age-old supremacy—for his nation. Bantin and Marak were war nations; did they obtain the secret they would use it against all the other worlds that abounded in the Universe.

The Universe was big. That was why Ennis was so sure there was atomic energy on this ship. For, even though it might have originated on a planet that was so tiny that *chemical energy*—although that was hard to visualize—would be sufficient to lift it out of the pull of gravity, to travel the distance that stretched between the stars only one thing would suffice.

He went back through the ship, trying to see what had happened.

There were pulps lying behind long tubes that pointed out through clever ports in the outer wall. He recognized them as weapons, worth looking into.

There must have been a battle. He visualized the scene. The forces that came from atomic energy must have warped even space in the vicinity. The ship pierced, the occupants killed, the controls wrecked, the vessel darting off at titanic speed, blindly into nothing. Finally it had come near enough to Heavyplanet to be enmeshed in its huge web of gravity.

Weeaao-o-ow! It was the wailing roar of his alarm siren, which brought him spinning around and dashing for his boat. Beyond, among the waves that leaped and fell so suddenly, he saw a long, low craft making way toward the derelict spaceship. He glimpsed a flash of color on the rounded, gray superstructure, and knew it for a battleship of Marak. Luck was going strong both ways; first good, now bad. He could easily have eluded the battleship in his own small craft, but he couldn't leave the derelict. Once lost to the enemy he could never regain it, and it was too valuable to lose.

The wind howled and buffeted about his head, and he strained his muscles to keep from being blasted away as he crouched there, half on his own boat and half on the derelict. The sun had set and the evening winds were beginning to

HEAVY PLANET

blow. The hulk scudded before them, its prow denting from the resistance of the water it pushed aside.

He thought furiously fast. With a quick motion he flipped the switch of the radiophone and called Shadden. He waited with fierce impatience until the voice of Shadden was in his ear. At last he heard it, then: "Shadden! This is Ennis. Get your glider, Shadden, fly to a45j on my route! Quickly! It's come, Shadden! But I have no time. Come!"

He flipped the switch off, and pounded the valve out of the bottom of his craft, clutching at the side of the derelict. With a rush the ocean came up and flooded his little boat and in an instant it was gone, on its way down to the bottom. That would save him from being detected for a short time.

Back into the darkness of the spaceship. He didn't think he had been noticed climbing through the opening. Where could he hide? Should he hide? He couldn't defeat the entire battleship singlehanded, without weapons. There were no weapons that could be carried anyway. A beam of concentrated actinic light that ate away the eyes and the nervous system had to be powered by the entire output of a battleship's generators. Weapons for striking and cutting had never been developed on a world where flesh was tougher than metal. Ennis was skilled in personal combat, but how could he overcome all that would enter the derelict?

Down again, into the dark chamber where the huge atomic generator towered over his head. This time he looked for something he had missed before. He crawled around it, peering into its recesses. And then, some feet above, he saw the opening, and pulled himself up to it, carefully, not to destroy the precious thing with his mass. The opening was shielded with a heavy, darkly transparent substance through which seeped a dim glow from within. He was satisfied then. Somehow, matter was still being disintegrated in there, and energy could be drawn off if he knew how.

There were leads—wires of all sizes, and busbars, and thick, heavy tubes that bent under their own weight. Some must lead in and some must lead out; it was not good to tamper with them. He chose another track. Upstairs again, and to the places where he had seen the weapons.

They were all mounted on heavy, rigid swivels. He carefully detached the tubes from the bases. The first time he tried it he was not quite careful enough, and part of the projector itself was ripped away, but next time he knew what he was doing and it came away nicely. It was a large thing, nearly as thick as his arm and twice as long. Heavy leads trailed from its lower end and a lever projected from behind. He hoped it was in working condition. He dared not try it; all he could do was to trace the leads back and make sure they were intact.

He ran out of time. There came a thud from the side, and then smaller thuds, as the boarding party incautiously leaped over. Once there was a heavy sound, as someone went all the way through the side of the ship.

"Idiots!" Ennis muttered, and moved forward with his weapon toward the stairway. Noises came from overhead, and then a loud crash buckled the plates of the ceiling. Ennis leaped out of the way, but the entire section came down, with two men on it. The floor sagged, but held for the moment. Ennis, caught beneath the downcoming mass, beat his way free. He came up with a girder in his hand, which he bent over the head of one of the Maraks. The man shook himself and struck out for Ennis, who took the blow rolling and countered with a buffet that left a black splotch on a skin that was like armor plate and sent the man through the opposite wall. The other was upon Ennis, who whirled with the quickness of one who maneuvers habitually under a pressure of ten thousand atmospheres, and shook the Marak from him, leaving him unconscious with a twist in a sensitive spot.

The first opponent returned, and the two grappled, searching for nerve centers to beat upon. Ennis twisted frantically, conscious of the real danger that the frail vessel might break to pieces beneath his feet. The railing of a staircase gave behind the two, and they hurtled down it, crashing through the steps to the floor below. Their weight and momentum carried them through. Ennis released his grip on the Marak, stopped his fall by grasping one of the girders that was part of the ship's framework. The other continued his devastating way down, demolishing the inner shell, and then the outer shell gave way with a grinding crash that ominously became a burbling rush of liquid.

Ennis looked down into the space where the Marak had fallen, hissed with a sudden intake of breath, then dove down himself. He met rising water, gushing in through a rent in the keel. He braced himself against a girder which sagged under his hand and moved onward against the rushing water. It geysered through the hole in a heavy stream that pushed him back and started to fill the bottom level of the ship. Against that terrific pressure he strained forward slowly, beating against the resisting waves, and then, with a mighty flounder, was at the opening. Its edges had been folded back upon themselves by the inrushing water, and they gaped inward like a jagged maw. He grasped them in a huge hand and exerted force. They strained for a moment and began to straighten. Irresistibly he pushed and stretched them into their former position, and then took the broken ends in his hands and squeezed. The metal grew soft under his grip and began to flow. The edges of the plate welded under that mighty pressure. He moved down the crack and soon it was watertight. He flexed his hands as he rose. They ached; even his strength was beginning to be taxed.

Noises from above; pounding feet. Men were coming down to investigate the commotion. He stood for a moment in thought, then turned to a blank wall, battered his way through it, and shoved the plates and girders back into position. Down to the other end of the craft, and up a staircase there. The corridor above was deserted, and he stole along it, hunting for the place he had left the weapon he had prepared. There was a commotion ahead as the Maraks found the unconscious man.

Two men came pounding up the passageway, giving him barely enough time to slip into a doorway to the side. The room he found himself in was a sleeping chamber. There were two red pulps there, and nothing that could help him, so he stayed in there only long enough to make sure that he would not be seen emerging into the hall. He crept down it again, with as little noise as possible. The racket ahead helped him; it sounded as though they were tearing the ship apart. Again he cursed their idiocy. Couldn't they see how valuable this was?

They were in the control room, ripping apart the machinery with the curiosity of children, wondering at the strange weakness of the paperlike metal, not realizing that, on the world where it was fabricated, it was sufficiently strong for any strain the builders could put upon it.

The strange weapon Ennis had prepared was on the floor of the passage, and just outside the control room. He looked anxiously at the trailing cables. Had they been stepped on and broken? Was the instrument in working condition? He had to get it and be away; no time to experiment to see if it would work.

A noise from behind, and Ennis again slunk into a doorway as a large Marak with a colored belt around his waist strode jarringly through the corridor into the control room. Sharp orders were barked, and the men ceased their havoc with the machinery of the room. All but a few left and scattered through the ship. Ennis' face twisted into a scowl. This made things more difficult. He couldn't overcome them all single-handed, and he couldn't use the weapon inside the ship if it was what he thought it was from the size of the cables.

A Marak was standing immediately outside the room in which Ennis lurked. No exit that way. He looked around the room; there were no other doors. A porthole in the outer wall was a tiny disk of transparency. He looked at it, felt it with his hands, and suddenly pushed his hands right through it. As quietly as he could, he worked at the edges of the circle until the hole was large enough for him to squeeze through. The jagged edges did not bother him. They felt soft, like a ragged pat of butter.

The Marak vessel was moored to the other side of the spaceship. On this side the wind howled blankly, and the sawtooth waves stretched on and on to a horizon that was many miles distant. He cautiously made his way around the glistening rotundity of the derelict, past the prow, straining silently against the vicious backward sweep of the water that tore at every inch of his body. The darker hump of the battleship loomed up as he rounded the curve, and he swam across the tiny space to grasp a row of projections that curved up over the surface of the craft. He climbed up them, muscles that were hard as carborundum straining to hold against all the forces of gravity and wind that fought him down. Near the top of the curve was a rounded, streamlined projection. He felt around its base and found a lever there, which he moved. The metal hump slid back, revealing a rugged swivel mounting with a stubby cylindrical projector atop it.

He swung the mounting around and let loose a short, sudden blast of white fire along the naked deck of the battleship. Deep voices yelled within and men sprang out, to fall back with abrupt screams clogged in their throats as Ennis caught them in the intolerable blast from the projector. Men, shielded by five thousand miles of atmosphere from actinic light, used to receiving only red and infra red, were painfully vulnerable to this frightful concentration of ultraviolet.

Noise and shouts burst from the derelict spaceship alongside, sweeping away eerily in the thundering wind that seemed to pound down upon them with new vigor in that moment. Heads appeared from the openings in the craft.

Ennis suddenly stood up to his full height, bracing himself against the wind, so dense it made him buoyant. With a deep bellow he bridged the space to the derelict. Then, as a squad of Maraks made their difficult, slippery way across the flank of the battleship toward him, and as the band that had boarded the spaceship crowded out on its battered deck to see what the noise was about, he dropped down into a crouch behind his ultraviolet projector, and whirled it around, pulling the firing lever.

That was what he wanted. Make a lot of noise and disturbance, get them all on deck, and then blow them to pieces. The ravening blast spat from the nozzle of the weapon, and the men on the battleship dropped flat on the deck. He found he could not depress the projector enough to reach them. He spun it to point at the spaceship. The incandescence reached out, and then seemed to waver and die. The current was shut off at the switchboard.

Ennis rose from behind the projector, and then hurtled from the flank of the battleship as he was struck by two Maraks leaping on him from behind the hump of the vessel. The three struck the water and sank, Ennis struggling violently. He was on the last lap, and he gave all his strength to the spurt. The water swirled around them in little choppy waves that fell more quickly than the eye could follow. Heavier blows than those from an Earthly trip hammer were scoring Ennis' face and head. He was in a bad position to strike back, and suddenly he became limp and sank below the surface. The pressure of the water around him was enormous, and it increased very rapidly as he went lower and lower. He saw the shadowy bulk of the spaceship above him. His lungs were fighting for air, but he shook off his pretended stupor and swam doggedly through the water beneath the derelict. He went on and on. It seemed as though the distance were endless following the metal curve. It was so big from beneath, and trying to swim the width without air made it bigger.

Clear, finally, his lungs drew in the saving breaths. No time to rest, though. He must make use of his advantage while it was his; it wouldn't last long. He swam along the side of the ship looking for an opening. There was none within reach from the water, so he made one, digging his stubby fingers into the metal, climbing up until it was safe to tear a rent in the thick outer and inner walls of the ship.

He found himself in one of the machine rooms of the second level. He went out into the corridor and up the stairway which was half-wrecked, and found himself in the main passage near the control room. He darted down it, into the room. There was nobody there, although the noises from above indicated that the Maraks were again descending. There was his weapon on the floor, where he had left it. He was glad that they had not gotten around to pulling that instrument apart. There would be one thing saved for intelligent examination.

The clatter from the descending crowd turned into a clamor of anger as they discovered him in the passageway. They stopped there for a moment, puzzled. He had been in the ocean, and had somehow magically reappeared within the derelict. It gave him time to pick up the weapon.

Ennis debated rapidly and decided to risk the unknown. How powerful the weapon was he did not know, but with atomic energy it would be powerful. He disliked using it inside the spaceship; he wanted to have enough left to float on the water until Shadden arrived; but they were beginning to advance on him, and he had to start something.

He pulled a lever. The cylinder in his arms jerked back with great force; a bolt of fierce, blinding energy tore out of it and passed with the quickness of light down the length of the corridor.

When he could see again there was no corridor. Everything that had been in the way of the projector was gone, simply disappeared.

Unmindful of the heat from the object in his hands, he turned and directed it at the battleship that was plainly outlined through the space that had been once the walls of the derelict. Before the men on the deck could move, he pulled the lever again.

And the winds were silenced for a moment. The natural elements were still in fear at the incredible forces that came from the destruction of atoms. Then with an agonized scream the hurricane struck again, tore through the spot where there had been a battleship.

Far off in the sky Ennis detected motion. It was Shadden, speeding in a glider.

Now would come the work that was important. Shadden would take the big machine apart and see how it ran. That was what history would remember.

LIFE-LINE
Astounding Science Fiction, August

by Robert A. Heinlein (1907–   )

More than any other single individual next to John Campbell himself, Robert A. Heinlein changed modern science fiction. Born in Butler, Missouri, he was in his early thirties when he began his sf career, which saw him become the greatest luminary of the Golden Age.

His "Future History" series (collected as THE PAST THROUGH TOMORROW, 1967) is one of the seminal works in the canon of science fiction. Although his political and social views have generated much controversy in the last twenty years, his emphasis on order, individualism, and discipline aroused little comment early in his career, with America in a struggle against an illegal, disorderly, and undisciplined fascism.

"Life-Line" was the first in the series and the first published science fiction of one of modern sf's founding fathers. It made him a star at once.

(Bob Heinlein gave me my very first alcoholic drink. It was a Cuba Libre. I sniffed at it suspiciously, but he assured me it was a Coca-Cola and I wouldn't dream of doubting the man who in a matter of months was suddenly the universally acknowledged "best writer" of science fiction. I drank it as though it was indeed a Coca-Cola and was promptly assailed by the most unpleasant symptoms. Although I had been my usually quiet self till then, I now crept into a corner to recover. Bob shouted, "No wonder he doesn't drink. It sobers him up!"—I still don't drink. IA)

The chairman rapped loudly for order. Gradually the catcalls and boos died away as several self-appointed sergeant-at-arms persuaded a few hot-headed individuals to sit down. The speaker on the rostrum by the chairman seemed unaware of the disturbance. His bland, faintly insolent face was impassive. The chairman turned to the speaker and addressed him in a voice in which anger and annoyance were barely restrained.

"Dr. Pinero"—the "Doctor" was faintly stressed—"I must apologize to you for the unseemly outburst during your remarks. I am surprised that my colleagues should so far forget the dignity proper to men of science as to interrupt a speaker, no matter"—he paused and set his mouth—"no matter how great the provocation." Pinero smiled in his face, a smile that was in some way an open insult. The chairman visibly controlled his temper and continued: "I am anxious that the program be concluded decently and in order. I want you to finish your remarks. Nevertheless, I must ask you to refrain from affronting our intelligence with ideas that any educated man knows to be fallacious. Please confine yourself to your discovery—if you have made one."

Pinero spread his fat, white hands, palms down. "How can I possibly put a new idea into your heads, if I do not first remove your delusions?"

The audience stirred and muttered. Someone shouted from the rear of the hall: "Throw the charlatan out! We've had enough."

The chairman pounded his gavel.

"Gentlemen! Please!"

Then to Pinero, "Must I remind you that you are not a member of this body, and that we did not invite you?"

Pinero's eyebrows lifted. "So? I seem to remember an invitation on the letterhead of the Academy."

The chairman chewed his lower lip before replying. "True. I wrote that invitation myself. But it was at the request of one of the trustees—a fine, public-spirited gentleman, but not a scientist, not a member of the Academy."

Pinero smiled his irritating smile. "So? I should have guessed. Old Bidwell, not so, of Amalgamated Life Insurance? And he wanted his trained seals to expose me as a fraud, yes? For if I can tell a man the day of his own death, no one will buy his pretty policies. But how can you expose me, if you will not listen to me first? Even supposing you had the wit to understand me? Bah! He has sent jackals to tear down a lion." He deliberately turned his back on them.

The muttering of the crowd swelled and took on a vicious tone. The chairman cried vainly for order. There arose a figure in the front row.

"Mr. Chairman!"

The chairman grasped the opening and shouted: "Gentlemen! Dr. van Rhein Smitt has the floor." The commotion died away.

The doctor cleared his throat, smoothed the forelock of his beautiful white hair, and thrust one hand into a side pocket of his smartly tailored trousers. He assumed his women's-club manner.

"Mr. Chairman, fellow members of the Academy of Science, let us have tolerance. Even a murderer has the right to say his say before the State exacts its tribute. Shall we do less? Even though one may be intellectually certain of the verdict? I grant Dr. Pinero every consideration that should be given by this august body to any unaffiliated colleague, even though"—he bowed slightly in Pinero's direction—"we may not be familiar with the university which bestowed his degree. If what he has to say is false, it cannot harm us. If what he has to say is true, we should know it." His mellow, cultivated voice rolled on, soothing and calming. "If the eminent doctor's manner appears a trifle inurbane of our tastes, we must bear in mind that the doctor may be from a place, or a stratum, not so meticulous in these matters. Now our good friend and benefactor has asked us to hear this person and carefully assess the merit of his claims. Let us do so with dignity and decorum."

He sat down to a rumble of applause, comfortably aware that he had enhanced his reputation as an intellectual leader. Tomorrow the papers would again mention the good sense and persuasive personality of "America's Handsomest University President." Who knows; maybe now old Bidwell would come through with that swimming-pool donation.

When the applause had ceased, the chairman turned to where the center of the disturbance sat, hands folded over his little round belly, face serene.

"Will you continue, Dr. Pinero?"

"Why should I?"

The chairman shrugged his shoulders. "You came for that purpose."

Pinero arose. "So true. So very true. But was I wise to come? Is there anyone here who has an open mind, who can stare a bare fact in the face without blushing? I think not. Even that so-beautiful gentleman who asked you to hear me out has already judged me and condemned me. He seeks order, not truth. Suppose truth defies order, will he accept it? Will you? I think not. Still, if I do not speak, you will win your point by default. The little man in the street will think that you little men have exposed me, Pinero, as a hoaxer, a pretender.

"I will repeat my discovery. In simple language, I have invented a technique to tell how long a man will live. I can give you advance billing of the Angel of Death. I can tell you when the Black Camel will kneel at your door. In five minutes' time, with my apparatus, I can tell any of you how many grains of sand are still left in your hour-glass." He paused and folded his arms across his chest. For a moment no one spoke. The audience grew restless.

Finally the chairman intervened, "You aren't finished, Dr. Pinero?"

"What more is there to say?"

"You haven't told us how your discovery works."

Pinero's eyebrows shot up. "You suggest that I should turn over the fruits of my work for children to play with? This is dangerous knowledge, my friend. I keep it for the man who understands it, myself." He tapped his chest.

"How are we to know that you have anything back of your wild claims?"

"So simple. You send a committee to watch me demonstrate. If it works, fine. You admit it and tell the world so. If it does not work, I am discredited, and will apologize. Even I, Pinero, will apologize."

A slender, stoop-shouldered man stood up in the back of the hall. The chair recognized him and he spoke.

"Mr. Chairman, how can the eminent doctor seriously propose such a course? Does he expect us to wait around for twenty or thirty years for someone to die and prove his claims?"

Pinero ignored the chair and answered directly.

"*Pfui!* Such nonsense! Are you so ignorant of statistics that you do not know that in any large group there is at least one who will die in the immediate future? I make you a proposition. Let me test each one of you in this room, and I will name the man who will die within the fortnight, yes, and the day and hour of his death." He glanced fiercely around the room. "Do you accept?"

Another figure got to his feet, a portly man who spoke in measured syllables. "I, for one, cannot countenance such an experiment. As a medical man, I have noted with sorrow the plain marks of serious heart trouble in many of our elder colleagues. If Dr. Pinero knows those symptoms, as he may, and were he to select as his victim one of their number, the man so selected would be likely to die on schedule, whether the distinguished speaker's mechanical egg timer works or not."

Another speaker backed him up at once. "Dr. Shepard is right. Why should we waste time on voodoo tricks? It is my belief that this person who calls himself *Dr.* Pinero wants to use this body to give his statements authority. If we participate in this farce, we play into his hands. I don't know what his racket is, but you can bet that he has figured out some way to use us for advertising his schemes. I move, Mr. Chairman, that we proceed with our regular business."

The motion carried by acclamation, but Pinero did not sit down. Amidst cries of "Order! Order!" he shook his untidy head at them, and had his say.

"Barbarians! Imbeciles! Stupid dolts! Your kind have blocked the recognition of every great discovery since time began. Such ignorant canaille are enough to start Galileo spinning in his grave. That fat fool down there twiddling his elk's tooth calls himself a medical man. Witch doctor would be a better term! That little bald-headed runt over there— You! You style yourself a philosopher, and prate about life and time in your neat categories. What do you know of either one? How can you ever learn when you won't examine the truth when you have a chance? Bah!" He spat upon the stage. "You call this an Academy of Science. I call it an undertakers' convention, interested only in embalming the ideas of your red-blooded predecessors."

He paused for breath and was grasped on each side by two members of the platform committee and rushed out the wings. Several reporters arose hastily from the press table and followed him. The chairman declared the meeting adjourned.

The newspapermen caught up with Pinero as he was going out by the stage door. He walked with a light, springy step, and whistled a little tune. There was no trace of the belligerence he had shown a moment before. They crowded about him. "How about an interview, doc?" "What d'yuh think of modern education?" "You certainly told 'em. What are your views on life after death?" "Take off your hat, doc, and look at the birdie."

He grinned at them all. "One at a time, boys, and not so fast. I used to be a newspaperman myself. How about coming up to my place?"

A few minutes later they were trying to find places to sit down in Pinero's messy bed-living room, and lighting his cigars. Pinero looked around and beamed. "What'll it be, boys? Scotch or Bourbon?" When that was taken care of he got down to business. "Now, boys, what do you want to know?"

"Lay it on the line, doc. Have you got something, or haven't you?"

"Most assuredly I have something, my young friend."

"Then tell us how it works. That guff you handed the profs won't get you anywhere now."

"Please, my dear fellow. It is my invention. I expect to make some money with it. Would you have me give it away to the first person who asks for it?"

"See here, doc, you've got to give us something if you expect to get a break in the morning papers. What do you use? A crystal ball?"

"No, not quite. Would you like to see my apparatus?"

"Sure. Now we're getting somewhere."

He ushered them into an adjoining room, and waved his hand. "There it is, boys." The mass of equipment that met their eyes vaguely resembled a medico's office X-ray gear. Beyond the obvious fact that it used electrical power, and that some of the dials were calibrated in familiar terms, a casual inspection gave no clue to its actual use.

"What's the principle, doc?"

Pinero pursed his lips and considered. "No doubt you are all familiar with the truism that life is electrical in nature. Well, that truism isn't worth a damn, but it will help to give you an idea of the principle. You have also been told that time is a fourth dimension. Maybe you believe it, perhaps not. It has been said so many times that it has ceased to have any meaning. It is simply a cliché that windbags use to impress fools. But I want you to try to visualize it now, and try to feel it emotionally."

He stepped up to one of the reporters. "Suppose we take you as an example. Your name is Rogers, is it not? Very well, Rogers, you are a space-time event having duration four ways. You are not quite six feet tall, you are about twenty inches wide and perhaps ten inches thick. In time, there stretches behind you more of this space-time event, reaching to, perhaps, 1905, of which we see a cross section here at right angles to the time axis, and as thick as the present. At the far end is a baby, smelling of sour milk and drooling its breakfast on its bib. At the other end lies, perhaps, an old man some place in the 1980s. Imagine this space-time event, which we call Rogers, as a long pink worm, continuous through the years. It stretches past us here in 1939, and the cross section we see appears as a single, discreet body. But that is illusion. There is physical continuity to this pink worm, enduring through the years. As a matter of fact, there is physical continuity in this concept to the entire race, for these pink worms branch off from other pink worms. In this fashion the race is like a vine whose branches intertwine and send out shoots. Only by taking a cross section of the vine would we fall into the error of believing that the shootlets were discreet individuals."

He paused and looked around at their faces. One of them, a dour, hard-bitten chap, put in a word.

"That's all very pretty, Pinero, if true, but where does that get you?"

Pinero favored him with an unresentful smile. "Patience, my friend. I asked you to think of life as electrical. Now think of our long, pink worm as a conductor of electricity. You have heard, perhaps, of the fact that electrical engineers can, by certain measurements, predict the exact location of a break in a transatlantic cable without ever leaving the shore. I do the same with our pink worms. By applying my instruments to the cross section here in this room I can tell where the break occurs; that is to say, where death takes place. Or, if you like, I can reverse the connections and tell you the date of your birth. But that is uninteresting; you already know it."

The dour individual sneered. "I've caught you, doc. If what you say about the race being like a vine fo pink worms is true, you can't tell birthdays, because the connection with the race is continuous at birth. Your electrical conductor reaches on back through the mother into a man's remotest ancestors."

Pinero beamed. "True, and clever, my friend. But you have pushed the analogy too far. It is not done in the precise manner in which one measures the length of an electrical conductor. In some ways it is more like measuring the length of a long corridor by bouncing an echo off the far end. At birth there is a sort of twist in the corridor, and, by proper calibration, I can detect the echo from that twist."

"Let's see you prove it."

"Certainly, my dear friend. Will you be a subject?"

One of the others spoke up. "He's called your bluff, Luke. Put up or shut up."

"I'm game. What do I do?"

"First write the date of your birth on a sheet of paper, and hand it to one of your colleagues."

Luke complied. "Now what?"

"Remove your outer clothing and step upon these scales. Now tell me, were you ever very much thinner, or very much fatter, than you are now? No? What did you weigh at birth? Ten pounds? A fine bouncing baby boy. They don't come so big any more."

"What is all this flubdubbery?"

"I am trying to approximate the average cross section of our long pink conductor, my dear Luke. Now will you seat yourself here? Then place this electrode in your mouth. No, it will not hurt you; the voltage is quite low, less than one micro-volt, but I must have a good connection." The doctor left him and went behind his apparatus, where he lowered a hood over his head before touching his controls. Some of the exposed dials came to life and a low humming came from the machine. It stopped and the doctor popped out of his little hide-away.

"I get sometime in February, 1902. Who has the piece of paper with the date?"

It was produced and unfolded. The custodian read, "February 22, 1902."

The stillness that followed was broken by a voice from the edge of the little group. "Doc, can I have another drink?"

The tension relaxed, and several spoke at once: "Try it on me, doc." "Me first, doc; I'm an orphan and really want to know." "How about it, doc? Give us all a little loose play."

He smilingly complied, ducking in and out of the hood like a gopher from its hole. When they all had twin slips of paper to prove the doctor's skill, Luke broke a long silence.

"How about showing how you predict death, Pinero?"

"If you wish. Who will try it?"

No one answered. Several of them nudged Luke forward. "Go ahead, smart guy. You asked for it." He allowed himself to be seated in the chair. Pinero changed some of the switches, then entered the hood. When the humming ceased he came out, rubbing his hands briskly together.

"Well, that's all there is to see, boys. Got enough for a story?"

"Hey, what about the prediction? When does Luke get his 'thirty'?"

Luke faced him. "Yes, how about it?"

Pinero looked pained. "Gentlemen, I am surprised at you. I give that information for a fee. Besides, it is a professional confidence. I never tell anyone but the client who consults me."

"I don't mind. Go ahead and tell them."

"I am very sorry, I really must refuse. I only agreed to show you how; not to give the results."

Luke ground the butt of his cigarette into the floor. "It's a hoax, boys. He probably looked up the age of every reporter in town just to be ready to pull this. It won't wash, Pinero."

Pinero gazed at him sadly. "Are you married, my friend?"

"No."

"Do you have anyone dependent on you? Any close relatives?"

"No. Why? Do you want to adopt me?"

Pinero shook his head. "I am very sorry for you, my dear Luke. You will die before tomorrow."

DEATH PUNCHES TIME CLOCK

... within twenty minutes of Pinero's strange prediction, Timons was struck by a falling sign while walking down Broadway toward the offices of the *Daily Herald* where he was employed.

Dr. Pinero declined to comment but confirmed the story that he had predicted Timons' death by means of his so-called chronovitameter. Chief of Police Roy.

Does the FUTURE worry you??????
Don't waste money on fortunetellers—
Consult
Dr. Hugo Pinero, Bio-Consultant
He will help you plan for the future by infallible
SCIENTIFIC METHODS
No Hocus-Pocus
No "Spirit" Messages....
$10,000 Bond posted in forfeit to back our predictions
Circular on request
SANDS of TIME, Inc.
Majestic Bldg., Suite 700
(adv.)

Legal Notice

To whom it may concern, greetings, I, John Cabot Winthrop III, of the firm of Winthrop, Winthrop, Ditmars and Winthrop, Attorneys-at-law, do affirm that Hugo Pinero of this city did hand to me ten thousand dollars in lawful money of the United States, and did instruct me to place it in escrow with a chartered bank of my selection with escrow instructions as follows:

The entire bond shall be forfeit, and shall forthwith be paid to the first client of Hugo Pinero and/or Sands of Time, Inc. who shall exceed his life tenure as predicted by Hugo Pinero by one per centum, or to the estate of the first client who shall fail of such predicted tenure in a like amount, whichever occurs first in point of time.

Subscribed and sworn,
John Cabot Winthrop III.

Subscribed and sworn to before
me this 2nd day of April, 1939.
Albert M. Swanson
Notary Public in and for this
county and State. My commission
expires June 17, 1939.

"Good evening, Mr. and Mrs. Radio Audience, let's go to press! Flash! Hugo Pinero, the Miracle Man from Nowhere, has made his thousandth death prediction without anyone claiming the reward he offered to the first person who catches him failing to call the turn. With thirteen of his clients already dead, it is mathematically certain that he has a private line to the main office of the Old Man with the Scythe. That is one piece of news I don't want to know about before it happens. Your coast-to-coast correspondent will *not* be a client of Prophet Pinero—"

The judge's watery baritone cut through the stale air of the courtroom. "Please, Mr. Weems, let us return to our subject. This court granted your prayer for a temporary restraining order, and now you ask that it be made permanent. In rebuttal, Dr. Pinero claims that you have presented no cause and asks that the injunction be lifted, and that I order your client to cease from attempts to interfere with what Pinero describes as a simple, lawful business. As you are not addressing a jury, please omit the rhetoric and tell me in plain language why I should not grant his prayer."

Mr. Weems jerked his chin nervously, making his flabby gray dewlap drag across his high stiff collar, and resumed:

LIFE-LINE

"May it please the honorable court, I represent the public—"

"Just a moment. I thought you were appearing for Amalgamated Life Insurance."

"I am, your honor, in a formal sense. In a wider sense I represent several other of the major assurance, fiduciary and financial institutions, their stockholders and policy holders, who constitute a majority of the citizenry. In addition we feel that we protect the interests of the entire population, unorganized, inarticulate and otherwise unprotected."

"I thought that I represented the public," observed the judge dryly. "I am afraid I must regard you as appearing for your client of record. But continue. What is your thesis?"

The elderly barrister attempted to swallow his Adam's apple, then began again: "Your honor, we contend that there are two separate reasons why this injunction should be made permanent, and, further, that each reason is sufficient alone.

"In the first place, this person is engaged in the practice of soothsaying, an occupation proscribed both in common law and statute. He is a common fortuneteller, a vagabond charlatan who preys on the gullibility of the public. He is cleverer than the ordinary gypsy palm reader, astrologer or table tipper, and to the same extent more dangerous. He makes false claims of modern scientific methods to give a spurious dignity to the thaumaturgy. We have here in court leading representatives of the Academy of Science to give expert witness as to the absurdity of his claims.

"In the second place, even if this person's claims were true—granting for the sake of argument such an absurdity"—Mr. Weems permitted himself a thin-lipped smile—"we contend that his activities are contrary to the public interest in general, and unlawfully injurious to the interests of my client in particular. We are prepared to produce numerous exhibits with the legal custodians to prove that this person did publish, or cause to have published, utterances urging the public to dispense with the priceless boon of life insurance to the great detriment of their welfare and to the financial damage of my client."

Pinero arose in his place. "Your honor, may I say a few words?"

"What is it?"

"I believe I can simplify the situation if permitted to make a brief analysis."

"Your honor," put in Weems, "this is most irregular."

"Patience, Mr. Weems. Your interests will be protected. It seems to me that we need more light and less noise in this matter. If Dr. Pinero can shorten the proceedings by speaking at this time, I am inclined to let him. Proceed, Dr. Pinero."

"Thank you, your honor. Taking the last of Mr. Weems' points first, I am prepared to stipulate that I published the utterances he speaks of—"

"One moment, doctor. You have chosen to act as your own attorney. Are you sure you are competent to protect your own interests?"

"I am prepared to chance it, your honor. Our friends here can easily prove what I stipulate."

"Very well. You may proceed."

"I will stipulate that many persons have canceled life-insurance policies as a result thereof, but I challenge them to show that anyone so doing has suffered any loss or damage therefrom. It is true that the Amalgamated has lost business through my activities, but that is the natural result of my discovery, which has made their policies as obsolete as the bow and arrow. If an injunction is granted on that ground, I shall set up a coal-oil-lamp factory, and then ask for an injunction against the Edison and General Electric companies to forbid them to manufacture incandescent bulbs.

"I will stipulate that I am engaged in the business of making predictions of death, but I deny that I am practicing magic, black, white or rainbow-colored. If to make predictions by methods of scientific accuracy is illegal, then the actuaries of the Amalgamated have been guilty for years, in that they predict the exact percentage that will die each year in any given large group. I predict death retail; the Amalgamated predicts it wholesale. If their actions are legal, how can mine be illegal?

"I admit that it makes a difference whether I can do what I claim, or not; and I will stipulate that the so-called expert witnesses from the Academy of Science will testify that I cannot. But they know nothing of my method and cannot give truly expert testimony on it—"

"Just a moment, doctor. Mr. Weems, is it true that your expert witnesses are not conversant with Dr. Pinero's theory and methods?"

Mr. Weems looked worried. He drummed on the table top, then answered, "Will the court grant me a few moments' indulgence?"

"Certainly."

Mr. Weems held a hurried whispered consultation with his cohorts, then faced the bench. "We have a procedure to suggest, your honor. If Dr. Pinero will take the stand and explain the theory and practice of his alleged method, then these distinguished scientists will be able to advise the court as to the validity of his claims."

The judge looked inquiringly at Pinero, who responded: "I will not willingly agree to that. Whether my process is true or false, it would be dangerous to let it fall into the hands of fools and quacks"—he waved his hand at the group of professors seated in the front row, paused and smiled maliciously—"as these gentlemen know quite well. Furthermore, it is not necessary to know the process in order to prove that it will work. Is it necessary to understand the complex miracle of biological reproduction in order to observe that a hen lays eggs? Is it necessary for me to re-educate this entire body of self-appointed custodians of wisdom—cure them of their ingrown superstitions—in order to prove that my predictions are correct?

"There are but two ways of forming an opinion in science. One is the scientific method; the other, the scholastic. One can judge from experiment, or one can blindly accept authority. To the scientific mind, experimental proof is all-important, and theory is merely a convenience in description, to be junked when it no longer fits. To the academic mind, authority is everything, and facts are junked when they do not fit theory laid down by authority.

"It is this point of view—academic minds clinging like oysters to disproved theories—that has blocked every advance of knowledge in history. I am prepared to prove my method by experiment, and, like Galileo in another court, I insist, 'It still moves!'

"Once before I offered such proof to this same body of self-styled experts, and they rejected it. I renew my offer; let me measure the life length of the members of the Academy of Science. Let them appoint a committee to judge the results. I will seal my findings in two sets of envelopes; on the outside of each envelope in one set will appear the name of a member; on the inside, the date of his death. In the other envelopes I will place names; on the outside I will place dates. Let the committee place the envelopes in a vault, then meet from time to time to open the appropriate envelopes. In such a large body of men some deaths may be expected, if Amalgamated actuaries can be trusted, every week or two. In such a fashion they will accumulate data very rapidly to prove that Pinero is a liar, or no."

He stopped, and thrust out his chest until it almost caught up with his little round belly. He glared at the sweating savants. "Well?"

The judge raised his eyebrows, and caught Mr. Weems' eye. "Do you accept?"

"Your honor, I think the proposal highly improper—"

The judge cut him short. "I warn you that I shall rule against you if you do not accept, or propose an equally reasonable method of arriving at the truth."

Weems opened his mouth, changed his mind, looked up and down the faces of the learned witnesses, and faced the bench. "We accept, your honor."

"Very well. Arrange the details between you. The temporary injunction is lifted and Dr. Pinero must not be molested in the pursuit of his business. Decision on the petition for permanent injunction is reserved without prejudice pending the accumulation of evidence. Before we leave this matter I wish to comment on the theory implied by you, Mr. Weems, when you claimed damage to your client. There has grown up in the minds of certain groups in this country the notion that because a man or corporation has made a profit out of the public for a number of years, the government and the courts are charged with the duty of guaranteeing such profit in the future, even in the face of changing circumstances and contrary to public interest. This strange doctrine is not supported by statute nor common law. Neither individuals nor corporations have any right to come into court and ask that the clock of history be stopped, or turned back."

Bidwell grunted in annoyance. "Weems, if you can't think up anything better than that, Amalgamated is going to need a new chief attorney. It's been ten weeks since you lost the injunction, and that little wart is coining money hand over fist. Meantime, every insurance firm in the country's going broke. Hoskins, what's our loss ratio?"

"It's hard to say, Mr. Bidwell. It gets worse every day. We've paid off thirteen big policies this week; all of them taken out since Pinero started operations."

A spare little man spoke up. "I say, Bidwell, we aren't accepting any new applicants for United, until we have time to check and be sure that they have not consulted Pinero. Can't we afford to wait until the scientists show him up?"

Bidwell snorted. "You blasted optimist! They won't show

him up. Aldrich, can't you face a fact? The fat little pest has something; how, I don't know. This is a fight to the finish. If we wait, we're licked." He threw his cigar into a cuspidor, and bit savagely into a fresh one. "Clear out of here, all of you! I'll handle this my own way. You, too, Aldrich. United may wait, but Amalgamated won't."

Weems cleared his throat apprehensively. "Mr. Bidwell, I trust you will consult me before embarking on any major change in policy?"

Bidwell grunted. They filed out. When they were all gone and the door closed, Bidwell snapped the switch of the interoffice announcer. "O.K.; send him in."

The outer door opened. A slight, dapper figure stood for a moment at the threshold. His small, dark eyes glanced quickly about the room before he entered, then he moved up to Bidwell with a quick, soft tread. He spoke to Bidwell in a flat, emotionless voice. His face remained impassive except for the live, animal eyes. "You wanted to talk to me?"

"Yes."

"What's the proposition?"

"Sit down, and we'll talk."

Pinero met the young couple at the door of his inner office.

"Come in, my dears, come in. Sit down. Make yourselves at home. Now tell me, what do you want of Pinero? Surely such young people are not anxious about the final roll call?"

The boy's pleasant young face showed slight confusion. "Well, you see, Dr. Pinero, I'm Ed Hartley and this is my wife, Betty. We're going to have . . . that is, Betty is expecting a baby and, well—"

Pinero smiled benignly. "I understand. You want to know how long you will live in order to make the best possible provision for the youngster. Quite wise. Do you both want readings, or just yourself?"

The girl answered, "Both of us, we think."

Pinero beamed at her. "Quite so. I agree. Your reading presents certain technical difficulties at this time, but I can give you some information now. Now come into my laboratory, my dears, and we'll commence."

He rang for their case histories, then showed them into his workshop. "Mrs. Hartley first, please. If you will go behind that screen and remove your shoes and your outer clothing, please."

He turned away and made some minor adjustments of his

apparatus. Ed nodded to his wife, who slipped behind the screen and reappeared almost at once, dressed in a slip. Pinero glanced up.

"This way, my dear. First we must weigh you. There. Now take your place on the stand. This electrode in your mouth. No, Ed, you mustn't touch her while she is in the circuit. It won't take a minute. Remain quiet."

He dove under the machine's hood and the dials sprang into life. Very shortly he came out, with a perturbed look on his face. "Ed, did you touch her?"

"No, doctor." Pinero ducked back again and remained a little longer. When he came out this time, he told the girl to get down and dress. He turned to her husband.

"Ed, make yourself ready."

"What's Betty's reading, doctor?"

"There is a little difficulty. I want to test you first."

When he came out from taking the youth's reading, his face was more troubled than ever. Ed inquired as to his trouble. Pinero shrugged his shoulders and brought a smile to his lips.

"Nothing to concern you, my boy. A little mechanical misadjustment, I think. But I shan't be able to give you two your readings today. I shall need to overhaul my machine. Can you come back tomorrow?"

"Why, I think so. Say, I'm sorry about your machine. I hope it isn't serious."

"It isn't, I'm sure. Will you come back into my office and visit for a bit?"

"Thank you, doctor. You are very kind."

"But, Ed, I've got to meet Ellen."

Pinero turned the full force of his personality on her. "Won't you grant me a few moments, my dear young lady? I am old, and like the sparkle of young folks' company. I get very little of it. Please." He nudged them gently into his office and seated them. Then he ordered lemonade and cookies sent in, offered them cigarettes and lit a cigar.

Forty minutes later Ed listened entranced, while Betty was quite evidently acutely nervous and anxious to leave, as the doctor spun out a story concerning his adventures as a young man in Tierra del Fuego. When the doctor stopped to relight his cigar, she stood up.

"Doctor, we really must leave. Couldn't we hear the rest tomorrow?"

"Tomorrow? There will not be time tomorrow."

"But you haven't time today, either. Your secretary has rung five times."

"Couldn't you spare me just a few more minutes?"

"I really can't today, doctor. I have an appointment. There is someone waiting for me."

"There is no way to induce you?"

"I'm afraid not. Come, Ed."

After they had gone, the doctor stepped to the window and stared out over the city. Presently, he picked out two tiny figures as they left the office building. He watched them hurry to the corner, wait for the lights to change, then start across the street. When they were part way across, there came the scream of a siren. The two little figures hesitated, started back, stopped and turned. Then the car was upon them. As the car slammed to a stop, they showed up from beneath it, no longer two figures, but simply a limp, unorganized heap of clothing.

Presently the doctor turned away from the window. Then he picked up his phone and spoke to his secretary.

"Cancel my appointments for the rest of the day. . . . No. . . . No one. . . . I don't care; cancel them."

Then he sat down in his chair. His cigar went out. Long after dark he held it, still unlighted.

Pinero sat down at his dining table and contemplated the gourmet's luncheon spread before him. He had ordered this meal with particular care, and had come home a little early in order to enjoy it fully.

Somewhat later he let a few drops of fiori d'Alpini roll around his tongue and trickle down his throat. The heavy, fragrant sirup warmed his mouth and reminded him of the little mountain flowers for which it was named. He sighed. It had been a good meal, an exquisite meal and had justified the exotic liqueur.

His musing was interrupted by a disturbance at the front door. The voice of his elderly maidservant was raised in remonstrance. A heavy male voice interrupted her. The commotion moved down the hall and the dining-room door was pushed open.

"Mia Madonna! Non si puo entrare! The master is eating!"

"Never mind, Angela. I have time to see these gentlemen. You may go."

Pinero faced the surly-faced spokesman of the intruders. "You have business with me; yes?"

"You bet we have. Decent people have had enough of your damned nonsense."

"And so?"

The caller did not answer at once. A smaller, dapper individual moved out from behind him and faced Pinero.

"We might as well begin." The chairman of the committee placed a key in the lock box and opened it. "Wenzell, will you help me pick out today's envelopes?" He was interrupted by a touch on his arm.

"Dr. Baird, you are wanted on the telephone."

"Very well. Bring the instrument here."

When it was fetched he placed the receiver to his ear. "Hello. . . . Yes; speaking. . . . What? . . . No, we have heard nothing. . . . Destroyed the machine, you say. . . . Dead! How? . . . No! No statement. None at all. . . . Call me later."

He slammed the instrument down and pushed it from him.

"What's up?"

"Who's dead now?"

Baird held up one hand. "Quiet, gentlemen, please! Pinero was murdered a few moments ago at his home."

"Murdered!"

"That isn't all. About the same time vandals broke into his office and smashed his apparatus."

No one spoke at first. The committee members glanced around at each other. No one seemed anxious to be the first to comment.

Finally one spoke up. "Get it out."

"Get what out?"

"Pinero's envelope. It's in there, too. I've seen it."

Baird located it, and slowly tore it open. He unfolded the single sheet of paper and scanned it.

"Well? Out with it!"

"One thirteen p.m. . . . today."

They took this in silence.

Their dynamic calm was broken by a member across the table from Baird reaching for the lock box. Baird interposed a hand.

"What do you want?"

"My prediction. It's in there—we're all in there."

"Yes, yes."

"We're all in there."

"Let's have them."

Baird placed both hands over the box. He held the eye of the man opposite him, but did not speak. He licked his lips. The corner of his mouth twitched. His hands shook. Still he did not speak. The man opposite relaxed back into his chair. "You're right, of course," he said.

"Bring me that wastebasket." Baird's voice was low and strained, but steady.

He accepted it and dumped the litter on the rug. He placed the tin basket on the table before him. He tore half a dozen envelopes across, set a match to them, and dropped them in the basket. Then he started tearing a double handful at a time, and fed the fire steadily. The smoke made him cough, and tears ran out of his smarting eyes. Someone got up and opened a window. When Baird was through, he pushed the basket away from him, looked down and spoke.

"I'm afraid I've ruined this table top."

ETHER BREATHER
Astounding Science Fiction, September

by Theodore Sturgeon (1918–)

Until the early seventies, Theodore Sturgeon (Edward H. Waldo) was the most heavily reprinted writer in the science fiction universe. This was a richly deserved honor, for he had produced a long line of outstanding, well-crafted stories featuring memorable characters. Working within the fantasy and science fiction genres, he excelled at both, and influenced an entire generation of writers, including Ray Bradbury.

Here is his first published story—one that exhibits all of the talent he would develop and nurture in succeeding years.

(Good Heavens! I've known Ted Sturgeon for forty years and never knew till now that that wasn't his real name. Are you sure, Marty? Anyway, an editor said to me once, "If you had to publish a collection of stories by Theodore Sturgeon, what would you call it?" I thought for a while and said, "Caviar!" The editor said triumphantly to someone else who was in the office, "See!!!" and that was indeed the name of the collection. IA)

Yes, Isaac, I'm sure. He legally changed his name to Sturgeon when his mother remarried.

It was "The Seashell." It *would* have to be "The Seashell." I wrote it first as a short story, and it was turned down. Then I made a novelette out of it, and then a novel. Then a short

short. Then a three-line gag. And it still wouldn't sell. It got to be a fetish with me, rewriting that "Seashell." After a while editors got so used to it that they turned it down on sight. I had enough rejection slips from that number alone to paper every room in the house of tomorrow. So when it sold—well, it was like the death of a friend. It hit me. I hated to see it go.

It was a play by that time, but I hadn't changed it much. Still the same pastel, froo-froo old "Seashell" story, about two children who grew up and met each other only three times as the years went on, and a little seashell that changed hands each time they met. The plot, if any, doesn't matter. The dialogue was—well, pastel. Naïve. Unsophisticated. Very pretty, and practically salesproof. But it just happened to ring the bell with an earnest young reader for Associated Television, Inc., who was looking for something about that length that could be dubbed "artistic"; something that would not require too much cerebration on the part of an audience, so that said audience could relax and appreciate the new polychrome technique of television transmission. You know; pastel.

As I leaned back in my old relic of an armchair that night, and watched the streamlined version of my slow-moving brainchild, I had to admire the way they put it over. In spots it was almost good, that "Seashell." Well suited for the occasion, too. It was a full-hour program given free to a perfume house by Associated, to try out the new color transmission as an advertising medium. I liked the first two acts, if I do say so as shouldn't. It was at the half-hour mark that I got my first kick on the chin. It was a two-minute skit for the advertising plug.

A tall and elegant couple were seen standing on marble steps in an elaborate theater lobby. Says she to he:

"And how do you like the play, Mr. Robinson?"

Says he to she: "It stinks."

Just like that. Like any radio-television listener, I was used to paying little, if any, attention to a plug. That certainly snapped me up in my chair. After all, it was my play, even if it was "The Seashell." They couldn't do that to me.

But the girl smiling archly out of my television set didn't seem to mind. She said sweetly, "I think so, too."

He was looking slushily down into her eyes. He said: "That goes for you, too, my dear. What *is* that perfume you are using?"

"Berbelot's *Doux Rêves*. What do you think of it?"

He said, "You heard what I said about the play."

I didn't wait for the rest of the plug, the station identification, and act three. I headed for my visiphone and dialed Associated. I was burning up. When their pert-faced switchboard girl flashed on my screen I snapped: "Get me Griff. Snap it up!"

"Mr. Griff's line is busy, Mr. Hamilton," she sang to me. "Will you hold the wire, or shall I call you back?"

"None of that, Dorothe," I roared. Dorothe and I had gone to high school together; as a matter of fact I had got her the job with Griff, who was Associated's head script man. "I don't care who's talking to Griff. Cut him off and put me through. He can't do that to me. I'll sue, that's what I'll do. I'll break the company. I'll—"

"Take it easy, Ted," she said. "What's the matter with everyone all of a sudden, anyway? If you must know, the man gabbing with Griff now is old Berbelot himself. Seems he wants to sue Associated, too. What's up?"

By this time I was practically incoherent. "Berbelot, hey? I'll sue him, too. The rat! The dirty—What are you laughing at?"

"He wants to sue you!" she giggled. "And I'll bet Griff will, too, to shut Berbelot up. You know, this might turn out to be really funny!" Before I could swallow that she switched me over to Griff.

As he answered he was wiping his heavy jowls with a handkerchief. "Well?" he asked in a shaken voice.

"What are you, a wise guy?" I bellowed. "What kind of a stunt is that you pulled on the commercial plug on my play? Whose idea was that, anyway? Berbelot's? What the—"

"Now, Hamilton," Griff said easily, "don't excite yourself this way." I could see his hands trembling—evidently old Berbelot had laid it on thick. "Nothing untoward has occurred. You must be mistaken. I assure you—"

"You pompous old sociophagus," I growled, wasting a swell two-dollar word on him, "don't call me a liar. I've been listening to that program and I know what I heard. I'm going to sue you. And Berbelot. And if you try to pass the buck onto the actors in that plug skit, I'll sue them, too. And if you make any more cracks about me being mistaken, I'm going to come up there and feed you your teeth. Then I'll sue you personally as well as Associated."

I dialed out and went back to my television set, fuming. The program was going on as if nothing had happened. As I cooled—and I cool slowly—I began to see that the last half of "The Seashell" was even better than the first. You know, it's poison for a writer to fall in love with his own stuff; but, by golly, sometimes you turn out a piece that really has something. You try to be critical, and you can't be. The Ponta Delgada sequence in "The Seashell" was like that.

The girl was on a cruise and the boy was on a training ship. They met in the Azores Islands. Very touching. The last time they saw each other was before they were in their teens, but in the meantime they had had their dreams. Get the idea of the thing? Very pastel. And they did do it nicely. The shots of Ponta Delgada and the scenery of the Azores were swell. Came the moment, after four minutes of ickey dialogue, when he gazed at her, the light of true, mature love dawning on his young face.

She said shyly, "Well—"

Now, his lines, as written—and I should know!—went:

"Rosalind . . . it *is* you, then, isn't it? Oh, I'm afraid"—he grasps her shoulders—"afraid that it can't be real. So many times I've seen someone who might be you, and it has never been . . . Rosalind, Rosalind, guardian angel, reason for living, beloved . . . belovèd—" Clinch.

Now, as I say, it went off as written, up to and including the clinch. But then came the payoff. He took his lips from hers, buried his face in her hair and said clearly: "I hate your————guts." And that "————" was the most perfectly enunciated present participle of a four-letter verb I have ever heard.

Just what happened after that I couldn't tell you. I went haywire, I guess. I scattered two hundred and twenty dollars' worth of television set over all three rooms of my apartment. Next thing I knew I was in a 'press tube, hurtling toward the three-hundred-story skyscraper that housed Associated Television. Never have I seen one of those 'press cars, forced by compressed air through tubes under the city, move so slowly, but it might have been my imagination. If I had anything to do with it, there was going to be one dead script boss up there.

And who should I run into on the 229th floor but old Berbelot himself. The perfume king had blood in his eye. Through the haze of anger that surrounded me, I began to realize that things were about to be very tough on Griff. And I was quite ready to help out all I could.

Berbelot saw me at the same instant, and seemed to read my thought. "Come on," he said briefly, and together we ran the gantlet of secretaries and assistants and burst into Griff's office.

Griff rose to his feet and tried to look dignified, with little success. I leaped over his glass desk and pulled the wings of his stylish open-necked collar together until he began squeaking.

Berbelot seemed to be enjoying it. "Don't kill him, Hamilton," he said after a bit. "I want to."

I let the script man go. He sank down to the floor, gasping. He was like a scared kid, in more ways than one. It was funny.

We let him get his breath. He climbed to his feet, sat down at his desk, and reached out toward a battery of push buttons. Berbelot snatched up a Dow-metal paper knife and hacked viciously at the chubby hand. It retreated.

"Might I ask," said Griff heavily, "the reason for this unprovoked rowdiness?"

Berbelot cocked an eye at me. "Might he?"

"He might tell us what this monkey business is all about," I said.

Griff cleared his throat painfully. "I told both you . . . er . . . gentlemen over the phone that, as far as I know, there was nothing amiss in our interpretation of your play, Mr. Hamilton, nor in the commercial section of the broadcast, Mr. Berbelot. After your protests over the wire, I made it a point to see the second half of the broadcast myself. Nothing was wrong. And as this is the first commercial color broadcast, it has been recorded. If you are not satisfied with my statements, you are welcome to see the recording yourselves, immediately."

What else could we want? It occurred to both of us that Griff was really up a tree; that he was telling the truth as far as he knew it, and that he thought we were both screwy. I began to think so myself.

Berbelot said, "Griff, didn't you hear that dialogue near the end, when those two kids were by that sea wall?"

Griff nodded.

"Think back now," Berbelot went on. "What did the boy say to the girl when he put his muzzle into her hair?"

" 'I love you,' " said Griff self-consciously, and blushed. "He said it twice."

Berbelot and I looked at each other. "Let's see that recording," I said.

Well, we did, in Griff's luxurious private projection room. I hope I never have to live through an hour like that again. If it weren't for the fact that Berbelot was seeing the same thing I saw, and feeling the same way about it, I'd have reported to an alienist. Because that program came off Griff's projector positively shimmering with innocuousness. My script was A-1; Berbelot's plugs were right. On that plug that had started everything, where the man and the girl were gabbing in the theater lobby, the dialogue went like this:

"And how do you like the play, Mr. Robinson?"

"Utterly charming . . . and that goes for you, too, my dear. What *is* that perfume you are using?"

"Berbelot's *Doux Rêves*. What do you think of it?"

"You heard what I said about the play."

Well, there you are. And by the recording, Griff had been right about the repetitious three little words in the Azores sequence. I was floored.

After it was over, Berbelot said to Griff: "I think I can speak for Mr. Hamilton when I say that if this is an actual recording, we owe you an apology; also when I say that we do not accept your evidence until we have compiled our own. I recorded that program as it came over my set, as I have recorded all my advertising. We will see you tomorrow, and we will bring that sound film. Coming, Hamilton?"

I nodded and we left, leaving Griff to chew his lip.

I'd like to skip briefly over the last chapter of that evening's nightmare. Berbelot picked up a camera expert on the way, and we had the films developed within an hour after we arrived at the fantastic "house that perfume built." And if I was crazy, so was Berbelot; and if he was, then so was the camera. So help me, that blasted program came out on Berbelot's screen exactly as it had on my set and his. If anyone ever took a long-distance cussing out, it was Griff that night. We figured, of course, that he had planted a phony recording on us, so that we wouldn't sue. He'd do the same thing in court, too. I told Berbelot so. He shook his head.

"No, Hamilton, we can't take it to court. Associated gave me that broadcast, the first color commercial, on condition that I sign away their responsibility for 'incomplete, or inadequate, or otherwise unsatisfactory performance.' They didn't quite trust that new apparatus, you know."

"Well, I'll sue for both of us, then," I said.

"Did they buy all rights?" he asked.

"Yes . . . damn! They got me, too! They have a legal right to do anything they want." I threw my cigarette into the electric fire, and snapped on Berbelot's big television set, tuning it to Associated's XZB.

Nothing happened.

"Hey! Your set's on the bum!" I said. Berbelot got up and began fiddling with the dial. I was wrong. There was nothing the matter with the set. It was Associated. All of their stations were off the air—all four of them. We looked at each other.

"Get XZW," said Berbelot. "It's an Associated affiliate, under cover. Maybe we can—"

XZW blared out at us as I spun the dial. A dance program, the new five-beat stuff. Suddenly the announcer stuck his face into the transmitter.

"A bulletin from Iconoscope News Service," he said conversationally. "FCC has clamped down on Associated Television and its stations. They are off the air. The reasons were not given, but it is surmised that it has to do with a little strong language used on the world première of Associated's new color transmission. That is all."

"I expected that," smiled Berbelot. "Wonder how Griff'll alibi himself out of that? If he tries to use that recording of his, I'll most cheerfully turn mine over to the government, and we'll have him for perjury."

"Sorta tough on Associated, isn't it?" I said.

"Not particularly. You know these big corporations. Associated gets millions out of their four networks, but those millions are just a drop in the bucket compared with the other pies they've got their fingers in. That color technique, for instance. Now that they can't use it for a while, how many other outfits will miss the chance of bidding for the method and equipment? They lose some advertising contracts, and they save by not operating. They won't even feel it. I'll bet you'll see color transmission within forty-eight hours over a rival network."

He was right. Two days later Cineradio had a color broadcast scheduled, and all hell broke loose. What they'd done to the Berbelot hour and my "Seashell" was really tame.

The program was sponsored by one of the antigravity industries— I forget which. They'd hired Raouls Stavisk, the composer, to play one of the ancient Gallic operas he'd exhumed. It was a piece called "Carmen" and had been practically forgotten for two centuries. News of it had created

ETHER BREATHER

quite a stir among music lovers, although, personally, I don't go for it. It's too barbaric for me. Too hard to listen to, when you've been hearing five-beat all your life. And those old-timers had never heard of a quarter tone.

Anyway, it was a big affair, televised right from the huge Citizens' Auditorium. It was more than half full—there were about 130,000 people there. Practically all of the select high-brow music fans from that section of the city. Yes, 130,000 pairs of eyes saw that show in the flesh, and countless millions saw it on their own sets; remember that.

Those that saw it at the Auditorium got their money's worth, from what I hear. They saw the complete opera; saw it go off as scheduled. The coloratura, Maria Jeff, was in perfect voice, and Stavisk's orchestra rendered the ancient tones perfectly. So what?

So, those that saw it at home saw the first half of the program the same as broadcast—of course. But—and get this—they saw Maria Jeff, on a close-up, in the middle of an aria, throw back her head, stop singing, and shout raucously: "The hell with this! Whip it up, boys!"

They heard the orchestra break out of that old two-four music—"Habañera," I think they called it—and slide into a wicked old-time five-beat song about "alco-pill Alice," the girl who didn't believe in eugenics. They saw her step lightly about the stage, shedding her costume—not that I blame her for that; it was supposed to be authentic, and must have been warm. But there was a certain something about the way she did it.

I've never seen or heard of anything like it. First, I thought that it was part of the opera, because from what I learned in school I gather that the ancient people used to go in for things like that. I wouldn't know. But I knew it wasn't opera when old Stavisk himself jumped up on the stage and started dancing with the prima donna. The televisors flashed around to the audience, and there they were, every one of them, dancing in the aisles. And I mean dancing. Wow!

Well, you can imagine the trouble that that caused. Cineradio, Inc., was flabbergasted when they were shut down by FCC like Associated. So were 130,000 people who had seen the opera and thought it was good. Every last one of them denied dancing in the aisles. No one had seen Stavisk jump on the stage. It just didn't make sense.

Cineradio, of course, had a recording. So, it turned out, did FCC. Each recording proved the point of its respective group. That of Cineradio, taken by a sound camera right there in the auditorium, showed a musical program. FCC's, photographed right off a government standard receiver, showed the riot that I and millions of others had seen over the air. It was too much for me. I went out to see Berbelot. The old boy had a lot of sense, and he'd seen the beginning of this crazy business.

He looked pleased when I saw his face on his house televisor. "Hamilton!" he exclaimed. "Come on in! I've been phoning all over the five downtown boroughs for you!" He pressed a button and the foyer door behind me closed. I was whisked up into his rooms. That combination foyer and elevator of his is a nice gadget.

"I guess I don't have to ask you why you came," he said as we shook hands. "Cineradio certainly pulled a boner, hey?"

"Yes and no," I said. "I'm beginning to think that Griff was right when he said that, as far as he knew, the program was on the up and up. But if he was right, what's it all about? How can a program reach the transmitters in perfect shape, and come out of every receiver in the nation like a practical joker's idea of paradise?"

"It can't," said Berbelot. He stroked his chin thoughtfully. "But it did. Three times."

"Three? When—"

"Just now, before you got in. The secretary of state was making a speech over XZM, Consolidated Atomic, you know. XZM grabbed the color equipment from Cineradio as soon as they were blacked out by FCC. Well, the honorable secretary droned on as usual for just twelve and a half minutes. Suddenly he stopped, grinned into the transmitter, and said, 'Say, have you heard the one about the traveling farmer and the salesman's daughter?' "

"I have," I said. "My gosh, don't tell me he spieled it?"

"Right," said Berbelot. "In detail, over the unsullied airwaves. I called up right away, but couldn't get through. XZM's trunk lines were jammed. A very worried-looking switchboard girl hooked up I don't know how many lines together and announced into them: 'If you people are calling up about the secretary's speech, there is nothing wrong with it. Now please get off the lines!' "

"Well," I said, "let's see what we've got. First, the broadcasts leave the studios as scheduled and as written. Shall we accept that?"

"Yes," said Berbelot. "Then, since so far no black-and-white broadcasts have been affected, we'll consider that this strange behavior is limited to the polychrome technique."

"How about the recordings at the studios? They were in polychrome, and they weren't affected."

Berbelot pressed a button, and an automatic serving table rolled out of its niche and stopped in front of each of us. We helped ourselves to smokes and drinks, and the table returned to its place.

"Cineradio's wasn't a television recording, Hamilton. It was a sound camera. As for Associated's . . . I've got it! Griff's recording was transmitted to his recording machines by wire, from the studios! It didn't go out on the air at all!"

"You're right. Then we can assume that the only programs affected are those in polychrome, actually aired. Fine, but where does that get us?"

"Nowhere," admitted Berbelot. "But maybe we can find out. Come with me."

We stepped into an elevator and dropped three floors. "I don't know if you've heard that I'm a television bug," said my host. "Here's my lab. I flatter myself that a more complete one does not exist anywhere."

I wouldn't doubt it. I never in my life saw a layout like that. It was part museum and part workshop. It had in it a copy of a genuine relic of each and every phase of television down through the years, right from the old original scanning-disk sets down to the latest three-dimensional atomic jobs. Over in the corner was an extraordinarily complicated mass of apparatus which I recognized as a polychrome transmitter.

"Nice job, isn't it?" said Berbelot. "It was developed in here, you know, by one of the lads who won the Berbelot scholarship." I hadn't known. I began to have real respect for this astonishing man.

"Just how does it work?" I asked him.

"Hamilton," he said testily, "we have work to do. I would be talking all night if I told you. But the general idea is that the vibrations sent out by this transmitter are all out of phase with each other. Tinting in the receiver is achieved by certain blendings of these out-of-phase vibrations as they leave this rig. The effect is a sort of irregular vibration—a vibration in the electromagnetic waves themselves, resulting in a totally new type of wave which is still receivable in a standard set."

"I see," I lied. "Well, what do you plan to do?"

"I'm going to broadcast from here to my country place up north. It's eight hundred miles away from here, which ought to be sufficient. My signals will be received there and automatically returned to us by wire." He indicated a receiver standing close by. "If there is any difference between what we send and what we get, we can possibly find out just what the trouble is."

"How about FCC?" I asked. "Suppose—it sounds funny to say it—but just suppose that we get the kind of strong talk that came over the air during my 'Seashell' number?"

Berbelot snorted. "That's taken care of. The broadcast will be directional. No receiver can get it but mine."

What a man! He thought of everything. "O.K.," I said. "Let's go."

Berbelot threw a couple of master switches and we sat down in front of the receiver. Lights blazed on, and through a bank of push buttons at his elbow, Berbelot maneuvered the transmitting cells to a point above and behind the receiver, so that we could see and be seen without turning our heads. At a nod from Berbelot I leaned forward and switched on the receiver.

Berbelot glanced at his watch. "If things work out right, it will be between ten and thirty minutes before we get any interference." His voice sounded a little metallic. I realized that it was coming from the receiver as he spoke.

The images cleared on the view-screen as the set warmed up. It gave me an odd sensation. I saw Berbelot and myself sitting side by side—just as if we were sitting in front of a mirror, except that the images were not reversed. I thumbed my nose at myself, and my image returned the compliment.

Berbelot said: "Go easy, boy. If we get the same kind of interference the others got, your image will make something out of that." He chuckled.

"Damn right," said the receiver.

Berbelot and I stared at each other, and back at the screen. Berbelot's face was the same, but mine had a vicious sneer on it. Berbelot calmly checked with his watch. "Eight forty-six," he said. "Less time each broadcast. Pretty soon the interference will start with the broadcast, if this keeps up."

"Not unless you start broadcasting on a regular schedule," said Berbelot's image.

It had apparently dissociated itself completely from Berbelot himself. I was floored.

Berbelot sat beside me, his face frozen. "You see?" he whispered to me. "It takes a minute to catch up with itself. Till it does, it is my image."

"What does it all mean?" I gasped.

"Search me," said the perfume king.

We sat and watched. And so help me, so did our images. They were watching *us!*

Berbelot tried a direct question. "Who are you?" he asked.

"Who do we look like?" said my image; and both laughed uproariously.

Berbelot's image nudged mine. "We've got 'em on the run, hey, pal?" it chortled.

"Stop your nonsense!" said Berbelot sharply. Surprisingly, the merriment died.

"Aw," said my image plaintively. "We don't mean anything by it. Don't get sore. Let's all have fun. *I'm* having fun."

"Why, they're like kids!" I said.

"I think you're right," said Berbelot.

"Look," he said to the images, which sat there expectantly, pouting. "Before we have any fun, I want you to tell me who you are, and how you are coming through the receiver, and how you messed up the three broadcasts before this."

"Did we do wrong?" asked my image innocently. The other one giggled.

"High-spirited sons o' guns, aren't they?" said Berbelot.

"Well, are you going to answer my questions, or *do I turn the transmitter off?*" he asked the images.

They chorused frantically: "We'll tell! We'll tell! Please don't turn it off!"

"What on earth made you think of that?" I whispered to Berbelot.

"A stab in the dark," he returned. "Evidently they like coming through like this and can't do it any other way but on the polychrome wave."

"What do you want to know?" asked Berbelot's image, its lip quivering.

"Who are you?"

"Us? We're . . . I don't know. You don't have a name for us, so how can I tell you?"

"Where are you?"

"Oh, everywhere. We get around."

Berbelot moved his hand impatiently toward the switch.

The images squealed: "Don't! Oh, please don't! This is fun!"

"Fun, is it?" I growled. "Come on, give us the story, or we'll black you out!"

My image said pleadingly: "Please believe us. It's the truth. We're everywhere."

"What do you look like?" I asked. "Show yourselves as you are!"

"We can't," said the other image, "because we don't 'look' like anything. We just . . . are, that's all."

"We don't reflect light," supplemented my image.

Berbelot and I exchanged a puzzled glance. Berbelot said, "Either somebody is taking us for a ride or we've stumbled on something utterly new and unheard-of."

"You certainly have," said Berbelot's image earnestly. "We've known about you for a long time—as you count time—"

"Yes," the other continued. "We knew about you some two hundred of your years ago. We had felt your vibrations for a long time before that, but we never knew just who you were until then."

"Two hundred years—" mused Berbelot. "That was about the time of the first atomic-powered television sets."

"That's right!" said my image eagerly. "It touched our brain currents and we could see and hear. We never could get through to you until recently, though, when you sent us that stupid thing about a seashell."

"None of that, now," I said angrily, while Berbelot chuckled.

"How many of you are there?" he asked them.

"One, and many. We are finite and infinite. We have no size or shape as you know it. We just . . . are."

We just swallowed that without comment. It was a bit big.

"How did you change the programs? How are you changing this one?" Berbelot asked.

"These broadcasts pass directly through our brain currents. Our thoughts change them as they pass. It was impossible before; we were aware, but we could not be heard. This new wave has let us be heard. Its convolutions are in phase with our being."

"How did you happen to pick that particular way of breaking through?" I asked. "I mean all that wisecracking business."

For the first time one of the images—Berbelot's—looked abashed. "We wanted to be liked. We wanted to come through to you and find you laughing. We knew how. Two hundred years of listening to every single broadcast, public and private, has taught us your language and your emotions and your ways of thought. Did we really do wrong?"

"Looks as if we have walked into a cosmic sense of humor," remarked Berbelot to me.

To his image: "Yes, in a way, you did. You lost three huge companies their broadcasting licenses. You embarrassed exceedingly a man named Griff and a secretary of state. You"—he chuckled—"made my friend here very, very angry. That wasn't quite the right thing to do, now, was it?"

"No," said my image. It actually blushed. "We won't do it any more. We were wrong. We are sorry."

"Aw, skip it," I said. I was embarrassed myself. "Everybody makes mistakes."

"That *is* good of you," said my image on the television screen. "We'd like to do something for you. And you, too, Mr.—"

"Berbelot," said Berbelot. Imagine introducing yourself to a television set!

"You can't do anything for us," I said, "except to stop messing up color televising."

"You really want us to stop, then?" My image turned to Berbelot's. "We have done wrong. We have hurt their feelings and made them angry."

To us: "We will not bother you again. Good-by!"

"Wait a minute!" I yelped, but I was too late. The viewscreen showed the same two figures, but they had lost their peculiar life. They were Berbelot and me. Period.

"Now look what you've done," snapped Berbelot.

He began droning into the transmitter: "Calling interrupter on polychrome wave! Can you hear me? Can you hear me? Calling—"

He broke off and looked at me disgustedly. "You dope," he said quietly, and I felt like going off into a corner and bursting into tears.

Well, that's all. The FCC trials reached a "person or persons unknown" verdict, and color broadcasting became a universal reality. The world has never learned, until now, the real story of that screwy business. Berbelot spent every night for three months trying to contact that ether-intelligence, without success. Can you beat it? It waited two hundred years for a chance to come through to us and then got its feelings hurt and withdrew!

My fault, of course. That admission doesn't help any. I wish I could do something—

PILGRIMAGE   *Amazing Stories,* October

by Nelson Bond (1908–   )

Another writer best known for his series characters (Lancelot Biggs, Meg the Priestess, Pat Pending), Nelson Bond was a steady, competent professional who occasionally attained brilliance. His best work can be found (if you can find the book) in NO TIME LIKE THE FUTURE, 1954.

"Meg the Priestess" was a significant series which consisted of only three stories (all in different magazines) that appeared from 1939–1941. It was one of the first series to feature a female protaganist, and this story began her adventures.

(I met Nelson Bond, only once, to my knowledge, and that was at the first world science fiction convention of 1939. He did me a great service some time later, though. I was unable to forget I was a fan and I argued with readers over my stories in the letter columns of the magazines—until Nelson dropped me a short note saying, "You're a writer, now, Isaac. Let the readers have their opinions."—And I followed his advice. IA)

In her twelfth summer, the illness came upon Meg and she was afraid. Afraid, yet turbulent with a strange feeling of exaltation unlike anything she had ever before known. She was a woman now. And she knew, suddenly and completely, that which was expected of her from this day on. Knew—and dreaded.

She went immediately to the *hoam* of the Mother. For such was the Law. But as she moved down the walk-avenue, she stared, with eyes newly curious, at the Men she passed. At their pale, pitifully hairless bodies. At their soft, futile hands and weak mouths. One lolling on the doorstep of 'Ana's *hoam,* returned her gaze brazenly; made a small, enticing gesture. Meg shuddered, and curled her lips in a refusal-face.

Only yesterday she had been a child. Now, suddenly, she was a woman. And for the first time, Meg saw her people as they really were.

The warriors of the Clan. She looked with distaste upon the tense angularity of their bodies. The corded legs, the grim, set jaws. The cold eyes. The brawny arms, scarred to the elbow with ill-healed cicatrices. The tiny, thwarted breasts, flat and hard beneath leather harness-plates. Fighters they were, and nothing else.

This was not what she wanted.

She saw, too, the mothers. The full-lipped, flabby breasted bearers of children, whose skins were soft and white as those of the Men. Whose eyes were humid; washed barren of all expression by desires too oft aroused, too often sated. Their bodies bulged at hip and thigh, swayed when they walked like ripe grain billowing in a lush and fertile field. They lived only that the tribe might live, might continue to exist. They reproduced.

This was not what she wanted.

Then there were the workers. Their bodies retained a vestige of womankind's inherent grace and nobility. But if their waists were thin, their hands were blunt-fingered and thick. Their shoulders were bent with the weight of labor, coarsened from adze and hod. Their faces were grim from the eternal struggle with an unyielding earth. And the earth, of which they had made themselves a part, had in return made itself a part of them. The workers' skin was browned with soil, their bodies stank of dirk and grime and unwashed perspiration.

No, none of these was what she wanted. None of these was what she would *have,* of that she was positively determined.

So great was Meg's concentration that she entered into the *hoam* of the Mother without crying out, as was required. Thus it was that she discovered the Mother making great magic to the gods.

In her right hand, the Mother held a stick. With it she scratched upon a smooth, bleached, calfskin scroll. From time to time she let the stick drink from a pool of midnight cupped in a dish before her. When she moved it again on the hide, it left its spoor; a spidery trail of black.

For a long moment Meg stood and watched, wondering. Then dread overcame her; fear-thoughts shook her body. She thought suddenly of the gods. Of austere Jarg, their leader; of lean Ibrim and taciturn Taamuz. Of far-seeing Tedhi, she whose laughter echoes in the roaring summer thunders. What wrath would they visit upon one who had spied into their secrets?

She covered her eyes and dropped to her knees. But there were footsteps before her, and the Mother's hands upon her shoulders. And there was but gentle chiding in the voice of the Mother as she said, "My child, know you not the Law? That all must cry out before entering the Mother's *hoam?*"

Meg's fear-thoughts went away. The Mother was good. It was she who fed and clothed the Clan; warmed them in dark winter and found them meat when meat was scarce. If she, who was the gods' spokesman on earth, saw no evil in Meg's unintentional prying—

Meg dared look again at the magic stick. There was a question in her eyes. The Mother answered that question.

"It is 'writing,' Meg. Speech without words."

Speech-without-words? Meg crept to the table; bent a curious ear over the spider-marks. But she heard no sound. Then the Mother was beside her again saying, "No, my child. It does not speak to the ears, but to the eyes. Listen, and I will make it speak through my mouth."

She read aloud.

"Report of the month of June, 3478 A.D. There has been no change in the number of the Jinnia Clan. We are still five score and seven, with nineteen Men, twelve cattle, thirty horses. But there is reason to believe that 'Ana and Sahlee will soon add to our number.

"Last week Darthee, Lina and Alis journeyed into the Clina territory in search of game. They met there several of the Durm Clan and exchanged gifts of salt and bacca. Pledges of friendship were given. On the return trip, Darthee was linberred by one of the Wild Ones, but was rescued by her companions before the strain could be crossed. The Wild One was destroyed.

"We have in our village a visitor from the Delwurs of the east, who says that in her territory the Wild Ones have almost disappeared. Illness she says, has depleted their Men—and she begs that I lend her one or two for a few months. I am thinking of letting her have Jak and Ralf, both of whom are proven studs—"

The Mother stopped. "That is as far as I had gone, my child, when you entered."

Meg's eyes were wide with wonder. It was quite true that Darthee, Lina and Alis had recently returned from a trip to China. And that there was now a visitor in camp. But how could the speech-without-words know these things, *tell* these things? She said, "But, Mother—will not the speech-without-words forget?"

"No, Meg. *We* forget. The books remember always."

"Books, Mother?"

"These are books." The Mother moved to the sleeping part of her *hoam;* selected one of a tumbled pile of calfskin scrolls. "Here are the records of our Clan from ages past— since the time of the Ancient Ones. Not all are here. Some have been lost. Others were ruined by flood or destroyed by fire.

"But it is the Mother's duty to keep these records. That is why the Mother must know the art of making the speech-without-words. It is hard work, my little one. And a labor without end—"

Meg's eyes were shining. The trouble that had been cold within her before was vanished now. In its place had come a great thought. A thought *so* great, *so* daring, that Meg had to open her lips twice before the words came.

"Is it—" she asked breathlessly, "Is it very hard to become a—Mother?"

The Mother smiled gently. "A very great task, Meg. But you should not think of such things. It is not yet time for you to decide—" She paused, looking at Meg strangely. "Or—is it, my child?"

Meg flushed, and her eyes dropped.

"It is, Mother."

"Then be not afraid, my daughter. You know the Law. At this important hour it is yours to decide what station in life will be yours. What is your wish, Meg? Would you be a warrior, a worker, or a breeding mother?"

Meg looked at the Clan leader boldly.

"I would be," she said, "a Mother!" Then, swiftly, "But not a breeding mother. I mean a *Clan* Mother—like you, O Mother!"

The Mother stared. Then the harsh lines melted from her face and she said, thoughtfully, "Thrice before has that request been made of me, Meg. Each time I have refused. It was Beth who asked first, oh, many years ago. She became a warrior, and died gallantly lifting the siege of Loovil. . . .

"Then Haizl. And the last time it was Hein. When I refused, she became the other type of mother.

"But I was younger then. Now I am old. And it is right that there should be someone to take my place when I am gone—" She stared at the girl intently.

"It is not easy, my daughter. There is much work to be done. Work, not of the body but of the mind. There are problems to be solved, many vows to be taken, a hard pilgrimage to be made—"

"All these," swore Meg, "would I gladly do, O Mother! If you will but let me—" Her voice broke suddenly. "But I cannot become anything else. I would not be a warrior, harsh and bitter. Nor a worker, black with dirt. And the breeders—I would as soon mate with one of the Wild Ones as with one of the Men! The thought of their soft hands—"

She shuddered. And the Clan Mother nodded, understanding. "Very well, Meg. Tomorrow you will move into this *hoam*. You will live with me and study to become the Jinnia Clan's next Mother. . . ."

So began Meg's training. Nor was the Mother wrong in saying that the task was not an easy one. Many were the times when Meg wept bitterly, striving to learn that which a Mother must know. There was the speech-without-words, which Meg learned to call "writing." It looked like a simple magic when the Mother did it. But that slender stick, which moved so fluidly beneath the Mother's aged fingers slipped and skidded and made ugly blotches of midnight on the hide whenever Meg tried to make spider-marks.

Meg learned that these wavering lines were not meaningless. Each line was made of "sentences," each sentence of "words," and each word was composed of "letters." And each letter made a sound, just as each combination of letters made a word-sound.

These were strange and confusing. A single letter, out of place, changed the whole meaning of the word ofttimes. Sometimes it altered the meaning of the whole sentence. But Meg's determination was great. There came, finally, the day when the Mother allowed her to write the monthly report in the Clan history. Meg was thirteen, then. But already she was older in wisdom than the others of her Clan.

It was then that the Mother began to teach her yet another

magic. It was the magic of "numbers." Where there had been twenty-six "letters," there were only ten numbers. But theirs was a most peculiar magic. Put together, ofttimes they formed other and greater numbers. Yet the same numbers taken away from each other formed still a third group. The names of these magics, Meg never did quite learn. They were strange, magical, meaningless terms. "Multiplication" and "subtraction." But she learned how to do them.

Her task was made the harder, for it was about this time that the Evil Ones sent a little pain-imp to torment her. He stole in through her ear one night while she was sleeping. And for many months he lurked in her head, above her eyes. Every time she would sit down to study the magic of the numbers, he would begin dancing up and down, trying to stop her. But Meg persisted. And finally the pain-imp either died or was removed. And Meg knew the numbers. . . .

There were rites and rituals to be learned. There was the Sacred Song which had to be learned by heart. This song had no tune, but was accompanied by the beating of the tribal drums. Its words were strange and terrible; echoing the majesty of the gods in its cryptic phrasing.

"O, Sakan! you see by Tedhi on his early Light—"

This was a great song. A powerful magic. It was the only tribal song Meg learned which dared name one of the gods. And it had to be sung reverently, lest far-seeing Tedhi be displeased and show her monstrous teeth and destroy the invoker with her mirthful thunders.

Meg learned, too, the tribal song of the Jinnia Clan. She had known it from infancy, but its words had been obscure. Now she learned enough to probe into its meaning. She did not know the meanings of some of the forgotten words, but for the most part it made sense when the tribe gathered on festive nights to sing, "Caamé back to over Jinnia—"

And Meg grew in age and stature and wisdom. In her sixteenth summer, her legs were long and firm and straight as a warrior's spear. Her body was supple; bronzed by sunlight save where her doeskin breech-cloth kept the skin white. Unbound, her hair would have trailed the earth, but she wore it piled upon her head, fastened by a netting woven by the old mothers, too ancient to bear.

The vanity-god had died long ages since, and Meg had no way of knowing she was beautiful. But sometimes, looking at her reflection in the pool as she bathed, she approved the soft curves of her slim young body, and was more than ever glad and proud that she had become a neophyte to the Mother. She liked her body to be this way. Why, she did not know. But she was glad that she had not turned lean and hard, as had those of her age who had become warriors. Or coarse, as had become the workers. Or soft and flabby, as were the breeding-mothers. Her skin was golden-brown, and pure gold where the sunlight burnished the fine down on her arms and legs, between her high, firm breasts.

And finally there came the day when the Mother let Meg conduct the rites at the Feast of the Blossoms. This was in July, and Meg had then entered upon her seventeenth year. It was a great occasion, and a great test. But Meg did not fail. She conducted the elaborate rite from beginning to end without a single mistake.

That night, in the quiet of their *hoam*, the Mother made a final magic. She drew from her collection of aged trophies a curl of parchment. This she blessed. Then she handed it to Meg.

"You are ready now, O my daughter," she said. "In the morning you will leave."

"Leave, Mother?" said Meg.

"For the final test. This that I give you is a map. A shower-of-places. You will see, here at this joining of mountain and river, our village in the heart of the Jinnia territory. Far off, westward and to the north, as here is shown, is the Place of the Gods. It is there you must go on pilgrimage before you return to take your place as Mother."

Now, at this last moment, Meg felt misgivings.

"But you, Mother?" she asked. "If I become Mother, what will become of you?"

"The rest will be welcome, daughter. It is good to know that the work will be carried on—" The aged Mother pondered. "There is much, yet, that you do not know, Meg. It is forbidden that I should tell you all until you have been to the Place of the Gods. There will you see, and understand—"

"The—the books?" faltered Meg.

"Upon your return you may read the books. Even as I read them when I returned. And all will be made clear to you. Even that final secret which the clan must not know—"

"I do not understand, Mother."

"You will, my daughter—later. And now, to sleep. For at dawn tomorrow begins your pilgrimage. . . ."

Off in the hills, a wild dog howled his melancholy farewell to the dying moon. His thin song clove the stirring silence of the trees, the incessant movement of the forest. Meg wakened at that cry; wakened and saw that already the red edge of dawn tinged the eastern sky.

She uncurled from the broad treecrotch in which she had spent the night. Her horse was already awake, and with restless movements was nibbling the sparse grass beneath the giant oak. Meg loosed his tether, then went to the spring she had found the night before.

There she drank, and in the little rill that trickled from the spring, bathed herself as best she could. Her ablutions finished, she set about making breakfast. There was not much food in her saddlebags. A side of rabbit, carefully saved from last night's dinner. Two biscuits, slightly dry now. A precious handful of salt. She ate sparingly, resolved to build camp early tonight in order to set a few game traps and bake another batch of biscuit.

She cleared a space, scratching a wide circle of earth bare of all leaves and twigs, then walking around it widdershins thrice to chase away the firedemon. Then she scratched the firestone against a piece of the black metal from the town of the Ancient Ones—a gift of the Mother—and kindled her little fire.

Two weeks had passed since Meg had left the Jinnia territory. She had come from the rugged mountainlands of her home territory, through the river valleys of the Hyan Clan. On the flat plains of the Yana section, she had made an error. Her map had shown the route clearly, but she had come upon a road built by the Ancient Ones. A road of white creet, still in fair repair. And because it was easier to travel on this highway than to thread a way through the jungle, she had let herself drift southward.

It was not until she reached the timeworn village of Slooie that friendly Zuries had pointed out her mistake. Then she had to turn northward and westward again, going up the Big River to the territory of the Demoys.

Now, her map showed, she was in Braska territory. Two more weeks—perhaps less than that—should bring her to her goal. To the sacred Place of the Gods.

Meg started and roused from her speculations as a twig snapped in the forest behind her. In one swift motion she had wheeled, drawn her sword, and was facing the spot from which the sound had come. But the green bushes did not tremble; no further crackling came from the underbrush. Her fears allayed, she turned to the important business of roasting her side of rabbit.

It was always needful to be on the alert. Meg had learned that lesson early; even before her second day's journey had led her out of Jinnia territory. For, as the Mother had warned, there were still many Wild Ones roaming through the land. Searching for food, for the precious firemetal from the ruined villages of the Ancient Ones—most of all for mates. The Wild Ones were dying out, slowly, because of their lack of mates. There were few females left among them. Most of the Wild Ones were male. But there was little in their shaggy bodies, their thick, brutish faces, their hard, gnarled muscles, to remind one of the Men.

A Wild One had attacked Meg in her second night's camp. Fortunately she had not yet been asleep when he made his foray—else her pilgrimage would have ended abruptly. Not that he would have killed her. The Wild Ones did not kill the women they captured. They took them to their dens. And— Meg had heard tales. A priestess could not cross her strain with a Wild One and still become a Mother.

So Meg had fought fiercely, and had been victorious. The Wild One's bones lay now in the Jinnia hills, picked bare by the vultures. But since that escape, Meg had slept nightly in trees, her sword clenched in her hand. . . .

The food was cooked now. Meg removed it from the spit, blew upon it, and began to eat. She had many things on her mind. The end of her pilgrimage was nigh. The hour when she would enter into the Place of the Gods, and learn the last and most carefully guarded secret.

That is why her senses failed her. That is why she did not even know the Wild One lurked near until, with a roar of throaty satisfaction, he had leaped from the shrubbery, seized her, and pinioned her struggling arms to her sides with tight grip.

It was a bitter fight, but a silent one. For all her slimness, Meg's body was sturdy. She fought pantherlike; using every weapon with which the gods had endowed her. Her fists, legs, teeth.

But the Wild One's strength was as great as his ardor was strong. He crushed Meg to him bruisingly; the stink of his sweat burning her nostrils. His arms bruised her breasts; choked the breath from her straining lungs. One furry arm tensed about her throat, cutting off the precious air.

Meg writhed, broke free momentarily, buried her strong

PILGRIMAGE

teeth in his arm. A howl of hurt and rage broke from the Wild One's lips. Meg tugged at her sword. But again the Wild One threw himself upon her; this time with great fists flailing. Meg saw a hammerlike hand smashing down on her, felt the shocking concussion of the Wild One's strength. A lightning flashed. The ground leaped up to meet her. Then all was silent. . . .

She woke, groaning weakly. Her head was splitting, and the bones of her body arched. She started to struggle to her feet; had risen halfway before she discovered with a burst of hope that she *could* move! She was not bound! Then the Wild One—

She glanced about her swiftly. She was still lying in the little glade where she had been attacked. The sun's full orb had crept over the horizon now, threading a lacework of light through the tiny glen. Her fire smouldered still. And beside it crouched a—a—

Meg could not decide what it was. It looked like a Man, but that of course was impossible. Its body was smooth and almost as hairless as her own. Bronzed by the sun. But it was not the pale, soft body of a man. It was muscular, hard, firm; taller and stronger than a warrior.

Flight was Meg's first thought. But her curiosity was even stronger than her fear. This was a mystery. And her sword was beside her. Whoever, or whatever, this Thing might be, it did not seem to wish her harm. She spoke to it.

"Who are you?" asked Meg. "And where is the Wild One?"

The stranger looked up, and a happy look spread over his even features. He pointed briefly to the shrubbery. Meg followed the gesture; saw lying there the dead body of the Wild One. Her puzzled gaze returned to the Man-thing.

"You killed him? Then you are not one of the Wild Ones? But I do not understand. You are not a man—"

"You," said the man-thing in a voice deeper than Meg had ever heard from a human throat, "talk too much. Sit down and eat, Woman!"

He tossed Meg a piece of her own rabbit-meat. Self unaware that she did so, Meg took it and began eating. She stared at the stranger as he finished his own repast, wiped his hands on his clout and moved toward her. Meg dropped her half-eaten breakfast, rose hastily and groped for her sword.

"Touch me not, Hairless One!" she cried warningly. "I am a priestess of the Jinnia Clan. It is not for such as you to—"

The stranger brushed by her without even deigning to hear her words. He reached the spot where her horse had been tethered; shook a section of broken rein ruefully.

"You women!" he spat. "Bah! You do not know how to train a horse. See—he ran away!"

Meg thought anger-thoughts. Her face burned with the sun, though the sun's rays were dim in the glade. She cried, "Man-thing, know you no better than to talk thus to a Woman and a master? By Jarg, I should have you whipped—"

"You talk too much!" repeated the Man-thing wearily. Once more he squatted on his hunkers; studied her thoughtfully. "But you interest me. Who are you? What are you doing so far from the Jinnia territory? Where are you going?"

"A priestess," said Meg coldly, "does not answer the questions of a Man-thing—"

"I'm not a Man-*thing*," said the stranger pettishly, "I am a Man. A Man of the Kirki tribe which lives many miles south of here. I am Daiv, known as He-who-would-learn. So tell me, Woman."

His candor confused Meg. Despite herself, she found the words leaving her lips. "I—I am Meg. I am making pilgrimage to the Place of the Gods. It is my final task ere I become Mother of my clan."

The Man's eyes appraised her with embarrassing frankness. "So?" he said. "Mother of a Clan? Meg, would you not rather stay with me and become mother of your own clan?"

Meg gasped. Men were the mates of Women—yes! But never had any Man the audacity to *suggest* such a thing. Matings were arranged by the Mother, with the agreement of the Woman. And surely this Man must know that priestesses did not mate.

"Man!" she cried, "Know you not the Law? I am soon to become a Clan Mother. Guard your words, or the wrath of the Gods—"

The Man, Daiv, made happy-sounds again. "It was I who saved you from the Wild One," he chuckled. "Not the Gods. In my land, Golden One, we think it does no harm to ask. But if you are unwilling—" he shrugged. "I will leave you now."

Without further adieu, he rose and started to leave. Meg's face reddened. She cried out angrily, "Man!"

He turned, "Yes?"

"I have no horse. How am I to get to the Place of the Gods?"

"Afoot, Golden One. Or are you Women too weak to make such a journey?"

He laughed again—and was gone.

For a long moment Meg stared after him, watching the green fronds close behind his disappearing form, feeling the stark desolation of utter aloneness close in upon her and envelop her. Then she did a thing she herself could not understand. She put down her foot upon the ground, hard, in an angry-movement.

The sun was high, and growing warmer. The journey to the Place of the Gods was longer, now that she had no mount. But the pilgrimage was a sacred obligation. Meg scraped dirt over the smoldering embers of her fire. She tossed her saddle-bags across her shoulder and faced westward. And she pressed on. . . .

The way was long; the day hot and tedious. Before the sun rode overhead, Meg was sticky with sweat and dust. Her feet were sore, and her limbs ached with the unaccustomed exercise of walking. By afternoon, every step was an agony. And while the sun was still too-strong-to-be-looked-at, she found a small spring of fresh water and decided to make camp there for the night.

She set out two seines for small game; took the flour and salt from her saddle-bags and set about making a batch of biscuit. As the rocks heated, she went to the stream and put her feet in it, letting the water-god lick the fever from her tender soles.

From where she sat, she could not see the fire. She had been there perhaps a half an hour when a strange, unfamiliar smell wrinkled her nostrils. It was at once a sweet-and-bitter smell; a pungent odor like strong herbs, but one that set the water to running in her mouth.

She went back to her camp hastily—and found there the Man, Daiv, once again crouching over her stone fireplace. He was watching a pot on the stones. From time to time he stirred the pot with a long stick. Drawing closer, Meg saw a brown water in the pot. It was this which made the aromatic smell. She would have called out to the Man, but he saw her first. And,

"Hello, Golden One!" he said.

Meg said stonily, "What are you doing here?"

The Man shrugged.

"I am Daiv. He-who-would-learn. I got to thinking about this Place of the Gods, and decided I too, would come and see it." He sniffed the brown, bubbling liquid; seemed satisfied. He poured some of it out into an earthen bowl and handed it to Meg. "You want some?"

Meg moved toward him cautiously. This might be a ruse of the Man from the Kirki tribe. Perhaps this strange, aromatic liquid was a drug. The Mother of the Clan had the secret of such drinks. There was one which caused the head to pucker, the mouth to dry and the feet to reel. . . .

"What is it?" she demanded suspiciously.

"Cawfi, of course." Daiv looked surprised. "Don't you know? But, no—I suppose the bean-tree would not grow in your northern climate. It grows near my land. In Sippe and Weezian territories. Drink it!"

Meg tasted the stuff. It was like its smell; strong and bitter, but strangely pleasing. Its heat coursed through her, taking the tired-pain from her body as the water of the spring had taken the burn from her feet.

"It's good, Man," she said.

"Daiv," said the Man. "My name is Daiv, Golden One."

Meg made a stern-look with her brows.

"It is not fitting," she said, "that a priestess should call a Man by his name."

Daiv seemed to be given to making happy-sounds. He made one again.

"You have done lots of things today that are not fitting for a priestess, Golden One. You are not in Jinnia now. Things are different here. And as for me—" He shrugged. "My people do things differently, too. We are one of the chosen tribes, you know. We come from the land of the Escape."

"The Escape?" asked Meg.

"Yes." As he talked, Daiv busied himself. He had taken meat from his pouch, and was wrapping this now in clay. He tossed the caked lumps into the embers of the crude oven. He had also some taters, which Meg had not tasted for many weeks. He took the skins off these, cut them into slices with his hunting-knife and browned the pieces on a piece of hot, flat rock. "The Escape of the Ancient Ones, you know."

"I—I'm not sure I understand," said Meg.

"Neither do I—quite. It happened many years ago. Before my father's father's father's people. There are books in the tribe Master's *hoam* which tell. I have seen some of them. . . .

"Once things were different, you know. In the days of the Ancient Ones, Men and Women were equal throughout the world. In fact, the Men were the Masters. But the Men were warlike and fierce—"

"Like the Wild Ones, you mean?"

"Yes. But they did not make war with clubs and spears, like the Wild Ones. They made war with great catapults that threw fire and flame and exploding death. With little bows that shot steel arrowheads. With gases that destroy, and waters that burn the skin.

"On earth and sea they made these battles, and even in the air. For in those days, the Ancient Ones had wings, like birds. They soared high, making great thunders. And when they warred, they dropped huge eggs of fire which killed others."

Meg cried sharply, "Oh—"

"Don't you believe me?"

"The taters, Daiv! They're burning!"

"Oh!" Daiv made a happy-face and carefully turned the scorching tater slices. Then he continued.

"It is told that there came a final greatest war of all. It was a conflict not only between the Clans, but between the forces of the entire earth. It started in the year which is known as nineteen and sixty—whatever *that* means—"

"I know!" said Meg.

Daiv looked at her with sudden respect. "You do? Then the Master of my tribe must meet you and—"

"It is impossible," said Meg. "Go on!"

"Very well. For many years this war lasted. But neither side could gain a victory. In those days it was the Men who fought, while the Women remained *hoam* to keep the Men's houses. But the Men died by thousands. And there came a day when the Women grew tired of it.

"They got together . . . all of them who lived in the civilized places. And they decided to rid themselves of the brutal Men. They stopped sending supplies and fire-eggs to the battling Men across the sea. They built walled forts, and hid themselves in them.

"The war ended when the Men found they had no more to fight with. They came back to their *hoams*, seeking their Women. But the Women would not receive them. There was bitter warfare once again—between the sexes. But the Women held their walled cities. And so—"

"Yes?" said Meg.

"The Men," said Daiv somberly, "became the Wild Ones of the forest. Mateless, save for the few Women they could linber.* Their numbers died off. The Clans grew. Only in a few places—like Kirki, my land—did humanity not become a matriarchy."

He looked at Meg. "You believe?"

Meg shook her head. Suddenly she felt very sorry for this stranger, Daiv. She knew, now, why he had not harmed her. Why, when she had been powerless before him, he had not forced her to become his mate. He was mad. Totally and completely mad. She said, gently, "Shall we eat, Daiv?"

Mad or not, there was great pleasure in having some company on the long, weary, remaining marches of her pilgrimage. Thus it was that Meg made no effort to discourage Daiv in his desire to accompany her. He was harmless, and he was pleasant company—for a Man. And his talk, wild as it was at times, served to pass boring hours.

They crossed the Braska territory and entered at last into the 'Kota country. It was here the Place of the Gods was— only at the far western end, near Yomin. And the slow days passed, turning into weeks. Not many miles did they cover in those first few days, while Meg's feet were tender and her limbs full of jumping little pain-imps. But when hard walking had destroyed the pain-imps, they traveled faster. And the time was drawing near. . . .

"You started, once, to tell me about the Escape, Daiv," said Meg one evening. "But you did not finish. What is the legend of the Escape?"

Daiv sprawled languidly before the fire. His eyes were dreamy.

"It happened in the Zoni territory," he said, "Not far from the lands of my own tribe. In those days was there a Mangod named Renn, who foresaw the death of the Ancient Ones. He built a gigantic sky-bird of metal, and into its bowels climbed two score Men and Women.

"They flew away, off there—" Daiv pointed to a shining white dot in the sky above. "To the evening star. But it is said that one day they will return. That is why our tribe tries to preserve the customs of the Ancient Ones. Why even misguided tribes like yours preserve the records—"

Meg's face reddened.

"Enough!" she cried. "I have listened to many of your tales without making comment, Daiv. But now I command you to tell me no more such tales as this. This is—this is blasphemy!"

*Linber—to kidnap (derived from Lindbergh?)—Ed.

"Blasphemy?"

"It is not bad enough that your deranged mind should tell of days when *Men* ruled the earth? Now you speak of a *Man*-god!"

Daiv looked worried. He said, "But, Golden One, I thought you understood that all the gods were Men—"

"Daiv!" Without knowing why she did so, Meg suddenly swung to face him; covered his lips with her hands. She sought the darkness fearfully; made a swift gesture and a swifter prayer. "Do not tempt the wrath of the Gods! I am a priestess, and I know. All the Gods are—*must* be—Women!"

"But why?"

"Why—why, because they are!" said Meg. "It could not be otherwise. All Women know the gods are great, good and strong. How, then, could they be men? Jarg, and Ibram, and Taamuz. The mighty Tedhi—"

Daiv's eyes narrowed in wonderthought.

"I do not know their names," he mused. "They are not gods of our tribe. And yet—Ibrim . . . Tedhi. . . ."

There was vast pity in Meg's voice.

"We have been comrades for a long journey, Daiv," she pleaded. "Never before, since the world began, have a Man and a Woman met as you and I. Often you have said mad, impossible things. But I have forgiven you because—well, because you are, after all, only a Man.

"But tomorrow, or the day after that, we should come to the Place of the Gods. Then will my pilgrimage be ended, and I will learn that which is the ultimate secret. Then I shall have to return to my Clan, to become the Mother. And so let us not spoil our last hours of comradeship with vain argument."

Daiv sighed.

"The elder ones are gone, and their legends tell so little. It may be you are right, Golden One. But I have a feeling that it is my tribal lore that does not err. Meg—I asked this once before. Now I ask again. Will you become my mate?"

"It is impossible, Daiv. Priestesses and Mothers do not mate. And soon I will take you back with me to Jinnia, if you wish. And I will see to it that you are taken care of, always, as a Man should be taken care of."

Daiv shook his head.

"I cannot, Meg. Our ways are not the same. There is a custom in our tribe . . . a mating custom which you do not know. Let me show you—"

He leaned over swiftly. Meg felt the mighty strength of his bronzed arms closing about her, drawing her close. And he was touching his mouth to hers; closely, brutally, terrifyingly.

She struggled and tried to cry out, but his mouth bruised hers. Angerthoughts swept through her like a flame. But it was not anger—it was something else—that gave life to that flame. Suddenly her veins were running with liquid fire. Her heart beat upon rising, panting breasts like something captive that would be free. Her fists beat upon his shoulders vainly . . . but there was little strength in her blows.

Then he released her, and she fell back, exhausted. Her eyes glowed with anger and her voice was husky in her throat. She tried to speak, and could not. And in that moment, a vast and terrible weakness trembled through Meg. She knew, fearfully, that if Daiv sought to mate with her, not all the priestessdom of the gods could save her. There was a body-hunger throbbing within her that hated his Manness . . . but cried for it!

But Daiv, too, stepped back. And his voice was low as he said, "Meg?"

She wiped her mouth with the back of her hand. Her voice was vibrant.

"What magic is that, Daiv? What custom is that? I hate it. I hate *you!* I—"

"It is the touching-of-mouths, Golden One. It is the right of the Man with his mate. It is my plea that you enter not the Place of the Gods, but return with me, now, to Kirki, there to become my mate."

For a moment, indecision swayed Meg. But then, slowly, "No! I must go to the Place of the Gods," she said.

And thus it was. For the next day Meg marked on the shower-of-places the last time that indicated the path of her pilgrimage. And at eventide, when the sun threw long, ruddy rays upon the rounded hills of black, she and Daiv entered into the gateway which she had been told led to the Place of the Gods.

It was here they lingered for a moment. There were many words each would have said to the other. But both knew that this was the end.

"I know no Law, Daiv," said Meg, "which forbids a Man from entering the Place of the Gods. So you may do so if you wish. But it is not fitting that we should enter together. Therefore I ask you to wait here while I enter alone.

PILGRIMAGE

"I will learn the secret there. And learning, I will go out by another path, and return to Jinnia."

"You will go—alone?"

"Yes, Daiv."

"But if you should—" he persisted.

"If by some strangeness I should change my mind," said Meg, "I will return to you—here. But it is unlikely. Therefore do not wait."

"I will wait, Golden One," said Daiv soberly, "until all hope is dead."

Meg turned away, then hesitated and turned back. A great sorrow was within her. She did not know why. But she knew of one magic that could hear her heart for the time.

"Daiv—" she whispered.

"Yes, Golden One?"

"No one will ever know. And before I leave you forever—could we once more do the—the touching-of-mouths?"

So it was that alone and with the recollection of a moment of stirring glory in her heart, Meg strode proudly at last into the Place of the Gods.

It was a wild and desolate place. Barren hills of sand rose about here, and of vegetation there was none save sparse weeds and scrubby stumps that flowered miserly in the bleak, chill air.

The ground was harsh and salt beneath her feet, and no birds sang an evening carillon in that drab wilderness. Afar, a wild dog pierced the sky with its lonely call. The great hills echoed that cry dismally.

Above the other hills towered a greater one. To this, with unerring footsteps, Meg took her way. She knew not what to expect. It might be that here a band of singing virgins would appear to her, guiding her to a secret altar before which she would kneel and learn the last mystery.

It might be that the gods themselves reigned here, and that she would fall in awe before the sweeping skirts of austere Jarg, to hear from the gods' own lips the secret she had come so far to learn.

Whatever it was that would be revealed to her, Meg was ready. Others had found this place, and had survived. She did not fear death. But—death-in-life? Coming to the Place of the Gods with a blasphemy in her heart? With the memory of a Man's mouth upon hers—

For a moment, Meg was afraid. She had betrayed her priestessdom. Her body was inviolate, but would not the gods search her soul and know that her heart had forgotten the Law; had mated with a Man?

But if death must be her lot—so be it. She pressed on.

So Meg turned through a winding path, down between two tortuous clefts of rock, and came at last unto the Place of the Gods. Nor could she have chosen a better moment for the ultimate reaching of this place. The sun's roundness had now touched the western horizon.

There was still light. And Meg's eyes, wondering, sought that light. Sought—and saw! And then, with awe in her heart, Meg fell to her knees.

She had glimpsed that-which-was-not-to-be-seen! The Gods themselves, standing in omnipotent majesty, upon the crest of the towering rock.

For tremulous moments Meg knelt there, whispering the ritual prayers of appeasement. At any moment she expected to hear the thunderous voice of Tedhi, or to feel upon her shoulder the judicial hand of Jarg. But there came no sound but the frenzied beating of her own heart, of the soft stirring of dull grasses, of the wind touching the grim rocks.

And she lifted her head and looked once more. . . .

It was they! A race recollection, deeper and more sure than her own haulting memory told her at once that she had not erred. This was, indeed, the Place of the Gods. And these were the Gods she faced—stern, implacable, everlasting. Carven in eternal rock by the hands of those long ago.

Here they were; the Great Four. Jarg and Taamuz, with ringletted curls framing their stern, judicial faces. Sad Ibrim, lean of cheek and hollow of eye. And far-seeing Tedhi, whose eyes were concealed behind the giant telescopes. Whose lips, even now, were peeled back as though to loose a peal of his thunderous laughter.

And the Secret?

But even as the question leaped to her mind, it had its answer. Suddenly Meg knew that there was no visitation to be made upon her here. There would be no circle of singing virgins, no communication from those great stone lips. For the Secret which the Mother had hinted . . . the Secret which the Clanswomen must not know . . . was a secret Daiv had confided to her during those long marches of the pilgrimage.

The Gods—were Men!

Oh, not men like Jak or Ralf, whose pale bodies were but the instruments through which the breeding mothers' bodies were fertilized! Nor male creatures like the Wild Ones.

PILGRIMAGE

But—Men like Daiv! Lean and hard of jaw, strong of muscle, sturdy of body.

Even the curls could not conceal the inherent masculinity of Jarg and Taamuz. And Tedhi's lip was covered with Manhair, clearcut and bristling above his happy-mouth. And Ibrim's cheeks were haired, even as Daiv's had been from time to time before he made his tribal cut-magic with a keen knife.

The gods, the rulers, the Masters of the Ancient Ones *had* been Men. It had been as Daiv said—that many ages ago the Women had rebelled. And now they pursued their cold and loveless courses, save where—in a few places like the land of Kirki—the old way still maintained.

It was a great knowledge, and a bitter one. Now Meg understood why the Mother's lot was so unhappy. Because only the Mother knew how artificial this new life was. How soon the Wild Ones would die out, and the captive Men along with them. When that day came, there would be no more young. No more Men *or* Women. No more civilization. . . .

The Gods knew this. That is why they stood here in the grey hills of 'Kota, sad, forlorn, forgotten. The dying gods of a dying race. That because of an ill-conceived vengeance humankind was slowly destroying itself.

There was no hope. Knowing, now, this Secret, Meg must return to her Clan with lips sealed. There, like the Mother before her, she must watch with haunted eyes the slow dwindling of their tiny number . . . see the weak and futile remnants of Man die off. Until at last—

Hope was not dead! The Mother had been wrong. For the Mother had not been so fortunate in her pilgrimage as had Meg. She had never learned that there were still places in the world where Man had preserved himself in the image of the Ancient Ones. In the image of the Gods.

But she, Meg, knew! And knowing, she was presented with the greatest choice a Woman could know.

Forward into the valley, lay the path through which she could return to her Clan. There she would become Mother, and would guide and guard her people through a lifetime. She would be all-wise, all-powerful, all-important. But she would be a virgin unto death; sterile with the sanctity of tradition.

This she might do. But there was yet another way. And Meg threw her arms high, crying out that the Gods might hear and decide her problem.

The Gods spoke not. Their solemn features, weighted with

the gravity of time, moved not nor spoke to her. But as she searched their faces piteously for an answer to her vast despair, there came to Meg a memory. It was a passage from the Prayer of Ibrim. And as her lips framed those remembered words, it seemed that the dying rays of the sun centered on Ibrim's weary face, and those great stone eyes were alive for a moment with understanding . . . and approval.

" . . . shall not perish from the earth, but have everlasting Life. . . ."

Then Meg, the priestess, decided. With a sharp cry that broke from her heart, she turned and ran. Not toward the valley, but back . . . back . . . back . . . on feet that were suddenly stumbling and eager. Back through the towering shadow of Mt. Rushmore, through a desolate grotto that led to a gateway wherein awaited the Man who had taught her the touching-of-mouths.

RUST *Astounding Science Fiction*, October

by Joseph E. Kelleam (1913–   )

> *Joseph E. Kelleam had a handful of stories in the sf magazines in the late thirties and early forties, then disappeared for almost fifteen years, resurfacing in the mid-fifties with a novel and later with a few more stories and three more novels. In addition to the present selection, a noteworthy story is "The Eagles Gather," Astounding, 1942. His later work did not fulfill the promise of these two.*
>
> *"Rust" vividly captures the mood of that portion of modern science fiction characterized by alienation and despair. World War II had not started when Kelleam wrote this story, but all the signs of a coming holocaust were there, and we think he was trying to warn us.*
>
> *(We were a small group as the Thirties waned, and we huddled together for comfort, caught as we were in the least regarded branch of that unregarded world of the pulp magazine. And yet even so it was possible to pass in the night. Kelleam's path and mine never crossed. IA)*

The sun, rising over the hills, cast long shadows across the patches of snow and bathed the crumbling ruins in the pale light. Had men been there they could have reckoned the month to be August. But men had gone, long since, and the sun had waned; and now, in this late period of the earth's age, the short spring was awakening.

Within the broken city, in a mighty-columned hall that still supported a part of a roof, life of a sort was stirring. Three grotesque creatures were moving, their limbs creaking dolefully.

X-120 faced the new day and the new spring with a feeling of exhilaration that nearly drove the age-old loneliness and emptiness from the corroded metal of what might be called his brain. The sun was the source of his energy, even as it had been the source of the fleshy life before him; and with the sun's reappearance he felt new strength coursing through the wires and coils and gears of his complex body.

He and his companions were highly developed robots, the last ever to be made by the Earthmen. X-120 consisted of a globe of metal, eight feet in diameter, mounted upon four many-jointed legs. At the top of this globe was a protuberance like a kaiser's helmet which caught and stored his power from the rays of the sun.

From the "face" of the globe two ghostly quartz eyes bulged. The globe was divided by a heavy band of metal at its middle, and from this band, at each side, extended a long arm ending in a powerful claw. This claw was like the pincers of a lobster and had been built to shear through metal. Four long cables, which served as auxiliary arms, were drawn up like springs against the body.

X-120 stepped from the shadows of the broken hall into the ruined street. The sun's rays striking against his tarnished sides sent new strength coursing through his body. He had forgotten how many springs he had seen. Many generations of twisted oaks that grew among the ruins had sprung up and fallen since X-120 and his companions had been made. Countless hundreds of springs had flitted across the dying earth since the laughter and dreams and follies of men had ceased to disturb those crumbling walls.

"The sunlight is warm," called X-120. "Come out, G-3a and L-1716. I feel young again."

His companions lumbered into the sunlight. G-3a had lost one leg, and moved slowly and with difficulty. The steel of his body was nearly covered with red rust, and the copper and aluminum alloys that completed his make-up were pitted with deep stains of greenish black. L-1716 was not so badly tarnished, but he had lost one arm; and the four auxiliary cables were broken and dangled from his sides like trailing wires. Of the three X-120 was the best preserved. He still had the use of all his limbs, and here and there on his body shone the gleam of untarnished metal. His masters had made him well.

The crippled G-3a looked about him and whined like an old, old man. "It will surely rain," he shivered. "I cannot stand another rain."

"Nonsense," said L-1716, his broken arms, scraping along the ground as he moved, "there is not a cloud in the sky. Already I feel better."

G-3a looked about him in fear. "And are we all?" he questioned. "Last winter there were twelve."

X-120 had been thinking of the other nine, all that had been left of the countless horde that men had once fashioned. "The nine were to winter in the jade tower," he explained. "We will go there. Perhaps they do not think it is time to venture out."

"I cannot leave my work," grated G-3a. "There is so little time left. I have almost reached the goal." His whirring voice was raised to a pitch of triumph. "Soon I shall make living robots, even as men made us."

"The old story," sighed L-1716. "How long have we been working to make robots who will take our places? And what have we made? Usually nothing but lifeless blobs of steel. Sometimes we have fashioned mad things that had to be destroyed. But never in all the years have we made a single robot that resembled ourselves."

X-120 stood in the broken street, and the sunlight made a shimmering over his rust-dappled sides.

"That is where we have failed," he mused as he looked at his clawlike arms. "We have tried to make robots like ourselves. Men did not make us for life; they fashioned us for death." He waved his huge lobster claw in the air. "What was this made for? Was it made for the shaping of other robots? Was it made to fashion anything? Blades like that were made for slaughter—nothing else."

"Even so," whined the crippled robot, "I have nearly succeeded. With help I can win."

"And have we ever refused to help?" snapped L-1716. "You are getting old, G-3a. All winter you have worked in that little dark room, never allowing us to enter."

There was a metallic cackle in G-3a's voice. "But I have nearly won. They said I wouldn't, but I have nearly won. I need help. One more operation. If it succeeds, the robots may yet rebuild the world."

Reluctantly X-120 followed the two back into the shadowy

ruins. It was dark in there; but their round, glassy eyes had been made for both day and night.

"See," squeaked old G-3a, as he pointed to a metal skeleton upon the floor. "I have remade a robot from parts that I took from the scrap heap. It is perfect, all but the brain. Still, I believe this will work." He motioned to a gleaming object upon a littered table. It was a huge copper sphere with two black squares of a tarlike substance set into it. At the pole opposite from these squares was a protuberance no larger than a man's fist.

"This," said G-3a thoughtfully, "is the only perfect brain that I could find. You see, I am not trying to create something; I am merely rebuilding. Those"—he nodded to the black squares—"are the sensory organs. The visions from the eyes are flashed upon these as though they were screens. Beyond those eyes is the response mechanism, thousands and thousands of photo-electric cells. Men made it so that it would react mechanically to certain images. Movement, the simple avoidance of objects, the urge to kill, these are directed by the copper sphere.

"Beyond this"—he gestured to the bulge at the back of the brain—"is the thought mechanism. It is what made us different from other machines."

"It is very small," mocked X-120.

"So it is," replied G-3a. "I have heard that it was the reverse with the brains of men. But enough! See, this must fit into the body—so. The black squares rest behind the eyes. That wire brings energy to the brain, and those coils are connected to the power unit which operates the arms and legs. That wire goes to the balancing mechanism—" He droned on and on, explaining each part carefully. "And now," he finished, "someone must connect it. I cannot."

L-1716 stared at his one rusty claw with confusion. Then both he and G-3a were looking at X-120.

"I can only try," offered the robot. "But remember what I said. We were not fashioned to make anything; only to kill."

Clumsily he lifted the copper sphere and its cluster of wires from the table. He worked slowly and carefully. One by one the huge claws crimped the tiny wires together. The job was nearly finished. Then the great pincers, hovering so carefully above the last wire, came into contact with another. There was a flash as the power short-circuited. X-120 reeled back. The copper sphere melted and ran before their eyes.

X-120 huddled against the far wall. "It is as I said," he moaned; "we can build nothing. We were not made to work at anything. We were only made for one purpose, to kill." He looked at his bulky claws, and shook them as though he might cast them away.

"Do not take on so," pacified old G-3a. "Perhaps it is just as well. We are things of steel, and the world seems to be made for creatures of flesh and blood—little, puny things that even I can crush. Still, that thing there"—he pointed to the metal skeleton which now held the molten copper like a crucible—"was my last hope. I have nothing else to offer."

"Both of you have tried," agreed L-1716. "No one could blame either of you. Sometimes of nights when I look into the stars, it seems that I see our doom written there; and I can hear the worlds laughing at us. We have conquered the earth, but what of it? We are going now, following the men who fashioned us."

"Perhaps it is better," nodded X-120. "I think it is the fault of our brains. You said that men made us to react mechanically to certain stimuli. And though they gave us a thought mechanism, it has no control over our reactions. I never wanted to kill. Yet, I have killed many men-things. And sometimes, even as I killed, I would be thinking of other things. I would not even know what had happened until after the deed was done."

G-3a had not been listening. Instead, he had been looking dolefully at the metal ruin upon the floor. "There was one in the jade tower," he said abruptly, "who thought he had nearly learned how to make a brain. He was to work all winter on it. Perhaps he has succeeded."

"We will go there," shrilled L-1716 laconically.

But even as they left the time-worn hall G-3a looked back ruefully at the smoking wreckage upon the floor.

X-120 slowed his steps to match the feeble gait of G-3a. Within sight of the tower he saw that they need go no farther. At some time during the winter the old walls had buckled. The nine were buried beneath tons and tons of masonry.

Slowly the three came back to their broken hall. "I will not stay out any longer," grumbled G-3a. "I am very old. I am very tired." He crept back into the shadows.

L-1716 stood looking after him. "I am afraid that he is nearly done," he spoke sorrowfully. "The rust must be within him now. He saved me once, long ago, when we destroyed this city."

"Do you still think of that?" asked X-120. "Sometimes it troubles me. Men were our masters."

"And they made us as we are," growled L-1716. "It was not our doing. We have talked of it before, you know. We were machines, made to kill—"

"But we were made to kill the little men in the yellow uniforms."

"Yes, I know. They made us on a psychological principle: stimulus, response. We had only to see a man in a yellow uniform and our next act was to kill. Then, after the Great War was over, or even before it was over, the stimulus and response had overpowered us all. It was only a short step from killing men in yellow uniforms to killing all men."

"I know," said X-120 wearily. "When there were more of us I heard it explained often. But sometimes it troubles me."

"It is all done now. Ages ago it was done. You are different, X-120. I have felt for long that there is something different about you. You were one of the last that they made. Still, you were here when we took this city. You fought well, killing many."

X-120 sighed. "There were small men-things then. They seemed so soft and harmless. Did we do right?"

"Nonsense. We could not help it. We were made so. Men learned to make more than they could control. Why, if I saw a man today, crippled as I am, I would kill him without thinking."

"L-1716," whispered X-120, "do you think there are any men left in the world?"

"I don't think so. Remember, the Great War was general, not local. We were carried to all parts of the earth, even to the smallest islands. The robots' rebellion came everywhere at almost the same time. There were some of us who were equipped with radios. Those died first, long ago, but they talked with nearly every part of the world." Suddenly he wearied of speech. "But why worry now. It is spring. Men made us for killing men. That was their crime. Can we help it if they made us too well?"

"Yes," agreed X-120, "it is spring. We will forget. Let us go toward the river. It was always peaceful and beautiful there."

L-1716 was puzzled. "What peace and beauty?" he asked.

"They are but words that men taught us. I have never known them. But perhaps you have. You were always different."

"I do not know what peace and beauty are, but when I think of them I am reminded of the river and of—" X-120 stopped suddenly, careful that he might not give away a secret he had kept so long.

"Very well," agreed L-1716, "we will go to the river. I know a meadow there where the sun always seemed warmer."

The two machines, each over twelve feet high, lumbered down the almost obliterated street. As they pushed their way over the débris and undergrowth that had settled about the ruins, they came upon many rusted skeletons of things that had once been like themselves. And toward the outskirts of the city they crossed over an immense scrap heap where thousands of the shattered and rusted bodies lay.

"We used to bring them here after—" said L-1716. "But the last centuries we have left them where they have fallen. I have been envying those who wintered in the jade tower." His metallic voice hinted of sadness.

They came at last to an open space in the trees. Farther they went and stood at the edge of a bluff overlooking a gorge and a swirling river below. Several bridges had once been there but only traces remained.

"I think I will go down to the river's edge," offered X-120.

"Go ahead. I will stay here. The way is too steep for me."

So X-120 clambered down a half-obliterated roadway alone. He stood at last by the rushing waters. Here, he thought, was something that changed the least. Here was the only hint of permanence in all the world. But even it changed. Soon the melting snow would be gone and the waters would dwindle to a mere trickle. He turned about and looked at the steep side of the gorge. Except for the single place where the old roadbed crept down, the sides rose sheer, their crests framed against the blue sky. These cliffs, too, were lasting.

Even in spring the cliffs and river seemed lonely and desolate. Men had not bothered to teach X-120 much of religion or philosophy. Yet somewhere in the combination of cells in his brain was a thought which kept telling him that he and his kind were suffering for their sins and for the sins of men before them.

And perhaps the thought was true. Certainly, men had

never conquered their age-old stupidity, though science had bowed before them. Countless wars had taken more from men than science had given them. X-120 and his kind were the culmination of this primal killer instinct.

In the haste of a war-pressed emergency man had not taken the time to refine his last creation, or to calculate its result. And with that misstep man had played his last card on the worn gaming table of earth. That built-in urge to kill men in yellow uniforms had changed, ever so slightly, to an urge to kill—men.

Now there were only X-120, his two crippled comrades, the heaps of rusted steel, and the leaning, crumbling towers.

He followed the river for several miles until the steep sides lessened. Then he clambered out, and wandered through groves of gnarled trees. He did not wish to go back to L-1716, not just yet. The maimed robot was always sad. The rust was eating into him, too. Soon he would be like G-3a. Soon the two of them would be gone. Then he would be the last. An icy surge of fear stole over him. He did not want to be left alone.

He lumbered onward. A few birds were stirring. Suddenly, almost at his feet, a rabbit darted from the bushes. X-120's long jointed arms swung swiftly. The tiny animal lay crushed upon the ground. Instinctively he stamped upon it, leaving only a bloody trace upon the new grass.

Then remorse and shame stole over him. He went on silently. Somehow the luster of the day had faded for him. He did not want to kill. Always he was ashamed, after the deed was done. And the age-old question went once more through the steel meshes of his mind: Why had he been made to kill?

He went on and on, and out of long habit he went furtively. Soon he came to an ivy-covered wall. Beyond this were the ruins of a great stone house. He stopped at what had once been a garden. Near a broken fountain he found what he had been seeking, a little marble statue of a child, weathered and discolored. Here, unknown to his companions, he had been coming for years upon countless years. There was something about this little sculpturing that had fascinated him. And he had been half ashamed of his fascination.

He could not have explained his feelings, but there was something about the statue that made him think of all the things that men had possessed. It reminded him of all the qualities that were so far beyond his kind. He stood looking at the statue for long. It possessed an ethereal quality that still defied time. It made him think of the river and of the overhanging cliffs. Some long-dead artist almost came to life before his quartz eyes.

He retreated to a nearby brook and came back with a huge ball of clay. This in spite of the century-old admonitions that all robots should avoid the damp. For many years he had been trying to duplicate the little statue. Now, once more, he set about his appointed task. But his shearlike claws had been made for only one thing, death. He worked clumsily. Toward sundown he abandoned the shapeless mass that he had fashioned and returned to the ruins.

Near the shattered hall he met L-1716. At the entrance they called to G-3a, telling him of the day's adventures. But no answer came. Together they went in. G-3a was sprawled upon the floor. The rust had conquered.

The elusive spring had changed into even a more furtive summer. The two robots were coming back to their hall on an afternoon which had been beautiful and quiet. L-1716 moved more slowly now. His broken cables trailed behind him, making a rustling sound in the dried leaves that had fallen.

Two of the cables had become entangled. Unnoticed, they caught in the branches of a fallen tree. Suddenly L-1716 was whirled about. He sagged to his knees. X-120 removed the cables from the tree. But L-1716 did not get up. "A wrench," he said brokenly; "something is wrong."

A thin tendril of smoke curled up from his side. Slowly he crumpled. From within him came a whirring sound that ended in a sharp snap. Tiny flames burst through his metal sides. L-1716 fell forward.

And X-120 stood over him and begged, "Please, old friend, don't leave me now." It was the first time that the onlooking hills had seen any emotion in centuries.

A few flakes of snow were falling through the air. The sky looked gray and low. A pair of crows were going home, their raucous cries troubling an otherwise dead world.

X-120 moved slowly. All that day he had felt strange. He found himself straying from the trail. He could only move now by going in a series of arcs. Something was wrong within him. He should be back in the hall, he knew, and not out in this dangerous moisture. But he was troubled, and all day he had wandered, while the snowflakes had fallen intermittently about him.

On he went through the gray, chill day. On and on until he came to crumbling wall, covered with withered ivy. Over this he went into a ruined garden, and paused at a broken fountain, before an old and blackened statue.

Long he stood, looking down at the carving of a little child, a statue that men had made so long before. Then his metal arm swung through the air. The marble shivered into a hundred fragments.

Slowly he turned about and retraced his steps. The cold sun was sinking, leaving a faint amethyst stain in the west. He must get back to the hall. Mustn't stay out in the wet, he thought.

But something was wrong. He caught himself straying from the path, floundering in circles. The light was paling, although his eyes had been fashioned for both day and night.

Where was he? He realized with a start that he was lying on the ground. He must get back to the hall. He struggled, but no movement came. Then, slowly, the light faded and flickered out.

And the snow fell, slowly and silently, until only a white mound showed where X-120 had been.

THE FOUR-SIDED TRIANGLE
Amazing Stories, November

by William F. Temple (1914–   )

William F. Temple was a former roommate of Arthur C. Clarke as well as former editor of the Journal of the British Interplanetary Society. In addition to this story, he is best known for his novel SHOOT AT THE MOON (1966) and the novelette "The Two Shadows" (Startling Stories, 1951).

"The Four-Sided Triangle" is about love and the duplication (not cloning) of life. The story was later expanded into an interesting novel (1949) and an underrated film (1953).

(In the Thirties, science fiction, to the American magazine-reading public at least, was a completely American phenomenon. We knew vaguely that the greatest science fiction writers, Jules Verne, H. G. Wells were not American, but that didn't count. When we held the first Science Fiction Convention, attended by Americans only, there was no hesitation in giving it the adjective "World." And yet even in those days there were important British writers: Eric Frank Russell, for instance. William F. Temple was another.)

Three people peered through a quartz window.

The girl was squashed uncomfortably between the two men, but at the moment neither she nor they cared. The object they were watching was too interesting.

The girl was Joan Leeton. Her hair was an indeterminate brown, and owed its curls to tongs, not to nature. Her eyes were certainly brown, and bright with unquenchable good humour. In repose her face was undistinguished, though far from plain; when she smiled, it was beautiful.

Her greatest attraction (and it was part of her attraction that she did not realise it) lay in her character. She was soothingly sympathetic without becoming mushy, she was very level-headed (a rare thing in a woman) and completely unselfish. She refused to lose her temper over anything, or take offence, or enlarge upon the truth in her favour, and yet she was tolerant of such lapses in others. She possessed a brain that was unusually able in its dealing with science, and yet her tastes and pleasures were simple.

William Fredericks (called 'Will') had much in common with Joan, but his sympathy was a little more disinterested, his humour less spontaneous, and he had certain prejudices. His tastes were reserved for what he considered the more worthy things. But he was calm and good-tempered, and his steadiness of purpose was reassuring. He was black-haired, with an expression of quiet content.

William Josephs (called 'Bill') was different. He was completely unstable. Fiery of hair, he was alternately fiery and depressed of spirit. Impulsive, generous, highly emotional about art and music, he was given to periods of gaiety and moods of black melancholia. He reached, at his best, heights of mental brilliance far beyond the other two, but long bouts of lethargy prevented him from making the best of them.

Nevertheless, his sense of humour was keen, and he was often amused at his own absurdly over-sensitive character; but he could not change it.

Both these men were deeply in love with Joan, and both tried hard to conceal it. If Joan had any preference, she concealed it just as ably, although they were aware that she was fond of both of them.

The quartz window, through which the three were looking, was set in a tall metal container, and just a few feet away was another container, identical even to the thickness of the window-glass.

Overhead was a complex assemblage of apparatus: bulbous, silvered tubes, small electric motors that hummed in various unexpected places, makeshift screens of zinc, roughly soldered, coils upon coils of wire, and a network of slung cables that made the place look like a creeper-tangled tropical jungle. A large dynamo churned out a steady roar in the corner, and a pair of wide sparkgaps crackled continuously, filling the laboratory with a weird, jumping blue light as the day waned outside the windows and the dusk crept in.

An intruder in the laboratory might have looked through the window of the other container and seen, standing on a steel frame in a cubical chamber, an oil painting of 'Madame Croignette' by Boucher, delicately illuminated by concealed lights. He would not have known it, but the painting was standing in a vacuum.

If he had squeezed behind the trio at the other container and gazed through their window he would have seen an apparently identical sight: an oil painting of 'Madame Croignette' by Boucher, standing on a steel frame in a vacuum, delicately illuminated by concealed lights.

From which he would probably not gather much.

The catch was that the painting at which the three were gazing so intently was not quite the same as the one in the first container—not yet. There were minute differences in colour and proportion.

But gradually these differences were righting themselves, for the whole of the second canvas was being built up atom by atom, molecule by molecule, into an exactly identical twin of the one which had felt the brush of Francis Boucher.

The marvellously intricate apparatus, using an adaption of a newly-discovered magnetic principle, consumed only a moderate amount of power in arranging the lines of sympathetic fields of force which brought every proton into position and every electron into its respective balancing orbit. It was a machine which could divert the flow of great forces without the ability to tap their energy.

'Any minute now!' breathed Will.

Bill rubbed his breath off the glass impatiently.

'Don't do that!' he said, and promptly fogged the glass over again. Not ungently, he attempted to rub a clear patch with Joan's own pretty nose. She exploded into laughter, fogging the glass hopelessly, and in the temporary confusion of this they missed seeing the event they had been waiting days for—the completion of the duplicate painting to the ultimate atom.

The spark-gaps died with a final snap, a lamp sprang into being on the indicator panel, and the dynamo began to run whirringly down to a stop.

They cleaned out the window, and there stood 'Madame Croignette' looking rather blankly out at them with wide brown eyes that exactly matched the sepia from Boucher's palette, and both beauty spots and every hair of her powdered wig in place to a millionth of a millimetre.

Will turned a valve, and there was the hiss of air rushing into the chamber. He opened the window, and lifted the painting out gingerly, as if he half-expected it to crumble in his hands.

'Perfect—a beauty!' he murmured. He looked up at Joan with shining eyes. Bill caught that look, and unaccountably checked the impulsive whoop of joy he was on the point of letting loose. He coughed instead, and leaned over Joan's shoulder to inspect 'Madame Croignette' more closely.

'The gamble's come off,' went on Will. 'We've sunk every cent into this, but it won't be long before we have enough money to do anything we want to do—anything.'

'Anything—except to get Bill out of bed on Sunday mornings,' smiled Joan, and they laughed.

'No sensible millionaire would get out of bed any morning,' said Bill.

The steel and glass factory of Art Replicas, Limited, shone like a diamond up in the green hills of Surrey. In a financial sense, it had actually sprung from a diamond—the sale of a replica of the Koh-i-noor. That had been the one and only product of Precious Stones, Limited, an earlier company which was closed down by the government when they saw that it would destroy the world's diamond market.

A sister company, Radium Products, was going strong up in the north because its scientific necessity was recognised. But the heart of the three company directors lay in Art Replicas, and there they spent their time.

Famous works of art from all over the world passed through the factory's portals, and gave birth to innumerable replicas of themselves for distribution and sale at quite reasonable prices.

Families of only moderate means found it pleasing to have a Constable or Turner in the dining room and a Rodin statuette in the hall. And this widely-flung ownership of *objets d'art,* which were to all intents and purposes the genuine articles, strengthened interest in art enormously. When people had lived with these things for a little while, they began to perceive the beauty in them—for real beauty is not always obvious at a glance—and to become greedy for more knowledge of them and the men who originally conceived and shaped them.

So the three directors—Will, Bill, and Joan—put all their energy into satisfying the demands of the world for art, and conscious of their part in furthering civilisation, were deeply content.

For a time.

Then Bill, the impatient and easily-bored, broke out one day in the middle of a Directors' Meeting.

'Oh to hell with the Ming estimates!' he cried, sweeping a pile of orders from the table.

Joan and Will, recognising the symptoms, exchanged wry glances of amusement.

'Look here,' went on Bill, 'I don't know what you two think, but I'm fed up! We've become nothing but dull business people now. It isn't our sort of life. Repetition, repetition, repetition! I'm going crazy! We're *research* workers, not darned piece-workers. For heaven's sake, let's start out in some new line!'

This little storm relieved him, and almost immediately he smiled too.

'But, really, aren't we?' he appealed.

'Yes,' responded Joan and Will in duet.

'Well, what about it?'

Will coughed, and prepared himself.

'Joan and I were talking about that this morning, as a matter of fact,' he said. 'We were going to suggest that we sell the factory, and retire to our old laboratory and re-equip it.'

Bill picked up the ink-pot and emptied it solemnly over the Ming estimates. The ink made a shining lake in the centre of the antique and valuable table.

'At last we're sane again,' he said. 'Now you know the line of investigation I want to open up. I'm perfectly convinced that the reason for our failure to create a living duplicate of any living creature was because the quotiety we assumed for the xy action—'

'Just a moment, Bill,' interrupted Will. 'Before we get on with that work, I——I mean, one of the reasons Joan and me wanted to retire was because—well—'

'What he's trying to say,' said Joan quietly, 'is that we plan to get married and settle down for a bit before we resume research work.'

Bill stared at them. He was aware that his cheeks were slowly reddening. He felt numb.

'Well!' he said. 'Well!' (He could think of nothing else. This was unbelievable! He must postpone consideration of it until he was alone, else his utter mortification would show.)

He put out his hand automatically, and they both clasped it.

'You know I wish you every possible happiness,' he said, rather huskily. His mind seemed empty. He tried to form some comment, but somehow he could not compose one sentence that made sense.

'I think we'll get on all right,' said Will, smiling at Joan. She smiled back at him, and unknowingly cut Bill to the heart.

With an effort, Bill pulled himself together and rang for wine to celebrate. He ordered some of the modern reconstruction of an exceedingly rare '94.

The night was moonless and cloudless, and the myriads of glittering pale blue points of the Milky Way sprawled across the sky as if someone had cast a handful of brilliants upon a black velvet cloth. But they twinkled steadily, for strong air currents were in motion in the upper atmosphere.

The Surrey lane was dark and silent. The only signs of life were the occasional distant glares of automobile headlights passing on the main highway nearly a mile away, and the red dot of a burning cigarette in a gap between the hedgerows.

The cigarette was Bill's. He sat there on a gate staring up at the array in the heavens and wondering what to do with his life.

He felt completely at sea, purposeless, and unutterably depressed. He had thought the word 'heartache' just a vague descriptive term. Now he knew what it meant. It was a solid physical feeling, an ache that tore him inside, unceasingly. He yearned to see Joan, to be with Joan, with his whole being. This longing would not let him rest. He could have cried out for a respite.

He tried to argue himself to a more rational viewpoint.

'I am a man of science,' he told himself. 'Why should I allow old Mother Nature to torture and badger me like this? I can see through all the tricks of that old twister. These feelings are purely chemical reactions, the secretions of the glands mixing with the blood-stream. My mind is surely strong enough to conquer that? Else I have a third-rate brain, not the scientific instrument I've prided myself on.'

He stared up at the stars glittering in their seeming calm

stability, age-old and unchanging. But were they? They may look just the same when all mankind and its loves and hates had departed from this planet, and left it frozen and dark. But he knew that even as he watched, they were changing position at a frightful speed, receeding from him at thousands of miles a second.

'Nature is a twister, full of illusions,' he repeated. . . .

There started a train of thought, a merciful anaesthetic in which he lost himself for some minutes.

Somewhere down in the deeps of his subconscious an idea which had, unknown to him, been evolving itself for weeks, was stirred, and emerged suddenly into the light. He started, dropped his cigarette, and left it on the ground.

He sat there stiffly on the gate and considered the idea.

It was wild—incredibly wild. But if he worked hard and long at it, there was a chance that it might come off. It would provide a reason for living, anyway, so long as there was any hope at all of success.

He jumped down from the gate and started walking quickly and excitedly along the lane back to the factory. His mind was already turning over possibilities, planning eagerly. In the promise of this new adventure, the heart-ache was temporarily submerged.

Six months passed.

Bill had retired to the old laboratory, and spent much of that time enlarging and re-equipping it. He added a rabbit pen, and turned an adjacent patch of ground into a burial-ground to dispose of those who died under his knife. This cemetery was like no cemetery in the world, for it was also full of dead things that had never died—because they had never lived.

His research got nowhere. He could build up, atom by atom, the exact physical counterpart of any living animal, but all such duplicates remained obstinately inanimate. They assumed an extraordinary life-like appearance, but it was frozen life. They were no more alive than waxwork images, even though they were as soft and pliable as the original animals in sleep.

Bill thought he had hit upon the trouble in a certain equation, but re-checking confirmed that the equation had been right in the first place. There was no flaw in either theory or practice as far as he could see.

Yet somehow he could not duplicate the force of life in action. Must he apply that force himself? How?

He applied various degrees of electrical impulses to the nerve centers of the rabbits, tried rapid alternations of temperatures, miniature 'iron lungs', vigorous massage—both external and internal—intra-venous and spinal injections of everything from adrenalin to even more powerful stimulants which his agile mind concocted. And still the artificial rabbits remained limp bundles of fur.

Joan and Will returned from their honeymoon and settled down in a roomy, comfortable old house a few miles away. They sometimes dropped in to see how the research was going. Bill always seemed bright and cheerful enough when they came, and joked about his setbacks.

'I think I'll scour the world for the hottest thing in female bunnies and teach her to do a hula-hula on the lab. bench,' he said. 'That ought to make some of these stiffs sit up!'

Joan said she was seriously thinking of starting an eating-house specialising in rabbit pie, if Bill could keep up the supply of dead rabbits. He replied that he'd already buried enough to feed an army.

Their conversation was generally pitched in this bantering key, save when they really got down to technicalities. But when they had gone, Bill would sit and brood, thinking constantly of Joan. And he could concentrate on nothing else for the rest of that day.

Finally, more or less by accident, he found the press-button which awoke life in the rabbits. He was experimenting with a blood solution he had prepared, thinking that it might remain more constant than the natural rabbit's blood, which became thin and useless too quickly. He had constructed a little pump to force the natural blood from a rabbit's veins and fill them instead with his artificial solution.

The pump had not been going for more than a few seconds before the rabbit stirred weakly and opened its eyes. It twitched its nose, and lay quite still for a moment, save for one foot which continued to quiver.

Then suddenly it roused up and made a prodigious bound from the bench. The thin rubber tubes which tethered it by the neck parted in midair, and it fell awkwardly with a heavy thump on the floor. The blood continued to run from one of the broken tubes, but the pump which forced it out was the rabbit's own heart—beating at last.

THE FOUR-SIDED TRIANGLE

The animal seemed to have used all its energy in that one powerful jump, and lay still on the floor and quietly expired.

Bill stood regarding it, his fingers still on the wheel of the pump.

Then, when he realised what it meant, he recaptured some of his old exuberance, and danced around the laboratory carrying a carboy of acid as though it were a Grecian urn.

Further experiments convinced him that he had set foot within the portals of Nature's most carefully guarded citadel. Admittedly he could not himself create anything original or unique in Life. But he could create a living image of any living creature under the sun.

A hot summer afternoon, a cool green lawn shaded by elms and on it two white-clad figures, Joan and Will, putting through their miniature nine-hole course. A bright-striped awning by the hedge, and below it, two comfortable canvas chairs and a little Moorish table with soft drinks. An ivy-covered wall of an old red-brick mansion showing between the trees. The indefinable smell of new-cut grass in the air. The gentle but triumphant laughter of Joan as Will foozled his shot.

That was the atmosphere Bill entered at the end of his duty tramp along the lane from the laboratory—it was his first outdoor excursion for weeks—and he could not help comparing it with the sort of world he had been living in: the benches and bottles and sinks, the eye-tiring field of the microscope, the sheets of calculations under the glare of electric light in the dark hours of the night, the smell of blood and chemicals and rabbits.

And he realised completely that science wasn't the greatest thing in life. Personal happiness was. That was the goal of all men, whatever way they strove to reach it.

Joan caught sight of him standing on the edge of the lawn, and came hurrying across to greet him.

'Where have you been all this time?' she asked. 'We've been dying to hear how you've been getting on.'

'I've done it,' said Bill.

'Done it? Have you really?' Her voice mounted excitedly almost to a squeak. She grabbed him by the wrist and hauled him across to Will. 'He's done it!' she announced, and stood between them, watching both their faces eagerly.

Will took the news with his usual calmness, and smilingly gripped Bill's hand.

'Congratulations, old lad,' he said. 'Come and have a drink and tell us all about it.'

They squatted on the grass and helped themselves from the table. Will could see that Bill had been overworking himself badly. His face was drawn and tired, his eyelids red, and he was in the grip of a nervous tension which for the time held him dumb and uncertain of himself.

Joan noticed this, too, and checked the questions she was going to bombard upon him. Instead, she quietly withdrew to the house to prepare a pot of the China tea which she knew always soothed Bill's migraine.

When she had gone, Bill, with an effort, shook some of the stupor from him, and looked across at Will. His gaze dropped, and he began to pluck idly at the grass.

'Will,' he began, presently, 'I'—He cleared his throat nervously, and started again in a none too steady voice. 'Listen, Will, I have something a bit difficult to say, and I'm not so good at expressing myself. In the first place, I have always been crazily in love with Joan.'

Will sat, and looked at him curiously. But he let Bill go on.

'I never said anything because—well, because I was afraid I wouldn't make a success of marriage. Too unstable to settle down quietly with a decent girl like Joan. But I found I couldn't go on without her, and was going to propose—when you beat me to it. I've felt pretty miserable since, though this work has taken something of the edge off.'

Will regarded the other's pale face—and wondered.

'This work held out a real hope to me. And now I've accomplished the major part of it. I can make a living copy of any living thing. Now—do you see *why* I threw myself into this research? *I want to create a living, breathing twin of Joan, and marry her!*'

Will started slightly. Bill got up and paced restlessly up and down.

'I know I'm asking a hell of a lot. This affair reaches deeper than a scientific curiosity. No feeling man can contemplate such a proposal without misgivings, for his wife and for himself. But honestly, Will, I cannot see any possible harm arising from it. Though, admittedly, the only good thing would be to make a selfish man happy. For heaven's sake, let me know what you think.'

Will sat contemplating, while the distracted Bill continued to pace.

Presently, he said, 'You are sure no physical harm could come to Joan in the course of the experiment?'

'Certain—completely certain,' said Bill.

'Then I personally have no objection. Anything but objection. I had no idea you felt that way, Bill, and it would make me, as well as Joan, very unhappy to know you had to go on like that.'

He caught sight of his wife approaching with a laden tray.

'Naturally, the decision rests with her,' he said. 'If she'd rather not, there's no more to it.'

'No, of course not,' agreed Bill.

But they both knew what her answer would be.

'Stop the car for a minute, Will,' said Joan suddenly, and her husband stepped on the foot-brake.

The car halted in the lane on the brow of the hill. Through a gap in the hedge the two occupants had a view of Bill's laboratory as it lay below in the cradle of the valley.

Joan pointed down. In the field behind the 'cemetery' two figures were strolling. Even at this distance, Bill's flaming hair marked his identity. His companion was a woman in a white summer frock. And it was on her that Joan's attention was fixed.

'She's alive now!' she whispered, and her voice trembled slightly.

Will nodded. He noticed her apprehension, and gripped her hand encouragingly. She managed a wry smile.

'It's not every day one goes to pay a visit to oneself,' she said. 'It was unnerving enough last week to see her lying on the other couch in the lab., dressed in my red frock—which *I* was wearing—so pale, and—Oh, it was like seeing myself dead!'

'She's not dead now, and Bill's bought her some different clothes, so cheer up,' said Will. 'I know it's a most queer situation, but the only possible way to look at it is from the scientific viewpoint. It's a unique scientific event. And it's made Bill happy into the bargain.'

He ruminated a minute.

'Wish he'd given us a hint as to how he works his resuscitation process, though,' he went on. 'Still, I suppose he's right to keep it a secret. It's a discovery which could be appallingly abused. Think of dictators manufacturing loyal, stupid armies from one loyal, stupid soldier! Or industrialists manufacturing cheap labour! We should soon have a world of robots, all traces of individuality wiped out. No variety, nothing unique—life would not be worth living.'

'No,' replied Joan, mechanically, her thoughts still on that white-clad figure down there.

Will released the brake, and the car rolled down the hill toward the laboratory. The two in the field saw it coming, and walked back through the cemetery to meet it. They reached the road as the car drew up.

'Hello, there!' greeted Bill. 'You're late—we've had the kettle on the boil for half an hour. Doll and I were getting anxious.'

He advanced into the road, and the woman in the white frock lingered hesitantly behind him. Joan tightened her lips and braced herself to face this unusual ordeal. She got out of the car, and while Will and Bill were grasping hands, she walked to meet her now living twin.

Apparently Doll had decided to face it in the same way, and they met with oddly identical expressions of smiling surface ease, with an undercurrent of curiosity and doubt. They both saw and understood each other's expression simultaneously, and burst out laughing. That helped a lot.

'It's not so bad, after all,' said Doll, and Joan checked herself from making the same instinctive remark.

'No, not nearly,' she agreed.

And it wasn't. For although Doll looked familiar to her, she could not seem to identify her with herself to any unusual extent. It was not that her apparel and hair-style were different, but that somehow her face, figure and voice seemed like those of another person.

She did not realise that hitherto she had only seen parts of herself in certain mirrors from certain angles, and the complete effect was something she had simply never witnessed. Nor that she had not heard her own voice outside her own head, so to speak—never from a distance of some feet.

Nevertheless, throughout the meal she felt vaguely uneasy, though she tried to hide it, and kept up a fire of witty remarks. And her other self, too, smiled at her across the table and talked easily.

They compared themselves in detail, and found they were completely identical in every way, even to the tiny mole on their left forearm. Their tastes, too, agreed. They took the same amount of sugar in their tea, and liked and disliked the same foodstuffs.

'I've got my eye on that pink iced cake,' laughed Doll. 'Have you?'

Joan admitted it. So they shared it.

'You'll never have any trouble over buying each other birthday or Christmas presents,' commented Will. 'How nice to know exactly what the other wants!'

Bill had a permanent grin on his face, and beamed all over the table all the time. For once he did not have a great deal to say. He seemed too happy for words, and kept losing the thread of the conversation to gaze upon Doll fondly.

'We're going to be married tomorrow!' he announced unexpectedly, and they protested their surprise at the lack of warning. But they promised to be there.

There followed an evening of various sorts of games, and the similar thought-processes of Joan and Doll led to much amusement, expecially in the guessing games. And twice they played checkers and twice they drew.

It was a merry evening, and Bill was merriest of all. Yet when they came to say goodnight, Joan felt the return of the old uneasiness. As they left in the car, Joan caught a glimpse of Doll's face as she stood beside Bill at the gate. And she divined that under that air of gaiety, Doll suffered the same uneasiness as she.

Doll and Bill were married in a distant registry office next day, using a fictitious name and birthplace for Doll to avoid any publicity—after all, no one would question her identity.

Winter came and went.

Doll and Bill seemed to have settled down quite happily, and the quartet remained as close friends as ever. Both Doll and Joan were smitten with the urge to take up flying as a hobby, and joined the local flying club. They each bought a single-seater, and went for long flights, cruising side by side.

Almost in self-protection from this neglect (they had no interest in flying) Bill and Will began to work again together, delving further into the mysteries of the atom. This time they were searching for the yet-to-be-discovered secret of tapping the potential energy which the atom held.

And almost at once they stumbled onto a new lead.

Formerly they had been able to divert atomic energy without being able to transform it into useful power. It was as if they had constructed a number of artificial dams at various points in a turbulent river, which altered the course of the river without tapping any of its force—though that is a poor and misleading analogy.

But now they had conceived, and were building, an amazingly complex machine which, in the same unsatisfactory analogy, could be likened to a turbine-generator, tapping some of the power of that turbulent river.

The 'river' however, was very turbulent indeed, and needed skill and courage to harness. And there was a danger of the harness suddenly slipping.

Presently, the others became aware that Doll's health was gradually failing. She tried hard to keep up her usual air of brightness and cheerfulness, but she could not sleep, and became restless and nervous.

And Joan, who was her almost constant companion, suddenly realised what was worrying that mind which was so similar to hers. The realisation was a genuine shock, which left her trembling, but she faced it.

'I think it would be a good thing for Doll and Bill to come and live here for a while, until Doll's better,' she said rather diffidently to Will one day.

'Yes, okay, if you think you can persuade them,' replied Will. He looked a little puzzled.

'We have far too many empty rooms here,' she said defensively. 'Anyway, I can help Doll if I'm with her more.'

Doll seemed quite eager to come, though a little dubious, but Bill thought it a great idea. They moved within the week.

At first, things did improve. Doll began to recover, and became more like her natural self. She was much less highly strung, and joined in the evening games with the other three with gusto. She studied Will's favourite game, backgammon, and began to enjoy beating him thoroughly and regularly.

And then Joan began to fail.

She became nerveless, melancholy, and even morose. It seemed as though through helping Doll back to health, she had been infected with the same complaint.

Will was worried, and insisted on her being examined by a doctor.

The doctor told Will in private: 'There's nothing physically wrong. She's nursing some secret worry, and she'll get worse until this worry is eased. Persuade her to tell you what it is—she refuses to tell me.'

She also refused to tell Will, despite his pleadings.

And now Doll, who knew what the secret was, began to

worry about Joan, and presently she relapsed into her previous nervous condition.

So it continued for a week, a miserable week for the two harassed and perplexed husbands, who did not know which way to turn. The following week, however, both women seemed to make an effort, and brightened up somewhat, and could even laugh at times.

The recovery continued, and Bill and Will deemed it safe to return to their daily work in the lab., completing the atom-harnessing machine.

One day Will happened to return to the house unexpectedly, and found the two women in each other's arms on a couch, crying their eyes out. He stood staring for a moment. They suddenly became aware of him, and parted, drying their eyes.

'What's up, Will? Why have you come back?' asked Joan, unsteadily, sniffing.

'Er—to get my slide-rule: I'd forgotten it,' he said. 'Bill wanted to trust his memory, but I think there's something wrong with his figures. I want to check up before we test the machine further. But—what's the matter with you two?'

'Oh, we're all right,' said Doll, strainedly and not very convincingly. She blew her nose, and endeavoured to pull herself together. But almost immediately she was overtaken by another burst of weeping, and Joan put her arms around her comfortingly.

'Look here,' said Will, in sudden and unusual exasperation, 'I've had about enough of this. You know what Bill and I are only too willing to deal with whatever you're worrying about. Yet the pair of you won't say a word—only cry and fret. How can we help if you won't tell us? Do you think we like to see you going on like this?'

'I'll tell you, Will,' said Joan quietly.

Doll emitted a muffled 'No!' but Joan ignored her, and went on: 'Don't you see that Bill has created another me in *every* detail? Every memory and every feeling? And because Doll thinks and feels exactly as I do, she's in love with you! She has been that way from the very beginning. All this time she's been trying to conquer it, to suppress it, and make Bill happy instead.'

Doll's shoulders shook with the intensity of her sobbing. Will laid his hands gently on them, consolingly. He could think of nothing whatever to say. He had not even dreamt of such a situation, obvious as it appeared now.

'Do you wonder the conflict got her down?' said Joan. 'Poor girl! I brought her here to be nearer to you, and that eased things for her.'

'But it didn't for you,' said Will, quietly, looking straight at her. 'I see now why you began to worry. Why didn't you tell me then, Joan?'

'How could I?'

He bit his lip, paced nervously over to the window, and stood with his back to the pair on the couch.

'What a position!' he thought. 'What can we do? Poor Bill!'

He wondered how he could break the sorry news to his best friend, and even as he wondered, the problem was solved for him.

From the window there was a view down the length of the wide, shallow valley, and a couple miles away the white concrete laboratory could just be seen nestling at the foot of one of the farther slopes. There were fields all around it, and a long row of great sturdy oak trees started from its northern corner.

From this height and distance the whole place looked like a table-top model. Will stared moodily at that little white box where Bill was, and tried to clarify his chaotic thoughts.

And suddenly, incredibly, before his eyes the distant white box spurted up in a dusty cloud of chalk-powder, and ere a particle of it had neared its topmost height, the whole of that part of the valley was split across by a curtain of searing, glaring flame. The whole string of oak trees, tough and amazingly deep-rooted though they were, floated up through the air like feathers of windblown thistledown before the blast of that mighty eruption.

The glaring flame vanished suddenly, like a light that had been turned out, and left a thick, brown, heaving fog in its place, a cloud of earth that had been pulverised. Will caught a glimpse of the torn oak trees falling back into this brown, rolling cloud, and then the blast wave, which had travelled up the valley, smote the house.

The window was instantly shattered and blown in, and he went flying backwards in a shower of glass fragments. He hit the floor awkwardly, and sprawled there, and only then did his laggard brain realise what had happened.

Bill's habitual impatience had at last been his undoing. He had refused to wait any longer for Will's return, and gone on with the test, trusting to his memory. And he had been wrong.

The harness had slipped.

THE FOUR-SIDED TRIANGLE

A man sat on a hill with a wide and lovely view of the country, bright in summer sunshine, spread before him. The rich green squares of the fields, the white ribbons of the lanes, the yellow blocks of haystacks and grey spires of village churches, made up a pattern infinitely pleasing to the eye.

And the bees hummed drowsily, nearby sheep and cattle made the noises of their kind, and a neighbouring thicket fairly rang with the unending chorus of a hundred birds.

But all this might as well have been set on another planet, for the man could neither see nor hear the happy environment. He was in hell.

It was a fortnight now since Bill had gone. When that grief had begun to wear off, it was succeeded by the most perplexing problem that had ever beset a member of the human race.

Will had been left to live with two women who loved him equally violently. Neither could ever conquer or suppress that love, whatever they did. They knew that.

On the other hand, Will was a person who was only capable of loving one of the women. Monogamy is deep-rooted in most normal people, and particularly so with Will. He had looked forward to travelling through life with one constant companion, and only one—Joan.

But now there were two Joans, identical in appearance, feeling, thought. Nevertheless, they were two separate people. And between them he was a torn and anguished man, with his domestic life in shapeless ruins.

He could not ease his mental torture with work, for since Bill died so tragically, he could not settle down to anything in a laboratory.

It was no easier for Joan and Doll. Probably harder. To have one's own self as a rival—even a friendly, understanding rival—for a man's companionship and affection was almost unbearable.

This afternoon they had both gone to a flying club, to attempt to escape for a while the burden of worry, apparently. Though neither was in a fit condition to fly, for they were tottering on the brink of a nervous breakdown.

The club was near the hill where Will was sitting and striving to find some working solution to a unique human problem which seemed quite unsoluble. So it was no coincidence that presently a humming in the sky caused him to lift dull eyes to see both the familiar monoplanes circling and curving across the blue spaces between the creamy, cumulus clouds.

He lay back on the grass watching them. He wondered which plane was which, but there was no means of telling, for they were similar models. And anyway, that would not tell him which was Joan and which was Doll, for they quite often used each other's planes, to keep the 'feel' of both. He wondered what they were thinking up there....

One of the planes straightened and flew away to the west, climbing as it went. Its rising drone became fainter. The other plane continued to bank and curve above.

Presently, Will closed his eyes and tried to doze in the warm sunlight. It was no use. In the darkness of his mind revolved the same old maddening images, doubts, and questions. It was as if he had become entangled in a nightmare from which he could not awake.

The engine of the plane overhead suddenly stopped. He opened his eyes, but could not locate it for a moment.

Then he saw it against the sun, and it was falling swiftly in a tailspin. It fell out of the direct glare of the sun, and he saw it in detail, revolving as it plunged so that the wings glinted like a flashing heliograph. He realised with a shock that it was but a few hundred feet from the ground.

He scrambled to his feet, in an awful agitation.

'Joan!' he cried, hoarsely. 'Joan!'

The machine continued its fall steadily and inevitably, spun down past his eye-level, and fell into the centre of one of the green squares of the fields below.

He started running down the hill even as it landed. As the sound of the crash reached him, he saw a rose of fire blossom like magic in that green square, and from it a wavering growth of black, oily smoke mounted into the heavens. The tears started from his eyes, and ran freely.

When he reached the scene, the inferno was past its worst, and as the flames died he saw that nothing was left, only black, shapeless, scattered things, unrecognisable as once human or once machine.

There was a squeal of brakes from the road. An ambulance had arrived from the flying club. Two men jumped out, burst through the hedge. It did not take them more than a few seconds to realise that there was no hope.

'Quick, Mr. Fredericks, jump in,' cried one of them, recognising Will. 'We must go straight to the other one.'

The other one!

Before he could question them, Will was hustled between

THE FOUR-SIDED TRIANGLE

them into the driving cabin of the ambulance. The vehicle was quickly reversed, and sped off in the opposite direction.

'Did—did the other plane—' began Will, and the words stuck in his throat.

The driver, with his eye on the road which was scudding under their wheels at sixty miles an hour, nodded grimly.

'Didn't you see, sir? They both crashed at exactly the same time, in the same way—tailspin. A shocking accident—terrible. I can't think how to express my sympathy, sir. I only pray that this one won't turn out so bad.'

It was as if the ability to feel had left Will. His thoughts slowed up almost to a standstill. He sat there numbed. He dare not try to think.

But, sluggishly, his thoughts went on. Joan and Doll had crashed at exactly the same time in exactly the same way. That was above coincidence. They must have both been thinking along the same lines again, and that meant they had crashed *deliberately!*

He saw now the whole irony of it, and groaned.

Joan and Doll had each tried to solve the problem in their own way, and each had reached the same conclusion without being aware what the other was thinking. They saw that one of them would have to step out of the picture if Will was ever to be happy. They knew that that one would have to step completely out, for life could no longer be tolerated by her if she had to lose Will.

And, characteristically, they had each made up their minds to be the self-sacrificing one.

Doll felt that she was an intruder, wrecking the lives of a happily married pair. It was no fault of hers: she had not asked to be created full of love for a man she could never have.

But she felt that she was leading an unnecessary existence, and every moment of it was hurting the man she loved. So she decided to relinquish the gift of life.

Joan's reasoning was that she had been partly responsible for bringing Doll into this world, unasked, and with exactly similar feelings and longings as herself. Ever since she had expected, those feelings had been ungratified, cruelly crushed and thwarted. It wasn't fair. Doll had as much right to happiness as she. Joan had enjoyed her period of happiness with Will. Now let Doll enjoy hers.

So it was that two planes, a mile apart, went spinning into crashes that were meant to appear accidental—and did, except to one man, the one who most of all was intended never to know the truth.

The driver was speaking again.

'It was a ghastly dilemma for us at the club. We saw 'em come down on opposite sides and both catch fire. We have only one fire engine, one ambulance. Had to send the engine to one, and rush this ambulance to the other. The engine couldn't have done any good at this end, as it happens. Hope it was in time where we're going!'

Will's dulled mind seemed to take this in quite detachedly. Who had been killed in the crash he saw? Joan or Doll? Joan or Doll?

Then suddenly it burst upon him that it was only the original Joan that he loved. That was the person whom he had known so long, around whom his affection had centred. The hair he had caressed, the lips he had pressed, the gay brown eyes which had smiled into his. He had never touched Doll in that way.

Doll seemed but a shadow of all that. She may have had memories of those happenings, but she had never actually experienced them. They were only artificial memories. Yet they must have seemed real enough to her.

The ambulance arrived at the scene of the second crash.

The plane had flattened out a few feet from the ground, and not landed so disastrously as the other. It lay crumpled athwart a burned and blackened hedge. The fire engine had quenched the flames within a few minutes. And the pilot had been dragged clear, unconscious, badly knocked about and burned.

They got her into the ambulance, and rushed her to a hospital.

Will had been sitting by the bedside for three hours before the girl in the bed had opened her eyes.

Blank, brown eyes they were, which looked at him, then at the hospital ward, without the faintest change of expression.

'Joan!' he whispered, clasping her free arm—the other was in a splint. There was no response of any sort. She lay back gazing unseeingly at the ceiling. He licked his dry lips. It couldn't be Joan after all.

'Doll!' he tried. 'Do you feel all right?'

Still no response.

'I know that expression,' said the doctor, who was standing by. 'She's lost her memory.'

THE FOUR-SIDED TRIANGLE

'For good, do you think?' asked Will, perturbed.

The doctor pursed his lips indicating he didn't know.

'Good lord! Is there no way of finding out whether she is my wife or my sister-in-law?'

'If you don't know, no one does, Mr. Fredericks,' replied the doctor. 'We can't tell which plane who was in. We can't tell anything from her clothes, for they were burned in the crash, and destroyed before we realized their importance. We've often remarked their uncanny resemblance. Certainly you can tell them apart.'

'I can't!' answered Will, in anguish. 'There is no way.'

The next day, the patient had largely recovered her senses, and was able to sit up and talk. But a whole tract of her memory had been obliterated. She remembered nothing of her twin, and in fact nothing at all of the events after the duplication experiment.

Lying on the couch in the laboratory, preparing herself under the direction of Bill, was the last scene she remembered.

The hospital psychologist said that the shock of the crash had caused her to unconsciously repress a part of her life which she did not want to remember. She could not remember now if she wanted to. He said she might discover the truth from her eventually, but if he did, it would take months—maybe even years.

But naturally her memories of Will, and their marriage, were intact, and she loved him as strongly as ever.

Was she Joan or Doll?

Will spent a sleepless night, turning the matter over. Did it really matter? There was only one left now—why not assume she was Joan, and carry on? But he knew that as long as doubt and uncertainty existed, he would never be able to recover the old free life he had had with Joan.

It seemed that he would have to surrender her to the psychologist, and that would bring to light all sorts of details which neither he, Joan, nor Bill had ever wished to be revealed.

But the next day something turned up which changed the face of things.

While he was sitting at the bedside, conversing with the girl who might or might not be Joan, a nurse told him a man was waiting outside to see him. He went, and found a police officer standing there.

Ever since the catastrophe which had wrecked Bill's laboratory, the police had been looking around that locality, searching for any possible clues.

Buried in the ground they had found a safe, burst and broken. Inside were the charred remains of books, papers, and letters. They had examined them, without gleaning much, and now the officer wished to know if Will could gather anything from them.

Will took the bundle and went through it. There was a packet of purely personal letters, and some old tradesmen's accounts, paid and receipted. These with the officer's consent, were destroyed. But also there were the burnt remains of three of Bill's experimental notebooks.

They were written in Bill's system of shorthand, which Will understood. The first two were old, and of no particular interest. The last, however—unfortunately the most badly charred of the three—was an account of Bill's attempts to infuse life into his replicas of living creatures.

The last pages were about the experiment of creating another Joan, and the last recognisable entry read:

'This clumsy business of pumping through pipes, in the manner of a blood transfusion, left a small scar at the base of Doll's neck, the only flaw in an otherwise perfect copy of Joan. I resented. . . .'

The rest was burned away.

To the astonishment of the police inspector, Will turned without saying a word and hurried back into the ward.

'Let me examine your neck, dear, I want to see if you've been biting yourself,' he said, with a false lightness.

Wondering, the girl allowed herself to be examined.

There was not the slightest sign of a scar anywhere on her neck.

'You are Joan,' he said, and embraced her as satisfactorily as her injuries would permit.

'I am Joan,' she repeated, kissing and hugging him back.

And at last they knew again the blessedness of peace of mind.

For once, Fate, which had used them so hardly, showed mercy, and they never knew that in the packet of Bill's receipted accounts, which Will had destroyed, was one from a plastic surgeon, which began:

'To removing operation scar from neck, and two days' nursing and attention.'

STAR BRIGHT *Argosy*, November

by Jack Williamson (1908–   )

Jack Williamson has been witness to the development of modern science fiction as reader, writer, and scholar. He has produced a solid body of work spanning fifty years, and has had little trouble in keeping up with the competition. Still writing today, he will always be remembered for his "Legion of Space" and "Seetee" stories, although there is much more in his canon, most notably THE HUMANOIDS (1949) and that wonderful fantasy, DARKER THAN YOU THINK (1940, in book form 1948). The best of his short fiction is available in THE BEST OF JACK WILLIAMSON, 1978.

Jack did not include this story in the latter collection, although he did select it for MY BEST SCIENCE FICTION STORY in 1949. He should have, because even though tastes change, this is a powerful story of hope, of desperation, and of a form of fulfillment.

(Once John Campbell took over Astounding and began to remold science fiction, many of the star writers of the previous decade fell by the way. There was the kind of slaughter we associate with the passing of the silents and the coming of the talkies. There were survivors, though, and one of the most remarkable of these was Jack Williamson whose Legion of Space had dazzled my teen-age years and who now went on to adapt himself, effortlessly, to Campbell's standards. IA)

Mr. Jason Peabody got off the street car. Taking a great, relieved breath of the open air, he started walking up Bannister Hill. His worried eyes saw the first pale star come out of the dusk ahead.

It made him grope back wistfully into the mists of childhood, for the magic of words he once had known. He whispered the chant of power:

> *Star light, star bright,*
> *First star I've seen tonight,*
> *I wish I may, I wish I might,*
> *Have the wish I wish tonight.*

Mr. Peabody was a brown, bald little wisp of a man. Now defiantly erect, his thin shoulders still betrayed the stoop they had got from twenty years of bending over adding machines and ledgers. His usually meek face now had a hurt and desperate look.

"I wish—"

With his hopeful eyes on the star, Mr. Peabody hesitated. His harried mind went back to the painful domestic scene from which he had just escaped. A wry little smile came to his troubled face.

"I wish," he told the star, "that I could work miracles!"

The star faded to a pale malevolent red.

"You've got to work miracles," added Mr. Peabody, "to bring up a family on a bookkeeper's pay. A family, that is, like mine."

The star winked green with promise.

Mr. Peabody still owed thirteen thousand dollars on the little stucco house, two blocks off the Locust Avenue car line: the payments were as easy as rent, and in ten more years it would be his own. Ella met him at the door, this afternoon, with a moist kiss.

Ella was Mrs. Peabody. She was a statuesque blonde, an inch taller than himself, with a remarkable voice. Her clinging kiss made him uneasy. He knew instantly, from twenty-two years of experience, that it meant she wanted something.

"It's good to be home, dear." He tried to start a counter-campaign. "Things were tough at the office today." His tired sigh was real enough. "Old Berg has fired until we're all doing two men's work. I don't know who will be next."

"I'm sorry, darling." She kissed him moistly again, and her

voice was tenderly sympathetic. "Now get washed. I want to have dinner early, because tonight is Delphian League."

Her voice was too sweet. Mr. Peabody wondered what she wanted. It always took her a good while to work up to the point. When she arrived there, however, she was likely to be invincible. He made another feeble effort.

"I don't know what things are coming to." He made a weary shrug. "Berg is threatening to cut our pay. With the insurance, and the house payments, and the children, I don't see how we'd live."

Ella Peabody came back to him, and put her soft arm around him. She smelled faintly of the perfume she had used on the evening before, faintly of kitchen odors.

"We'll manage, dear," she said bravely.

She began to talk brightly of the small events of the day. Her duties in the kitchen caused no interruption. Her remarkable voice reached him clearly, even through the closed bathroom door.

With an exaggerated show of fatigue, Mr. Peabody settled himself into an easy chair. He found the morning paper—which he never had time to read in the morning—opened it, and then dropped it across his knees as if too tired to read. Feebly attempting another diversion, he asked:

"Where are the children?"

"William is out to see the man about his car."

Mr. Peabody forgot his fatigue.

"I told William he couldn't have a car," he said, with some heat. "I told him he's too young and irresponsible. If he insists on buying some pile of junk, he'll have to pay for it himself. Don't ask me how."

"And Beth," Mrs. Peabody's voice continued, "is down at the beauty shop." She came to the kitchen door. "But I have the most thrilling news for you, darling!"

The lilt in her voice told Mr. Peabody to expect the worst. The dreaded moment had come. Desperately he lifted the paper from his knees, became absorbed in it.

"Yes, dear," he said. "Here—I see the champ is going to take on this Australian palooka, if—"

"Darling, did you hear me?" Ella Peabody's penetrating voice could not be ignored. "At the Delphian League tonight, I'm going to read a paper on the Transcendental Renaissance. Isn't that a perfectly gorgeous opportunity?"

Mr. Peabody dropped the paper. He was puzzled. The

liquid sparkle in her voice was proof enough that her moment of victory was at hand. Yet her purpose was still unrevealed.

"Ella, dear," he inquired meekly, "what do you know about the Transcendental Renaissance?"

"Don't worry about that, darling. The young man at the library did the research and typed the paper for me, for only ten dollars. But it's so sweet of you to want to help me, and there's one thing that you can do."

Mr. Peabody squirmed uncomfortably in his chair. The trap was closing, and he could see no escape.

"I knew you'd understand, darling." Her voice had a little tender throb. "And you know I didn't have a decent rag to wear. Darling, I'm getting that blue jersey that was in the window of the Famous. It was marked sixty-nine eighty, but the manager let me have it for only forty-nine ninety-five."

"I'm awfully sorry, dear," Mr. Peabody said slowly. "But I'm afraid we simply can't manage it. I'm afraid you had better send it back."

Ella's blue eyes widened, and began to glitter.

"Darling!" Her throbbing voice broke. "Darling—you must understand. I can't read my paper in those disgraceful old rags. Besides, it has already been altered."

"But, dear—we just haven't got the money."

Mr. Peabody picked up his paper again, upside down. After twenty-two years, he knew what was to come. There would be tearful appeals to his love and his pride and his duty. There would be an agony of emotion, maintained until he surrendered.

And he couldn't surrender: that was the trouble. In twenty-two years, his affection had never swerved seriously from his wife and his children. He would have given her the money, gladly; but the bills had to be paid tomorrow.

He sighed with momentary relief when an unfamiliar motor horn honked outside the drive. William Peabody slouched, in ungraceful indolence, through the side door.

William was a lank, pimpled sallow-faced youth, with unkempt yellow hair and prominent buck teeth. Remarkably, in spite of the fact that he was continually demanding money for clothing, he always wore the same dingy leather jacket and the same baggy pants.

Efforts to send him to the university, to a television school, and to a barber college, had all collapsed for want of William's cooperation.

"Hi, Gov." He was filling a black college-man pipe. "Hi, Mom. Dinner up?"

"Don't call me Gov," requested Mr. Peabody, mildly. "William!" He had risen and walked to the window, and his voice was sharper. "Whose red roadster is that in the drive?"

William dropped himself into the easy chair which Mr. Peabody had just vacated.

"Oh, the car?" He exhaled blue smoke. "Why, didn't Mom tell you, Gov? I just picked it up."

Mr. Peabody's slight body stiffened.

"So you bought a car? Who's going to pay for it?"

William waved the pipe, carelessly.

"Only twenty a month," he drawled. "And it's a real buy, Gov. Only eighty thousand miles, and it's got a radio. Mom said you could manage it. It will be for my birthday, Gov."

"Your birthday is six months off."

Silver, soothing, Mrs. Peabody's voice floated from the kitchen:

"But you'll still be paying for it when his birthday comes, Jason. So I told Bill it would be all right. A boy is so left out these days, if he hasn't a car. Now, if you will just give me the suit money—"

Mr. Peabody began a sputtering reply. He stopped suddenly, when his daughter Beth came in the front door. Beth was the bright spot in his life. She was a tall slim girl, with soft sympathetic brown eyes. Her honey-colored hair was freshly set in exquisite waves.

Perhaps it was natural for father to favor daughter. But Mr. Peabody couldn't help contrasting her cheerful industry to William's idleness. She was taking a business course, so that she would be able to keep books for Dr. Rex Brant, after they were married.

"Hello, Dad." She came to him and put her smooth arms around him and gave him an affectionate little squeeze. "How do you like my new permanent? I got it because I have a date with Rex tonight. I didn't have enough money, so I said I would leave the other three dollars at Mrs. Larkin's before seven. Have you got three dollars, Dad?"

"Your hair looks pretty, dear."

Mr. Peabody patted his daughter's shoulder, and dug cheerfully into his pocket. He never minded giving money to Beth—when he had it. Often he regretted that he had not been able to do more for her.

"Thanks, Dad." Kissing his temple, she whispered, "You dear!"

Tapping out his black pipe, William looked at his mother.

"It just goes to show," he drawled. "If it was Sis that wanted a car—"

"I told you, son," Mr. Peabody declared positively, "I'm not going to pay for that automobile. We simply haven't the money."

William got languidly to his feet.

"I say, Gov. You wouldn't want to lose your fishing tackle."

Mr. Peabody's face stiffened with anxiety.

"My fishing tackle?"

In twenty-two years, Mr. Peabody had actually found the time and money to make no more than three fishing trips. He still considered himself, however, an ardent angler. Sometimes he had gone without his lunches, for weeks, to save for some rod or reel or special fly. He often spent an hour in the back yard, casting at a mark on the ground.

Trying to glare at William, he demanded hoarsely:

"What about my fishing tackle?"

"Now, Jason," interrupted the soothing voice of Mrs. Peabody, "don't get yourself all wrought up. You know you haven't used your old fishing tackle in the last ten years."

Stiffly erect, Mr. Peabody strode toward his taller son.

"William, what have you done with it?"

William was filling his pipe again.

"Keep your shirt on, Gov," he advised. "Mom said it would be all right. And I had to have the dough to make the first payment on the bus. Now don't bust an artery. I'll give you the pawn tickets."

"Bill!" Beth's voice was sharp with reproof. "You *didn't*—"

Mr. Peabody, himself, made a gasping incoherent sound. He started blindly toward the front door.

"Now, Jason!" Ella's voice was silver with a sweet and unendurable reason. "Control yourself, Jason. You haven't had your dinner—"

He slammed the door violently behind him.

This was not the first time in twenty-two years that Mr. Peabody had fled to the windy freedom of Bannister Hill. It was not even the first time he had spoken a wish to a star. While he had no serious faith in that superstition of his childhood, he still felt that it was a very pleasant idea.

An instant after the words were uttered, he saw the shooting star. A tiny point of light, drifting a little upward through the purple dusk. It was not white, like most falling stars, but palely green.

It recalled another old belief, akin to the first. If you saw a falling star, and if you could make a wish before the star went out, the wish would come true. Eagerly, he caught his breath.

"I wish," he repeated, "I could do miracles!"

He finished the words in time. The star was still shining. Suddenly, in fact, he noticed that its greenish radiance was growing brighter.

Far brighter! And exploding!

Abruptly, then, Mr. Peabody's vague and wistful satisfaction changed to stark panic. He realized that one fragment of the green meteor, like some celestial bullet, was coming straight at him! He made a frantic effort to duck, to shield his face with his hand—

Mr. Peabody woke, lying on his back on the grassy hill. He groaned and lifted his head. The waning moon had risen. Its slanting rays shimmered from the dew on the grass.

Mr. Peabody felt stiff and chilled. His clothing was wet with the dew. And something was wrong with his head. Deep at the base of his brain, there was a queer dull ache. It was not intense, but it had a slow, unpleasant pulsation.

His forehead felt oddly stiff and drawn. His fingers found a streak of dried blood, and then the ragged, painful edge of a small wound.

"Golly!"

With that little gasping cry, he clapped his hand to the back of his head. But there was no blood in his hair. That small leaden ache seemed close beneath his hand, but there was no other surface wound.

"Great golly!" whispered Mr. Peabody. "It has lodged in my brain!"

The evidence was clear enough. He had seen the meteor hurtling straight at him. There was a tiny hole in his forehead, where it must have entered. There was none where it could have emerged.

Why hadn't it already killed him? Perhaps because the heat of it had cauterized the wound. He remembered reading a believe-it-or-not about a man who had lived for years with a bullet in his brain.

A meteor lodged in his brain! The idea set him to shuddering. He and Ella had met their little ups and downs, but his life had been pretty uneventful. He could imagine being shot by a bandit or run over by a taxi. But this—

"Better go to Beth's Dr. Brant," he whispered.

He touched his bleeding forehead, and hoped the wound would heal safely. When he tried to rise, a faintness seized him. A sudden thirst parched his throat.

"Water!" he breathed.

As he sank giddily back on his elbow, that thirst set in his mind the image of a sparkling glass of water. It sat on a flat rock, glittering in the moonlight. It looked so substantial that he reached out and picked it up.

Without surprise, he drank. A few swallows relieved his thirst, and his mind cleared again. Then the sudden realization of the incredible set him to quivering with reasonless panic.

The glass dropped out of his fingers, and shattered on the rock. The fragments glittered mockingly under the moon. Mr. Peabody blinked at them.

"It was real!" he whispered. "I made it real—out of nothing. A miracle—I worked a miracle!"

The word was queerly comforting. Actually, he knew no more about what had happened than before he had found a word for it. Yet much of its disquieting unfamiliarity was dispelled.

He remembered a movie that the Englishman, H. G. Wells, had written. It dealt with a man who was able to perform the most surprising and sometimes appalling miracles. He had finished, Mr. Peabody recalled, by destroying the world.

"I want nothing like that," he whispered in some alarm, and then set out to test his gift. First he tried mentally to lift the small flat rock upon which the miraculous glass had stood.

"Up," he commanded sharply. "Up!"

The rock, however, refused to move. He tried to form a mental picture of it, rising. Suddenly, where he had tried to picture it, there was another and apparently identical rock.

The miraculous stone crashed instantly down upon its twin, and shattered. Flying fragments stung Mr. Peabody's face. He realized that his gift, whatever his nature, held potentialities of danger.

"Whatever I've got," he told himself, "it's different from what the man had in the movie. I can make things—small things, anyhow. But I can't move them." He sat up on the wet grass. "Can I—unmake them?"

He fixed his eyes upon the fragments of the broken glass.

"Go!" he ordered. "Go away—vanish!"

They shimmered unchanged in the moonlight.

"No," concluded Mr. Peabody, "I can't unmake things."

That was, in a way, too bad.

He made another mental note of caution. Large animals and dangerous creations of all kinds had better be avoided. He realized suddenly that he was shivering in his dew-soaked clothing. He slapped his stiff hands against his sides, and wished he had a cup of coffee.

"Well—why not?" He tried to steady his voice against a haunting apprehension. "Here—a cup of coffee!"

Nothing appeared.

"Come!" he shouted. "Coffee!"

Still there was nothing. And doubt returned to Mr. Peabody. Probably he had just been dazed by the meteor. But the hallucinations had looked so queerly real. That glass of water, glittering in the moonlight on the rock—

And there it was again!

Or another, just like it. He touched the glass uncertainly, sipped at the ice-cold water. It was as real as you please. Mr. Peabody shook his bald aching head, baffled.

"Water's easy," he muttered. "But how do you get coffee?"

He let his mind picture a heavy white cup, sitting in its saucer on the rock, steaming fragrantly. The image of it shimmered oddly, half-real.

He made a kind of groping effort. There was a strange brief roaring in his head, beyond that slow painful throb. And suddenly the cup was real.

With awed and trembling fingers, he lifted it. The scalding coffee tasted like the cheaper kind that Ella bought when she was having trouble with the budget. But it was coffee.

Now he knew how to get the cream and sugar. He simply pictured the little creamer and the three white cubes, and made that special grasping effort—and there they were. And he was weak with a momentary unfamiliar fatigue.

He made a spoon and stirred the coffee. He was learning about the gift. It made no difference what he said. He had only the power to *realize* the things he pictured in his mind. It required a peculiar kind of effort, and the act was accompanied by that mighty, far-off roaring in his ears.

The miraculous objects, moreover, had all the imperfections of his mental images. There was an irregular gap in the heavy saucer, behind the cup—where he had failed to complete his picture of it.

Mr. Peabody, however, did not linger long upon the mechanistic details of his gift. Perhaps Dr. Brant would be able to explain it: he was really a very clever young surgeon. Mr. Peabody turned to more immediate concerns.

He was shivering with cold. He decided against building a miraculous fire, and set out to make himself an overcoat. This turned out to be more difficult than he had anticipated. It was necessary to picture clearly the fibers of the wool, the details of buttons and buckle, the shape of every piece of material, the very thread in the seams.

In some way, moreover, the process of materializing was very trying. He was soon quivering with a strange fatigue. The dull little ache at the base of his brain throbbed faster. Again he sensed that roaring beyond, like some Niagara of supernal power.

At last, however, the garment was finished. Attempting to put it on, Mr. Peabody discovered that it was a very poor fit. The shoulders were grotesquely loose. What was worse, he had somehow got the sleeves sewed up at the cuffs.

Wearily, his bright dreams dashed a little, he drew it about his shoulders like a cloak. With a little care and practice, he was sure, he could do better. He ought to be able to make anything he wanted.

Feeling a tired contentment, Mr. Peabody started back down Bannister Hill. Now he could go home to a triumphant peace. His cold body anticipated the comforts of his house and his bed. He dwelt pleasantly upon the happiness of Ella and William and Beth, when they should learn about his gift.

He pushed the ungainly overcoat into a trash container, and swung aboard the car. Fumbling for change to pay the twenty-cent fare, he found one lone dime. A miraculous twin solved the problem. He relaxed on the seat with a sigh of quiet satisfaction.

His son, William, as it happened, was the first person to whom Mr. Peabody attempted to reveal his unusual gift. William was sprawled in the easiest chair, his sallow face decorated with scraps of court plaster. He woke with a start. His eyes rolled glassily. Seeing Mr. Peabody, he grinned with relief.

"Hi, Gov," he drawled. "Got over your tantrum, huh?"

STAR BRIGHT

Consciousness of the gift lent Mr. Peabody a new authority.

"Don't call me Gov." His voice was louder than usual. "I wasn't having a tantrum." He felt a sudden apprehension. "What has happened to you, William?"

William fumbled lazily for his pipe.

"Guy crocked me," he drawled. "Some fool in a new Buick. Claims I was on his side of the road. He called the cops, and had a wrecker tow off the bus.

"Guess you'll have a little damage suit on your hands, Gov. Unless you want to settle for cash. The wrecker man said the bill would be about nine hundred. . . . Got any tobacco, Gov?"

The old helpless fury boiled up in Mr. Peabody. He began to tremble, and his fists clenched. After a moment, however, the awareness of his new power allowed him to smile. Things were going to be different now.

"William," he said gravely, "I would like to see a little more respect in your manner in the future." He was building up to the dramatic revelation of his gift. "It was your car and your wreck. You can settle it as you like."

William gestured carelessly with his pipe.

"Wrong as usual, Gov. You see, they wouldn't sell *me* the car. I had to get Mom to sign the papers. So you can't slip out of it that easy, Gov. You're the one that's liable. Got any tobacco?"

A second wave of fury set Mr. Peabody to dancing up and down. Once more, however, consciousness of the gift came to his rescue. He decided upon a double miracle. That ought to put William in his place.

"There's your tobacco." He gestured toward the bare center of the library table. "Look!" He concentrated upon a mental image of the red tin container. "Presto!"

William's mild curiosity changed to a quickly concealed surprise. Lazily he reached for the tin box, drawling:

"Fair enough, Gov. But that magician at the Palace last year pulled the same trick a lot slicker and quicker—" He looked up from the open can, with a triumphant reproof. "Empty, Gov. I call that a pretty flat trick."

"I forgot." Mr. Peabody bit his lip. "You'll find half a can on my dresser."

As William ambled out of the room, he applied himself to a graver project. In his discomfiture and general excitement, he failed to consider a certain limitation upon acts of creation, miraculous or otherwise, existing through Federal law.

His flat pocketbook yielded what was left of the week's pay. He selected a crisp new ten-dollar bill, and concentrated on it. His first copy proved to be blank on the reverse. The second was blurred on both sides. After that, however, he seemed to get the knack of it.

By the time William came swaggering back, lighting up his pipe, there was a neat little stack of miraculous money on the table. Mr. Peabody leaned back in his chair, closing his eyes. That pulsing ache diminished again, and the roar of power receded.

"Here, William," he said in a voice of weary triumph. "You said you needed nine hundred to settle for your wreck."

He counted off the bills, while William stared at him, mouth open and buck teeth gleaming.

"Whatsis, Gov?" he gasped. A note of alarm entered his voice. "Where have you been tonight, Gov? Old Berg didn't leave the safe open?"

"If you want the money, take it," Mr. Peabody said sharply. "And watch your language, son."

William picked up the bills. He stared at them incredulously for a moment, and then stuffed them into his pocket and ran out of the house.

His mind hazy with fatigue, Mr. Peabody relaxed in the big chair. A deep satisfaction filled him. This was one use of the gift which hadn't gone wrong. There was enough of the miraculous money left so that he could give Ella the fifty dollars she wanted. And he could make more, without limit.

A fly came buzzing into the lamplight. Watching it settle upon a candy box on the table, and crawl across the picture of a cherry, Mr. Peabody was moved to another experiment. A mere instant of effort created another fly!

Only one thing was wrong with the miraculous insect. It looked, so far as he could see, exactly like the original. But, when he reached his hand toward it, it didn't move. It wasn't alive.

Why? Mr. Peabody was vaguely bewildered. Did he merely lack some special knack that was necessary for the creation of life? Or was that completely beyond his new power, mysteriously forbidden?

He applied himself to experiment. The problem was still unsolved, although the table was scattered with lifeless flies and the inert forms of a cockroach, a frog, and a sparrow, when he heard the front door.

Mrs. Peabody came in. She was wearing the new blue suit. The trim lines of it seemed to give a new youth to her ample figure, and Mr. Peabody thought that she looked almost beautiful.

She was still angry. She returned his greeting with a stiff little nod, and started regally past him toward the stair. Mr. Peabody followed her anxiously.

"That's your new suit, Ella? You look pretty in it."

With a queen's dignity, she turned. The lamplight shimmered on her blonde indignant head.

"Thank you, Jason." Her voice was cool. "I had no money to pay the boy. It was most embarrassing. He finally left it, when I promised to take the money to the store in the morning."

Mr. Peabody counted off ten of the miraculous bills.

"Here it is, dear," he said. "And fifty more."

Ella was staring, her jaw hanging.

Mr. Peabody smiled at her.

"From now on, dear," he promised her, "things are going to be different. Now I'll be able to give you everything that you've always deserved."

Puzzled alarm tensed Ella Peabody's face, and she came swiftly toward him.

"What's this you say, Jason?"

She saw the lifeless flies that he had made, and then started back with a little muffled cry from the cockroach, the frog, and the sparrow.

"What are these things?" Her voice was shrill. "What are you up to?"

A pang of fear struck into Mr. Peabody's heart. He perceived that it was going to be difficult for other people to understand his gift. The best plan was probably a candid demonstration of it.

"Watch, Ella. I'll show you."

He shuffled through the magazines on the end of the table. He had learned that it was difficult to materialize anything accurately from memory alone. He needed a model.

"Here." He had found an advertisement that showed a platinum bracelet set with diamonds. "Would you like this, my dear?"

Mrs. Peabody retreated from him, growing pale.

"Jason, are you crazy?" Her voice was quick and apprehensive. "You know you can't pay for the few things I simply must have. Now—this money—diamonds—I don't understand you!"

Mr. Peabody dropped the magazine on his knees. Trying to close his ears to Ella's penetrating voice, he began to concentrate on the jewel. This was more difficult than the paper money had been. His head rang with that throbbing pain. But he completed that peculiar final effort, and the thing was done.

"Well—do you like it, my dear?"

He held it toward her. The gleaming white platinum had a satisfying weight. The diamonds glittered with a genuine fire. But she made no move to take it.

Her bewildered face went paler. A hard accusing stare came into her eyes. Suddenly she advanced upon him, demanding:

"Jason, where did you get that bracelet?"

"I—I made it." His voice was thin and husky. "It's—miraculous."

Her determined expression made that statement sound very thin, even to Mr. Peabody.

"Miraculous lie!" She sniffed the air. "Jason, I believe you are drunk!" She advanced on him again. "Now I want to know the truth. What have you done? Have you been—stealing?"

She snatched the bracelet from his fingers, shook it threateningly in front of him.

"Now where did you get it?"

Looking uneasily about, Mr. Peabody saw the kitchen door opening slowly. William peered cautiously through. He was pale, and his trembling hand clutched a long bread knife.

"Mom!" His whisper was hoarse. "Mom, you had better watch out! The Gov is acting plenty weird. He was trying to pull some crummy magic stunts. And then he gave me a bale of queer."

His slightly bulging eyes caught the glitter of the dangling bracelet, and he started.

"Hot ice, huh?" His voice grew hard with an incredible moral indignation. "Gov, cantcher remember you got a decent respectable family? Hot jools, and pushing the queer! Gov, how could you?"

"Queer?" The word croaked faintly from Mr. Peabody's dry throat. "What do you mean—queer?"

"The innocence gag, huh?" William sniffed. "Well, let me

tell you, Gov. Queer is counterfeit. I thought that dough looked funny. So I took it down to a guy at the pool hall that used to shove it. A mess, he says. A blind man could spot it. It ain't worth a nickel on the dollar. It's a sure ticket, he says, for fifteen years!"

This was a turn of affairs for which Mr. Peabody had not prepared himself. An instant's reflection told him that, failing in his confusion to distinguish the token of value from the value itself, he had indeed been guilty.

"Counterfeit—"

He stared dazedly at the tense suspicious faces of his wife and son. A chill of ultimate frustration was creeping into him. He collected himself to fight it.

"I didn't—didn't think," he stammered. "We'll have to burn the money that I gave you, too, Ella."

He mopped at his wet forehead, and caught his breath.

"But look." His voice was louder. "I've still got the gift. I can make anything I want—out of nothing at all. I'll show you. I'll make—I'll make you a brick of gold."

His wife retreated, her face white and stiff with dread. William made an ominous flourish with the bread knife, and peered watchfully.

"All right, Gov. Strut your stuff."

There couldn't be any crime about making real gold. But the project proved more difficult than Mr. Peabody had expected. The first dim outlines of the brick began to waver, and he felt sick and dizzy.

The steady beat of pain filled all his head, stronger than it had ever been. The rush of unseen power became a mighty hurricane, blowing away his consciousness. Desperately, he clutched at the back of a chair.

The massive yellow ingot at last shimmered real, under the lamp. Mopping weakly at the sweat on his face, Mr. Peabody made a gesture of weary triumph and sat down.

"What's the matter, darling?" his wife said anxiously. "You look so tired and white. Are you ill?"

William's hands were already clutching at the yellow block. He lifted one end of it, with an effort, and let it fall. It made a dull solid thud.

"Gosh, Gov!" William whispered. "It *is* gold!" His eyes popped again, and narrowed grimly. "Better quit trying to string us, Gov. You cracked a safe tonight."

"But I made it." Mr. Peabody rose in anxious protest. "You saw me."

Ella caught his arm, steadied him.

"We know, Jason," she said soothingly. "But now you look so tired. You had better come up to bed. You'll feel better in the morning."

Digging into the gold brick with his pocket knife, William cried out excitedly:

"Hey, Mom! Lookit—"

With a finger on her lips and a significant nod, Mrs. Peabody silenced her son. She helped Mr. Peabody up the stairs, to the door of their bedroom, and then hurried back to William.

Mr. Peabody undressed wearily and put on his pajamas. With a tired little sigh, he snuggled down under the sheets and closed his eyes.

Naturally he had made little mistakes at first, but now everything was sure to be all right. With just a little more practice, he would be able to give his wife and children all the good things they deserved.

"Daddy?"

Mr. Peabody opened his eyes, and saw Beth standing beside the bed. Her brown eyes looked wide and strange, and her voice was anxious.

"Daddy, what dreadful thing has happened to you?"

Mr. Peabody reached from beneath the sheet, and took her hand. It felt tense and cold.

"A very wonderful thing, Bee, dear," he said. "Not dreadful at all. I simply have a miraculous gift. I can create things. I want to make something for you. What would you like, Bee? A pearl necklace, maybe?"

"Dad—darling!"

Her voice was choked with concern. She sat down on the side of the bed, and looked anxiously into his face. Her cold hand quivered in his.

"Dad, you aren't—insane?"

Mr. Peabody felt a tremor of ungovernable apprehension.

"Of course not, daughter. Why?"

"Mother and Bill have been telling me the most horrid things," she whispered, staring at him. "They said you were playing with dead flies and a cockroach, and saying you could work miracles, and giving them counterfeit money and stolen jewelry and a fake gold brick—"

"Fake?" He gulped. "No; it was real gold."

Beth shook her troubled head.

STAR BRIGHT

"Bill showed me," she whispered. "It looks like gold on the outside. But when you scratch it, it's only lead."

Mr. Peabody felt sick. He couldn't help tears of frustration from welling into his eyes.

"I tried," he sobbed. "I don't know why everything goes wrong." He caught a determined breath, and sat up in bed. "But I *can* make gold—real gold. I'll show you."

"Dad!" Her voice was low and dry and breathless. "Dad, you *are* going insane." Quivering hands covered her face. "Mother and Bill were right," she sobbed faintly. "But the police—oh, I can't stand it!"

"Police?" Mr. Peabody leaped out of bed. "What about the police?"

The girl moved slowly back, watching him with dark, frightened eyes.

"Mother and Bill phoned them, before I came in. They think you're insane, and mixed up in some horrid crimes besides. They're afraid of you."

Twisting his hands together, Mr. Peabody padded fearfully to the window. He had an instinctive dread of the law, and his wide reading of detective stories had given him a horror of the third degree.

"They mustn't catch me!" he whispered hoarsely. "They wouldn't believe, about my gift. Nobody does. They'd grill me about the counterfeit and the gold brick and the bracelet. Grill me!" He shuddered convulsively. "Bee, I've got to get away!"

"Dad, you mustn't." She caught his arm, protestingly. "They'll catch you, in the end. Running away will only make you seem guilty."

He pushed away her hand.

"I've got to get away, I tell you. I don't know where. If there were only someone who would understand—"

"Dad, listen!" Beth clapped her hands together, making a sound from which he started violently. "You must go to Rex. He can help you. Will you Dad?"

After a moment, Mr. Peabody nodded.

"He's a doctor. He might understand."

"I'll phone him to expect you. And you get dressed."

He was tying his shoes, when she ran back into the room. "Two policemen, downstairs," she whispered. "Rex said he would wait up for you. But now you can't get out—"

Her voice dropped with amazement, as a coil of rope appeared magically upon the carpet. Mr. Peabody hastily knotted one end of it to the bedstead, and tossed the other out the window.

"Goodby, Bee," he gasped. "Dr. Rex will let you know."

She hastily thumb-bolted the door, as an authoritative hammering began on the other side. Mrs. Peabody's remarkable voice came unimpeded through the panels:

"Jason! Open the door, this instant. Ja-a-a-son!"

Mr. Peabody was still several feet from the ground when the miraculous rope parted unexpectedly. He pulled himself out of a shattered trellis, glimpsed the black police sedan parked in front of the house, and started down the alley.

Trembling from the peril and exertion of his flight across the town, he found the door of Dr. Brant's modest two-room apartment unlocked. He let himself in quietly. The young doctor laid aside a book and stood up, smiling, to greet him.

"I'm glad to see you, Mr. Peabody. Won't you sit down and tell me about yourself?"

Breathless, Mr. Peabody leaned against the closed door. He thought that Brant was at once too warm and too watchful. It came to him that he must yet step very cautiously to keep out of a worse predicament than he had just escaped.

"Beth probably phoned you to expect a lunatic," he began. "But I'm not insane, doctor. Not yet. I have simply happened to acquire a unique gift. People won't believe that it exists. They misunderstand me, suspect me."

Depite his effort for a calm, convincing restraint, his voice shook with bitterness.

"Now my own family has set the police on me!"

"Yes, Mr. Peabody." Dr. Brant's voice was very soothing. "Now just sit down. Make yourself comfortable. And tell me all about it."

After snapping the latch on the door, Mr. Peabody permitted himself to sink wearily into Brant's easy chair. He met the probing eyes of the doctor.

"I didn't mean to do wrong." His voice was still protesting, ragged. "I'm not guilty of any deliberate crime. I was only trying to help the ones I loved."

"I know," the doctor soothed him.

A sharp alarm stiffened Mr. Peabody. He realized that Brant's soothing professional manner was intended to calm a dangerous madman. Words would avail him nothing.

"Beth must have told you what they think," he said desperately. "They won't believe it, but I can create. Let me show you."

Brant smiled at him, gently and without visible skepticism. "Very well. Go on."

"I shall make you a goldfish bowl."

He looked at a little stand, that was cluttered with the doctor's pipes and medical journals, and concentrated upon that peculiar, painful effort. The pain and the rushing passed, and the bowl was real. He looked inquiringly at Brant's suave face.

"Very good, Mr. Peabody. "Now can you put the fish in it?"

"No." Mr. Peabody pressed his hands against his dully aching head. "It seems that I can't make anything alive. That is one of the limitations that I have discovered."

"Eh?"

Brant's eyes widened a little. He walked slowly to the small glass bowl, touched it gingerly, and put a testing finger into the water it contained. His jaw slackened.

"Well." He repeated the word, with increasing emphasis. "Well, well, *well!*"

His staring gray eyes came back to Mr. Peabody. "You are being honest with me? You'll give your word there's no trickery? You materialized this object by mental effort alone?"

Mr. Peabody nodded.

It was Brant's turn to be excited. While Mr. Peabody sat quietly recovering his breath, the lean young doctor paced up and down the room. He lit his pipe and let it go out, and asked a barrage of tense-voiced questions.

Wearily, Mr. Peabody tried to answer the questions. He made new demonstrations of his gift, materializing a nail, a match, a cube of sugar, and a cuff link that was meant to be silver. Commenting upon the leaden color of the latter, he recalled his misadventures with the gold brick.

"A minor difficulty, I should think—always assuming that this is a fact."

Brant took off his rimless glasses, and polished them nervously. "Possibly due merely to lack of familiarity with atomic structure.... But—my word!"

He began walking the floor again.

All but dead with fatigue, Mr. Peabody was mutely grateful at last to be permitted to crawl into the doctor's bed. Despite that small dull throbbing in his brain, he slept soundly.

And up in the heavens a bright star winked, greenly.

Brant, if he slept at all, did so in the chair. The next morning, wrinkled, hollow-eyed, dark-chinned, he woke Mr. Peabody; refreshed his bewildered memory with a glimpse of a nail, a match, a cube of sugar, and a lead cuff link; and inquired frantically whether he still possessed the gift.

Mr. Peabody felt dull and heavy. The ache at the back of his head was worse, and he felt reluctant to attempt any miracles. He remained able, however, to provide himself with a cup of inexplicable coffee.

"Well!" exclaimed Brant. "Well, well, well! All through the night I kept doubting even my own senses. My word—it's incredible. But what an opportunity for medical science!"

"Eh?" Mr. Peabody started apprehensively. "What do you mean?"

"Don't alarm yourself," Brant said soothingly. "Of course we must keep your case a secret, at least until we have data enough to support an announcement. But, for your sake as well as for science, you must allow me to study your new power."

Nervously, he was polishing his glasses.

"You are my uncle," he declared abruptly. "Your name is Homer Brown. Your home is in Pottsville, upstate. You are staying with me for a few days, while you undergo an examination at the hospital."

"Hospital?"

Mr. Peabody began a feeble protest. Ever since Beth was born, he had felt a horror of hospitals. Even the odor, he insisted, was enough to make him ill.

In the midst of his objections, however, he found himself bundled into a taxi.

Brant whisked him into the huge gray building, past nurses and interns. There was an endless series of examinations; from remote alert politeness that surrounded him, he guessed that he was supposed to be insane. At last Brant called him into a tiny consultation room, and locked the door.

His manner was suddenly respectful—and oddly grave.

"Mr. Peabody, I must apologize for all my doubts," he said. "The X-ray proves the incredible. Here, you may see it for yourself."

He made Mr. Peabody sit before two mirrors, that each reflected a rather gruesome-looking skull. The two images emerged into one. At the base of the skull, beyond the staring eye sockets, Brant pointed out a little ragged black object.

"That's it."

"You mean the meteor?"

"It is a foreign body. Naturally, we can't determine its true nature, without recourse to brain surgery. But the X-ray shows the scars of its passage through brain tissue and frontal bone—miraculously healed. It is doubtless the object which struck you."

Mr. Peabody had staggered to his feet, gasping voicelessly.

"Brain surgery!" he whispered hoarsely. "You aren't—"

Very slowly, Brant shook his head.

"I wish we could," he said gravely. "But the operation is impossible. It would involve a section of the cerebrum itself. No surgeon I know would dare attempt it."

Gently, he took Mr. Peabody's arm. His voice fell.

"It would be unfair to conceal from you the fact that your case is extremely serious."

Mr. Peabody's knees were shaking.

"Doctor, what do you mean?"

Brant pointed solemnly at the X-ray films.

"That foreign body is radioactive," he said deliberately. "I noticed that the film tended to fog, and you sound like hail on the Geiger counter." The doctor's face was tense and white.

"You understand that it can't be removed," he said. "And the destructive effect of its radiations upon the brain tissue will inevitably be fatal, within a few weeks."

He shook his head, while Mr. Peabody stared uncomprehendingly.

Brant's smile was tight, bitter.

"Your life, it seems, is the price you must pay for your gift."

Mr. Peabody let Brant take him back to the little apartment. The throbbing in his head was an incessant reminder that the rays of the stone were destroying his brain. Despair numbed him, and he felt sick with pain.

"Now that I know I'm going to die," he told the doctor, "there is just one thing I've got to do. I must use the gift to make money enough so that my family will be cared for."

"You'll be able to do that, I'm sure," Brant agreed. Filling a pipe, he came to Mr. Peabody's chair. "I don't want to excite your hopes unduly," he said slowly. "But I want to suggest one possibility."

"Eh?" Mr. Peabody half rose. "You mean the stone might be removed?"

Brant was shaking his head.

"It can't be, by any ordinary surgical technique," he said.

"But I was just thinking: your extraordinary power healed the wound it made in traversing the brain. If you can acquire control over the creation and manipulation of living matter, we might safely attempt the operation—depending on your gift to heal the section."

"There's no use to it." Mr. Peabody sank wearily back into Brant's easy chair. "I've tried, and I can't make anything alive. The power was simply not granted me."

"Nonsense," Brant told him. "The difficulty, probably, is just that you don't know enough biology. A little instruction in bio-chemistry, anatomy, and psysiology ought to fix you up."

"I'll try," Mr. Peabody agreed. "But first my family must be provided for."

After the doctor had given him a lesson on the latest discoveries about atomic and molecular structures, he found himself able to create objects of the precious metals, with none of them turning out like the gold brick.

For two days he drove himself to exhaustion, making gold and platinum. He shaped the metal into watch cases, old-fashioned jewelry, dental work, and medals, so that it could be disposed of without arousing suspicion.

Brant took a handful of the trinkets to a dealer in old gold. He returned with five hundred dollars, and the assurance that the entire lot, gradually marketed, would net several thousand.

Mr. Peabody felt ill with the pain and fatigue of his creative efforts, and he was still distressed with a fear of the law. He learned from the newspapers that the police were watching his house, and he dared not even telephone his daughter Beth.

"They all think I'm insane; even Beth does," he told Brant. "Probably I'll never see any of them again. I want you to keep the money, and give it to them after I am gone."

"Nonsense," the young doctor said. "When you get a little more control over your gift, you will be able to fix everything up."

But even Brant had to admit that Mr. Peabody's increasing illness threatened to cut off the research before they had reached success.

Unkempt and hollow-eyed, muttering about "energy-conversion" and "entropy-reverse," and "telurgic psi capacity," Brant sat up night after night while Mr. Peabody slept, plowing through heavy tomes on relativity and atomic physics and parapsychology trying to discover a sane explanation of the gift.

"I believe that roaring you say you hear," he told Mr. Peabody, "is nothing less than a sense of the free radiant energy of cosmic space. The radioactive stone has somehow enabled your brain—perhaps by stimulation of the psychophysical faculty that is rudimentary in all of us—has enabled you to concentrate and convert that diffuse energy into material atoms."

Mr. Peabody shook his fevered, throbbing head.

"What good is your theory to me?" Despair moved him to a bitter recital of his case.

"I can work miracles, but what good has the power done me? It has driven me from my family. It has made me a fugitive from justice. It has turned me into a sort of guinea pig, for your experiments. It is nothing but a headache—a real one, I mean. And it's going to kill me, in the end."

"Not," Brant assured him, "if you can learn to create living matter."

Not very hopefully, for the pain and weakness that accompanied his miraculous efforts were increasing day by day. Mr. Peabody followed Brant's lectures in anatomy and physiology. He materialized blobs of protoplasm and simple cells and bits of tissue.

The doctor evidently had grandiose ideas of a miraculous human being. He set Mr. Peabody to studying and creating human limbs and organs. After a few days, the bathtub was filled with a strange lot of miraculous debris, swimming in a preservative solution.

Then Mr. Peabody rebelled.

"I'm getting too weak, doctor," he insisted faintly. "My power is somehow—going. Sometimes it seems that things are going to flicker out again, instead of getting real. I know I can't make anything as large as a human being."

"Well, make something small," Brant told him. "Remember, if you give up, you are giving up your life."

And presently, with a manual of marine biology on his knees, Mr. Peabody was forming small miraculous goldfish in the bowl he had made on the night of his arrival. They were gleaming, perfect—except that they always floated to the top of the water, dead.

Brant had gone out. Mr. Peabody was alone before the bowl, when Beth slipped silently into the apartment. She looked pale and distressed.

"Dad!" she cried anxiously. "How are you?" She came to him, and took his trembling hands. "Rex warned me on the phone not to come: he was afraid the police would follow me. But I don't think they saw me. And I had to come, Dad. I was so worried. But how are you?"

"I think I'll be all right," Mr. Peabody lied stoutly, and tried to conceal the tremor in his voice. "I'm glad to see you, dear. Tell me about your mother and Bill."

"They're all right. But Dad, you look so ill!"

"Here, I've something for you." Mr. Peabody took the five hundred dollars out of his wallet, and put it in her hands. "There will be more, after—later."

"But, Dad—"

"Don't worry, dear, it isn't counterfeit."

"It isn't that." Her voice was distressed. "Rex has tried to tell me about these miracles. I don't understand them, Dad; I don't know what to believe. But I do know we don't want the money you make with them. None of us."

Mr. Peabody tried to cover his hurt.

"But my dear," he asked, "how are you going to live?"

"I'm going to work, next week," she said. "I'm going to be a reception clerk for a dentist—until Rex has an office of his own. And Mom is going to take two boarders, in the spare room."

"But," said Mr. Peabody, "there is William."

"Bill already has a job," Beth informed him. "You know the fellow he ran into? Well, the man has a garage. He let Bill go to work for him. Bill gets fifty a week, and pays back thirty for the accident. Bill's doing all right."

The way she looked when she said it made it clear to Mr. Peabody that there had been a guiding spirit in his family's remarkable reformation—and that Beth had had a lot to do with it. Mr. Peabody smiled at her gratefully to show that he understood, but he said nothing.

She refused to watch him demonstrate his gift.

"No, Dad." She moved back almost in horror from the little bowl with the lifeless goldfish floating in it. "I don't like magic, and I don't believe in something for nothing. There is always a catch to it."

She came and took his hand again, earnestly.

"Dad," she begged softly, "why don't you give up this gift? Whatever it is. Why don't you explain to the police and your boss, and try to get your old job back?"

Mr. Peabody shook his head, with a wry little smile.

"I'm afraid it wouldn't be so easy, explaining," he said. "But I'm ready to give up the gift—whenever I can."

"I don't understand you, Dad." Her face was trembling. "Now I must go. I hope the police didn't see me. I'll come back, whenever I can."

She departed, and Mr. Peabody wearily returned to his miraculous goldfish.

Five minutes later the door was flung unceremoniously open. Mr. Peabody looked up, startled. And the gleaming ghost of a tiny fish, half-materialized, shimmered and vanished.

Mr. Peabody had expected to see Brant, returning. But four policemen, two in plain clothes, trooped into the room. They triumphantly informed him that he was under arrest, and began searching the apartment.

"Hey, Sergeant!" came an excited shout from the bathroom. "Looks like Doc Brant is in the ring, too. And it ain't only jewel-robbery and fraud and counterfeiting. It's murder—with mutilation!"

The startled officers converged watchfully upon Mr. Peabody, and handcuffs jingled. Mr. Peabody, however, was looking curiously elated for a man just arrested under charge of the gravest of crimes. The haunting shadow of pain cleared from his face, and he smiled happily.

"Hey, they're gone!" It was the patrolman in the bathroom. His horror-tinged excitement had changed to bewildered consternation. "I saw 'em, a minute ago. I swear it. But now there ain't nothing in the tub but water."

The sergeant stared suspiciously at Mr. Peabody, who looked bland but exhausted. Then he made a few stinging remarks to the bluecoat standing baffled in the doorway. Finally he swore with much feeling.

Mr. Peabody's hollow eyes had closed. The smile on his face softened into weary relaxation. The detective sergeant caught him, as he swayed and fell. He had gone to sleep.

He woke next morning in a hospital room. Dr. Brant was standing beside the bed. In answer to Mr. Peabody's first alarmed question, he grinned reassuringly.

"You are my patient," he explained. "You have been under my care for an unusual case of amnesia. Very convenient disorder, amnesia. And you are doing very well."

"The police?"

Brant gestured largely.

"You've nothing to fear. There's no evidence that you were

guilty of any criminal act. Naturally they wonder how you came into possession of the counterfeit; but certainly they can't prove you made it. I have already told them that, as a victim of amnesia, you will not be able to tell them anything."

Mr. Peabody sighed and stretched himself under the sheets, gratefully.

"Now, I've got a couple of questions," Brant said. "What was it that happened so fortunately to the debris in the bathtub? And to the stone in your head? For the X-ray shows that it is gone."

"I just undid them," Mr. Peabody said.

Brant caught his breath, and nodded very slowly.

"I see," he said at last. "I suppose the inevitable counterpart of creation must be annihilation. But how did you do it?"

"It came to me, just as the police broke in," Mr. Peabody said. "I was creating another one of those damned goldfish, and I was too tired to finish it. When I heard the door, I made a little effort to—well, somehow let it go, push it away."

He sighed again, happily.

"That's the way it happened. The goldfish flickered out of existence; it made an explosion in my head, like a bomb. That gave me the feel of unmaking. Annihilation, you call it. Much easier than creating, once you get the knack of it. I took care of the things in the bathroom, and the stone in my brain."

"I see." Brant took a restless turn across the room, and came back to ask a question. "Now that the stone is gone," he said, "I suppose your remarkable gift is—lost?"

It was several seconds before Mr. Peabody replied. Then he said softly:

"It was lost."

That statement, however, was a lie. Mr. Peabody had learned a certain lesson. The annihilation of the meteoric stone had ended his pain. But, as he had just assured himself by the creation and instant obliteration of a small goldfish under the sheets, his power was intact.

Still a bookkeeper, Mr. Peabody is still outwardly very much the same man as he was that desperate night when he walked upon Bannister Hill. Yet there is now a certain subtle difference in him.

A new confidence in his bearing has caused Mr. Berg to increase his responsibilities and his pay. The yet unsolved mysteries surrounding his attack of amnesia cause his family and his neighbors to regard him with a certain awe. William now only very rarely calls him "Gov."

Mr. Peabody remains very discreet in the practice of his gift. Sometimes, when he is quite alone, he ventures to provide himself with a miraculous cigarette. Once, in the middle of the night, a mosquito which had tormented him beyond endurance simply vanished.

And he has come, somehow, into the possession of a fishing outfit which is the envy of his friends—and which he now finds time to use.

Chiefly, however, his gift is reserved for performing inexplicable tricks for the delight of his two grandchildren, and the creation of tiny and miraculous toys.

All of which, he strictly enjoins them, must be kept secret from their parents, Beth and Dr. Brant.

MISFIT *Astounding Science Fiction*, November

by Robert A. Heinlein

Heinlein's second story (in this volume and his second published), "Misfit" contains all the elements that made him great—attention to detail, narrative flow, young protaganist, and interesting social extrapolation. The "Cosmic Construction Corps" owes an obvious debt to the depression-era CCC. There was to be a great deal more from where this came from—for evidence, see Volume II, 1940.

(No one ever dominated the science fiction field as Bob did in the first few years of his career. It was a one-man phenomenon that will probably never be repeated. The field has grown too large, its nature too varied, its writers too many for any one person to overshadow it. IA)

> ". . . for the purpose of conserving and improving our interplanetary resources, and providing useful, healthful occupations for the youth of this planet."
> Excerpt from the enabling act, H.R. 7118, setting up the Cosmic Construction Corps.

"Attention to muster!" The parade ground voice of a First Sergeant of Space Marines cut through the fog and drizzle of a nasty New Jersey morning. "As your names are called, answer 'Here', step forward with your baggage, and embark. Atkins!"

"Here!"

"Austin!"

"Hyar!"

"Ayres!"

"Here!"

One by one they fell out of ranks, shouldered the hundred and thirty pounds of personal possessions allowed them, and trudged up the gangway. They were young—none more than twenty-two—in some cases luggage outweighed the owner.

"Kaplan!"

"Here!"

"Keith!"

"Heah!"

"Libby!"

"Here!" A thin gangling blonde had detached himself from the line, hastily wiped his nose, and grabbed his belongings. He slung a fat canvas bag over his shoulder, steadied it, and lifted a suitcase with his free hand. He started for the companionway in an unsteady dog trot. As he stepped on the gangway his suitcase swung against his knees. He staggered against a short wiry form dressed in the powder-blue of the Space Navy. Strong fingers grasped his arm and checked his fall.

"Steady, son. Easy does it." Another hand readjusted the canvas bag.

"Oh, excuse me, uh"—the embarrassed youngster automatically counted the four bands of silver braid below the shooting star—"Captain. I didn't—"

"Bear a hand and get aboard, son."

"Yes, sir."

The passage into the bowels of the transport was gloomy. When the lad's eyes adjusted he saw a gunner's mate wearing the brassard of a Master-at-Arms, who hooked a thumb towards an open air-tight door.

"In there. Find your locker and wait by it." Libby hurried to obey. Inside he found a jumble of baggage and men in a wide low-ceilinged compartment. A line of glow-tubes ran around the junction of bulkhead and ceiling and trisected the overhead; the soft roar of blowers made a background to the voices of his shipmates. He picked his way through heaped luggage, and located his locker, seven-ten, on the far wall outboard. He broke the seal on the combination lock, glanced at the combination, and opened it. The locker was very small, the middle of a tier of three. He considered what he should keep in it. A loudspeaker drowned out the surrounding voices and demanded his attention:

"Attention! Man all space details; first section. Raise ship in twelve minutes. Close air-tight doors. Stop blowers at minus two minutes. Special orders for passengers; place all gear on deck, and lie down on red signal light. Remain down until release is sounded. Masters-at-Arms check compliance."

The gunner's mate popped in, glanced around and immediately commenced supervising rearrangement of the baggage. Heavy items were lashed down. Locker doors were closed. By the time each boy had found a place on the deck and the Master-at-Arms had okayed the pad under his head, the glow-tubes turned red and the loudspeaker brayed out.

"All hands—Up Ship! Stand by for acceleration." The Master-at-Arms hastily reclined against two cruise bags, and watched the room. The blowers sighed to a stop. There followed two minutes of dead silence. Libby felt his heart commence to pound. The two minutes stretched interminably. Then the deck quivered and a roar like escaping high-pressure steam beat at his ear drums. He was suddenly very heavy and a weight lay across his chest and heart. An indefinite time later the glow-tubes flashed white, and the announcer bellowed:

"Secure all getting underway details; regular watch, first section." The blowers droned into life. The Master-at-Arms stood up, rubbed his buttocks and pounded his arms, then said:

"Okay, boys." He stepped over and undogged the airtight door to the passageway. Libby got up and blundered into a bulkhead, nearly falling. His legs and arms had gone to sleep, besides which he felt alarmingly light, as if he had sloughed off at least half of his inconsiderable mass.

For the next two hours he was too busy to think, or to be homesick. Suitcases, boxes, and bags had to be passed down into the lower hold and lashed against angular acceleration. He located and learned how to use a waterless water closet. He found his assigned bunk and learned that it was his only eight hours in twenty-four; two other boys had the use of it too. The three sections ate in three shifts, nine shifts in all—twenty-four youths and a master-at-arms at one long table which jam-filled a narrow compartment off the galley.

After lunch Libby restowed his locker. He was standing before it, gazing at a photograph which he intended to mount on the inside of the locker door, when a command filled the compartment:

"Attention!"

Standing inside the door was the Captain flanked by the Master-at-Arms. The Captain commenced to speak. "At rest, men. Sit down. McCoy, tell control to shift this compartment to smoke filter." The gunner's mate hurried to the communicator on the bulkhead and spoke into it in a low tone. Almost at once the hum of the blowers climbed a half-octave and stayed there. "Now light up if you like. I'm going to talk to you.

"You boys are headed out on the biggest thing so far in your lives. From now on you're men, with one of the hardest jobs ahead of you that men have ever tackled. What we have to do is part of a bigger scheme. You, and hundreds of thousands of others like you, are going out as pioneers to fix up the solar system so that human beings can make better use of it.

"Equally important, you are being given a chance to build yourselves into useful and happy citizens of the Federation. For one reason or another you weren't happily adjusted back on Earth. Some of you saw the jobs you were trained for abolished by new inventions. Some of you got into trouble from not knowing what to do with the modern leisure. In any case you were misfits. Maybe you were called bad boys and had a lot of black marks chalked up against you.

"But everyone of you starts even today. The only record you have in this ship is your name at the top of a blank sheet of paper. It's up to you what goes on that page.

"Now about your job—We didn't get one of the easy repair-and-recondition jobs on the Moon, with week-ends at Luna City, and all the comforts of home. Nor did we draw a high-gravity planet where a man can eat a full meal and expect to keep it down. Instead we've got to go out to Asteroid HS-5388 and turn it into Space Station E-M3. She has no atmosphere at all, and only about two percent Earth-surface gravity. We've got to play human fly on her for at least six months, no girls to date, no television, no recreation that you don't devise yourselves, and hard work every day. You'll get space sick, and so homesick you can taste it, and agoraphobia. If you aren't careful, you'll get ray-burnt. Your stomach will act up, and you'll wish to God you'd never enrolled.

"But if you behave yourself, and listen to the advice of the old spacemen, you'll come out of it strong and healthy, with a little credit stored up in the bank, and a lot of knowledge and experience that you wouldn't get in forty years on Earth. You'll be men, and you'll know it.

"One last word. It will be pretty uncomfortable to those that aren't used to it. Just give the other fellow a little consideration, and you'll get along all right. If you have any complaint and can't get satisfaction any other way, come see me. Otherwise, that's all. Any questions?"

One of the boys put up his hand. "Captain?" he enquired timidly.

"Speak up, lad, and give your name."

"Rogers, sir. Will we be able to get letters from home?"

"Yes, but not very often. Maybe every month or so. The chaplain will carry mail, and any inspection and supply ships."

The ship's loudspeaker blatted out, "All hands! Free flight in ten minutes. Stand by to lose weight." The Master-at-Arms supervised the rigging of grab-lines. All loose gear was made fast, and little cellulose bags were issued to each man. Hardly was this done when Libby felt himself get light on his feet—a sensation exactly like that experienced when an express elevator makes a quick stop on an upward trip, except that the sensation continued and became more intense. At first it was a pleasant novelty, then it rapidly became distressing. The blood pounded in his ears, and his feet were clammy and cold. His saliva secreted at an abnormal rate. He tried to swallow, choked, and coughed. Then his stomach shuddered and contracted with a violent, painful, convulsive reflex and he was suddenly, disastrously nauseated. After the first excruciating spasm, he heard McCoy's voice shouting.

"Hey! Use your sick-kits like I told you. Don't let that stuff get in the blowers." Dimly Libby realized that the admonishment included him. He fumbled for his cellulose bag just as a second temblor shook him, but he managed to fit the bag over his mouth before the eruption occurred. When it subsided, he became aware that he was floating near the overhead and facing the door. The chief Master-at-Arms slithered in the door and spoke to McCoy.

"How are you making out?"

"Well enough. Some of the boys missed their kits."

"Okay. Mop it up. You can use the starboard lock." He swam out.

McCoy touched Libby's arm. "Here, Pinkie, start catching them butterflies." He handed him a handful of cotton waste, then took another handful himself and neatly dabbed up a globule of the slimy filth that floated about the compartment. "Be sure your sick-kit is on tight. When you get sick, just stop and wait until it's over." Libby imitated him as best as he could. In a few minutes the room was free of the worst of the sickening debris. McCoy looked it over, and spoke:

"Now peel off them dirty duds, and change your kits.

Three or four of you bring everything alone to the starboard lock."

At the starboard spacelock, the kits were put in first, the inner door closed, and the outer opened. When the inner door was opened again the kits were gone—blown out into space by the escaping air. Pinkie addressed McCoy,

"Do we have to throw away our dirty clothes too?"

"Huh uh, we'll just give them a dose of vacuum. Take 'em into the lock and stop 'em to those hooks on the bulkheads. Tie 'em tight."

This time the lock was left closed for about five minutes. When the lock was opened the garments were bone dry—all the moisture boiled out by the vacuum of space. All that remained of the unpleasant rejecta was a sterile powdery residue. McCoy viewed them with approval. "They'll do. Take them back to the compartment. Then brush them—hard—in front of the exhaust blowers."

The next few days were an eternity of misery. Homesickness was forgotten in the all-engrossing wretchedness of spacesickness. The Captain granted fifteen minutes of mild acceleration for each of the nine meal periods, but the respite accentuated the agony. Libby would go to a meal, weak and ravenously hungry. The meal would stay down until free flight was resumed, then the sickness would hit him all over again.

On the fourth day he was seated against a bulkhead, enjoying the luxury of a few remaining minutes of weight while the last shift ate, when McCoy walked in and sat down beside him. The gunner's mate fitted a smoke filter over his face and lit a cigarette. He inhaled deeply and started to chat.

"How's it going, bud?"

"All right, I guess. This spacesickness—Say, McCoy, how do you ever get used to it?"

"You get over it in time. Your body acquires new reflexes, so they tell me. Once you learn to swallow without choking, you'll be all right. You even get so you like it. It's restful and relaxing. Four hours sleep is as good as ten."

Libby shook his head dolefully. "I don't think I'll ever get used to it."

"Yes, you will. You'd better anyway. This here asteroid won't have any surface gravity to speak of; the Chief Quartermaster says it won't run over two per cent Earth normal.

That ain't enough to cure spacesickness. And there won't be any way to accelerate for meals either."

Libby shivered and held his head between his hands.

Locating one asteroid among a couple of thousand is not as easy as finding Trafalgar Square in London—especially against the star-crowded backdrop of the galaxy. You take off from Terra with its orbital speed of about nineteen miles per second. You attempt to settle into a composite conoid curve that will not only intersect the orbit of the tiny fast-moving body, but also accomplish an exact rendezvous. Asteroid HS-5388, 'Eighty-eight,' lay about two and two-tenths astronomical units out from the sun, a little more than two hundred million miles; when the transport took off it lay beyond the sun better than three hundred million miles. Captain Doyle instructed the navigator to plot the basic ellipsoid to tack in free flight around the sun through an elapsed distance of some three hundred and forty million miles. The principle involved is the same as used by a hunter to wing a duck in flight by 'leading' the bird in flight. But suppose that you face directly into the sun as you shoot; suppose the bird cannot be seen from where you stand, and you have nothing to aim by but some old reports as to how it was flying when last seen?

On the ninth day of the passage Captain Doyle betook himself to the chart room and commenced punching keys on the ponderous integral calculator. Then he set his orderly to present his compliments to the navigator and to ask him to come to the chartroom. A few minutes later a tall heavyset form swam through the door, steadied himself with a grabline and greeted the captain.

"Good morning, Skipper."

"Hello, Blackie." The Old Man looked up from where he was strapped into the integrator's saddle. "I've been checking your corrections for the meal time accelerations."

"It's a nuisance to have a bunch of ground-lubbers on board, sir."

"Yes, it is, but we have to give those boys a chance to eat, or they couldn't work when we got there. Now I want to decelerate starting about ten o'clock, ship's time. What's our eight o'clock speed and co-ordinates?"

The Navigator slipped a notebook out of his tunic. "Three hundred fifty-eight miles per second; course is right ascension fifteen hours, eight minutes, twenty-seven seconds, declination minus seven degrees, three minutes; solar distance one

MISFIT

hundred and ninety-two million four hundred eighty thousand miles. Our radial position is twelve degrees above course, and almost dead on course in R.A. Do you want Sol's co-ordinates?"

"No, not now." The captain bent over the calculator, frowned and chewed the tip of his tongue as he worked the controls. "I want you to kill the acceleration about one million miles inside Eighty-eight's orbit. I hate to waste the fuel, but the belt is full of junk and this damned rock is so small that we will probably have to run a search curve. Use twenty hours on deceleration and commence changing course to port after eight hours. Use normal asymptotic approach. You should have her in a circular trajectory abreast of Eighty-eight, and paralleling her orbit by six o'clock tomorrow morning. I shall want to be called at three."

"Aye aye, sir."

"Let me see your figures when you get 'em. I'll send up the order book later."

The transport accelerated on schedule. Shortly after three the Captain entered the control room and blinked his eyes at the darkness. The sun was still concealed by the hull of the transport and the midnight blackness was broken only by the dim blue glow of the instrument dials, and the crack of light from under the chart hood. The Navigator turned at the familiar tread.

"Good morning, Captain."

"Morning, Blackie. In sight yet?"

"Not yet. We've picked out half a dozen rocks, but none of them checked."

"Any of them close?"

"Not uncomfortably. We've overtaken a little sand from time to time."

"That can't hurt us—not on a stern chase like this. If pilots would only realize that the asteroids flow in fixed directions at computable speeds nobody would come to grief out here." He stopped to light a cigarette. "People talk about space being dangerous. Sure, it used to be; but I don't know of a case in the past twenty years that couldn't be charged up to some fool's recklessness."

"You're right, Skipper. By the way, there's coffee under the chart hood."

"Thanks; I had a cup down below." He walked over by the lookouts at stereoscopes and radar tanks and peered up at the star-flecked blackness. Three cigarettes later the lookout nearest him called out.

"Light ho!"

"Where away?"

His mate read the exterior dials of the stereoscope. "Plus point two, abaft one point three, slight drift astern." He shifted to radar and added, "Range seven nine oh four three."

"Does that check?"

"Could be, Captain. What is her disk?" came the Navigator's muffled voice from under the hood. The first lookout hurriedly twisted the knobs of his instrument, but the Captain nudged him aside.

"I'll do this, son." He fitted his face to the double eye guards and surveyed a little silvery sphere, a tiny moon. Carefully he brought two illuminated cross-hairs up until they were exactly tangent to the upper and lower limbs of the disc. "Mark!"

The reading was noted and passed to the Navigator, who shortly ducked out from under the hood.

"That's our baby, Captain."

"Good."

"Shall I make a visual triangulation?"

"Let the watch officer do that. You go down and get some sleep. I'll ease her over until we get close enough to use the optical range finder."

"Thanks, I will."

Within a few minutes the word had spread around the ship that Eighty-eight had been sighted. Libby crowded into the starboard troop deck with a throng of excited mess mates and attempted to make out their future home from the view port. McCoy poured cold water on their excitement.

"By the time that rock shows up big enough to tell anything about it with your naked eye we'll all be at our grounding stations. She's only about a hundred miles thick, yuh know."

And so it was. Many hours later the ship's announcer shouted:

"All hands! Man your grounding stations. Close all airtight doors. Stand by to cut blowers on signal."

McCoy forced them to lie down throughout the ensuing two hours. Short shocks of rocket blasts alternated with nauseating weightlessness. Then the blowers stopped and check valves clicked into their seats. The ship dropped free for a few moments—a final quick blast—five seconds of falling, and a short, light, grinding bump. A single bugle note came over the announcer, and the blowers took up their hum.

McCoy floated lightly to his feet and poised, swaying, on his toes. "All out, troops—this is the end of the line."

A short chunky lad, a little younger than most of them, awkwardly emulated him, and bounded toward the door, shouting as he went, "Come on, fellows! Let's go outside and explore!"

The Master-at-Arms squelched him. "Not so fast, kid. Aside from the fact that there is no air out there, go right ahead. You'll freeze to death, burn to death, and explode like a ripe tomato. Squad leader, detail six men to break out spacesuits. The rest of you stay here and stand by."

The working party returned shortly loaded down with a couple of dozen bulky packages. Libby let go the four he carried and watched them float gently to the deck. McCoy unzipped the envelope from one suit, and lectured them about it.

"This is a standard service type, general issue, Mark IV, Modification 2." He grasped the suit by the shoulders and shook it out so that it hung like a suit of long winter underwear with the helmet lolling helplessly between the shoulders of the garment. "It's self-sustaining for eight hours, having an oxygen supply for that period. It also has a nitrogen trim tank and a carbon-dioxide-water-vapor cartridge filter."

He droned on, repeating practically verbatim the description and instructions given in training regulations. McCoy knew these suits like his tongue knew the roof of his mouth; the knowledge had meant his life on more than one occasion.

"The suit is woven from glass fibre laminated with nonvolatile asbestocellutite. The resulting fabric is flexible, very durable; and will turn all rays normal to solar space outside the orbit of Mercury. It is worn over your regular clothing, but notice the wire-braced accordion pleats at the major joints. They are so designed as to keep the internal volume of the suit nearly constant when the arms or legs are bent. Otherwise the gas pressure inside would tend to keep the suit blown up in an erect position, and movement while wearing the suit would be very fatiguing.

"The helmet is moulded from a transparent silicone, leaded and polarized against too great ray penetration. It may be equipped with external visors of any needed type. Orders are to wear not less than a number-two amber on this body. In addition, a lead plate covers the cranium and extends on down the back of the suit, completely covering the spinal column.

"The suit is equipped with two-way telephony. If your radio quits, as these have a habit of doing, you can talk by putting your helmets in contact. Any questions?"

"How do you eat and drink during the eight hours?"

"You don't stay in 'em any eight hours. You can carry sugar balls in a gadget in the helmet, but you boys will always eat at the base. As for water, there's a nipple in the helmet near your mouth which you can reach by turning your head to the left. It's hooked to a built-in canteen. But don't drink any more water when you're wearing a suit than you have to. These suits ain't got any plumbing."

Suits were passed out to each lad, and McCoy illustrated how to don one. A suit was spread supine on the deck, the front zipper that stretched from neck to crotch was spread wide and one sat down inside this opening, whereupon the lower part was drawn on like long stockings. Then a wiggle into each sleeve and the heavy flexible gauntlets were smoothed and patted into place. Finally an awkward backward stretch of the neck with shoulders hunched enabled the helmet to be placed over the head.

Libby followed the motions of McCoy and stood up in his suit. He examined the zipper which controlled the suit's only opening. It was backed by two soft gaskets which would be pressed together by the zipper and sealed by internal air pressure. Inside the helmet a composition mouthpiece for exhalation led to the filter.

McCoy bustled around, inspecting them, tightening a belt here and there, instructing them in the use of the external controls. Satisfied, he reported to the conning room that his section had received basic instruction and was ready to disembark. Permission was received to take them out for thirty minutes acclimatization.

Six at a time, he escorted them through the air lock, and out on the surface of the planetoid. Libby blinked his eyes at the unaccustomed luster of sunshine on rock. Although the sun lay more than two hundred million miles away and bathed the little planet with radiation only one fifth as strong as that lavished on mother Earth, nevertheless the lack of atmosphere resulted in a glare that made him squint. He was glad to have the protection of his amber visor. Overhead the sun, shrunk to penny size, shone down from a dead black sky in which unwinking stars crowded each other and the very sun itself.

The voice of a mess mate sounded in Libby's earphones, "Jeepers! That horizon looks close. I'll bet it ain't more'n a mile away."

Libby looked out over the flat bare plain and subconsciously considered the matter. "It's less," he commented, "than a third of a mile away."

"What the hell do you know about it, Pinkie? And who asked you, anyhow?"

Libby answered defensively, "As a matter of fact, it's one thousand six hundred and seventy feet, figuring that my eyes are five feet three inches above ground level."

"Nuts. Pinkie, you are always trying to show off how much you think you know."

"Why, I am not," Libby protested. "If this body is a hundred miles thick and as round as it looks: why, naturally the horizon *has* to be just that far away."

"Says *who?*"

McCoy interrupted.

"Pipe down! Libby is a lot nearer right than you were."

"He is exactly right," put in a strange voice. "I had to look it up for the navigator before I left control."

"Is that so?"—McCoy's voice again—"If the Chief Quartermaster says you're right, Libby, you're right. How did you know?"

Libby flushed miserably. "I—I don't know. That's the only way it could be."

The gunner's mate and the quartermaster stared at him but dropped the subject.

By the end of the 'day' (ship's time, for Eighty-eight had a period of eight hours and thirteen minutes), work was well under way. The transport had grounded close by a low range of hills. The Captain selected a little bowl-shaped depression in the hills, some thousand feet long and half as broad, in which to establish a permanent camp. This was to be roofed over, sealed, and an atmosphere provided.

In the hill between the ship and the valley, quarters were to be excavated; dormitories, mess hall, officers' quarters, sick bay, recreation room, offices, store rooms, and so forth. A tunnel must be bored through the hill, connecting the sites of these rooms, and connecting with a ten foot airtight metal tube sealed to the ship's portside air-lock. Both the tube and tunnel were to be equipped with a continuous conveyor belt for passengers and freight.

Libby found himself assigned to the roofing detail. He helped a metalsmith struggle over the hill with a portable atomic heater, difficult to handle because of a mass of eight hundred pounds, but weighing here only sixteen pounds. The rest of the roofing detail were breaking out and preparing to move by hand the enormous translucent tent which was to be the 'sky' of the little valley.

The metalsmith located a landmark on the inner slope of the valley, set up his heater, and commenced cutting a deep horizontal groove or step in the rock. He kept it always at the same level by following a chalk mark drawn along the rock wall. Libby enquired how the job had been surveyed so quickly.

"Easy," he was answered, "two of the quartermasters went ahead with a transit, leveled it just fifty feet above the valley floor, and clamped a searchlight to it. Then one of 'em ran like hell around the rim, making chalk marks at the height at which the beam struck."

"Is this roof going to be just fifty feet high?"

"No, it will average maybe a hundred. It bellies up in the middle from the air pressure."

"Earth normal?"

"Half Earth normal."

Libby concentrated for an instant, then looked puzzled. "But look—This valley is a thousand feet long and better than five hundred wide. At half of fifteen pounds per square inch, and allowing for the arch of the roof, that's a load of one and an eighth billion pounds. What fabric can take that kind of a load?"

"Cobwebs."

"Cobwebs?"

"Yeah, cobwebs. Strongest stuff in the world, stronger than the best steel. Synthetic spider silk. This gauge we're using for the roof has a tensile strength of four thousand pounds a running inch."

Libby hesitated a second, then replied, "I see. With a rim about eighteen hundred thousand inches around, the maximum pull at the point of anchoring would be about six hundred and twenty-five pounds per inch. Plenty safe margin."

The metalsmith leaned on his tool and nodded. "Something like that. You're pretty quick at arithmetic, aren't you, bud?"

Libbly looked startled. "I just like to get things straight."

They worked rapidly around the slope, cutting a clean smooth groove to which the 'cobweb' would be anchored and sealed. The white-hot lava spewed out of the discharge vent and ran slowly down the hillside. A brown vapor boiled off the surface of the molten rock, arose a few feet and sublimed almost at once in the vacuum to white powder which settled to the ground. The metalsmith pointed to the powder.

"That stuff 'ud cause silicosis if we let it stay there, and breathed it later."

"What do you do about it?"

"Just clean it out with the blowers of the air conditioning plant."

Libby took this opening to ask another question. "Mister—?"

"Johnson's my name. No mister necessary."

"Well, Johnson, where do we get the air for this whole valley, not to mention the tunnels? I figure we must need twenty-five million cubic feet or more. Do we manufacture it?"

"Naw, that's too much trouble. We brought it in with us."

"On the transport?"

"Uh huh, at fifty atmospheres."

Libby considered this. "I see—that way it would go into a space eighty feet on a side."

"Matter of fact it's in three specially constructed holds—giant air bottles. This transport carried air to Ganymede. I was in her then—a recruit, but in the air gang even then."

In three weeks the permanent camp was ready for occupancy and the transport cleared of its cargo. The storerooms bulged with tools and supplies. Captain Doyle had moved his administrative offices underground, signed over his command to his first officer, and given him permission to proceed on 'duty assigned'—in this case; return to Terra with a skeleton crew.

Libby watched them take off from a vantage point on the hillside. An overpowering homesickness took possession of him. Would he ever go home? He honestly believed at the time that he would swap the rest of his life for thirty minutes each with his mother and with Betty.

He started down the hill toward the tunnel lock. At least

the transport carried letters to them, and with any luck the chaplain would be by soon with letters from Earth. But tomorrow and the days after that would be no fun. He had enjoyed being in the air gang, but tomorrow he went back to his squad. He did not relish that—the boys in his squad were all right, he guessed, but he just could not seem to fit in.

This company of the C.C.C. started on its bigger job; to pock-mark Eighty-eight with rocket tubes so that Captain Doyle could push this hundred-mile marble out of her orbit and herd her in to a new orbit between Earth and Mars, to be used as a space station—a refuge for ships in distress, a haven for life boats, a fueling stop, a naval outpost.

Libby was assigned to a heater in pit H-16. It was his business to carve out carefully calculated emplacements in which the blasting crew then set off the minute charges which accomplished the major part of the excavating. Two squads were assigned to H-16, under the general supervision of an elderly marine gunner. The gunner sat on the edge of the pit, handling the plans, and occasionally making calculations on a circular slide rule which hung from a lanyard around his neck.

Libby had just completed a tricky piece of cutting for a three-stage blast, and was waiting for the blasters, when his phones picked up the gunner's instructions concerning the size of the charge. He pressed his transmitter button.

"Mr. Larsen! You've made a mistake!"

"Who said that?"

"This is Libby. You've made a mistake in the charge. If you set off that charge, you'll blow this pit right out of the ground, and us with it."

Marine Gunner Larsen spun the dials on his slide rule before replying, "You're all het up over nothing, son. That charge is correct."

"No, I'm not, sir," Libby persisted, "you've multiplied where you should have divided."

"Have you had any experience at this sort of work?"

"No, sir."

Larsen addressed his next remark to the blasters. "Set the charge."

They started to comply. Libby gulped, and wiped his lips with his tongue. He knew what he had to do, but he was afraid. Two clumsy stiff-legged jumps placed him beside the blasters. He pushed between them and tore the electrodes from the detonator. A shadow passed over him as he worked, and Larsen floated down beside him. A hand grasped his arm.

"You shouldn't have done that, son. That's direct disobedience of orders. I'll have to report you." He commenced reconnecting the firing circuit.

Libby's ears burned with embarrassment, but he answered back with the courage of timidity at bay. "I had to do it, sir. You're still wrong."

Larsen paused and ran his eyes over the dogged face. "Well,—it's a waste of time, but I don't like to make you stand by a charge you're afraid of. Let's go over the calculation together."

Captain Doyle sat at his ease in his quarters, his feet on his desk. He stared at a nearly empty glass tumbler.

"That's good beer, Blackie. Do you suppose we could brew some more when it's gone?"

"I don't know, Cap'n. Did we bring any yeast?"

"Find out, will you?" He turned to a massive man who occupied the third chair. "Well, Larsen, I'm glad it wasn't any worse than it was."

"What beats me, Captain, is how I could have made such a mistake. I worked it through twice. If it had been a nitro explosive, I'd have known off hand that I was wrong. If this kid hadn't had a hunch, I'd have set it off."

Captain Doyle clapped the old warrant officer on the shoulder. "Forget it, Larsen. You wouldn't have hurt anybody; that's why I require the pits to be evacuated even for small charges. These isotope explosives are tricky at best. Look what happened in pit A-9. Ten days' work shot with one charge, and the gunnery officer himself approved that one. But I want to see this boy. What did you say his name was?"

"Libby, A.J."

Doyle touched a button on his desk. A knock sounded at the door. A bellowed "Come in!" produced a stripling wearing the brassard of Corpsman Mate-of-the-Deck.

"Have Corpsman Libby report to me."

"Aye aye, sir."

Some few minutes later Libby was ushered into the Captain's cabin. He looked nervously around, and noted Larsen's presence, a fact that did not contribute to his peace of mind. He reported in a barely audible voice, "Corpsman Libby, sir."

The Captain looked him over. "Well, Libby, I hear that

you and Mr. Larsen had a difference of opinion this morning. Tell me about it."

"I—I didn't mean any harm, sir."

"Of course not. You're not in any trouble; you did us all a good turn this morning. Tell me, how did you know that the calculation was wrong? Had any mining experience?"

"No, sir. I just saw that he had worked it out wrong."

"But how?"

Libby shuffled uneasily. "Well, sir, it just seemed wrong— It didn't fit."

"Just a second, Captain. May I ask this young man a couple of questions?" It was Commander "Blackie" Rhodes who spoke.

"Certainly. Go ahead."

"Are you the lad they call 'Pinkie'?"

Libby blushed. "Yes, sir."

"I've heard some rumors about this boy." Rhodes pushed his big frame out of his chair, went over to a bookshelf, and removed a thich volume. He thumbed through it, then with open book before him, started to question Libby.

"What's the square root of ninety-five?"

"Nine and seven hundred forty-seven thousandths."

"What's the cube root?"

"Four and five hundred sixty-three thousandths."

"What's its logarithm?"

"Its what, sir?"

"Good Lord, can a boy get through school today without knowing?"

The boy's discomfort became more intense. "I didn't get much schooling, sir. My folks didn't accept the Covenant until Pappy died, and we had to."

"I see. A logarithm is a name for a power to which you raise a given number, called the base, to get the number whose logarithm it is. Is that clear?"

Libby thought hard. "I don't quite get it, sir."

"I'll try again. If you raise ten to the second power— square it—it gives one hundred. Therefore the logarithm of a hundred to the base ten is two. In the same fashion the logarithm of a thousand to the base ten is three. Now what is the logarithm of ninety-five?"

Libby puzzled for a moment. "I can't make it come out even. It's a fraction."

"That's okay."

"Then it's one and nine hundred seventy-eight thousandths—just about."

Rhodes turned to the Captain. "I guess that about proves it, sir."

Doyle nodded thoughtfully. "Yes, the lad seems to have intuitive knowledge of arithmetical relationships. But let's see what else he has."

"I am afraid we'll have to send him back to Earth to find out properly."

Libby caught the gist of this last remark. "Please, sir, you aren't going to send me home? Maw 'ud be awful vexed with me."

"No, no, nothing of the sort. When your time is up, I want you to be checked over in the psychometrical laboratories. In the meantime I wouldn't part with you for a quarter's pay. I'd give up smoking first. But let's see what you can do."

In the ensuing hour the Captain and the Navigator heard Libby: one, deduce the Pythagorean proposition; two, derive Newton's laws of motion and Kepler's laws of ballistics from a statement of the conditions in which they obtained; three, judge length, area, and volume by eye with no measurable error. He had jumped into the idea of relativity and non-rectilinear space-time continua, and was beginning to pour forth ideas faster than he could talk, when Doyle held up a hand.

"That's enough, son. You'll be getting a fever. You run along to bed, now, and come see me in the morning. I'm taking you off field work."

"Yes, sir."

"By the way, what is your full name?"

"Andrew Jackson Libby, sir."

"No, your folks wouldn't have signed the Covenant. Good night."

"Good night, sir."

After he had gone, the two older men discussed their discovery."

"How do you size it up, Captain?"

"Well, he's a genius, of course—one of those wild talents that will show up once in a blue moon. I'll turn him loose among my books and see how he shapes up. Shouldn't wonder if he were a page-at-a-glance reader, too."

"It beats me what we turn up among these boys—and not a one of 'em any account back on Earth."

Doyle nodded. "That was the trouble with these kids. They didn't feel needed."

Eighty-eight swung some millions of miles further around the sun. The pock-marks on her face grew deeper, and were lined with durite, that strange close-packed laboratory product which (usually) would confine even atomic disintegration. Then Eighty-eight received a series of gentle pats, always on the side headed along her course. In a few weeks' time the rocket blasts had their effect and Eighty-eight was plunging in an orbit toward the sun.

When she reached her station one and three-tenths the distance from the sun of Earth's orbit, she would have to be coaxed by another series of pats into a circular orbit. Thereafter she was to be known as E-M3, Earth-Mars Space Station Spot Three.

Hundreds of millions of miles away two other C.C.C. companies were inducing two other planetoids to quit their age-old grooves and slide between Earth and Mars to land in the same orbit as Eighty-eight. One was due to ride this orbit one hundred and twenty degrees ahead of Eighty-eight, the other one hundred and twenty degrees behind. When E-M1, E-M2, and E-M3 were all on station no hard-pushed traveler of the spaceways on the Earth-Mars passage would ever again find himself far from land—or rescue.

During the months that Eighty-eight fell free toward the sun, Captain Doyle reduced the working hours of his crew and turned them to the comparatively light labor of building a hotel and converting the little roofed-in valley into a garden spot. The rock was broken down into soil, fertilizers applied, and cultures of anaerobic bacteria planted. Then plants, conditioned by thirty-odd generations of low gravity at Luna City, were set out and tenderly cared for. Except for the low gravity, Eighty-eight began to feel like home.

But when Eighty-eight approached a tangent to the hypothetical future orbit of E-M3, the company went back to maneuvering routine, watch on and watch off, with the Captain living on black coffee and catching catnaps in the plotting room.

Libby was assigned to the ballistic calculator, three tons of thinking metal that dominated the plotting room. He loved the big machine. The Chief Fire Controlman let him help adjust it and care for it. Libby subconsciously thought of it as a person—his own kind of person.

On the last day of the approach, the shocks were more frequent. Libby sat in the right-hand saddle of the calculator and droned out the predictions for the next salvo, while

MISFIT

gloating over the accuracy with which the machine tracked. Captain Doyle fussed around nervously, occasionally stopping to peer over the Navigator's shoulder. Of course the figures were right, but what if it didn't work? No one had ever moved so large a mass before. Suppose it plunged on and on—and on. Nonsense! It couldn't. Still he would be glad when they were past the critical speed.

A marine orderly touched his elbow. "Helio from the Flagship, sir."

"Read it."

"Flag to Eighty-eight; private message, Captain Doyle; am lying off to watch you bring her in.—Kearney."

Doyle smiled. Nice of the old geezer. Once they were on station, he would invite the Admiral to ground for dinner and show him the park.

Another salvo cut loose, heavier than any before. The room trembled violently. In a moment the reports of the surface observers commenced to trickle in. "Tube nine, clear!" "Tube ten, clear!"

But Libby's drone ceased.

Captain Doyle turned on him. "What's the matter, Libby? Asleep? Call the polar stations. I have to have a parallax."

"Captain—" The boy's voice was low and shaking.

"Speak up, man!"

"Captain—the machine isn't tracking."

"Spiers!" The grizzled head of the Chief Fire Controlman appeared from behind the calculator.

"I'm already on it, sir. Let you know in a moment."

He ducked back again. After a couple of long minutes he reappeared. "Gyros tumbled. It's a twelve hour calibration job, at least."

The Captain said nothing, but turned away, and walked to the far end of the room. The Navigator followed him with his eyes. He returned, glanced at the chronometer, and spoke to the Navigator.

"Well, Blackie, if I don't have that firing data in seven minutes, we're sunk. Any suggestions?"

Rhodes shook his head without speaking.

Libby timidly raised his voice. "Captain—"

Doyle jerked around. "Yes?"

"The firing data is tube thirteen, seven point six three; tube twelve, six point nine oh; tube fourteen, six point eight nine."

Doyle studied his face. "You sure about that, son?"

"It *has* to be that, Captain."

Doyle stood perfectly still. This time he did not look at Rhodes but stared straight ahead. Then he took a long pull on his cigarette, glanced at the ash, and said in a steady voice,

"Apply the data. Fire on the bell."

Four hours later, Libby was still droning out firing data, his face grey, his eyes closed. Once he had fainted but when they revived him he was still muttering figures. From time to time the Captain and the Navigator relieved each other, but there was no relief for him.

The salvos grew closer together, but the shocks were lighter.

Following one faint salvo, Libby looked up, stared at the ceiling, and spoke.

"That's all, Captain."

"Call the polar stations!"

The reports came back promptly, "Parallax constant, sidereal-solar rate constant."

The Captain relaxed into a chair. "Well, Blackie, we did it—thanks to Libby!" Then he noticed a worried, thoughtful look spread over Libby's face. "What's the matter, man? Have we slipped up?"

"Captain, you know you said the other day that you wished you had Earth-normal gravity in the park?"

"Yes. What of it?"

"If that book on gravitation you lent me is straight dope, I think I know a way to accomplish it."

The Captain inspected him as if seeing him for the first time. "Libby, you have ceased to amaze me. Could you stop doing that sort of thing long enough to dine with the Admiral?"

"Gee, Captain, that would be swell!"

The audio circuit from Communications cut in.

"Helio from Flagship: 'Well done, Eighty-eight.' "

Doyle smiled around at them all. "That's pleasant confirmation."

The audio brayed again.

"Helio from Flagship: 'Cancel last signal, stand by for correction.' "

A look of surprise and worry sprang into Doyle's face—then the audio continued:

"Helio from Flagship: 'Well done, E-M3.' "